Frances Gordon is t........... ....s.. actor and
after a convent education worked in newspapers and
the legal profession. She now lives and writes in
Staffordshire. She is the author of four acclaimed fantasy
novels, written under the name of Bridget Wood.

BLOOD RITUAL is also available from Headline:
'A superior example of the vampire genre . . a pleasure
from start to finish' *Time Out*
'A chilling, blood-curdling novel' *Peterborough
Evening Telegraph*

The Devil's Piper

Frances Gordon

Extract from *The Oxford Companion to Music* by Percy Scholes,
10th ed. 1970, p. 1042, used by permission of Oxford University Press.

The right of Frances Gordon to be identified as the Author of
the Work has been asserted by her in accordance with the
Copyright, Designs and Patents Act 1988.

First published in Great Britain in 1995
by HEADLINE BOOK PUBLISHING
First published in paperback in 1996
by HEADLINE BOOK PUBLISHING

A HEADLINE FEATURE paperback

10 9 8 7 6 5 4 3 2 1

ISBN 0 7472 4924 5

Typeset by CBS, Felixstowe, Suffolk

Printed and bound in Great Britain by
Mackays of Chatham PLC, Chatham, Kent

HEADLINE BOOK PUBLISHING
A division of Hodder Headline PLC
338 Euston Road, London NW1 3BH

For my brother Tony,
because of the music.

Extract from *The Oxford Companion to Music*: (OUP).

In early ecclesiastical music, (fourth to sixteenth century), the melodic use of the tritone was forbidden, as was also, though less stringently, its inversion, the diminished fifth. Early theorists called it the 'devil in music' – *Diabolus in Musica.*

Chapter One

Temple and Newman
Solicitors and Notaries Public,
Lincoln's Inn Fields
London

19 October 199-

Dear Mr West
re: ESTATE OF P B WEST DECEASED

I am pleased to inform you that Probate has finally been granted in respect of your father's estate and the enclosed Statement shows the monies which you can expect to receive. We have deducted our own charges for the handling of this matter, together with the fees for your own divorce from Mrs E West. This, as you know, became absolute last month. However, you will see that a modest sum remains due to you, along with the cottage, which forms part of your father's estate, and which was purchased in 1932 by your grandfather, Mr Jude Weissman. I regret that the Title Deeds are not as comprehensive as I should wish, but no doubt this is due to Mr Weissman being in Vienna at the time of the purchase, and also he employed Irish solicitors for the transaction. Matters were further complicated by your father's decision to change the family's name from Weissman to West in

1953, although I cannot say I blame him for that.

I understand that you have recently resigned your post with the Music Faculty at Stornforth University, and that you intend to live in the cottage. The Abstract of Title is at best sparse, and there is no proper record of past transfers, so that we have had to prepare a completely new Abstract. (See item No.4(c) on the attached account.) This missing information led to a small confusion regarding the ownership of and responsibility for the eastern boundary which abuts the grounds of a monastery, but I am glad to say that despite the quite remarkable age of the monastery, the monks were able to provide surprisingly detailed Deeds for inspection. The matter has been amicably resolved in our favour, the Father Abbot having undertaken to make good a section of dilapidated retaining wall.

Your Title now appears to be sound and although I understand the cottage has not been lived in since the unfortunate business in the Forties and must therefore be in a near-derelict condition, at least the property is as yet unencumbered by any mortgage.

Yours etc.

M B TEMPLE

Stornforth University
21 October 199-

Dear Mr Temple

I cannot imagine where you obtain your information, but since it appears that my overturning of the tables in the Money Lenders' Temple last month (see New Testament) has reached your ears by some nefarious and invisible means, I shall be grateful for whatever crumbs fall from the rich man's table, no matter how modest, although to call them modest is an exercise in meiosis. Your own account renders me bereft of speech, which my former superiors would tell you is no mean feat and if the erstwhile Madame West succeeds in her financial demands, my bankruptcy will probably be announced next week. Between the orange wife and the litigious gentlemen of your profession I shall be lucky to be left with a pound of flesh to call my own.

What do you mean by saying that the sparse nature of the Title Deeds is probably due to my grandfather having employed Irish solicitors? Are Irish solicitors inferior to English ones? Or merely less venal, which I can see would make them lesser mortals in your eyes. I don't know that I much care for the idea of having an ancient Order of monks for neighbours, but at least I shall be spared late night parties and loud rock music.

Do I detect a note of sarcasm in the comment that the cottage is as yet unencumbered by mortgage?

Please let me know when I can have the keys.

Yours etc.

    ISAREL WEST

Temple and Newman
Solicitors and Notaries Public,
Lincoln's Inn Fields
London

25 October 199-

Dear Mr West
re: ESTATE OF P B WEST DECEASED

The above matter having at last been completed,

we beg to enclose our cheque in settlement.

I understand that the keys to Mr Weissman's property are held in Curran Glen itself, and I enclose a letter of authority for you to present to Mr Edward Mahoney whose firm acted for your grandfather, and who is now its sole partner.

If in fact you do wish to mortgage the property we would, of course, be happy to make suitable arrangements on your behalf.

With good wishes,

Yours etc.

M B TEMPLE

Stornforth University
27 October 199-

Dear Mr Temple

Since when did the derelict cottage of dubious Title become a property? I suspect it was since the sordid matter of a mortgage was raised.

No thank you, I will dree my own weird.

With good wishes to you as well,

ISAREL WEST

It pleased Isarel to take the route to the cottage that Jude himself would have taken so many years earlier. He knew only the barest details about it, other than it had been acquired in the Nineteen Thirties – 1932 had old Temple said? – when Jude was a young man. Within the family, it had been spoken of simply as 'Your grandfather's cottage', and Isarel had never done more than vaguely visualise it as somewhere on the west coast.

But as he came out of Shannon airport, driving the small hire car – enough money left for that at least! – and

4

following the directions sent by the apparently efficient Edward Mahoney, he realised that Curran Glen was much farther west than he had thought.

'Beyond civilisation,' his father had once said. 'Overlooking Liscannor Bay. Quite impractical, of course.'

Jude would probably not have cared about the uncivilised and impractical situation of his cottage, and Jude's grandson, setting out to re-discover it over fifty years later, did not care either.

Jude would have driven out here almost as a matter of course: in the Thirties cars had been getting commonplace, and he had already made more than sufficient money to own one.

But in Jude's day the roads would have been little better than widened cart tracks, and he would not have had to cope with the constant drone of traffic and the smell of petrol fumes. Isarel frowned and concentrated on getting the journey over as quickly as possible. Over the hills and far away . . . Yes, as far away as possible. Worlds and light years away from greedy grasping females and soulless faculty professors who preached about Art but practised Accountancy. The beginnings of a grin curved his lips. It had been good to tell them what he thought of them. It had been almost worth the loss of his lectureship.

Over hill, over dale. The ribbon of road unwound before him, sometimes fringed by woodland, sometimes by fields. Thorough bush, thorough brier . . . Was it out here, surrounded by ancient fey Celtic magic that Jude had conceived the eerie '*Devil's Piper*' Suite? It had acquired such a sinister reputation, that most musicians and conductors fought shy of it and the critics used the word 'darkness' about it. It had never been played in public since Jude had played it inside Eisenach Castle in Northern Germany over half a century ago, although there were one or two rather pale recordings still in circulation. Isarel had heard it on Radio Three about a year ago, part of a concert of compositions that traditionally had a faintly Satanic connection. Jude's beautiful brilliant music, filled with images of pouring blue and purple shadows, soaked in creeping menace, had been offered, halfway between apology and amusement, as something of a curio, cobwebby with age and creaking with disuse. 'A storm petrel,' said the announcer in the carefully expressionless tone of one who would be torn into pieces by wild horses galloping in four different directions before admitting to a belief in superstition. 'The Macbeth of the Music World,' he had added for good measure, at which point Isarel had thrown a book at the radio and stalked out of the room.

He pushed away the memories and turned into the main street of the next town he came to, drawing up on the forecourt of a small supermarket. He piled food and provisions into a wire basket, hesitating over things like eggs and cheese, unsure whether the cottage would have a workable fridge, or even electricity. He bought them anyway, but added several packs of wax candles and half a dozen boxes of matches in case, and moved on to the wine section. Was he going to drown his glory in a shallow cup and sell his reputation for a song? He supposed he had already done that and pretty irrevocably as well. The Grape had employed its Logic absolute on the jarring Sects of Academe, or was it warring Sects? There was probably not a lot of difference. Damn the plebeian professors in Stornforth and curse Liz and her selfish greedy ladder-climbing. He added several bottles of whiskey and a case of wine, because if he was really going to drown in the shallow cup he might as well do it with panache. He wedged the cartons of food on the back seat, consulted the directions, and set off again.

As he rounded a curve in the road, there was the far-off glint of water with the sun on it over on the left, and there was a scent of something smoky and autumnal on the air. Peat fires? Peat burning in the hearths, and smoky Irish whiskey and the soft rainfall that the Irish had the insolence to call mist. A sudden longing for something – happiness? – spiked across his mind, and then vanished, because the village was ahead: sheltered by a fold of cliff from the coast road. There was a huddle of rooftops forming a winding village street and fields and scattered white farmhouses.

And dominating it all, the grey stones and clerestory windows and towering spires of the monastery.

Curran Glen.

It was thorough bush, thorough brier with a vengeance now. As Isarel turned off the small village street, which was little more than a handful of shops, a Post Office and a pub, the tarmac disappeared and gave way to a dusty cart track. He could see the silhouette of the monastery more clearly now: there was a high wall surrounding it but as Isarel drove on he glimpsed cloisters and a small gatehouse, and what looked like a chapter house. He wondered in a half-interested way, where the eastern boundary, the cause of M B Temple's dispute, was situated.

A little farther along was a signpost leaning drunkenly on a post, and reading 'No Thoroughfare', and Isarel experienced an unexpected jolt of ownership. Mine. Whatever is at the end of this overgrown cart track, it's mine. He thought it would be better by far than the small furnished campus flat at Stornforth, and infinitely better than the characterless neo-Georgian house in a cul-de-sac that Liz had demanded and got, and then filled with beige carpets and white anaglypta walls and featureless furniture in blond ash and smoked glass. She had had the bad taste to screw her lover in their bed, and the even worse taste to let Isarel catch them doing it. Isarel had enjoyed that last gesture of sending her the Title Deeds to the house and he had torn up her sickly-sweet note in which she had wished him happiness, the bitch. He hoped she would marry her Sales Director with his false bonhomie and boastful tales and he hoped they would make one another thoroughly miserable.

The monastery was on his left now, and there was a winding bouncing drive for several hundred yards, with bushes and thrusting thickthorn hedges pushing against the sides of the car and whippy branches that painted sappy green smears on the windscreen. Isarel engaged second gear and drove grimly on.

When he wound down the car window birdsong flooded in, and there was the scent of peat fires again. *I am coming home . . .* The thought thrust unbidden into his mind and he pushed it aside impatiently. The solicitor – what was his name? – was to meet him here at six o'clock. Isarel glanced at his watch. Five forty. Plenty of time to explore on his own.

And then it was there. Set back from the track a little, standing behind a tangle of brier and blackberry, with a white wicket gate, half off its hinges.

Jude's house.

It was much larger and considerably older than Isarel had expected, and it was certainly worthy of a grander name than cottage. A red brick four-square house with the tall flat windows of the Regency, and crumbling stone pillars on each side of the front door. The brick had long since mellowed into a dark soft red, the colour beloved of Titian and Burne Jones for their roseate-skinned, full-cheeked ladies, and the sun was setting behind the house, bathing it in a fiery glow and dissolving the windows into molten gold. Isarel switched off the ignition and the silence closed down, broken only by the evening birdsong and the faint ticking of the cooling engine.

Some kind of creeper covered the lower portions – a pity if that had to be stripped away, but it might have weakened the brickwork – and now that the sun was sliding below the horizon, he could see the dereliction. The upper windows had shutters, half falling away, and all the window frames were rotten and crumbling. As he had thought the brickwork was soft and powdery where the mortar had dried and flaked off, and there was an ominous dip in the roofline. He made a quick calculation of his finances and scowled.

The garden was a tangled mass of thrusting rose bay willow and rank grass, but to one side were ragged-headed wild roses, and immense bushes of lilac and lavender. In full summer they would scent the air for miles around. On the other side was surely the remains of a herb garden: was there rosemary there? Rosemary, that's for remembrance . . . It would hardly be remembrance for Jude, especially out here where memories would be long. Elder would be more in keeping. Judas, the traitor, hanged on an elder tree . . . Isarel frowned and turned back to the house, searching for electricity or telephone cables. Nothing. Isolation with a vengeance, then. Alone and in the sea of life enisl'd . . . What kind of a benighted place had he come to, for God's sake?

But the feeling of *I am coming home*, and the feeling of something tremendous just beyond hearing and just out of vision, was still with him, and he was suddenly fiercely glad that he had arrived early and that he could be on his own with the house until the solicitor arrived.

Tacked onto the sagging gate was an oblong of wood with a name – 'Mallow' – and a rusting chain that snapped in two when he lifted it. Isarel had not known the name of

9

Jude's house, and the old resonance of the word pleased him. It was a purple word, a soft violet-tinted word. If you wrote music about mallows you would give it a dark velvety feel: a minor key but a rich wine-dark one . . .

If you wrote music . . .

He had not written a note since the day he had walked out of Liz's Habitat bedroom, but now, without the least warning, the music was with him again, pushing its way up in his mind: something golden and warm and something that was laced with such allure that it was almost sexual in quality. Follow me over the hills and far away . . .

Jude haunting his days as he had haunted his nights all those years ago?

It was nothing more than tiredness: the flight here, the drive through unfamiliar country. Too much wine the night before. Well, all right, maybe it was a little that he was coming to Jude's house. But if Jude walked anywhere, he would surely not walk here. This had been his hideaway, his retreat. This had been where he had brought his women.

He walked round the house, looking into the windows, putting up a hand to block his own reflection, trying to make out the shadowy outlines of furniture. Probably woodworm and death watch beetle had long since made matchwood of the furniture, but so far as he could see, there were at least chairs to sit on and a table to eat off.

He progressed to the window on the left-hand side of the front door, but before he could make out the contents of that room, there was the sound of another car coming up the rough track behind him, and he turned his back on the house and went down the track to meet the solicitor.

Edward Mahoney had not seemed very keen to stay, or even to enter Mallow.

He had handed Isarel a bunch of keys, conscientiously

10

labelled with things like 'Garden Door', and 'Cellar', and 'Small Scullery', and then he had gone. Another appointment, he had said, his eyes sliding away from Isarel, determinedly turning his back on the house. And then his family expecting him for supper – Mr West would no doubt excuse him from giving the guided tour? It was said with the slight quirkiness of the Irish, but for all that, there was a note of genuine anxiety. Mr Edward Mahoney quite clearly did not want to enter Mallow, and so far from wanting to enter it was he, that he did not even want to be in its vicinity for long.

Haunted after all? Isarel grinned, and picked out the key labelled 'Main Door'.

The lock slid open and he stepped inside.

Edward Mahoney walked up the nice, neat drive of his garden and turned the latch of his own front door. He was very glad indeed to have left the tumbledown Weissman estate behind, and he was extremely relieved that he had so adroitly managed to avoid actually going inside. He would not have entered that house after dark if the Furies had been at his heels. He would prefer not to enter it in full daylight either, really. Not that anyone had ever seen anything, not so far as Edward knew and he did not, of course, believe in such nonsense. But you had to expect that there would be a few stories about a place empty for so long.

He permitted himself a touch of complacency. The past weeks had been tricky, what with the finicking English solicitor in Lincoln's Inn making every kind of difficulty, and what with this Mr West's father – Jude's son, that was – having changed the family's name in the Fifties, although that was no more than Edward would have done himself given the scandal.

Isarel West had been younger than he had been expecting:

no more than thirty or so. You tended to think of university lecturers as elderly, of course, and probably West was one of these modern aggressive clever young men you heard about. Edward had no time for them, although he frowned, remembering Isarel West's disquieting likeness to the photographs of Jude at the height of his fame. Thin-faced and dark-haired. The kind of intense dark eyes that foolish young girls sometimes found attractive. It might be as well to ensure that Moira was not thrust into any kind of contact with Mr West, not that the child would be interested, she did not bother with boys or nonsense about pop groups or film actors.

He let himself into his house and stood smiling, waiting for his womenfolk to put aside whatever they had been doing, and come running out to welcome him home.

Chapter Two

The minute that Isarel stepped over the threshold, he was aware of relief that Edward Mahoney had gone. The scent of age billowed out from the house and folded about him, so strong that for a minute it was like a solid wall and Isarel felt his senses blur.

But this was not the musty dankness of damp or rot and there was nothing sad or sordid about it. This was age at its best and most evocative: a pot-pourri of old seasoned timbers and long-ago peat fires and a lingering scent of dried lavender. A gentler age when ladies embroidered and wrote letters on hot-pressed notepaper and painted dainty water-colours and practised their music.

Music . . . The faint stirring came again, rippling the surface of his mind like the puckering of thin silk.

Follow me, come with me . . . Over the frozen mountaintops, across the glassy lakes . . .

So he was suffering from *delirium tremens* now. So it was something that a good many people had long since predicted. He turned back to the house.

A staircase wound up from the hall to the upper floors: the stairs were uncarpeted and at some time the boards had been polished until they resembled new-run honey with the sun on it. There were elaborately carved newel posts and a small half landing where the evening light filtered through.

On the right of the hall, a door was partly open into a

long shrouded room. The evening light was in here as well: great pouring swathes of purple dusk softening the neglect. The once-lovely wallpaper was peeling from the walls, and the plaster mouldings on the ceiling had fallen to the floor in a shower of tiny dry crumbs and the curtains, which might have been any colour at all, had faded to indeterminate grey. But there was a deep window seat covered in the same faded velvet as the curtains, and if you sat on it you would be able to look through the jutting bow window over a small orchard. There were several deep armchairs and a small rosewood desk, and although the fireplace was probably choked with starlings' nests, it was square and substantial-looking and chimneys could be swept. So far so good. He would far rather have this elegant dereliction than fifty of Liz's symmetrical lounges.

The kitchen gave him pause: cooking facilities there were, but they were provided by a huge black range. Isarel, accustomed to electric cookers where you turned a switch, or microwave ovens where you set a dial, eyed it doubtfully. Alongside it was an immense dresser, probably built into the house – probably its main king post for heaven's sake! – and at the centre was a scrubbed-top table. A thick layer of dust covered everything, but Isarel had the uncomfortable feeling that if he put out a hand he would find that the range was still faintly warm, and that he had only just missed hearing the sound of the kettle singing on the hob. He shivered and went back through the wood-scented hall into the cascading twilight. He would cope with the practicalities first and then he would think about the delusions.

The scented dusk had given way to night proper as he unloaded the cartons of food and the whiskey. He unpacked the candles first, lighting several and standing them on window ledges and tables. It took longer than he thought to carry everything in and store it all away. Just off the kitchen was a massive stone-floored larder with an old-fashioned mesh-fronted meat safe, and a marble slab for cheese and butter. There were plates and cups and cutlery in a drawer and when he tried the water in the deep square sink, although it ran rusty to start with – bodies in the sewerage? don't be ridiculous! – after a time it came clear and pure. He rinsed the dust from plates and cups and set them on the dresser to dry. He would make himself a sandwich and pour a tumbler of whiskey before exploring further.

If he was going to suffer from DTs he might as well do the thing properly.

It was remarkable what food and drink did for you. Isarel rinsed the plates and knives, re-filled the tumbler with whiskey, lit several more candles and walked across the hall to explore the rest of his domain. The leaping candle flame sent his own shadow dancing across the ceiling, and there was a moment – heart-stopping – when he thought that a second shadow walked with him. A creature wearing a deep hood that concealed its face, a creature that dragged itself painfully along, deep-sleeved arms outstretched and then lifted, ready to snatch up a victim . . .

The candle burned up and the illusion vanished, and Isarel pushed open the door to the room on the other side of the hall.

The same drifting scent of age, the same neglect. A darker room this, probably once papered in something vaguely William Morris. He made out the ghosts of huge cabbage roses and twining vines on the wall. Lovely. It was faded and there were damp patches here and there, but it beat emulsioned woodchip any day.

At the far end, positioned beneath the window that looked out over the tangle of Mallow's garden, was a low

15

gleaming shape. Satinwood and ebony, and the pale shimmer of ivory teeth.

Jude's piano.

The shadows were quiescent as he drew the piano stool with the faded velvet seat forward, but he again had the impression that he was not alone, and that something crouched in the shadows, near to the window. Something that was huddled into one of the pools of darkness, the cowl of its robe shadowing its face, but that lifted its head and turned towards him as he touched the keys . . .

Isarel swore and lit another candle from the stub of the first and the shadows receded again. Damn Edward Mahoney and his alacrity to beat a retreat and damn M B Temple in London with his stories about ancient Orders of Monks and Abbeys of incalculable age.

Under the piano was an elaborate brass box, probably used for music sheets. Isarel stared at it, and felt his heart give a great bound, and then resume a painful, too-rapid beating. Jude's music. It might be empty, of course. Or whatever was in it might have been long since destroyed. Mildew, damp, mice. Vandals. Would vandals bother to steal music? Moving as if through a dream now, he dragged the box from under the piano, where the candlelight fell across the tarnished surface. Not brass after all, thought Isarel. Silver? And supposing it's locked? If it's locked I'll break it open.

The box was not locked but the lid was sealed with the accreted dust of years. Isarel tore several layers of skin from his hands prising it up, but at length, with a groan that rasped against his already-raw nerves, the lid came slowly up, with a faint breath of dry air being exhaled. As if something was sighing with regret. As if it had lain buried here for a long time and did not want to be woken. Isarel's hand was shaking as he reached inside.

A thick pile of yellowing music paper: score sheets, some professionally printed, some not. Brahms, Mozart, Liszt. Beethoven piano concertos. Jude's extravagant, elaborate writing sprawled in the margins of almost every one. The edges were crumbling and flaking with age, and Isarel lifted them out with extreme care.

And there, under them all, the ink faded to pale brown, was the one he had wanted to find and perversely hoped not to.

Jude Weissman's original score for the infamous music he had written over half a century earlier and played in Eisenach Castle.

The *Devil's Piper.*

Edward Mahoney's evening had not gone quite as he had expected.

He was accustomed to his supper being ready for him as soon as he arrived, and surely to goodness it was not unreasonable for a man to expect his supper to be on the table at the correct time of an evening. He felt obliged to administer a gentle rebuke.

Supper was a family event: he insisted on it. He had no patience with nonsense about the girls wanting to be off with harum-scarum friends or pleas to attend youth clubs or school orchestra practices. A good Catholic family ate the evening meal together.

It was annoying that the delay and Mary's nervous apology should mar the time of the day that Edward liked best: entering his own house and seeing his womenfolk come running to greet him, vying for his attention. But after all, it was not wholly spoiled. The twins, Rosa and Angela, came running as soon as they heard his key in the lock, just as they always did, clattering down the stair, leaving their schoolwork behind, and calling out that Father was home, here was Father and they had such a lot to tell him! Edward expanded with red-faced pleasure, and looked up the stairs, expectantly. He liked seeing the twins, of course, noisy scrambling pair that they were, but it was Moira, his lovely precious Moira that he really wanted to see.

She came slowly down to him, with the slight halting step that so distressed them all. She was wearing one of her thin cotton shirts tonight; Edward could see the outline of her breasts quite clearly. He drew in his breath sharply, and bent over to kiss her, anticipating it, savouring the closeness. There was nothing wrong in a fond paternal kiss.

Club foot, they had called Moira's disability at the hospital; not a very severe case fortunately, and there was no reason why the child, so pretty and intelligent, could not lead an almost normal life. No games unfortunately, although swimming might be possible. But other than that a perfectly normal and fulfilled life.

Edward had not paid such absurdities any attention; he had been courteous but firm, and although Moira had perforce to attend St Asaph's from the age of five on, he had seen to it that Mary fetched and took her every day. There would be no walking home with a giggling group of giddy schoolgirls at four o'clock every afternoon, very likely eyeing boys and all manner of nonsense! Edward had seen the behaviour of some of St Asaph's girls from his office window in the village square, and very bold it was.

Later, he had resisted the representations of the nuns to allow Moira to try for a university place, perhaps even to read law so that she could come into the firm with her father, wouldn't that be a fine thing? they had said. Edward had been surprised that the nuns should consider such a thing, because of course a child with Moira's disability could not cope with life in Dublin, the very idea! Moira would stay at home where her daddy could keep her safe. He thought, but did not say, that having her with him all the time was precisely what he had always wanted; in any case, he was certainly not going to permit her to go stravaging off to a university, where she would be ogled by lusty-eyed boys who would want to stroke her breasts and take her clothes off to satisfy their hot, thrusting bodies. Unthinkable in connection with his precious girl.

The image of Moira in the bed of some lout was something he dwelled on quite often. Moira, naked on a bed, her red hair tumbling down her white shoulders . . . The image slid insidiously into his consciousness now, as Moira accepted her evening kiss and smiled at him, and said supper would not be long.

He left them to see to the serving of his food, and went out to take a turn in the garden. It was cool and autumnal and a tiny wind was soughing in the trees over towards Mallow. Edward stood at the end of the garden, looking across to the forest and there, in front of the blurred silhouette of the trees, was the denser shape that was the house. A ramshackle place it was although Edward dared say something might be made of it, always supposing that West had the money to do it, which was unlikely. Everyone in Curran Glen knew that Jude Weissman's money had long since vanished, and the amount passed to the heir had been scandalously small. Edward, dealing importantly with the London solicitors, knew how much Isarel West had inherited to the penny.

The wind was oddly resonant tonight. Edward could have almost thought it was bearing thin silvery music on the air. He looked back at Mallow, a crouching bulk in front of the forest, and a prickle of unease brushed his scalp. And then he remembered that Isarel West was a musician like Jude.

There was absolutely no reason why the thin silvery music drifting on the night air should produce a feeling of unease.

Isarel was fathoms deep in Jude's music, the mist-wreathed purple-shadowed eeriness of the *Devil's Piper* pouring from the piano almost of its own volition. The Bluthner was painfully out of tune and if there was such a thing as a good tuner out here he would have to be called in, because although some things would have to be economised on, Jude's piano was not going to be one of them.

Isarel's father had hidden Jude's musical scores in the attic of their house, but Isarel had found them when he was eight, and the crumbling yellowed sheets had fascinated him. He had copied Jude's marvellous work carefully on to fresh notation paper, working by the light of a torch in his bedroom when he was supposed to be asleep, and then stealing into the study at the back of the house where the jangly upright piano was kept. For some reason he had never understood, he had never played Jude's music when his parents were in the house; despite that, by the time he was eleven, he knew all of his grandfather's compositions absolutely by heart.

But he had never found the score to the *Devil's Piper*.

Jude had written the instructions: *allegro maestoso*, for the first movement, meaning fast but stately, but to Isarel, the entrance of the Piper, the enigmatic myth-shrouded creature, was soaked in menace. Could you instruct that a piece of music was played menacingly? What about *con malicia*. With malice . . .

Excitement gripped him as the music poured into the dark room, like a torrent of crimson and gold, streaked here

20

and there with dark malevolence. He had been unable to feel strongly about anything since he found Liz in bed with her Sales Director, and since he discovered the Faculty Heads fiddling the Departmental allowance and cursed them all for a set of tone-deaf provincials on the last memorable day. Even the violent drinking bouts that had ended in several unknown beds had failed to move him.

But the emotions were all fiercely there again: violent feeling tearing through his mind. It beat the faceless bodies in crumpled beds any day. It was like a mental orgasm. Was it how Jude had felt when he was creating this? How near to him was Jude now?

Isarel's mind was alight and alive with soaring joy, as if huge spotlights were illuminating it, and the patterns tumbled out through his hands on to the out-of-tune piano. There was a grisliness in the music: an element of fee-fi-fo-fum – seven-league boots and a tread that would shake the ground as it came . . . A feeling of something beckoning with a long crooked finger . . . It was a little like Wagner at his most menacing or even Mahler at his darkest. Menacing . . . Malicious . . . That word again. Something sleeping inside the music – almost as if somebody had *hidden* it there! – something was awakening . . . Something ancient and dark, but so irresistible that you would follow it anywhere . . .

Over hill, over dale . . . thorough bush, thorough brier . . . Through famine and flood and hell's fire-drenched furnaces . . .

The images poured scaldingly through his mind. A prowling beckoning dance, the music weaving in and out of the streets and in and out of men's minds, calling them into the streets. The faceless daemons and devils who danced through the Middle Ages, forcing victims into the streets, forcing them to dance on the medieval cobblestones until they dropped . . . The Plague Piper wearing his glaring red mask of agony, leading his victims to the twin Towers of Fever and Madness . . . The dancing, jeering demons, following him down into the town . . .

The legends cascaded out of the music as easily as if a door had been opened on a packed-tight cupboard; they walked in the shadowy old house, tapping their skeletal feet, dancing as they came.

Tap-tap-tap . . .

The sound was so absolutely in time with the music, that for a while Isarel did not realise that it was a separate thing. He was enrapt in the tumbling images, in the intricate footsteps of Jude's creation, he was drawing the death-figure out of its lair and forcing it into the light.

A minor theme was coming in now, something contrapuntal, so that you were more aware of evil uncoiling . . . Springs to catch woodcocks, music to snare souls . . . Come out and die . . .

Tap-tap-tap . . . He's riding down into the town, thought Isarel, his black hair falling unheeded over his brow. This is Jude's creation. Am I Jude? Or is he controlling me, haunting me as he did when I was a child . . . Oh God, all those nights when I lay awake and felt his presence in the bedroom with me. I think he's here now.

Tap-tap-tap . . .

Horses' hoofs? – No, of course not, they're cloven hoofs, cloven for satyrs and fauns . . . And devils.

Tap-tap-tap . . .

This time he did hear it and it jerked him back into the present. He wheeled round on the piano stool, his eyes on the inner door that led to the square hall, and which he had not completely shut, his heart pounding.

Someone was tapping lightly on the outside door. Was

it? Was someone standing in Mallow's deep old porch, trying to get in?

Tap-tap . . . Let-me-in . . .

Isarel glanced at his watch and saw with a start of surprise that it was ten o'clock. Two hours since he had sat down. Not late by many standards: certainly not late by Stornforth's standards, where people studied into the night and burned midnight oil almost permanently, but probably very late indeed for this Irish backwater.

The tapping came again, louder now, as if it might be nearer. Somewhere overhead? Or in the hall, just beyond the half-open door of this room? Had someone got into the house earlier and hidden until darkness fell? It was unspeakably sinister to think that someone might have been in the house with him all the time he had eaten his makeshift meal, all the time he had been falling deeper and deeper into the strange compelling music.

The sound came again, and Isarel's heart began to beat erratically as he remembered the darkness outside and Mallow's isolation and the lack of a telephone.

There was a dragging sound as well now; as if someone (something?) was making a slow painful way towards him. Outside? Or in? Isarel stayed where he was, his eyes raking the shadows, every sense straining to hear and understand. There it came again. Something that could only creep its poor lame way through the world . . . Something warped and distorted . . .

Was the door to the music-room being pushed slowly open from the hall? He snatched up the nearest candle and was across the room in five seconds. He was not overly anxious to tackle an intruder on his own, but he was damned if he would be crept up on in the dark.

He threw back the door of the music room so that it crashed against the wall, and stood for a moment, scanning

23

the hall. Nothing. He glanced up at the stair. Was something there, crouching just above him on the half landing? No. There was only the shadow cast by an old blanket chest – a hope chest didn't they call it? Why should he remember something so trivial at such a moment? He looked back at the outer door, and saw how the red and blue fanlight, relic of Jude's own era, cast a harlequin shadow across the bare floor. There was nothing there. Had he imagined the whole thing? At once, as if in mocking answer the sound came again.

No-you-did-not . . . And the dragging limping footsteps came nearer.

Isarel held the candle up and went steadily up the shadowy stairway.

Chapter Three

In the end, Edward's supper had not been as late as all that. He drank his coffee benevolently, and wanted to know how his Moire Silk would be spending her evening. Perhaps they could have one of their cosy games of Scrabble which they so enjoyed, and then sometimes there was a television programme to be watched together. Edward smiled indulgently while he waited to hear would it be Scrabble or Trivial Pursuit, and felt the smile die as Moira started to explain about spending the evening working on a project which the monks had undertaken, and with which they had requested her assistance.

'The tracing of religious music down the centuries.' Moira had been curled on a humpty by the fire, half in and half out of the light, but she leaned forward, hugging her bent knees. 'As far back as the Levites singing in the Temple and David playing soothing music for King Saul. And Brother Ciaran was telling me a legend about a Temple ha— A Temple lady called Susannah in first century Jerusalem, who possessed a piece of music thought to have power over the dead. Very interesting.' She had just managed not to say harlot which Father would have said was an unbecoming word for a lady to use. Moira sometimes wondered what century he thought he was living in.

She said carefully, 'The monks want to produce a

booklet about it all, and if it's good enough maybe even sell it: so many cathedrals have little bookstalls now. Father Abbot asked Mother Bernadette if I could help with the research or even some of the actual writing.' Moira faltered into silence, because it was disconcerting when Father stared at her in this way. What had he thought of the idea? Please let him agree to it.

Edward was thinking: red hair, washed to molten flame by the firelight. Red hair was supposed to denote a passionate nature, although Mary had never really liked that side of marriage. No, there had never been anything passionate there, but then in Mary the red was palest ginger-cat, and in Moira it was vibrant copper. And it brushes her shoulders and curls over one breast . . . Had anyone ever touched her breasts? Had anyone tried to? He would not allow her to be despoiled by clumsy clodhopping boys with hot-breathed appetites and groping hands.

He said, 'And what has Mother Bernadette to say to all this?'

'She thought it was a very good idea.' It was infuriating to hear the pleading note come into her voice and Moira sat up a bit straighter. 'It will be very interesting, and I do think I can be of help. Brother Ciaran said I could make use of the Abbey library.' Surely, oh please, he could find nothing to object to in this?

Edward did not want his Moire Silk spending time in Curran Glen Abbey – he did not really want her spending time anywhere other than with him – but to object might have sounded unreasonable, which would have been short-sighted, or peevish, which would have been unattractive. And he did not want to offend the monks who had several times consulted him professionally over matters of boundaries and the quarterly rents and tied cottages on their land. Edward had been amazed at the speed with which Father Abbot settled Mahoney & Company's accounts, although it had to be said that Father Abbot always checked the calculations with an eagle eye first. Edward had not forgotten the very embarrassing incident when a total had been incorrect and he had had to go up to the Abbey and apologise personally. You could trust the Roman Catholic Church to make you feel inefficient as well as greedy; there had been absolutely no need for Father Abbot to recite the parable of the rich man and the unjust steward, with a side excursion into the worship of Mammon by way of extra reprimand. Edward had come away red-faced with indignation.

No, the Brothers could not be offended, although it was a pity that this scheme of Father Abbot's should bring Moira into contact with so many men, even though Edward was inclined to absolve most of the monks from possessing any lingering carnal appetites. Unfortunately you would have to except Brother Ciaran who frequented the Black Boar – although not during Lent it had to be admitted – and was far worldlier than any monk had any right to be, and who appeared to treat the most sacred of subjects with shocking nonchalance. Edward had never trusted Brother Ciaran and it made him feel a bit uneasy to think of Ciaran – to think of any of the monks! – spending perhaps several hours at a time with Moira; shut into the warm dim Abbey library with the scents of old leather and woodsmoke and centuries of learning. It was not the smallest use to think that most celibates were virtual neuters like Father Abbot himself, or dear old Brother Cuthbert who was about eighty, or Brother Daniel who was plump and genial. It was not the likes of Father Abbot or Daniel that Edward feared; it was the others: the ones who knew very well indeed about carnal desire and who waged a more or less ongoing fight against it. Like Ciaran. The unwelcome

27

suspicion that Moira found Ciaran attractive had more than once flickered on Edward's mind.

He supposed he would have to agree to this musical project, but he would take his own steps to see that his little girl was not brought into contact with Ciaran more than was absolutely necessary. And so he smiled at Moira and said benevolently, Well, they would have to see; perhaps it might be possible, although they would have to be sure it was not too tiring for her.

As he spoke, he heard, very faintly, the sounds of the Abbey bell chiming for Vespers and saw the sudden brightness in Moira's eyes. It was to be hoped she was not wondering if it was Ciaran up there in the bell tower, and harbouring foolish fancies about him.

Brother Daniel was on bell-ringing duty tonight, and he was going to get the job done as quickly as ever possible and go back down into the chapel with the others.

He did not like being on bell duty, because he always found the bell tower a touch eerie. Well, he found it very eerie indeed if the truth were told. Probably it was because the tower was the oldest part of the Abbey, set apart from the main buildings, so that you had to cross the quadrangle and unlock the door from outside. Probably it was because the tower was directly over the crypt, as well.

As soon as he was inside and had climbed up the tower steps and then up the little rung-ladder that debouched into the floor of the bell-ringing chamber, he always scrambled for the light switch as quickly as possible. He tried very hard to preserve an inner calm on these nights but being up here in the dark gave him the shudders. You were so awesomely conscious of the immense bronze mouths of the bells far above you and until you could switch on the electric light they had brought up here in 1940 when

28

Curran Glen was electrified, you had the nastiest feeling that someone was standing silently in the dark watching you.

The climb up the stairs was becoming more arduous as he got older, and he reached the ringing chamber a bit out of breath. As he pressed down the switch, flooding the small boarded loft with light, he noticed a musty smell up here – he had not noticed it when he came up to ring for the mid-day Angelus, but he would make a note to get it washed down in the morning. It was really very nasty indeed. Daniel reached up to unlatch the little clerestory window to let in the clean night air and as he did so, he caught, like tinkling icicles on the air, the sound of soft piano music. He stood for a minute listening, and then remembered that the grandson of the notorious Jude Weissman was supposed to be coming to Mallow. Presumably he was already here, then. Daniel had been only a young boy when Jude had lived in Curran Glen, but he knew the legend. The older monks could remember how Jude used to fling wide Mallow's windows, and how his strange beautiful music drifted across the summer nights. It would be rather nice if the grandson did the same. It was very nice indeed to think of Mallow being lived in again. He turned to the tassel-ended sallies of the bells.

For Vespers – for all of the Daily Offices – the monks used the small sweet bell which their Tudor forbears had had cast in 1536 as a memorial to the dead Katherine of Aragon, and which had a thin clear treble. Daniel gave the statutory twelve notes – not one for each of the Apostles, as so many people thought, but in remembrance of the twelve brothers who had brought the Order to Ireland from Cremona in the twelfth century. Daniel had always rather liked the story of how they had travelled here under the leadership of the Order's Founder, Simon of Cremona.

29

He stood for a few minutes before embarking on the second 'reminder' bell. This was the part he disliked, because you could still hear the faint echo of the bells from the first ringing, and if you craned your neck, you could see straight up into the bell tower. You could see the immense bronze mouths of the bells themselves, only two others besides little sweet Aragon, although Father Abbot had wondered should they have a new one cast to commemorate Vatican II. Daniel concentrated on the different bells and their histories, which were all very interesting. There was gentle silvery Aragon, of course, but there was also Siege which had been presented to the Abbey in the eighteenth century to mark the ending of the Troubles, and then there was Victory, the immense wide-mouthed four-ton Victory, commemorating Waterloo. The monks seldom used Victory for the daily Offices and never for Vespers, not since uncharitably minded people down in the town had said that while it was all very stirring not to say historic to hear Victory's huge solemn note, when the wind was in the wrong quarter it spoiled the evening's episode of *Connelly's Hotel*.

It was time for the reminder ring. Six short swift chimes, and he would do it briskly and then he would go down from the tower and join the others for Vespers. He was reaching for the tassel-ended sallie of Aragon when he heard the sound.

A scraping. Hard stone against hard stone. Daniel whipped round, scanning the shadows. Something up here after all? But there was nothing to be seen and he shook his head angrily. Imagination.

And there it came again. A dull clanging. And beneath it something lighter. Something dry and rustling. Like old bones being rubbed together. Like ancient, sucked-dry flesh stirring . . . Something creeping out of the grave and feeling its blind fumbling way towards him . . . His heart began to pound, and a vague fluttering tightened about his chest. He waited, willing the silence to go on, praying that there had been nothing moving in the bell tower other than his own too-active imagination.

The sound came again almost immediately; a kind of harsh grating. As if something was being dislodged. As if stones were being dislodged. Daniel stood very still and his mind received the image of an immense slab of stone or rock being moved. Yes, but where? And then, as if in answer, he felt it vibrate upwards, as if it came from beneath, as if it was echoing up the walls.

Underneath . . .

Sweat sprang out on his brow, and he thought: the crypt! There's something moving in the crypt!

Moira thought she had just about managed to persuade Father into letting her help the monks with their project, which was almost more than she had dared hope for.

It was absurd how uncomfortable Father was making her feel these days. He had a way of looking at her lately which was – this was the odd bit – but it was exactly the way that road workers or building site men looked at you if you walked past them in the height of summer when you wore your thinnest skimpiest cotton shirts and skirts, so that you found yourself glancing guiltily down in case a button had come undone or a zip had slid open.

Since she had left school, Moira had taken to wearing cotton trousers or long flowing skirts of thin Indian cotton or silk – what some people called ethnic clothes – to hide the clumsy club foot. It had been rather fun to discover this method of making it less noticeable, but Father did not like the outfits: Drifty and bitty, he said and wouldn't she look nicer in a well-cut cotton frock or a suit with a proper waist

31

and buttons? There was a new Laura Ashley shop opening in Galway – they'd make a little expedition there together – and there were such things as mail order catalogues from places like Harvey Nichols. And had she really to wear her hair long and flowing as if she was no better than a tinker's child?

Moira would have looked ridiculous in the things Father wanted for her, and if you had red hair you might as well admit to it and let it grow. Bryony O'Rourke, whom the nuns had said was the giddiest girl St Asaph's had ever known, but who everybody agreed was the best-looking and the best company, said there was a new expression: if you've got it, flaunt it. I'll flaunt it, Moira had thought, rebelliously. And long hair was fun, because you could twist it up on top with little tendrils escaping over your neck, or thread it with beads. Father said she looked like a gypsy and why not have it cut and shaped into a nice bob, and Mother had wanted to make her a blouse with darts at the bust and a Peter Pan collar. Nobody Moira knew ever got wolf whistles by wearing a homemade blouse with a Peter Pan collar and having a shaped bob, and when you had a club foot and knew you walked with an ugly limp the wolf whistles were pretty gratifying.

She went out into the garden for a breath of air after supper, which was about as far as she ever managed to get in the evening. Tim Shaughnessey, who was the son of Dr Shaughnessey and thought by all the girls to be the sexiest boy in Curran Glen, had once asked could he take her to the cinema and maybe a bite of supper afterwards – actually coming up to the house to ask Father's permission for Heaven's sake! – but Father had not permitted it. 'Our little girl is not very strong,' he had said, making it sound as if it was a virtue. 'And I am afraid she is rather nervous

32

of going out after dark. A little homebird.' From then on Tim Shaughnessey had started taking out Bryony O'Rourke, and smiled at Moira in an embarrassed way when they met.

Three or four times a year there were discos and cheese-and-French-bread suppers at the Black Boar, and Moira had asked could she attend one of these – Bryony and the others were going and it would be a great night. But Father had embarked on one of his confidential little talks, saying that since she would not be able to dance people would wonder why she was there, which might be distressing. He could not bear his little girl to be upset, he had said emotionally, and it had been impossible to explain that you did not actually have to dance: you went to meet up with people and have a few glasses of wine or lager, and join in the fun. Moira had not asked again, because it was not worth hearing about dance-hall tarts, and having Mother join in and say that in her day there had been a nasty name for girls who went to dances not intending to dance. Moira had wondered what decade they both thought they were living in, because life seemed to have stopped for them around 1940.

As she was going outside, Father called to her to be sure to put on her fleecy-lined coat, and Moira clenched her teeth and waited for him to say, 'the one that makes you look like Daddy's little teddy bear'. He said it, dead on cue, and Moira clenched her teeth. If Tim Shaughnessey had heard *that* he would never have got as far as suggesting the cinema and supper at Murphy's.

It was cool and quiet in the garden. Moira sent up a prayer that Father would not come out to join her and stand a bit too close so that his thigh was pressing against hers.

She could see Mallow House from here, a dark crouching outline against the trees. It had been empty for as long as Moira could remember, and everyone at St Asaph's had giggled about it and vied to tell the scariest stories, because it was supposed to be haunted by the ghost of Jude Weissman, who had been executed for treason after the Second World War. One term, several of the girls at St Asaph's had a dare to go up to Mallow, and came back bragging that they had broken a window and got inside, and danced in Jude's music room, which everyone said was where the ghost walked, and played 'Chopsticks' on his piano.

'But did you see the ghost?' Moira had asked, round-eyed, and the girls had doubled over with laughter and dug one another in the ribs, and said, Sure hadn't they seen plenty, and then gone on exaggeratedly lurching walks around the common room, moaning and wringing their hands, helpless with mirth. Bryony O'Rourke, who usually went one better than everyone else, had dragged her school tie to one side and jerked it upwards in her hand, with the idea of portraying a hanged man, but unfortunately Mother Fidelia had come in at that very minute and clapped her hands in horror and said, Did they think the good Lord gave them voices to shriek like banshees while people were trying to study, and if Madame O'Rourke thought her poor father was working his fingers to the bone just to give his daughter school uniforms to make a pig's breakfast of, her wits had flown straight out of the window! Moira had never really found out if Mallow was haunted by Jude Weissman, and she did not think that Bryony O'Rourke and her crowd had found out either.

She sighed and turned to go back inside before Father could come hurrying out to ask why she was standing out here in the dark by herself.

Chapter Four

Ciaran was late for Vespers and nearly missed it altogether because he was closeted in Father Abbot's study with a lady.

He had not been surprised when Father Abbot had asked him to receive the young woman who was apparently seeking permission to camp in the Abbey's western meadow, because Father Abbot was inclined to be wary of females. 'Deal with her for me, Ciaran, will you?' he had said. 'If she lives in a caravan she might be one of these New Age Travellers which would terrify me so much that I shouldn't know what to say to her. And you've more experience at handling women than I have.'

The New Age lady was punctual to the minute and she shook hands with Ciaran which was unexpected because most females avoided physical contact with monks.

'Brother Ciaran?' She pronounced it correctly which pleased him. 'I'm Kate Kendal. Thank you for agreeing to see me.'

Her voice was very cool and very English and very well bred. It was a voice that Ciaran associated with Oxford double-firsts and Cheltenham Ladies' College rather than with someone who lived in a caravan in a field. He motioned to her to sit down in the visitor's chair, and took the seat behind Father Abbot's desk, considerably intrigued.

Kate Kendal was pale and thin with long straight black

hair and slanting cheekbones. Her eyes were so wide apart that they were almost grotesque and Ciaran who had been, as Father Abbot had wilily pointed out, very used to women indeed before entering the Order, was unable to decide if she was startlingly beautiful or very nearly ugly. She was wearing tight black trousers and leather boots, with a loose jacket made of squares of different-coloured chenille: maroon and violet and indigo. There was a faint, feminine scent about her: nothing so definite as sprayed-on perfume, but a clean-hair, clean-skin aura.

Ciaran said, 'You're asking permission for temporary occupancy of our meadow, Miss Kendal, is that right? Or should I say Mrs?' She was not wearing a wedding ring, but that meant nothing at all; Ciaran could list in double figures the women he had known who took wedding rings on and off their fingers with an alacrity that bordered on the promiscuous.

'Kate will do.' She regarded him thoughtfully and then said, 'First of all, I'm concerned that I don't commit any kind of trespass, and I'm hoping you'll give me permission to camp on your land for two or three weeks. I can pay rent, of course. It can't be much but I never heard of the Catholic Church turning down any offer of money.'

'Oh, we never refuse a good offer,' said Ciaran, at once. 'Father Abbot thought you were a New Age Traveller and it terrified him. But you're not, are you?'

She smiled, 'Nothing so unconventional. I'm on my own here. I'm quite law-abiding, I promise, and there won't be any loud music or ill-tended cooking fires or drugs.'

'How did you know we owned the land?' said Ciaran. 'Most people believe that it's common land, never parcelled out to tenants under the old manorial laws. In fact it's still in our tenure.'

'I looked up Titles to the land in Galway,' said Kate. 'Part of my research. The monks are still manorial overlords.'

'We are, although not many people know it. And yes, Ms Kendal, it does have a beautifully feudal ring to it.'

Kate smiled suddenly. 'How did you know what I was thinking?'

'You have a very expressive face.' He sat back. 'Would you mind if I asked your reasons for wanting to be here?'

'Of course not. That's the second point. I'm researching ancient liturgical music, and your Abbey has an unusual reputation in that area.'

She stopped and Ciaran said thoughtfully, 'Has it indeed?'

'According to some of the stuff I've found, you're one of the few religious houses in Ireland still using the Ambrosian plainsong in its original form,' said Kate. 'I thought that if I could be given permission to use your library to see what manuscripts you might have referring to the Abbey's founding, or even its actual founder—?'

They looked at one another. 'Early plainsong?' said Ciaran at last.

'Yes. Dating to around AD 350.' There was an unmistakable note of defensiveness now.

Ciaran said softly, 'I'm prepared to acknowledge you know what you're talking about, but apart from that I think you're a terrible liar, Kate. Because whatever else you're up to you certainly aren't here to research into early Church music.'

Kate hesitated and then grinned. 'Trust a religious to spot a spurious tale,' she said. 'I thought I'd done it so well.'

'You had. But I was trained to spot a lie at twenty paces.'

'Police?'

'Nothing so respectable. The dusty purlieus of the law.'

'You were a solicitor? – no, that's wrong – A barrister? Yes, of course you were. I can see you persuading witnesses into being indiscreet,' said Kate.

'Oh, I've brought to light a few indiscretions in my time, Ms Kendal,' rejoined Ciaran blandly. 'And I've caused one or two as well.'

'That I can believe.'

Ciaran studied her. 'You know, I wish you'd tell me what this is really about,' he said.

'I can't. It's a – a private quest. I'm almost certainly chasing a chimera, but I'm vain enough not to want to be proved wrong in public.' She paused, and then said, 'I expect you're used to scholars and historians with obsessions. The geographical location of the Lost Atlantis, or was Christ a space traveller – I probably shouldn't have said that to a monk.'

'Why not, it's an intriguing theory,' said Ciaran at once. 'But I recognise an attempt to turn the conversation in a different direction.'

Kate looked at him. 'It's all right,' she said suddenly. 'I mean, you can trust me. I'm not doing anything illegal or even immoral.' The grin showed again. 'Well, not immoral very often and never publicly. Is that bell summoning you to something?'

'It is.' It was the first Vespers bell, in fact. Ciaran, who should have been on his way to the chapel and composing his mind for the evening prayers, stayed where he was. After a moment, he said, 'Listen now, I think there's a dozen reasons why I shouldn't give permission for you to use the library, but I can't bring any one of them to mind. We could let you in for a couple of hours – unfortunately no more, Father Abbot's a bit strict – but it would be free tomorrow morning. Would that do? There're a couple of early accounts about the Abbey's founder, I'll get the librarian to put them out for you. I can't think of any reason why you shouldn't take a few notes,' he said. 'And – should we say five punts a week for the field?'

'Very acceptable on both counts,' said Kate at once. 'The rent's a peppercorn, you know.'

'Well, the Church never despises the peppercorns of this world.'

'Thank you very much. Will you take a cheque for two weeks now?'

'I will indeed.'

She wrote the cheque quickly and her fingers brushed his as she handed it over. Ciaran felt the faintest prickle of electricity across his skin, and in the same moment, Kate's eyes flew upwards to meet his, and he knew she had felt it as well. For the first time, a trace of colour touched the high cheekbones.

And then she stood up, and the moment passed, and Ciaran was left with nothing more than the impression of cool deliberate efficiency. Just as well, of course. As he opened the door for her, he said, 'Will you let me know how your work progresses? We're interested in everything concerning the Abbey's history.'

'Of course.' She met his eyes squarely, and then grinned.

'Of course you won't,' said Ciaran.

'No. But thank you for trusting me. Are you going to be late for whatever that bell was for?'

'Vespers. Yes I am, but it won't be the first time and they'll start without me. I'll see you out.'

Vespers, with its formal evening prayers, was a good meeting time; a gathering together of all the various strands and fragments of the entire Abbey before going in to

39

supper in the long cool refectory. Supper followed immediately afterwards, and since Father Abbot believed it to be the mark of a civilised community to have conversations at meals, there was no Rule of Silence at table. You brought to the table the amusing or interesting or encouraging things you had encountered during your day, and you knew that everyone else would be doing the same. It was an exchanging, said the monks, pleased with the small unconventionality. A stepping outside of the Rule for an hour. Several people said rather caustically that if there was to be any stepping outside the Rule you could usually look to Ciaran to be at the forefront, but others said, No, it was more that Ciaran did not notice the Rule in the first place.

Ciaran reached his stall only a few minutes late, and heard with pleasure the familiar swell of the monks' voices and the resonance of the organ. The twilight was already slanting through the south quatrefoil and lying across the chapel's polished oak floor. His stall faced the window that looked out on the quadrangle and at each of the Offices throughout the day he could see how the shadow of the bell tower lengthened across the old cobbled square. At Vespers during the summer it just touched the ivy-clad library wing, but at this time of year the bell tower was shrouded in darkness.

It was not shrouded in darkness tonight. The small clerestory window near the top of the tower was open, and light poured outwards from it. Ciaran frowned and then dragged his concentration back to the plainchant. Probably whoever was on bell duty had simply forgotten to switch off the light. This was entirely reasonable until Ciaran remembered that Brother Daniel was bell ringer this week, and Daniel was a very methodical monk indeed. It was just about conceivable that he had missed it when he locked the

40

outside tower door, which was not something any of them ever forgot, on account of stray cats and weasels getting in. On one memorable occasion a tinker had spent the night in the chapel, sleeping in Father Abbot's own stall and urinating in the font, which had meant that the Bishop had to re-consecrate the whole chapel and everything had to be swabbed down with Jeyes' fluid.

Ciaran thought there would be nothing wrong, but it would not hurt to just look across the quadrangle when Vespers was over, to make sure the outside door to the tower was closed. Aside from tinkers and cats, monks were ordinary people and like anybody else they could fall down stairs. Dear old Brother Cuthbert, eighty if he was a day and the Abbey's Sub-Prior, had some years ago slipped on a too-highly-polished section of floor in the chapel and knocked himself out on the altar rail and it had been an hour and a half before anyone missed him. Ciaran glanced round the chapel, but saw that after all, Daniel was in his stall, his head bowed in prayer, his face in shadow inside the hood of his gown.

It was unusual for any of them to pull the hood up, but perhaps Daniel had caught a cold in the draughty bell loft.

Ciaran slipped across the quadrangle after the service, and into the bell tower. The others were already going in to the refectory, but he would not be missed for the few minutes this would take.

The tower door was ajar which was so unlike Daniel that the prickle of unease increased. Ciaran hesitated, and then pushed the door wide. It was odd how you could hear a thin humming from the bells in here, even from the ground. As if they were singing quietly to themselves up there in the dark.

He would just look into the bell chamber to make sure

there was nothing wrong and then he would come straight back down and switch off the lights. It felt extraordinarily eerie in here, and it was getting eerier by the minute. Supposing a tramp had got in again and was lying up here, out of his mind on meths?

As he walked across the tiny wooden-floored vestibule towards the stair leading up to the bell loft, he heard a faint moan and spun round at once. Something behind him!

It was then that he saw that the door leading down to the crypt was open.

Daniel had managed to crawl to the foot of the stair, but he had not been able to get any farther; Ciaran understood this at once, and horror flooded over him.

Whoever had attacked Daniel had stripped him of his woollen robe and he was clad only in the cotton undershirt and shorts which most of the monks wore as under-garments. He was huddled over, his hands covering his face, but Ciaran could see that he was breathing, even though it was the struggling shallow breathing of one in extreme pain. He instantly thought: heart attack! because it was easy to visualise an intruder falling on Daniel, stripping him and leaving him for dead. Entirely believable said the upper half, the logical half of his mind.

But the other half, the half that owed nothing at all to logic, said, insidiously: *yes, but he is in the crypt. In the CRYPT* . . .

Ciaran frowned and made an abrupt movement as if to push the silvery voice away. He bent over Daniel's prone body, trying to take his hands away from his face, trying to speak soothingly. He felt the cold fingers stiffen resistantly, and Daniel groaned again and a shuddering spasm wracked his body.

'Who—'

42

'It's Brother Ciaran. You're all right, Daniel,' said Ciaran immediately. 'You're just inside the bell tower, and you're quite safe. But I'll have to fetch help.'

Daniel said, 'There was something here—'

'A tramp,' said Ciaran at once. 'I think you've been attacked. But whoever it was is gone, and we'll get you to the infirmary—' He reached for Daniel's hands again, and as he did so, Daniel gave another of the deep dreadful moans.

'No— You don't understand what he did—'

As Ciaran pulled Daniel's hands away from his face, he felt horror slam into the pit of his stomach.

Daniel's face was smeary and crusted with blood, the flesh torn and hanging in bloodied tatters. Whatever had attacked him had gouged deep wounds into his cheeks and neck, the worst still oozing blood, but some beginning to dry and crust over.

But where his eyes had been were two deep bloody wounds, and as Ciaran stared, his mind spinning with sick horror, blood and thick viscous eye fluid welled up and spilled over Daniel's mutilated face, running down over his chin.

Daniel moaned again and turned his face as if trying to see. Ciaran thought: oh dear God, he is trying to see, but his eyes are no longer there to see with. Whatever attacked him, didn't just claw his face.

It clawed his eyes. It almost clawed them out. That's why he wouldn't take his hands away. He's been lying down here trying to hold his eyes in place with his hands.

Ciaran regarded his two superiors in Father Abbot's small firelit study and said, 'I don't believe it and I can't believe it. It's centuries since anyone gave any credence to that old legend.'

43

'Legends are often rooted in fact, Ciaran. And you yourself saw what had been done to Daniel. Clawed and mutilated.'

Ciaran repressed a shudder and said, 'How is he?'

'Brother John's staying with him in the infirmary and he'll let us know if there's any change.' This was Cuthbert. Sub-Prior and the Abbey's oldest inhabitant. 'They're hopeful that he'll recover, although of course his eyes are gone—'

'Yes.' Ciaran chewed his lower lip thoughtfully and then said, 'I suppose we're thinking it was a tramp who attacked him.'

'Why would a tramp steal a monastic habit?' said Father Abbot.

'Why not if it was better than what he had?'

'Excuse me, Brother Ciaran, but there's something I don't think you've had time to consider.' Cuthbert was so trusting he would take up the cudgels on behalf of the devil himself if Satan were to put forward a plausible case over a pot of tea in the parlour, but he could occasionally be unexpectedly cynical.

'Yes?'

'Daniel was attacked immediately after the first Vespers ring,' said Cuthbert. 'He must have been.'

'He can't have been,' said Ciaran at once. 'I saw him at Vespers myself. He came down to the chapel and then went back to the bell tower.' He stopped. 'But he wasn't in the bell tower when I found him. He was in the crypt at the top of the stair.'

'And,' said Cuthbert, leaning forward, 'why would he have gone back to the tower in the first place?'

'Because he forgot to switch off the light,' said Ciaran. 'I saw it myself from the chapel. My stall looks onto the quadrangle and I could see it. He must have left the light on

44

after he rang Vespers. It's easily done.'

'Yes, but he didn't ring Vespers, not completely,' said Cuthbert. 'He rang the first call, but he was attacked before he could ring the reminder.'

'Are you sure? We're all so used to the bells that we hear them without knowing we hear them. I'm sounding like Irving,' said Ciaran crossly.

'Daniel rang the first call,' said Cuthbert. 'Most people heard it – I heard it myself, because I was working in the library, and I thought, Ah, that's the first call—'

'Well, you would hear it in the library, it adjoins the tower—'

'—and I thought, Oh good, I'll just have time to put St Thomas Aquinas back in his proper place, because as you know, Father, St Thomas lives on one of the very top shelves, under "A" as you'd expect, only it means getting onto the library steps and reaching up—'

'It doesn't actually matter about putting St Thomas back, Cuthbert—'

'—and it takes me a bit of time, because I'm not as agile as I once was, in fact I'm a bit creaky especially on steps. But I like to leave the library in order,' said Cuthbert firmly. 'And I thought, well, I'm all right for a minute or two because the second call hasn't sounded yet and until it does I can take my time.'

'Which you did.'

'Which I did,' agreed Cuthbert. 'But while I was taking my time, I was listening for the second call and it didn't come.'

'Forgive me, Brother, but are you absolutely sure about that?'

'My hearing might not be as sharp as it used to be,' said Cuthbert injured, 'but I can still hear Aragon ringing Vespers, especially when I'm only in the library.'

'I'm sorry,' said Ciaran at once.

'I didn't hear it because it wasn't rung,' explained Cuthbert, and Father Abbot said slowly,

'If that's true, then Daniel must have been attacked between the two calls.'

'He can't have been,' said Ciaran at once.

'Why not?'

'Because he was at Vespers. He was in his stall. I thought afterwards that he'd seen the bell tower light on as I did and gone across to—' He stopped again and then said slowly, 'Daniel couldn't have seen the light. Not from the chapel. His stall's on the dexter side, looking inwards.'

'Exactly, Brother.'

'But that means that he never came out of the bell tower.'

'Exactly,' said Cuthbert again.

'Then,' said Ciaran in a voice of horror, 'who was it who was in Daniel's stall at Vespers?'

'It was a tramp,' said Ciaran, clinging to his original idea. 'Father Abbot, Cuthbert, you know it must have been a tramp.'

'Would a tramp have put on Daniel's robe and come down to stand in Daniel's stall and take part in Vespers?'

'Yes, Father, and whoever it was, he knew the plainchant, because my own stall's only two along and I could hear that he was singing. How many outsiders would know our plainchant?' demanded Cuthbert, and Ciaran said thoughtfully,

'That's true. It isn't even Gregorian, it's the old Ambrosian chant.'

'And Daniel sounded a bit different,' said Cuthbert.

'How?'

'Well,' said Cuthbert rather reluctantly, 'I remember

46

thinking, My word, Brother Daniel sounds as if he's caught a bad cold in that draughty bell tower this week. And then I got a whiff of what I thought was camphorated oil or that evil-smelling cough stuff that Brother John keeps in the infirmary, only I can see now that I was simply associating it with the harsh voice.'

Ciaran said slowly, 'I noticed a smell in the bell tower, as well. Like disease. Or as if—'

'Yes?'

'As if a door had been opened on a chamber sealed off for centuries,' said Ciaran unwillingly.

There was a sudden charged silence. Then Ciaran said, 'That doesn't preclude a tramp, Father. They're all a bit—'

'No, but we have to remember where Daniel was found,' said Father Abbot. 'We have to remember that he was found actually in the crypt, and that he had been clawed. *Clawed*.' He frowned, and then said, 'And whoever attacked him came down into the chapel and joined in Vespers. He sang the plainchant – our own Ambrosian chant that dates back to eleventh century Italy. That Simon of Cremona brought to Ireland.'

He looked at Ciaran, and Ciaran said, 'And he had the hood pulled up. He had to keep his face hidden.'

'Well?' said Father Abbot. 'Doesn't that suggest one very particular thing to you? Something that had to conceal its face, something that left the stench of death in its wake— Something that knew the eleventh century plainchant. Above all, something that clawed our poor Daniel.'

He stopped, and Ciaran, staring at him, said in a half whisper, 'You're going to open up the tomb.'

Chapter Five

A cold dry breath of wind ruffled the papers on Father Abbot's desk, and Ciaran knelt down to replenish the fire. The ticking of the clock on the mantel suddenly seemed much louder.

At last, Ciaran said, 'Father Abbot, that – that thing that's buried in the crypt has been there for hundreds of years. It'll be a mouldering skeleton. A heap of bones. Nobody believes in the legend any more, and even if we do—'

He stopped and Father Abbot said, 'Even if we do . . .?'

'It needs the music to wake it,' said Ciaran. 'The – what did they used to call it? – the *Black Chant,* and— dear God, isn't this the most ridiculous conversation ever!' He made an impatient gesture. 'I hear what I'm saying but I don't believe I'm saying it,' said Ciaran.

'The tomb is there,' said Father Abbot. 'The tomb of Ahasuerus.' With the pronouncing of the name, a sudden silence closed down on the room, and Ciaran had the feeling that something outside had crept up to the uncurtained windows and was standing just out of sight, listening. The feeling was so strong that he crossed the room and looked out. Something moving out there? But there was nothing, and Ciaran drew the curtains and came back into the room.

'I'll give you the tomb,' he said, resuming his seat. 'I'll

even give you the *Black Chant*. Too many intelligent people have believed in it.'

'Mozart believed in it, didn't he?' said Cuthbert unexpectedly. 'The *Chant* and the legend of the devil's piper?'

'So it's said. Wasn't he a Freemason?' said Father Abbot.

'I've no idea. What's that got to do with it?'

'Only that they've kept some odd secrets over the centuries.'

'So,' said Ciaran caustically, 'has the Roman Catholic Church.'

'Oh yes.'

'But the music vanished hundreds of years ago!' said Ciaran. 'We all know that. And even if you believe in it – even if you truly believe that a piece of music exists that has power over that thing in the tomb – do you really believe there's a musician in today's world with sufficient fire in his belly or passion in his soul to re-create it?'

'I'll tell you who could have done it,' said Cuthbert. 'He's dead now. God keep him, but he could have done it. The grandfather of that young man who's just come to Mallow House. Jude Weissman.'

'Judas,' said Ciaran, softly.

'Well, we didn't call him that in those days, of course. But he wrote something while he was here that people said had an oddness to it. Father Abbot – your predecessor, that was, Father – always wondered if the tomb influenced him, Mallow being so near and all. I remember him quite well,' said Cuthbert. 'He played the Abbey's organ for us one Easter, which considering he was Jewish was very generous, I thought, because I don't know that I'd go into a synagogue. He played Bach, I think it was. And some Handel. He was a very brilliant young man, although he

49

was supposed to be a bit erratic. We used to hear him sometimes in the summer when the windows of the house were open. Only very faintly, but it was there. The scent of lilac and Jude Weissman's music. The two always go together for me,' said Cuthbert, with unexpected poetry. 'We all prayed for him later, when they said he was a traitor, and we offered up Masses for the repose of his soul after they executed him. He left a wife and small child. It was all very terrible.'

Father Abbot said thoughtfully, 'Is it possible that the grandson has inherited his gifts?'

'And found the *Chant* by accident and played it tonight? But that would be impossible,' said Ciaran. 'Wouldn't it? If the *Chant* does exist, no one could find it unless they knew about it? And if they found it, they'd certainly know about it.'

He looked at Cuthbert for confirmation, but Cuthbert said thoughtfully, 'I'm not so sure. I wouldn't swear that some of these modern pop music people haven't occasionally hit a nerve.'

Ciaran smiled for the first time. 'Cuthbert, you never cease to amaze me. What on earth do you know about pop music?'

'Only that it occasionally drives young people to drugs or suicide,' said Cuthbert. 'And that's it's always much too loud.'

Ciaran said slowly, 'You could be right about pop music and the *Black Chant*, Cuthbert. There was a case a year or so ago where a young man blasted out his brains with a shotgun and his family tried to prove that there was some kind of subliminal message in the pop group he followed. They even went to Court over it, I think.'

'People forget that the devil is extremely clever,' said Cuthbert seriously. 'They think of him – if they think of him at all – as a persuasive gentleman with horns and a forked tail, but if he went about today's world looking like that, people would only think it was a gimmick to sell central heating. If he's in the world today – and of course he is – he'll be in all the things that lower people's resistance. Drugs and drink, and excuse me, Father Abbot, but sex.'

Ciaran said suddenly, 'Daniel wasn't sexually assaulted, was he?' and the ugly words jarred on the gentle scholarly ambience of the room. Cuthbert, shocked, drew in his breath and said: bless them and save them all, certainly not. 'Whatever else has been said about Ahasuerus, it's never been said he wasn't a gentleman.'

'It's never been said the Prince of Darkness wasn't a gentleman either,' said Ciaran caustically. 'But if Ahasuerus is such a gentleman, would he have injured Daniel so violently?'

'He might,' said Father Abbot at last. 'He might if there was a struggle of some kind. If Ahasuerus had broken out and Daniel tried to stop him. We'll know more when Daniel regains consciousness. In the meantime—' He stopped and then said, 'In the meantime, there's the tomb.' He glanced uneasily to the window, and Ciaran thought: so he heard it, as well. 'We'll have to open the tomb, I'm afraid,' said Father Abbot. 'Or at least, see if it's been disturbed.'

He stood up, and Ciaran said, 'Now? You're going to go down to the crypt *now*?'

'Bless me, is that altogether wise, Father? I don't want to interfere, but it's very nearly dead of night—'

Father Abbot said very firmly, 'We can't delay. We don't dare delay. If that thing has really woken—' He broke off, and then said, 'Ciaran, you'll come with me?'

'Into the jaws of—' Ciaran stopped and spread his

51

hands. 'It's the maddest thing I ever heard of, but I'll come with you.'

'We needn't wake the others. I don't want to worry them until we know if there's anything to worry about.'

'I'll come as well if you want me,' said Cuthbert.

'Would you, Cuthbert? Three of us would manage better than two.'

'Yes, and that vault hasn't been unsealed since – dear me, Brother John Joseph in seventeen fifty, and that was only to repair a bit of chipped stonework. We'll need the proper tools,' said Cuthbert, becoming practical. 'And candles as well, because there's no electricity down there, you do know that, do you, Father?'

'I do know there's no electricity, Cuthbert.'

'And,' said Ciaran in an expressionless voice, 'precious little sanity either. Very well, *en avant*, Father.'

It was not quite what the novelists called the witching hour, but it was close enough. Ciaran supposed that if you were going to commit a foolhardy act, you might as well do it with the full complement of midnight chimes – or at least ten o'clock chimes – from the clock tower and with only the flickering light of a candle to see by.

As they crossed the quadrangle he again had the feeling that they were being watched, and he paused, holding his candle aloft, shielding it from the sighing night wind with one hand. I believe there is something out there, he thought. But there was nothing to see except the Abbey's own black shadows, and there was no sound except the wind stirring the dry leaves on the ground, and he turned back to where Cuthbert was unlocking the outer door of the tower.

The crypt stairs, up which Daniel had managed to drag himself, twisted round and down. They were dark and enclosed and narrow, and the candle flames burned up

52

strongly in the dry air, throwing their three shadows onto the ancient stones, exaggerated and grotesque. The stone steps were worn away at the centre, and Ciaran felt a shiver of awe at this evidence of age. As they went down, he found himself turning round several times to scan the shadowy stairs above. The feeling of being silently followed was very strong indeed.

And then Cuthbert was saying in a matter-of-fact voice, 'It's over there, I believe. Directly ahead.'

'I don't think we're going to miss it, Cuthbert.'

Ciaran could feel the centuries of goodness and the decades of prayer and sacred music receding. Like water streaming off the oiled feathers of a seabird. An albatross or a storm petrel . . . Why did I think of storm petrels? A bird of ill-omen on my right hand . . . Yes, but what sits, invisible, on my left? And supposing the tomb is tenantless . . .?

He shivered again and at once Father Abbot said, 'The atmosphere is not good here.'

'There's no air,' said Ciaran shortly.

'That's not what I meant.'

'I know.'

Cuthbert was setting more candles at intervals on the floor, using the melting wax to stand them upright. 'Light,' he said. 'Very important.'

'Important for what? Grave-desecration?'

'For fighting back any kind of darkness,' said Cuthbert with complete seriousness, and Ciaran at once said, 'Forgive me, Brother.'

He looked about him at the shadowy crypt, the low archways of stone, the shelves of rock at the sides, and drew breath to frame a prayer. As he did so, Father Abbot's hand came down on his arm.

There in front of them, shrouded in twisting darkness,

was a crouching black bulk: a waist-high rectangle of dark stone, roughly eight feet in length and four or five feet wide.

The tomb of Ahasuerus.

It was more conventional than Ciaran remembered, although he was no longer sure if he had in fact seen it properly until now. There was no reclining figure on the lid, but whoever had constructed the tomb had apparently spent some time in Eastern countries, for there was a strong resemblance to the sarcophagi of the Egyptians. But Ahasuerus wasn't Egyptian, thought Ciaran, puzzled. I don't believe the legend, not entirely, but I know what it says, and in every version Ahasuerus was a Jew, he was the rebel High Priest of the Temple . . .

Whatever Ahasuerus had been in life, in death he lay inside a long elaborate stone sepulchre, embellished with ancient symbols of light, including the Aryan swastika – the real thing, not the later distortion of the Nazis, thought Ciaran, with awe – and with Celtic and Pictish crosses as well as the conventional crucifix, the *crux commissa* representing Christ's gibbet.

At his side, Father Abbot said softly, 'They bound him to the grave with every symbol of light they could find and still he escaped. The tomb is the original one, of course, but the inner coffin was made several hundred years later. Or so the legend says,' he added.

'Is he – forgive me, Father – but was his body *embalmed*?'

'I have no idea.'

As the three men walked slowly forward, their eyes never leaving the crouching outline of the tomb, dense pools of darkness slithered across the floor at its base. And then Father Abbot murmured a prayer and held up the candle and the shadows seemed to dissolve and trickle away.

Even before they reached it, they could see that the stone lid had been dislodged – from beneath? thought Ciaran, atavistic fear prickling his skin – and as they approached, a faint drift of corruption breathed outwards from the yawning blackness of the interior. The breath of the grave, thought Ciaran and felt a knot of sickness form at the pit of his stomach.

He drew in a deep breath, his free hand closing about the crucifix he wore at his waist and he was grateful when Father Abbot said in a perfectly ordinary voice, 'Do you both see the inscription on the side? In the bas-relief near the top?'

Ciaran held his candle up so that the warm glow fell across the side of the sepulchre. In a soft voice, he read the inscription.

'"*Non omnis moriar multaque pars mei Vitabit Libitinam. I shall not wholly die; large residues shall escape the Queen of Death*".' He looked at Father Abbott. 'So he really did claim immortality?'

'Apparently.' Father Abbot studied the carved words for a moment, and then said quietly, 'It's believed that it was our founders, the ancient *Fratres Cruciferi* Order, who caused those words to be engraved on the sepulchre.'

Ciaran looked back at the tomb, and felt once more the creeping fear. *Non omnis moriar* . . . He drew in a deep breath, and held up the candle.

The warm flickering light fell across the stone sepulchre, and the horror reared up and lashed against the minds of the three men.

The immense stone lid had been pushed aside so that it lay at right angles to the elaborate stone sepulchre. Inside was a smaller, more conventional coffin: wooden and unexpectedly flimsy, as if it might have been constructed hurriedly, in immense secrecy.

The inside of the stone tomb reeked of death and despair and agony. The wooden lid of the inner coffin had been flung aside, and a thin layer of discoloured linen lay discarded as if whatever had lain under it had pushed it aside and sat up.

The tomb was empty.

The fire in Father Abbot's study had hardly burned down at all, but Ciaran stacked more logs of wood on to it before taking a seat.

Cuthbert was glad to see Ciaran replenish the fire because hadn't the crypt been a nasty draughty place and their experience a very terrible one indeed.

'And with your permission, Father, we'll take a little drop of the brandy that the infirmary keeps for medicinal purposes. I've fetched it in for us.'

'I suppose,' said Ciaran, accepting the brandy gratefully, 'I suppose that it isn't all a series of coincidences? Could the lid have been moved by anything ordinary? Settlement in the foundations? Vandals? Have we had workmen in—?'

'The tomb was empty, Ciaran.'

'I'm not forgetting that.' Ciaran frowned, and then said, 'Listen now, could Ahasuerus – could anyone – have got out of that tomb from the inside? Rolled back the stone? I didn't mean that to sound quite so Biblical, Father.'

'The stone wouldn't be that heavy. And if you were trapped—'

'Could Daniel have helped him?' asked Cuthbert hesitantly. 'Was that why Ahasuerus clawed him?'

'I shouldn't think so. If Daniel heard something in the crypt, it's more likely that he'd go for help,' said Ciaran. 'I know I would. I wouldn't investigate that crypt after darkness unless I'd got at least two other people with me, and certainly not if I thought something was prowling about down there. Isn't it more likely that Daniel encountered – whatever it was – and was flung aside?' He made an impatient gesture. 'I'm beginning to sound as if I believe in all this,' he said.

Father Abbot said softly, 'Didn't you see the marks, Ciaran?'

'I— yes.' Ciaran looked at the older man. 'But I hoped no one else had,' he said.

'What— Father Abbot, Brother Ciaran, what marks?'

In a voice scraped raw with pity, Ciaran said, 'On the underside of the coffin lid were claw marks. Where – whatever was inside – had fought to get out.'

The silence came down again, heavy and stifling, but at length, Father Abbot said, 'The *Fratres Cruciferi* believed they had entombed Ahasuerus for ever. They thought Ahasuerus would never walk in the world again.' He paused, and then said, 'But as we know, they were wrong. Ahasuerus's last furious threat came true.'

'*Non omnis moriar . . .*' said Ciaran gently, 'I shall not wholly die.'

Chapter Six

Ahasuerus had hated the *Fratres Cruciferi* far more than he had thought it possible to hate anyone.

The *Cruciferi* had called themselves mission monks but Ahasuerus had known from the beginning that they were nothing more than greedy mendicant friars who had seen an opportunity to bring riches and prominence to their small impoverished brotherhood.

There had been twelve of them in Jerusalem on the day he was sentenced, but only five had been in the Judgement Hall. They had sat quietly listening, and, when the terrible sentence was finally pronounced, they had looked across at him with such self-righteousness that Ahasuerus had thought he would be damned if he would give them the satisfaction of seeing him break. The words of the sentence had struck against his mind so violently that for a moment the Judges and Elders who formed the Council of the Sanhedrin had blurred and wavered and sick dread had closed about him.

And then all of the old arrogance – the arrogance that the Elders had so deplored in him – had come surging to his rescue, and he had been able to stand straight and eye the Sanhedrin defiantly and uncaringly. It had been then he had flung the threat at them.

'I shall not wholly die . . . large residues shall escape the Queen of Death.' He heard with delight that his voice held all the arrogance he could wish, and he saw that only a small proportion of them recognised the words of the Roman philosopher and writer, Horace, and this had lent him further courage, for he had always been able to outwit the stupid sheep-creatures.

'I shall return!' he said in a low threatening voice, and felt the bolt of fear go through the Temple.

For a moment there was a terrible silence, and Ahasuerus had smiled, because for all their self-importance not one knew how to respond. It had been then the leader of the *Cruciferi* had stepped forward, speaking into the horrified silence and saying unctuously that if the Judges would permit, he and his brothers would undertake to convey the High Priest's body to a place of secrecy after death.

The Judges had glanced at one another from the corners of their eyes and Ahasuerus had seen the relief in their faces. They had asked what the monks had in mind, and they had stressed the need for secrecy. The threat to return was a vain boast, of course, but nevertheless— They looked across to Ahasuerus, half scared, half defiant. Nevertheless, they said firmly, the High Priest had consorted with the harlot-sorceress, Susannah – he had actually been caught in blatant and sacrilegious fornication with her on the high altar. The possibility that the threat might not be an idle one must therefore be in the forefront of their minds. Ahasuerus's coffin must be so well concealed that if he woke his return to the world would be barred by insuperable obstacles. His mutilated body must be lost so completely that the world would never know it had existed.

The monks had appeared undeterred, although Ahasuerus had seen the youngest frame the dread word 'immortality' silently, and shiver.

Also, said the Judges, the name of Ahasuerus was to be erased from every chronicle and every annal ever written by the Temple Scribes. Stonemasons were already waiting to begin the task of taking his name from the tablets. It would be as if he had never existed and if he was remembered at all, it would be as the renegade, the rebel High Priest who had been cast out of the Temple.

The monks conferred in low voices and then said they could do what was required. After death had finally taken place, they said, their expressions solemn but their hands curving greedily, they would seal the body into a stone tomb which they would carve with a warning, lest it should one day be found, and which they would also embellish with symbols of light.

'Christian symbols of light,' said the Judges, at once, their eyes cold, and the monks had glanced uneasily over their shoulders and said, Christian symbols, certainly. But would the Sanhedrin not consider that the creature, Susannah, the High Priest's partner in the sinful act, was believed to traffick with gods that owed nothing to the Christian beliefs? Would it not be better – would it not be *safer* to allow for all eventualities? They would advise that it was so, they said, unctuously.

There was a thoughtful silence, and then the Judges said, 'You are perhaps right in what you say. And then?'

And then, said the monks, they would take the stone tomb with them on their journey out of Jordan; they could let it be thought that they were transporting the body of a fellow monk to a resting place with his family. And although their vows naturally prevented them from accepting payment for the small service, if the Temple cared to further their Order's work, God would surely look kindly on the journey.

Ah. The single syllable was non-committal and the monks exchanged glances. And the journey itself? asked the Judges.

Well, said the spokesman, they had intended to go

towards the west when they left Jerusalem; partly across the old Persian and Isphahan caravan routes, but partly by sea. There was no reason, was there, why this was not acceptable?

There was no reason that anyone could think of.

Very well then, that would be the journey, although they would of course avoid Pharaoh's Egypt and travel north through Turkey and Greece, crossing the Aegean Sea and trusting to the trade winds to be favourable. They thought they would not be challenged.

And the threat made by the doomed High Priest? asked the Judges. The threat to return after death?

The monks permitted themselves small smiles. Surely only an angry boast, they said. The Elders themselves had said it was so, only a short while ago and it could not be otherwise. But they would bear it in mind: they would look for a desolate mountain cavern, or a bottomless pit in a remote forest, or a fathomless lake and they would consign the stone coffin into oblivion for ever.

Ahasuerus, the renegade High Priest of the Temple, the scholar and the sinner and the rebel would vanish from history as completely as if he had never lived.

No one in the world would ever hear of him again.

Isarel had searched Mallow from cellar to attic and found nothing, other than the rather unpleasant evidence of mice in the former and bats in the latter. You could set traps for mice or get a cat, but he suspected that bats might be a protected species. Be damned to that, thought Isarel crossly, going back downstairs, and reaching for the whiskey bottle again. If there's such a thing as a Pest Control Company out here, it can poison the evil little bastards with my blessing, never mind if twenty Dracula Societies or fifty Preservation Groups set up protest camps on the doorstep!

The tapping had probably been nothing more than the wind in the trees after all. There was a huge old oak whose branches were close to one of the upstairs windows, and it was perfectly possible that the branches had tapped against the pane. It was rather a friendly thing if you looked at it sensibly. Isarel drained the whiskey in his tumbler and resolved to look at it thus.

As he re-crossed the hall back to the music room, he stopped in mid-stride, his heart resuming its earlier thudding, icy sweat sliding between his shoulder blades. This time he was not imagining it. This time there was something outside the door.

Whatever it was, it was standing on the other side of the door, darkly silhouetted against the chequered blue and red fanlight. Isarel stood perfectly still and waited, and as he did so, whoever (whatever?) was outside seemed to gather itself together as if making up its mind to a particular course of action. The brass knocker was lifted and let to fall, echoing with breath-snatching loudness in the quiet house.

Anger rose up in Isarel without warning, because how dared anyone come up to his house at – what was it now? a quarter to midnight, for heaven's sake! – and rap so peremptorily on the door? Without a thought for caution which ought to have dictated a firm enquiry through the bolted door first, Isarel strode forward and flung wide the door.

On the threshold, his uncovered head the colour of pale horse-chestnuts in the moonlight, a square glossy beard emphasising his lean features, stood the figure of a monk.

Isarel stared and then said, 'Yes? What do you want?' And was glad to hear that he sounded ordinarily impatient, as anyone might sound on being dragged away from an absorbing piece of work, or as any householder might sound on being summoned to his own front door on a dark night. The word 'householder' gave him unexpected confidence. My house. My fortress. How dare you come knocking in the middle of the night!

'Well?' Curiosity was replacing the fear and Isarel held the candle challengingly aloft and said sharply, 'Who the hell are you?'

There was a silence, during which Isarel had time to remember all over again Mallow's desolate situation, and then the monk said, not making it a question, but a statement: 'Would you forgive the lateness of the hour.'

'Lateness! Jesus God, it's nearly midnight!' said Isarel.

'I know. But I saw you had lights burning in the downstairs rooms.' A pause. 'I should like to talk to you, Mr West.'

A madman. Some kind of religious lunatic, probably. This made Isarel feel a bit better, but not much, because if he had to be at the mercy of a madman he would very much prefer it to be within calling distance of help. And whoever the madman was, he was in possession of Isarel's name. Isarel said, 'What do you want?' again.

'May I come in?' said the monk, and it occurred to Isarel that he had the soft beguiling voice of so many southern Irishmen, but that his eyes were cool and very intelligent.

And the one thing you never did, the absolute last thing any sane reasoning person ever did was to invite into his house the unknown stranger who tapped on his door in the middle of the night and requested admittance. Wild notions of devil worship, unfrocked priests who had to wait for your polite invitation to cross your threshold before they killed you in some gruesome ritual of their own, flashed across Isarel's mind.

He said, 'Who are you?' and waited, and after what

seemed to be a long time, the monk said, 'My name is Ciaran O'Connor.'

He glanced over his shoulder to the dark countryside and then looked back at Isarel and said, 'Would you invite me in, Mr West?'

There were a number of things that could be done. The most obvious was to say, 'Sod off,' and slam the door hard and then beat it out the back and get help. The next most obvious was to engage the man in polite conversation and edge your way round until you had manoeuvred yourself on the other side, within reach of the car. Isarel tried to remember if he had pocketed the ignition keys and thought he had not.

The worst possible thing of all would be to say, 'Please come in,' and hold wide the door.

Isarel heard himself say, 'Come in.'

And held wide the door.

Chapter Seven

Isarel did not recall offering his uninvited guest a seat; he had not, in fact, asked him to do more than step into the hall, and yet somehow they were both seated in the music room, with Jude's piano melting into the shadows and extra candles lit and set on each side of the mantelpiece. The fire had been replenished and wine had been offered and poured.

Ciaran said, 'This is very good wine, Mr West.'

'If you're going to drink yourself into oblivion, you might as well do so with style.'

'Is that your aim? To drink yourself into oblivion?'

'Possibly. The red stream of life that creates the tide of unknowing. What's it got to do with you?' Isarel re-filled his glass and lounged back in his chair, which sagged and was falling to pieces like everything else in Mallow, but which was surprisingly comfortable. 'And why are you here?'

Ciaran leaned forward. 'You are Jude Weissman's grandson, aren't you?' he said.

'Have you brought a distraint on the furniture?'

'No.'

'Or a writ to possess the house? Or a set of scales to weigh a pound of carrion flesh against three thousand outstanding ducats or even vulgar Irish punts?'

'I have not.'

'You never know with Jude,' said Isarel. 'Some of the stories about him— Still, if you're neither bailiff nor tipstaff?'

'I am not.'

'Then,' said Isarel, 'I admit to being Jude Weissman's grandson. What about it?'

'Earlier tonight you played his piano.'

'May not a man bring forth the music of the gods or even his grandfather? As a matter of fact I did play it, but I don't see what it's got to do with you.'

Isarel drained his glass and re-filled it, and Ciaran said, 'Should you object to telling me what you played?'

'Not in the least,' said Isarel blandly. 'It was a variation on a theme.' He regarded his guest unblinkingly, and for the first time, Ciaran smiled.

'The classic evasion,' he said.

'I'm not being evasive, I'm being offensive.' Isarel drank his wine. 'I suppose you will tell me what you want at some point, will you? Or do I call the police – what do they call them here, *guarda*, isn't it? – and have you forcibly removed.'

'But,' said Ciaran, 'Mallow has no phone.'

'Screw that, I'll summon the Pope and a wagonload of Rabbis if I have to—'

Ciaran said, 'My brother monks and I would like to engage your services, Mr West. We will pay you, of course.'

Isarel's eyebrows went up. 'Rome wants me, does it?' he said, sarcastically. 'And can Rome afford me?'

'Rome always affords the things it wants.'

'So I've heard. But,' said Isarel, 'I don't give private recitals to women's institutes or church coffee mornings.'

Ciaran studied him for a moment and then said, 'I think I'll have to tell you the whole truth.'

'Does anybody in the world ever tell anybody else in the world the whole truth? What is truth? quoth Jesting Pilate. But go ahead,' said Isarel. 'Set forth thy tale and tarry not the time – you aren't tarrying it much anyway, are you? It's nearly midnight.'

'Well,' said Ciaran, 'it's a story to harrow up a soul, sure enough, leave aside it being a fragment from the life of dreams.'

He eyed Isarel who grinned and said, with energy, 'Bested, by God and in my own house, never mind in my cups! Only I am allowed to mangle up the quotations of the great, didn't you know that, Brother Ciaran? More wine?'

'Thank you.'

'You're extraordinarily intemperate for a monk.'

'So I am. But I think, Mr West, that by the time we have finished, we shall both be glad of the wine.'

'You might as well drop the formality,' said Isarel. 'I can't get properly drunk and listen to fairy stories, and especially not truths, with somebody who keeps calling me "Mr West".'

Ciaran grinned and leaned back in the sagging comfortable chair. 'The truth does sound a bit like a fairy story,' he said.

'Then say on. The floor's yours. It's a bit dusty and the joists in that corner have gone but for the moment it's yours,' said Isarel. 'Start with "once upon a time" and go on from there.'

'Once upon a time,' said Ciaran, sitting back and eyeing with approval the leaping fire in the hearth and the way it reflected on the half-full bottle, 'there was a piece of music which was supposed to possess strange and ancient powers. My brother monks and I know it as the *Black Chant*. Have you heard of it at all?'

'Yes, of course. Anyone who ever studied music would have done.'

'Tell me what you know.'

Isarel, his interest unexpectedly caught, said, 'It's a piece of music that makes use of a chord known as the *el diablo*. The *Black Chant* is supposed to have been written around the *el diablo*, and it was once thought to have power over minds. The medievals called the chord the *diabolus in musica* and they knew it as a tritone – that's an interval of three tones with an augmented fourth. They believed it could summon the devil. But the legend of the *Chant* itself is immensely old, and half the folk tales of Europe seem to be based on it in one way or another: Faust trading with Mephistopheles for eternal youth and Marguerite in his bed – Orpheus with his lyre, charming the denizens of hell into giving him back his lady . . . The eighteenth-century composer, Giuseppe Tartini is supposed to have heard it in a dream in which he believed he had sold his soul to the devil in return for it. Tartini called the music the Devil's Trill.'

'You're very knowledgeable,' said Ciaran, and Isarel shrugged.

'I grew up with music. And it used to be my profession, although God knows whether I can claim to have a profession any longer.' He sipped his wine, thoughtfully. 'It's rather an interesting legend, and it's remarkable how it keeps cropping up. Browning had fun with it of course – most people know about the Piper of Hamlin – but there's other versions: the Black Man of Saxony who lured children from their homes: the Man of the Mountains who charmed an entire village into following him into his master's lair – I forget why, but he had some sinister intent. They're all more or less similar variations of the same theme: a piece of music, occasionally a musical instrument that calls to men's souls and holds them in thrall. It's grand stirring stuff, marvellous for horror fiction and plays and films. I don't remember who wrote the original Phantom of the Opera but he was probably influenced by the legend – Lloyd-Webber cashed in on it later of course and good for him. None of it's meant to be taken seriously.'

Ciaran said softly, 'But there have been people down the ages who have encountered it in its raw form, and who have taken it very seriously indeed.' He sipped his wine, and then said, 'There's one strand of that legend you haven't mentioned.'

'What?'

Ciaran said very deliberately, 'Jude Weissman.'

There was an abrupt silence. Isarel was conscious all over again of Mallow's desolate situation. Who is this Ciaran O'Connor? How do I know I can trust him? On the mantelpiece, the clock he had wound up a lifetime ago ticked steadily on. At last, he said, '*Jude* believed in the *Black Chant*?'

'I think he not only believed in it,' said Ciaran levelly, 'I think he found it while he was living here at Mallow.'

There was another of the silences, and then Isarel said, 'What makes you think he found it?'

'What makes you think he didn't?'

Isarel stared at him, a dozen different emotions churning in his mind. After a moment, he got up and went to stand in the deep bow window that jutted out over Mallow's darkling gardens. His head was turned away from the light and he was clearly struggling with some powerful emotion. Ciaran waited and after a moment Isarel turned back into the room. He lit two more candles from the stubs of the ones on the mantel, and set them on one of the packing cases under the window.

'Listen,' he said, and, flinging up the lid of the piano, began to play.

The music poured into the silence like cascading silk, like molten gold, and even played like this on an out-of-tune piano, it was the most compelling music that Ciaran had ever heard in his life, and it was also the most frightening. This was music you would die for and music you would kill for. Music you would sell your soul for if only it would go on . . . A Beckoning. This is it, thought Ciaran, transfixed. I'm hearing the *Black Chant*. The music that drew Ahasuerus out of the tomb.

He had no idea how long the music lasted, although he thought afterwards that it was not very long. Ten minutes? Perhaps a little more.

Even when Isarel stopped the spell lingered and Ciaran felt an abrupt sense of loss. He sat very still, and then Isarel got up to replenish the guttering candles and reality returned. Ciaran said, 'When it stops, the spell fades. The rough magic taken back, the book drowned fathoms deep . . . That was it, wasn't it? The *Black Chant*.'

Isarel had returned to the piano as if he needed to draw warmth from it. His face was in shadow and when he spoke again, his voice was devoid of expression.

'What I've just played is part of the *Devil's Piper* suite.'

'Jude's *Devil's Piper*?'

'Yes. I found his score earlier tonight.' He looked at Ciaran, his eyes still in shadow. 'Jude was a charismatic conductor and a brilliant composer and an extraordinary musician,' said Isarel. 'He was only twenty-four when he wrote the *Devil's Piper*, but he could already hold a concert hall in the palm of his hand. Women in the audience used to faint. He had a mesmeric quality, or so it's said.'

He stopped, and Ciaran said suddenly, 'You're afraid of him, aren't you? Or at least, you're afraid of his memory.'

'Yes. He haunts me. He always has done.' Isarel frowned and, reaching across to re-fill the wine glasses, said in a dismissive voice, 'But I don't understand what any of this has to do with you or your Abbey. Or what it is you want from me.'

'Our present Order dates from about a thousand years after the death of Christ,' said Ciaran. 'And the Abbey itself was built in the twelfth century. When our Founder came to Curran Glen, he brought with him a tomb, a stone sarcophagus with an inner coffin of wood. When the Abbey was built, the tomb was locked into the crypt. It was to be sealed away from the world for ever and perpetually guarded.'

'Why?'

'Because the creature inside it was believed to have been cursed with immortality.'

'"Cursed" with it? Isn't immortality the greatest prize of all?'

'It's the greatest burden anyone could ever have to bear,' said Ciaran, very seriously, and Isarel stared at him.

'Yes, of course. I wasn't thinking. Flippancy has become a way of life. I don't think I believe in immortal things in coffins, but we'll let that pass. By the way could we call it "suspended animation" or would that offend your story-teller's soul?'

'It's probably a more accurate description anyway,' said Ciaran.

'I don't know about accuracy, but it'd be easier to swallow. Where did the tomb come from?'

'A place in Northern Italy called Cremona. Our Founder left an account of how he came into possession of it, but it's very incomplete and it's difficult to piece the story together. What we do know is that around eleven hundred and something a certain Cosimo Amati of Cremona played the *Chant* and that it called up a creature he believed to be the devil—'

'Just a minute, are we talking about the Amati dynasty that had Guarneri and Stradivari as pupils?'

'We are.'

'Jesus God, if Stradivari was involved in the *Chant* that gives the thing an even wider dimension.'

Isarel stared at Ciaran, who said, absent-mindedly, 'Don't blaspheme. We don't know how Cosimo Amati got his hands on the music or why he used it. But according to Brother Simon's account he played it in his house one night – deliberately and calculatedly – and something came to his house in answer to it.'

'Simon was your Founder?'

'Yes. And according to his account, Cosimo was unable to control the creature he'd summoned, and he sought Simon's help.'

Isarel said promptly, 'Baron Frankenstein and the monster getting away. People never learn.'

'Quite.'

'Or something from the Arabian Nights. Genies or jinns who become troublesome and have to be corked into bottles for a thousand and one nights. Go on. How did Simon cork up this particular jinn?'

'We don't know,' said Ciaran. 'We know that Simon and Cosimo both believed the creature had been compelled to answer the music. We know they returned it to the tomb and that Simon brought the tomb to Ireland and Curran Glen. What we don't know is how they got him back in the tomb.'

'So the music's a one-way ticket,' said Isarel thoughtfully. 'It calls the creature up, but it doesn't necessarily send it back. Go on.'

'Simon created an Order of Guardians of the tomb. Christian in belief and way of life, but who in addition to their vows to God, must also vow to guard the tomb and re-inter Ahasuerus if he wakes.'

A log broke apart in the hearth, making both men jump. Isarel caught a movement on the edges of his vision, and he turned sharply because just for a moment it had seemed as if a dark hunched figure was crouching behind them. 'Ahasuerus,' he said softly. 'I don't believe any of this, of course, but—'

'Yes?'

'Naming him makes him unexpectedly real,' said Isarel.

'My Church believes that in order to exorcize a demon, you must first name him,' said Ciaran, and then seeing Isarel's expression, he smiled. 'Demons can have names like Fear, Jealousy, Despair, Violence—'

'All right, you've named this particular demon and he's called Ahasuerus. But you can't seriously expect me to believe that a creature who's been dead for a thousand years can wake and walk in answer to a sequence of music—'

'It doesn't matter whether you believe it or not,' said Ciaran. 'It's happened. Earlier tonight one of our monks was attacked and left for dead. His eyes were clawed out by something extremely savage.'

'A homicidal immortal yet. Didn't anyone see this savage gentleman? I thought you were supposed to guard him.'

'Actually most of us did see him although we didn't realise. He was among us during Vespers, but he was hooded and robed to hide his face. At some point he was mutilated,' said Ciaran expressionlessly. 'We don't know the details, but we know his face was spoiled.'

Isarel regarded Ciaran and then said politely, 'Yes, I should have known he'd be horribly scarred. All the best immortals are. I thought you looked alert when I mentioned Phantom of the Opera.'

Ciaran smiled again, but said, 'When we went down to the crypt, we found the tomb disturbed.' He looked very directly at Isarel. 'The stone lid was pushed back and the inner coffin was empty.' He paused. 'And earlier tonight, you had played the *Chant*.'

There was a sudden silence. Isarel stared at Ciaran. 'You think I called him out of the tomb?' he said, staring. 'My God, you really do think it, don't you? And now you want me to play it again to get him back. That's why you're here. I always thought the Catholic Church was rife with superstition, but in all my sinful Jewish life I've never heard such a load of uncircumcised balls—' He stopped as Ciaran made an abrupt movement. 'What is it?'

Ciaran said, 'There's something outside in the hall.'

And then Isarel heard it as well.

The slow dragging of footsteps. And the whispering of a long robe across the bare oak floorboards.

For a moment neither of them moved. The footsteps outside stopped, and Isarel thought that perhaps after all he had been mistaken. Then Ciaran pointed silently to the half-closed door into the hall.

On the bare dusty floor, thrown into sharp relief by the candlelight, was the black elongated shadow of a crouching figure standing in the hall. Isarel felt icy fingers trace a path down his spine. The shadow had a monkish look as if it was wearing a long robe, and the head was covered by a cowl.

The mutilated creature cursed with immortality . . . Ahasuerus hiding his spoiled face from the world . . . Yes,

74

but I don't believe it. And if I don't believe it, it can't be happening.

In a whisper so soft that Isarel barely caught it, Ciaran said, 'Stand next to me. When I signal, fling the door open. Ready?'

'Of course I'm not ready! Ready for what, for God's sake?'

'We've got to force him back into the tomb,' said Ciaran. 'Can you play the music again?'

'But you don't know how to get him back in the tomb—' Isarel broke off and shook his head incredulously. 'I don't believe I'm saying this.'

'I don't believe you're saying it either. I don't believe it's happening.'

'Will he even follow the music?'

'How do I know!' said Ciaran in a furious whisper. 'I'm boxing as blind as you are! But he's followed it once already and if you play it again—'

'How?' demanded Isarel. 'Hell's teeth, Ciaran, I can't drag the Bluthner across the fields on the off chance that an escaped corpse will go obediently after it, and—' Isarel stopped as memory stirred. He made a quick gesture, signalling: wait a minute, and crossed swiftly to the packing cases under the window. His thoughts were in chaos, but there was the memory of having brought to Ireland, along with everything else, one of the few things that had come down from Jude and that Isarel would never have relinquished to anyone in the world.

The shofar. The sweet-toned harmonic Hebrew trumpet, referred to numerous times in the Bible, once used to sound battle calls and still used in some modern synagogues. It was many years since Isarel had been inside a synagogue, or indeed any appointed place of worship, but he regarded the shofar as something very nearly sacred. He would certainly never have left it behind in England for Liz and her Sales Director who would probably have hung it on the wall alongside a fake hunting horn.

He had not played it since he had lectured to a post-graduate class on Jewish music and he was not at all sure if he could remember how to play it, never mind reproduce Jude's music on it. He was certainly not sure if he believed any of this extravagant tale of ancient curses and maimed creatures forced to walk the world.

But something was standing in the dark hall beyond the warm circle of candlelight, and if Ciaran was to be believed, something was loose in Curran Glen that had already savaged a man.

And if there was a shred of truth in Ciaran's remarkable story, if anything could lure the immortal Ahasuerus, Cosimo Amati's out-of-control demon, back to the tomb, then it would surely be the Hebrew shofar.

Chapter Eight

Cosimo Amati knew all the stories about over-reaching, under-estimating fools who lured demons and then failed to control them, and he was not going to add to their number.

He had gone about his preparations very carefully indeed, and he had not told anyone what he was going to do in case of failing and being laughed at. You had to be cunning, you had to be secretive and sly about these things. But there the music was and there the legend was, and he was going to take his courage in both hands and see whether it was all true or only a burned-out myth.

Aside from that, it would be very gratifying if he could be the one to banish the plague-rats from Cremona, especially when everyone in the town had prayed until they dropped and Heaven must be weary of their pleas for deliverance from the evil diseased things.

It would be really be very satisfying if he was destined to go down in Cremona's history as the man who saved an entire town. 'Cosimo Amati,' people would say in years to come. 'My word, what courage. My word, our forefathers had cause to be grateful to him.' His mind roamed pleasurably between a plaque in the Cathedral (which would be nice for his descendants), and a yearly pension from the City fathers, (which would be of more immediate benefit).

After much furrowing of his brow he decided to use his workroom which was a long, low-ceilinged room, a half-cellar in fact, with the windows at street level so that people could not look in on you unless they bent down on all fours which was not something you needed to worry about at midnight. And if Isabella awoke and found him not in their bed, she would only think he was working late again. She would smile the thin enigmatic smile that always drove him demented – he suspected it drove half of Cremona demented as well, although naturally Isabella, dear innocent girl, would not realise it – and she would turn over and go back to sleep.

He stacked his half-finished lutes and the lyres at the far end of the workroom, leaning them carefully against the wall, because several were commissioned works and Cosimo was not going to forego any of his patrons' payments, not if he found himself entertaining Satan and the entire hierarchy of devils.

He arranged a small velvet cushion to sit on, because while it was all very well to be large-minded and loftily say you were going to call up the Servant of the ancient music and order him to save your city, you did not want to get a splinter in your buttocks in the process. Uncharitable people said that Cosimo was fat, but Cosimo thought of himself as nicely rounded which meant that there was plenty of flesh for recalcitrant splinters. He smoothed the velvet and turned to set out the candles. Everything had to be in accordance with the ancient ritual: Cosimo had made a list, which he consulted anxiously at intervals.

As he made his preparations, he thought it was surely a terrible desecration to light the thick repulsive candles made from dead men's fat and the brains of a still-born child. These had been the hardest items to acquire, because when you were a respected lute-maker and a responsible member of Cremona's little community, you could not go rummaging about in graveyards. In the end, he had engaged the services of the two men who pulled the plague-cart through Cremona's streets at curfew each night, swearing them to secrecy under threat of punishment of the most gruesome kind. Earlier that evening, directly after supper, he had pounded the nasty substances together, shuddering and sickened, but not flinching because a man ought not to flinch from any worthwhile task, and more to the point the stuff had cost a disgracefully large sum of money.

As the candle flames burned up their stench filled the room, driving out the ordinary, safe-feeling workaday scents. This was eerily in accordance with the ancient legend: Isabella, spinning the tale for him one night, singing the cool silvery sequence of notes in her high sweet voice, had said her grandmother always told how, if you ever dared to use the ritual and summon the Creature, its stench would drive out all else. The devil trailed its own aura with it, Isabella's grandmother had said: at least, that was the belief handed down and down through the women of their family, and you could believe it or not, just as you chose.

Cosimo seated himself on the velvet cushion, the candles burning up strongly and smelling very nasty indeed by this time. He could almost imagine there was a whiff of horse manure about them which was odd, because the two carters would not have dared to cheat a man of Cosimo's standing, especially not when he had paid them so well.

It was not supposed to matter what instrument was used: Isabella had said that if the music was played in correct sequence, the Servant had to come, that was the legend. Perhaps the candles and the melted corpse-fat did not really matter either. Perhaps they were only trappings, tricks to dazzle the gullible.

Cosimo took a deep breath and lifted the lyre in his

79

hands. It was the oldest one he possessed, and it was made not from polished wood, but from human bone. It felt cool and light to his touch and it was rather a grisly feeling to know that the bones had once belonged to a person who had walked and danced and laughed. For a moment he could almost fancy that he felt a ripple of life from it.

This was going to be it. This was going to be the playing of the devil's music, the incantation that Isabella's family called the *Black Chant*, and that they had guarded over the centuries; the music that her grandmother believed had been forged in the blood of Lucifer and seared in the fire-drenched furnaces of his domain. Cosimo had memorised Isabella's sweet cool song and had hummed it to himself a number of times to be sure he got it right. He had done this very softly and he had been careful never to hum it after sunset, because it did not do to take chances with these matters.

And now he was going to play the musical sequence that would reach the devil's Servant slumbering in his deep unknown tomb and that would draw him into the old house in Cremona and force him to obey the bidding of the one who summoned him.

He took a deep breath and plucked out the sequence of notes.

The first thing that Ahasuerus was aware of was the music trickling into his mind like coloured water trickling through cracks in a wall. Marvellous enchanted music: *come with me and come to me . . . dance to my piping and follow me into hell and beyond . . .*

The second thing was the feeling that he was waking from a long, long sleep. He remained motionless, letting the memories seep into his mind.

The cellar beneath the Temple where he had been chained

and manacled and left without food and only a few sips of water. The travesty of a trial, and then the Sanhedrin's grisly sentence of death and the horrified gasps of the listeners. And above all, the monks: the *Fratres Cruciferi*, sly-eyed, greedy-fingered, waiting until they could shoulder their burden and receive their blood-tainted payment. Had they done so? Towards the end Ahasuerus had been blind and deaf with agony and so near to death he had been almost beyond thought, but he had known that the monks were on the edges of the crowd, their black robes turning them into the carrion crows they were. Had they carried out their promise to take his unmarked tomb to the depths of a bottomless pit, or the subterrenean hall of some lonely mountain? Was that where he was now? He thought the monks would have kept their word: they had been a little afraid of him – they had certainly flinched when he had flung that last threat at them – 'I shall return!' They would have taken the mutilated body of the High Priest and carried it to a dark desolate resting place.

But now the music was calling him back: Susannah's music that she had coaxed or bullied or seduced out of the old Scribe, and whose history stretched so far back that no one could trace it, and that Susannah said would stretch just as far forward. Time was like a great unrolling carpet and if you possessed the knowledge, you could walk back and forth on its surface. Perhaps the Nazarene had possessed the knowledge? Susannah had said, slyly, and Ahasuerus had stared at her, his mind tumbling, not daring to believe, but caught for a moment by the dazzling allure of such an idea.

Whether Christ had had the knowledge or not, he had never known and he never would know. But lying in the dark silence, the music soaking into his bones and his mind, he knew now that Susannah had not lied and delight poured through his whole being. Her promise was coming true; she had guarded the music, and after his death and hers, she had passed it on and passed it down, so that at some future neither of them could see it would call them both back into the world.

Ahasuerus opened his eyes. The darkness and the silence were absolute and there was the feeling of being in a narrow, enclosed space. Memory unrolled a little more, and he saw again the stone sarcophagus, the waiting sepulchre on the edge of the crowd that had gathered to witness his execution. Its massive lid had been propped against its side and the interior yawned blackly. Even through the choking death agonies he had been aware of black bitter fury, because they might at least have hidden that from him until he was dead.

And now he was inside it. He was entombed in the elaborate stone coffin that the greedy friars had prepared for him. How long had he been here? He had no idea, and it did not matter yet.

He moved for the first time, and cried out with the pain that flooded his body. His cry was harsh and weak, but it was a terrible sound in the dark silent tomb. He moaned in agony as the congealed blood moved in his arms and legs, and his moans echoed eerily in the confined space and came back mockingly at him.

The tomb-stench was stifling and Ahasuerus drew in a breath, and felt the winding-sheet sucked into his mouth, stinking of mildew. Disgusting! He choked, retching, and spat out shreds of the rotting cloth, forcing his mind to concentrate, forcing back the mists that clung to his brain. It was like pushing through a shaled-on crust, like fighting out of a membraneous sac, but he was doing it.

Overcoming death . . . Climbing out of the tomb.

With the thought he reached upwards, and at once his

hands met resistance. The stone lid? Yes, of course. They had not nailed it down, because stone could not be nailed, but it was a huge heavy slab and it would be squarely across the tomb and it would take every ounce of his strength to move it. Panic gripped him, and he thought: I can't do it! I'm trapped! Susannah, you wanton bitch, did you unknowingly sentence me to a far worse death than the Sanhedrin's? A silent lonely death in the blackness of the tomb. Am I to end as a ravening madman, screaming with hunger and thirst, blind and deaf, my mind splintered into insanity?

He pushed upwards again and this time there was a rasp of sound, stone scraping against stone, the faintest scratch imaginable. But Ahasuerus heard it, and dizzy gratitude flooded his mind, so that for a moment the darkness was shot with light. Moveable. It may take hours or days, but I shall move it. I shall get out.

Slowly, with many pauses to gather his slowly returning strength, he inched the stone lid aside; not trying to overturn it which would surely be beyond him, but sliding it to one side. To begin with the progress was so painful and so slow that he thought after all he would never do it, but to be trapped down here until he went slowly mad was so gruesome a prospect that fierce determination gave him extra strength. Eventually, sweat soaking his hair and his skin, a faint dim line of light appeared. The sweetest thing I ever thought to see. Only a little more and I can grasp the edge and gain more purchase . . . Only a very little more . . .

And then he was pushing the lid across and the light was stronger and there was a dry stale stench gusting into his face. Ahasuerus sat up cautiously. He was light-headed and he was trembling and weak, as if every muscle had been beaten with knotted scourges, but his mind was clearing. He drew in a deep breath and looked about him.

First, the practicalities. The where and how and what. The where was necessarily first: he was somewhere underground, somewhere that was nearly airless and that reeked of death and age and old, old bones. His eyes were adjusting now, and he could see that the stone tomb was ledged on a rock shelf, and that in dislodging the lid he had dislodged what looked to be corpses, heavy soft bodies wrapped in winding sheets. Was this some kind of burial pit? He glanced upwards to the rock ceiling, and quite suddenly understood where he was. Catacombs. The brothers of the *Cruciferi Order*, may they rot in living torment, had put him in a catacomb cavern.

So. So the curs had brought his murdered body down here, together with paupers and plague-corpses and criminals, and all the other poor creatures who could not afford proper burial. He could smell the stench of too-ripe meat, like fruit bursting and leaking its rottenness.

But he could sense, far above him, fresh clean air. He forced himself to climb out of the stone tomb, pushing back the press of bodies as he did so. He had no idea of where he was; he might be just outside Jerusalem, or he might be just outside of anywhere. How far would those greedy monks have taken his sepulchre? He glanced at it. As he had thought, it was lying on a shelf of rock, with more shelves above and below, each one stacked with corpses, some of them incompletely shrouded, the winding sheets loosened and trailing. He turned his back on it and set off through the tunnels.

Ahasuerus had no idea how long it took him to find his way out of the catacombs. His eyes were still only partially adjusted to the light, and he could scarcely see. His whole world and his every sense was focused on the hewn-out rock of the caverns and on the piles of half-rotting corpses.

There was nothing by which to measure time and the thick smothering stench of decay was everywhere. As he walked on, his feet making no sound on the hard rock floor, he could hear the dripping of water somewhere over his head and it was a terrible and a desolate sound. I am the only living creature here. Yes, but I am returning to the world.

He padded on, seeing that he was coming to the newer part of the catacombs, seeing that the burials were more recent. The deeper part had been drenched in the stench and the feel of crumbled bones, and there had been a sprinkling of grey bone-dust on the ground. But there was a stench of putrefaction in his nostrils now, and the winding sheets of these later bodies were wet and stained with the leaking body decay within . . .

Ahasuerus stopped abruptly and bent over, retching, his forehead beaded with sweat. But if I am sweating it is a living sweat and if I am sick being sick is a living experience. Susannah, you were right about the music . . . Awe, tinged with fear, brushed his mind.

And then directly ahead of him was a slanting ray of light: sweet dark blue twilight, pouring in from over his head. With it, he smelt the clean pure air of the world again. Almost there!

He broke into a half-run, and then he was standing in the pouring twilight, at the mouth of the caves and the cool clean night air was filling his lungs, and the grave-stench was behind him, but nothing had ever tasted or felt so good: not the best wine in all the world, not the body of a woman you loved.

He was out of the catacomb city of the dead.

Chapter Nine

Isarel's first notes on the shofar were hesitant, and after a moment he lowered the instrument and half closed his eyes, reaching for the cadences of Jude's music. I can do it, he thought. I believe I can do it. When he lifted the shofar to his lips for the second time, he did so with authority.

And this time it was there; between one breathspace and the next, it was there. Like hitting a nerve. Dead in the gold.

The *Devil's Piper*, the magical beckoning that Jude had discovered, that some long-ago member of the Amati dynasty had used to summon a creature he had believed to be a demon.

The *Black Chant*.

On the rim of his vision, Isarel saw Ahasuerus's shadow tense, and he thought: in another minute I shall see him. Panic churned and his heart began to race. In another minute he'll be before us: the sinister figure of all those stories. The doomed creature chained to the world forever, bound to answer the music ... I don't believe any of it, said Isarel's mind fiercely.

No? Then why are you playing Jude's music?

Ciaran moved then, flinging the door back against the wall, and standing in the dark hall was the robed, hunched-over figure of a man, his face hidden by the deep hood. Every nightmare, every imagined horror, thought Isarel, struggling for calm. The silent intruder who steals into your house, so stealthy that you never hear him until you round a corner and there he is in front of you.

I don't believe any of this, said his mind, again. I don't believe I'm taking part in this charade. This silver-tongued Irish monk is probably a con-man and that's his accomplice. Once I'm out of the house they'll ransack it, or they'll take possession: lock and bar the doors and windows, and claim squatters' rights. Why would anyone want to squat in Mallow for God's sake?

Ciaran was pulling open the outer door and the moonlight was sliding bars of cold brilliance on the scarred oak. We're moon-mad, thought Isarel. Moonstruck lunacy, that's what this is.

But of their own volition Isarel's hands were lifting the shofar again, and the music was spinning. Music that walked the thin line between evil and good, and between seduction and allure.

As they went into the night, Isarel looked back and saw the huddled figure come lurching out of the shadows after them. Ahasuerus walked awkwardly, almost cowering inside the enveloping robe as if fearful that it might be snatched from him. He dragged one foot as he came, and Isarel suddenly found this limping gait unbearably painful.

But he walked purposefully on, through the roughish track that wound between the sparse trees and down the narrow path that led towards the Abbey. There was a vague memory of the English solicitors talking about shared boundaries and the resolving of responsibilities for upkeep. Then this must still be Mallow's land, and the Abbey must be only on the other side of a wall or a fence. Would they go down on to the highroad and in at the gates? For a mad moment, he visualised them all climbing over a wall, amicably helping one another. Mind you don't trip over your robe, Ahasuerus. Just hold the shofar for a minute, would you, while I vault across. And now down here and let's put you back in the tomb.

Ciaran was walking ahead of them, and a tiny part of Isarel's mind was aware of a spurt of too-shrill amusement that he should be entering an Irish Catholic monastery in this way, and that he should be entering such a place at all.

With the playing of the music, memory had yielded other things now, and the haunting words that Jude had put to part of the *Piper* music were singing through his brain.

*'I know a charm that will call up the spirits of the
     gloaming . . .
That will soothe pain with sound, and agony with
     air;
I know a charm that will remove the veils from the
     communing shades . . .
That will stay the poor unhousell'd souls from
     roaming . . .
And tempt the wild woodland magic from the glades.
But it will do no good unless you believe it . . .'*

It was plagiarism at its most obvious and its most defiant, of course: Jude had unrepentantly plundered *Midsummer Night's Dream* and *The Tempest*, and Clemence Dane's *Will Shakespeare* and probably Maeterlinck and Spenser as well if you went deeply enough. And then he had rolled the stolen threads up into one brilliant coruscating sphere. The sphere was hollow and the hybrid phrases were counterfeit, but it did not stop any of it from raking at Isarel's senses half a century after Jude had written it.

The Abbey was ahead now – some kind of gate in the wall was there? – and Isarel quickened his steps. Would the doors be open? Yes, fool, the door is always open for those who ask . . . No, that's something else. Is this the low door in the wall that the philosophers and the dreamers and the poets wrote about? I believe I'm slightly light-headed. Hallucinating with tiredness. The drive across Ireland. The whiskey and wine. God yes, the wine. Delirium tremens at last, that's what this is. Seeing things that aren't there, manipulating charms I don't believe in.

Luring the unhousell'd soul back to the tomb.

It was impossible to forget Jude's words and it was impossible to avoid the analogies. I'm the Pied Piper, thought Isarel, the Black Man of Saxony . . . The doomed Erik in *Phantom*, luring his lady – what was her name? – down to the sewers beneath the Paris Opera House. Shall we get the scene where the mask's ripped aside?

A dim light burned at the Abbey's heart and Isarel saw it with thankfulness. Almost there. Over the water-jump, down the straight and home. Is he following? Oh God, yes of course he is.

He risked one quick look over his shoulder – and that'll probably turn me into a pillar of salt! – and saw that Ahasuerus was certainly following. He looked like a creature made up of the twisting shadows: Isarel could almost believe that the shadows had reared up to trail after him, but whatever else was happening, Ahasuerus was following the music. Because even if I don't believe in the charm, he does, thought Isarel. It's the belief that counts, remember? and the poor sod believes. Is that what this is about? He hasn't lain in the Abbey cellars for a thousand years at all, and he hasn't risen from the grave either.

But he might think he has. And Ciaran might think it as well. What if they're a couple of escaped psychopaths? What if it isn't an Abbey but a lunatic asylum? What would happen if I threw down the shofar and ran like hell down to the village? I won't do it, of course. But I don't know why I won't do it. And there's the music, that's real enough. Jude, what have you bequeathed to me, you bastard?

They were through the gate and ahead of them was an ancient stone arch with cloisters beyond, and as they crossed to the bell tower and Ciaran unlocked the door, Isarel glanced upwards. Bells and cats and looking glasses! They all have an eerie inverted life. I wouldn't like to be in that bell tower now. And then he realised that they would not be up there, they would be somewhere far more frightening.

They would be beneath it. They were going down into the ancient foundations: into the stone crypt that Simon of Cremona had constructed a thousand years ago for the immortal thing he had trapped and brought to Ireland.

Ahasuerus would be with them as he had been with Simon last time. Only this time he would be outside the tomb.

As they entered the crypt, Ciaran saw that the tomb was exactly as he and the others had left it. The stone slab rested on the sarcophagus' edge, and there was still the aching desolation. He moved quickly, setting down hastily lit candles, feeling a shiver of dank coldness pass over his skin as the tiny flames burned up.

He felt as if he had passed through several worlds and several years since he had come down here with Father Abbot and Cuthbert. Four hours, had it been? Five? I'm trusting Isarel West very fully, he thought, suddenly. He's Jude's grandson and he knew the music. He glanced at Isarel again, and thought: I suppose it's all right. Well, it will have to be, because I can't think what else to do. And Mother of God, how do I get Ahasuerus back into the tomb? He moved across the stone floor until he was standing with his back to the gaping tomb, facing the stair.

They could hear the dragging footsteps above them now, and then a pause as Ahasuerus stopped at the head of the stair. Ciaran's heart was pounding and he could feel sweat trickling between his shoulder blades. He glanced at Isarel and saw that his face was white and set, but that he still held the shofar to his lips.

Ahasuerus was on the stair. He's just out of sight, thought Ciaran, his eyes aching with the effort of watching the dark stairway. He's just beyond those shadows, and in another minute he'll be here, he'll be in the crypt and then I shall have to force him back into the tomb. Panic gripped him. I can't do it! he thought. And then: but I must! I took the vow! God help me to keep it! He's dragging himself down the stair now. And several layers beneath his fear, he was aware of a thrill of something quite different; he was thinking that after all the legends had all been true, the myths and the old stories. There is a piece of music with magical qualities, thought Ciaran, and there is an immortal creature bound by it, and I'm hearing the music and I'm seeing the creature.

Isarel was behind the tomb, facing the stair. His features were lit from below by the candles, and the flickering glow showed up the hollows and the angles of his thin face and scooped out black pits where his eyes were. A prickle of atavistic fear brushed Ciaran's skin. Just for a moment it might have been Jude himself standing there: the dark charismatic Judas, stepped down from one of the old black-and-white photographs or scratchy newsreels. Playing the demonic music, sending it spinning and shivering through the crypt, soaking into the stones, licking the groyned arches above them, running in and out of the cracked flags at their feet.

And then Ahasuerus's shadow fell on to the stair wall: exaggerated out of all proportion in the flickering candlelight, toweringly tall but hunched-over and filled with such menace that both men felt a lurch of fresh fear. Harsh ragged breathing filled the enclosed space.

Twisting down the dark stair came the robed hooded figure they had glimpsed at Mallow. There was the glint of eyes deep in the hood, and Ahasuerus stood watching them for a moment before moving slowly and unwillingly across the stone floor. Ciaran thought it was as if Ahasuerus was being drawn to the tomb by silver cords and with the thought he could almost see them: thin glistening strands, sticky cobweb strings pulling him back to the grave . . .

He thought: of course he's fighting it. He'll fight it with every shred of strength he has and he'll fight me as well, and how can I blame him for it? It's why he fought Daniel earlier, not because he's a killer – all the legends say he was never a killer – but he'll fight to stay out of the tomb. This is much worse than I feared. He touched the crucifix about his neck for reassurance and began to edge along the wall, forcing Ahasuerus to yield ground. Could he back him up to the tomb? Could it be as easy? But it was the only thing he could think of. The candles flickered wildly as the two men moved, and there was a sharp acrid tang as the nearest one guttered. But you did not need much light to send someone into the darkness of the tomb for ever.

Ciaran had not dared to take his eyes from Ahasuerus but he sensed that Isarel was tiring – unfamiliar music, he thought. He's struggling to maintain it.

Isarel was indeed struggling. The music itself was not so very difficult, but playing it unceasingly on the seldom-used shofar was beginning to take its toll. His mind was spinning between fear and panic but beneath it he was conscious of a dark stirring, and of something brushing his mind, exactly as it had done when he played Jude's piano at Mallow.

He had seen, as Ciaran had seen, that Ahasuerus was unable to resist the music, and he guessed that Ciaran was simply walking forward and forcing Ahasuerus back. I believe he's going to do it, thought Isarel, his heart thumping with anticipation and fear. And then he remembered that Ciaran had no idea of what would send Ahasuerus back into his strange living death. Would it be sufficient simply to push him into the tomb and drag across the stone lid?

Ahasuerus was turning his head from side to side as if seeking a means of escape and Isarel felt another tug of pity. At any minute Ciaran will bound forward, he thought. He'll leap across the floor and he'll push him back and down.

Down and down into hell, and say I sent thee thither . . .

Ahasuerus was backing away, shaking his head as if pleading dumbly with his captors and several times he looked round, as if scanning the shadows for a way out. His hands were no longer folded in the sleeves of his gown, and Isarel saw him hold them out in a gesture of entreaty.

Let me go free . . .

The shadowy crypt was beginning to blur and waver, and the candles were dissolving into discs of incandescence. Like looking at something through water. Isarel blinked and dragged his mind to focus on the music. At any minute Ciaran would spring, and when he does I must be there with him, thought Isarel. I must be at his side to help him, bang! no delay.

But even though he was so tightly keyed up mentally and physically, when Ciaran did move, it took him by surprise.

Ciaran lunged forward – like a rugger tackle! thought Isarel startled – and sent Ahasuerus toppling backwards.

A howl rent the air as Ahasuerus went down into the

tomb, his hands flailing. The long sleeves of the robe fell back, and Isarel felt as if something had slammed into the base of his throat.

Where Ahasuerus's hands should have been, were distorted lumps of flesh, fingerless travesties, the rudimentary thumbs bearing narrow thick nails that tapered to points, so that the terrible hands had the semblance of pincers, nippers.

The hand with no heart in it, the claw, the paw, the flipper, the fin . . . The greedy clutch with the heat of sin . . . *Rubente dextera* . . . With his red hands . . . Only there are no hands, thought Isarel, sickened, only lobster-claws . . . Ciaran said something about a monk's eyes being gouged out . . .

Ahasuerus was howling, great tearing screams of furious anger and hatred that swooped and spun and echoed all about the crypt, filling it with harsh agony. He was scrabbling at the sides of the deep stone trough, and Isarel dropped the shofar and moved swiftly to the tomb's foot.

The slab was heavier than he had expected and it was awkward. Ciaran had thrust one hand deep into the tomb, pushing Ahasuerus in and forcing him down, and Isarel saw the terrible pitiful hands blindly clawing out. One of the thick ugly nails tore into Ciaran's wrist, and Ciaran flinched and let out an oath and then leaned over again, blood running down between his fingers.

Ahasuerus was fighting Ciaran like a demon, like the devil he had once been thought to be, but the tomb was deep and he had fallen backwards straight into the inner coffin. There was a moment when the claw-hands scraped at the tomb's sides, clawing frantically for purchase, and then Ciaran had snatched up the coffin lid and forced it into place, and he and Isarel were dragging at the immense stone slab. There was the harsh rasp of stone against stone, and then a dull clanging that reverberated through the crypt.

The muffled clang as the sepulchre re-sealed was so final, so symbolic – a door shutting out the world and the light for ever! – that it tore unbearably at Isarel's already-raw nerves, and he leaned over the tomb gasping, wiping the sweat from his face with the back of his hand. The agony and the pity of it washed over him in cold shuddering waves.

Ciaran's face was ashen and his lips were set in a grim line, and although both his hands were bleeding from the deep clawed wounds, they were perfectly steady. He set the small silver crucifix at the head of the stone tomb and made the sign of the cross over it. Isarel heard him murmur a prayer and turned away, picking up the shofar, not embarrassed exactly, but feeling excluded.

After a moment, he said, 'Will that do it? Will it keep him there?'

'Truly I have no idea.' Ciaran glanced at Isarel. 'The inner lid was hammered down with nails before,' he said.

'And even then he broke out?'

'Yes.'

'Do we snuff the candles?'

Ciaran hesitated, and then said, 'Yes. Yes, no light's needed down here any more.'

As they quenched the candles, one by one, the shadows seemed to start forward, and leap across the ancient tomb.

Ciaran said suddenly, 'If I had any sense, I suppose I'd leave them to burn and hope they'd set fire to the whole place.' He sent Isarel a sideways glance. 'It would put paid to Ahasuerus once and for all,' he said.

Isarel said, 'Did you see his face?'

Ciaran paused, and then said, 'No. Did you?'

'No.'

'Why did you ask?'

'I'm not sure,' said Isarel, slowly. 'I think I was wondering what he was like – to begin with, I mean. I wondered what turned him into that dreadful thing you forced into the coffin.' He frowned, and with a return to his customary off-hand manner, said, 'Of course I still don't believe any of it.'

'Of course not. Neither do I,' said Ciaran politely.

'Are your hands much hurt?'

'Nothing some sticking plaster won't put right.'

They went out of the bell tower into the cool, sweet night air, and Ciaran stopped to turn the key in the immense iron lock.

Neither of them heard the faint scratching sounds that came from the creature trapped in the soundless darkness of the tomb.

Chapter Ten

Kate thought Brother Ciaran had not been aware that she had been watching as he entered the bell tower with the other two monks, and he had certainly not been aware that she had followed him to Mallow House.

She had not precisely lied to Ciaran at their meeting, but she had certainly left the essential bits out. Such as the fact that she had already been watching the Abbey for three nights. Probably she was guilty of what Ciaran would have called a sin of omission. Kate felt her lips curve in a reluctant half-grin, because it might be rather interesting to listen to Ciaran on the subject of sin, sometime. If he's a true celibate, I'm the Archbishop of Canterbury, thought Kate. How on earth did someone like that end up in a monastery? Well, it's nothing to do with me.

On each of the three nights, the Abbey had subsided into its quiet, innocent darkness, and Kate had gained nothing other than a feeling of cold and desolation, and a sneaking suspicion that she might be chasing a will-o'-the-wisp after all. She had no clear idea of what she was watching for: some kind of medieval tomb-ritual at midnight? – now that's *really* bizarre, Kate!

But tonight the Abbey had not been shrouded in darkness. Tonight lights had burned very late indeed, and Kate, trying to remember the Abbey's layout, thought they came from Father Abbot's study. Something's happening, she thought.

She climbed over the lych gate, and as she went under the stone arch leading to the inner courtyard, she heard soft footsteps and a murmur of voices. She dodged back into the shadows and as she did so, three robed and cowled figures, each carrying a lit candle, crossed the courtyard and went towards the bell tower on the farthest side. Two were older monks and there was the faint glint of a pectoral cross from the taller, but the third was unmistakably Ciaran himself. Her whole being sprang to attention. The midnight tomb-ritual after all? Should she go after them? No, it was too dangerous: she would wait to see what happened next.

When they came back out so quickly, she was relieved she had not followed, but when Ciaran came out of Father Abbot's study a short time later, she went after him, keeping at a distance but keeping him in sight. He went through under the stone arch and through the lych gate towards Mallow House and Kate hesitated, because trespassing on the grounds of an ordinary private house seemed somehow much worse than trespassing on monastery land. And late as it was, there might be a perfectly innocent explanation for all this. Vague notions of deathbed confessions went through her mind. Did monks administer the Last Rites? But there had been that curious little procession into the bell tower.

But when Isarel started to play the Bluthner, Kate forgot about trespassing, and even forgot about being caught. The music poured through the dark tangled gardens, and lashed against her senses like a huge icy torrent. This is it! This is the music! So I was right all along – the music is somehow tied up with the Abbey! For a moment her mind refused to function, and then she crept up to the sketchily curtained window with the flickering candlelight beyond. This is the ancient music of the legends, thought Kate, feeling it cascade into her mind. This is the evil, beautiful beckoning that slices into people's souls and topples them into madness and suicide. I've found it and now I can— Oh God, Ciaran's coming out! He's coming out but the music's still continuing. And there's someone with him.

She ducked into the shadow of the thickthorn hedge, her heart racing. She could not see the face of the man with Ciaran, but he was moving swiftly and with a kind of angry impatience, and Kate had the impression that he was a few years younger than Ciaran, perhaps about her own age. She leaned forward, trying to see the instrument he was using; a large flute or a recorder, was it? The music ebbed and flowed, and Kate experienced a surge of emotion that was half fear, but half triumph, because this was the thing she had spent the last three years chasing.

It was then she saw the limping shape following the two men.

Ciaran went purposefully towards the Abbey, going through the stone arch again and across the quadrangle to the bell tower.

They're going in, thought Kate. They're going in to the Abbey, and that creature's following them. No, I'm wrong, it's following the music. This is the Pied Piper re-played, of course, and I'm not believing any of it. But it's the kind of thing I came here to see and now I am seeing it I've got to admit it's pretty potent stuff. I wonder who Ciaran's companion is? I've got this far – what do I do now? Follow them into the tower, you fool.

Her body was ahead of her mind, and she was already crossing the quadrangle, seeing that the door was ajar, seeing that she could step inside quite easily. As she approached, she could still hear the music very faintly. As if it was calling to her to come in. Kate hesitated. Alice down the rabbit hole? Or Red Riding Hood into grandmother's cottage? Either way, here I go.

It was cold and dim in the tower and there was the mustiness of extreme age. Kate felt the darkness and the music reaching for her, as if it was enticing her inside. Lift the latch, my dear, and turn the key and step into the nightmare. Whatever else this was, it definitely wasn't Alice following the White Rabbit.

Inside the tower door was the tiniest of tiny, bare halls, no more than six feet square, and on her right was a shallow set of stairs, obviously leading up into the belfry. But directly ahead of the door a stair wound downwards, and a thin flickering light seeped up from it. Kate could hear the music coming upwards, very faintly. Then the musician, whoever he was, was still playing. She advanced cautiously, but almost at once froze, the breath catching in her throat in terror. Going down the stair, casting an immense grotesque shadow on the wall, was the hooded creature that had followed the music, so dreadfully deformed-looking and sinister that Kate felt horrified repulsion wash over her. Certainly not Alice. More like Nosferatu.

She glanced over her shoulder. Could she hide in the bell tower itself and come down to investigate after Ciaran and the other man had gone? Yes, she could.

She was setting foot on the first step when without warning the music shut off, and from beyond the dark stair came a low agonised groan, and then a dreadful, shrieking cry of agony. Kate felt the back of her neck prickling. Something terrible was happening. Her instinctive response was to run towards the cries but she hesitated, because she had no idea of who was on whose side. And then hard on the heels of the scream came an echoing clang, a huge reverberating noise that spun and shivered within the narrow tower. There was a low warning thrum from the bells far above her. The sound's disturbed them, thought Kate, glancing towards the belfry stair.

Ciaran and the other man were coming back up, talking in low voices, saying something about snuffing the candles, and Kate crouched into the curve of the tower stair, trying to hear. Ciaran's voice was soft but it was unmistakable. Nice. The other man sounded English rather than Irish. She found herself praying they would not search the tower.

I'll go down after they've left, she thought. I don't really believe any of the ancient legend, I'm only here to disprove it. But I'll just find out what that creature was and what they did with it, and then I'll be satisfied. I'll eliminate the impossible and then I'll concentrate on the improbable. Of course you will, Holmes, my dear fellow.

She had reached this point when there was another sound, and Kate started up, stark terror rushing in. She had thought she had been so cool and dispassionate about all this and so she had.

But she had not allowed for this one thing.

Ciaran had locked the door of the tower from outside.

Kate went down the tower stair as if demons were at her heels.

Locked. He's locked the door. She took a deep breath, her eyes fixed on the door. It was important not to give way to panic, because even if the door was locked there would be another way out.

As she reached for the iron ring handle her hands were shaking. Don't let it be locked, please God, don't let it be locked. And if it is – it won't be – but if it is, let there be another way out.

She closed both hands about the handle and at once

knew it was immovable. Stuck? No, you fool, it's locked, you knew it was all the time. Try turning the other way. No. Absolutely fast. Ciaran locked it – I heard him do it. Sensible, of course, even at this time of night. Especially at this time of night. The tower stood a little apart from the main Abbey, with its own entrance. Curran Glen was probably more law-abiding than most, but it would have its share of tramps and vagrants and it would not be difficult for someone to creep in for a night's sleep. The monks probably had a rule that the tower was always kept locked. I'm locked in for the night.

Kate sank down to the ground, hugging her knees, trying to think. Locked in for the night. Locked in with the great silent iron-tongued bells over her head.

And the creature of the ancient legends below.

Ahasuerus had come out on a narrow shelf of rock that looked down on to a dusty road fringed with trees. It was colder than he had expected and there was a fresh moist feeling to the air.

He curled against the rock wall of the catacombs, absorbing the new clean world, deciding what to do and watching the few travellers going to and fro below him. In the main they were in groups of threes and fours, but occasionally lone men – never women – walked by. So that had not changed since Jerusalem. He began to watch more closely, marking what the travellers wore and how they moved. Can I copy all of that? What language do they speak? The highroad was wider and better marked than any he remembered, and he thought a very great number of years must have passed.

Night shrouded the landscape, which was unfamiliar but rather interesting. He thought the music was somewhere to his left, and narrowing his eyes he could see the outlines of buildings and houses – not quite like any he had ever encountered, but plainly places for people to live and gather.

He would have to resist the music for a little longer yet, if he could. He was still clad only in the linen garment they had used to lay him in the coffin and the marks of his execution were visible. He felt again the hatred against the Judges and the sanctimonious monks.

It was easy enough to wait for the next solitary traveller, and then to stalk him through the night. Ahasuerus leapt on the man as they passed into the cover of some trees, stunning him with a blow to the head, and dragging him to the side of the road. It was astonishingly easy. He stripped the man's clothes from him, finding amongst them a purse of coins which were unfamiliar but which were clearly tokens that could be exchanged for food and wine. He looked back at his victim. Dead? No, only knocked out of his senses for a few hours. Then I haven't turned into a murderer yet.

He straightened up and looked about him. No one to be seen. And the music was tugging at his mind again. Susannah's music. The smile that had fascinated the females who had come to the Temple; curved his lips. Susannah's music, calling him back, pulling him into an unknown world. He was conscious of a sudden excitement.

He donned the unconscious man's clothes, arranging them as nearly like the other travellers as he could. All right? Yes, he thought he would pass. He had no idea how far he had to travel to reach the music – he thought its pull would guide him – but it could not be so very far. And he had acceptable clothes now and money. If necessary he could purchase food and wine on the road; it would be easy enough to watch how it was done and copy. The thought of an unknown tongue gave him pause, but if he encountered anyone on the road, he could surely present himself as a traveller, a pilgrim from a distant land. He would learn as he went.

He was aware of the excitement spiralling a little higher. A new world. Unknown people and strange customs.

But Susannah might be here.

To begin with, Cosimo thought that nothing was going to happen. The music shivered and spun all about the workroom, and the candles flickered wildly, giving out a sickly sulphurous stench.

Sulphur . . . When he comes, he'll come straight from hell, thought Cosimo, torn between a wish that he would succeed and a devout hope that nothing would happen.

The shadows thickened and all about him Cremona slept. Or did it? Was that a footstep outside? Someone going untimely and stealthily home? Someone creeping back home after a night in a strange bed? Cremona was no worse and no better than anywhere else and you got fornication and adultery in the unlikeliest of places. Cosimo was glad to know that Isabella would never behave so wantonly, despite the looks of the young men who came to be apprenticed to him. He had now and then permitted them to escort her to some place of entertainment on occasions when he could not do so himself. He trusted Isabella completely, of course.

He thought that several hours had passed since he had played the music for the first time, but he was not sure because he seemed to have entered into a kind of half-world where the only thing that mattered was the steady burning of the six flames, and the inexorable shortening of the candles. He had played the *Chant* at regular intervals which he had thought would be sufficient.

He shifted uncomfortably on the velvet cushion, which

was beginning to seem very much thinner than when he had first sat on it. Two of the candles were almost guttering now. He leaned over to re-kindle them and as he did so, a dog went sniffing and scrabbling along the street outside. Shortly afterwards a beggar dragged his way along the cobbled pavement, muttering as he went and Cosimo's heart lurched. But the beggar went on his way, and a little while after that, the faint chiming of the monastery bell from the outskirts of the town broke through his consciousness.

He had no idea how long it was before the night rustlings and the soft stirrings coalesced into something definite. Something that came slowly along the street, not hesitant, but wary. Cosimo sat very straight and very still, his eyes on the window and, scarcely daring to breathe, plucked out the music's pattern again.

A shadow fell across the window as if someone had stopped outside. Cosimo faltered in his playing, not daring to move, his eyes on the door. Was it opening? Was it being pushed slowly to?

And then without the least warning the door fell back and he was there. Cloaked and robed, his arms crossed on his breast, a pilgrim's deep hood hiding his face.

The Nameless One whose body had lain beneath the ancient City of Cremona for nearly a thousand years had risen from the grave and come in answer to the music.

Exactly as the legend had always foretold.

Kate crouched in the tiny vestibule at the top of the crypt stairs, the outer door at her back, staring at the stair to the crypt. She had formulated and discarded half a dozen plans for getting out of the bell tower, and several times she had almost given way to panic.

Because you'd better face it, Kate, at the foot of those

dark stairs, inside the Abbey's crypt, is the Devil's Piper himself. The creature bound by the music; his name's Ahasuerus and you might as well admit you know it, you might as well stop pretending. You've known his name all along, and you knew what Ciaran and the other man were doing as well. Back into the grave before sunrise. Crucifix and silver bullet and stake-through-the-heart time. Yes, but I didn't believe it – correction, I didn't want to believe it. Only it's time to be honest now. And how the hell am I going to get out of here?

It was impossible not to give way to the grisliest kind of nightmare visions: Ahasuerus shut into the crypt . . . Maybe creeping up the stair toward her . . . No, they'd have shut him away. That was what she had heard, the huge, dull clanging was the sound of the tomb being closed.

She was becoming cramped and cold, but she was afraid to move from the door. If she went up into the bell tower it would mean she could not keep watch on the crypt. To go down to the crypt itself, with no means of running away, was unthinkable.

Had that been a sound from below? She scrambled to her feet and pressed back against the locked door, her eyes on the stair. Something scratching at a coffin lid? Something tapping to be let out? She looked at the tower stair again. It was rather horridly reminiscent of every sinister legend ever written or read or imagined. Child Rowland and the dark tower of the foul fiend Flibbertigibbet . . . The Glamis monster prowling its dark fortress and weaving its dark bloody history . . . The ogres of Grimm sniffing out humans . . . Stop it!

Would the tower provide a means of escape? Maybe she could climb through a window and go down the walls. Or ring the bells to indicate an emergency, like World War Two when the ringing of church bells had been the alarm signal for the German invasion? The bell-ringing would work spectacularly, but the trouble was that Kate was not supposed to be here. The monks would presumably hand her over to the Irish police, because although she had not done anything especially criminal, she had certainly broken into the premises, and the Irish authorities might take a very serious view of somebody breaking into a monastery. They might politely ask her to leave the country. Deport her as an undesirable. And the end of it would be that she would never find out about Ahasuerus and the music.

She looked back at the tower again. Ringing the bells was out, but what about climbing through a window?

Going up into the bell tower was a very eerie experience indeed. Kate had brought a small torch with her, but in fact there was more light than she had expected and at each twist in the narrow stair a slit of a window was set into the stone wall. Moonlight trickled in, and Kate, constantly listening for any sound from the crypt, paused at each turn in the stair, looking out. This was not such a very high tower; it was not Salisbury Cathedral or Lichfield, but it was quite high. Could she bring herself to climb out of one of the windows? She thought she could. But how would she get down the outside wall? She would need to lower herself by a rope and—

A rope.

She sped up the final stretch of spiral steps and on up the vertical loft ladder into the ringing chamber. Ropes . . . She scrabbled for the torch again. And there in the thin light of the torch, hanging down from the great bells overhead, were four ropes.

Kate had not brought many implements on the spying expedition but she turned out the pockets of her jacket. A torch and a small knife with the blade protected by a thick leather sheath. It was hardly le Carré or Bond standard issue, but it might serve her purpose. She put the torch back and looked at the dangling ropes. If she was going to cut off one of those, she would have to cut it off as near to the bells as possible. She thought that even the lowest window was twenty-odd feet from the ground and she would need all the length she could get. She took a deep breath and grasped the rungs of the vertical ladder.

There was only a thin spill of moonlight now, and Kate went up the ladder more by feel than sight. As she neared the belfry a wind stirred, bringing with it a sour ancient odour, as if the bells themselves were breathing their iron breaths down on to her. Child Rowland going into Shakespeare's dark tower and smelling the blood of an Englishman . . .

The belfry was smaller than she had expected and the bells were directly over her head now. Kate glanced up and at once wished she had not done so because she was looking straight up into the bells themselves and it was like looking into the yawning maws of huge iron-tongued monsters. All the better to deafen you. All the better to gobble you up, my dear. Don't look.

There was no floor up here, only wooden staging, and it was cramped and awkward, and it would be dreadfully easy to miss your footing and tumble between the joists. It was open on all four sides, which she had more or less expected, but the apertures were not as large as she had feared and it would probably be virtually impossible to fall out. But the wind that had soughed in and out of the narrow stair was much stronger and much colder up here; it tore through the tower, whipping Kate's hair against her face and stinging her eyes. She gasped and crouched on the top of the ladder, holding on to the rungs with one hand for ballast, determinedly not looking upwards, concentrating on the ropes. Each one was pulled taut from under the bell and looped around a system of pulleys bolted to the joists before vanishing down into the ringing chamber below.

The wind was tapping gently against the bells so that there was a soft low humming, so quiet you were not sure if you were really hearing it. The wind did not quite disturb the bells but you had the feeling that it was very close to doing so. At any minute they might rear up and shriek their brazen call across Curran Glen. The ropes swayed slightly in the wind.

There was a really blood-chilling story about somebody having offended a bell, and the bell pursuing the miscreant across a bleak snow-covered landscape and killing him. The really spine-tingling part was when the bell was found quietly back in its place next day, apparently a guileless and inanimate lump of metal, but with its mouth dripping blood. Like a cat, innocent-eyed, but licking gore-smeared jowls. Kate wished she had not remembered it.

She would not think about anything except cutting through one of the ropes and escaping. The nearest rope was slightly thinner than the others and it might be fractionally easier to sever. Probably it was from the smallest bell. As Kate grasped it there was the faintest vibration from above. She felt sweat break out between her shoulder blades.

It would not be necessary to be particularly technical or practical about this, but it would be necessary to be deft. All she had to do was hack the rope off. Probably all the ropes were attached to the bells by some kind of pulley system, so that if you could climb on to the bells themselves it would be possible to unhook the ropes and let them snake down.

Kate thought she was as practical as most women today,

but she did not think she was sufficiently practical – all right, sufficiently brave! – to climb on to the back of a cluster of centuries-old bells and try to fathom the pulley system in the dark.

By dint of pulling up some slack with one hand, and holding the fall of the rope firmly between her knees, it was possible to slice through the rope without disturbing the bells. The rope was supple and strong and it ought to hold her weight. She cut doggedly, and felt the strands part and let the rope slither down through the holes in the floor. It fell with a soft thud into the ringing chamber below. So far so good. Now for the descent.

She chose the lowest window possible. It was probably still dangerously high up in the tower, but she thought she could face climbing through. The frame seemed sound and tough – the monks were apparently as careful of their Abbey as they were of their souls – and after knotting the rope firmly several times around the frame, she flung it out and then swung one leg over the sill.

It took a shorter time than she had thought and it was much easier than she had feared to lower herself to the ground. As her feet touched the grassy quadrangle, she breathed a huge sigh of relief and stepped back, eyeing the dangling rope. There was nothing she could do about it, the monks would find it at first light, but there was absolutely nothing to connect her with it. And if she could be brazen enough to keep her morning appointment for the library research, and act as if nothing had happened, she would probably get away with the whole thing.

But somehow she was going to have to get the key to the bell tower and go down into the crypt.

She was going to have to find out whether Ahasuerus was alive inside the tomb.

Chapter Eleven

Moira had hardly slept because she was looking forward so much to her first day at the Abbey's musical project. It was probably something that would rank as a very small event in most people's lives, but Moira thought it was going to be interesting. It would be creative in its own small way and more to the point it would get her away from Father for a few hours.

She had not wanted Edward to collect her at the end of the afternoon, but there had been no getting out of it. He had wagged his finger over breakfast and given one of his indulgent smiles and said, Nonsense, he would be wanting to hear all about the businesswoman's day and he would walk up to the Abbey when he himself finished in his office. He would be there to the tick and Moira was not to have turned into a high-flying career lady in a pin-striped suit by that time!

Mother had looked up from pouring out Father's coffee to smile and nod, and Moira had smiled dutifully as well, although it was going to be a terrible bore if Father insisted on fetching her home each day. She had been looking forward to walking back from the Abbey on her own: it was dusk by five o'clock and it was the nicest part of the day with everywhere swathed in violet and purple. You could pretend you were in the long-ago Ireland when it had been called by another name, and when half-human creatures

111

prowled the woods and the land was peopled with heroes and giants and warrior queens. You could not do any of that if Father was there because he would be solicitously telling you to look where you stepped, and asking was the walk too much for you and saying he must have a word with the Roads Department about laying a sensible bit of tarmac because the path was in a shocking state. Moira could not dream about Irish legends with Father talking about tarmac and Roads Departments.

Brother Matthew, who was the librarian, answered the door when she rather timidly pulled the bellrope shortly after lunch, and escorted her to the library.

'And now will you mind being left by yourself?' he said. 'Everything's in its proper place, because we had a young lady in this morning researching early plainsong – rather a coincidence, isn't it? – and she left everything very tidily indeed, in fact a sight tidier than most of the Brothers, I'm ashamed to say.'

Moira asked if people from outside often used the library.

'Well, we get post-graduate students working for doctoral theses or sometimes people writing books on local folklore, but we try to be a bit careful because some of the manuscripts are very old and irreplaceable. Now, Brother Ciaran said he'd leave you out some notes, but I can't see— oh yes, look, over here. And you'll like a cup of tea later, I expect? No, it's no trouble at all, a pot's always made about four o'clock, it's one of Father Abbot's little indulgences, I'll fetch it along myself.'

Moira did not in the least mind being left on her own, although she had been secretly looking forward to seeing Ciaran. Brother Ciaran. The library was narrow and rather dim and there were latticed windows that looked out over a small quadrangle with a stone bench at the centre. The walls were lined with books and there was one of the little wheeled contraptions that you pulled along while you were searching the top shelves. There were two or three leather-topped desks placed directly under the windows, but it was still necessary to switch on the wall lights.

The books were stacked a bit haphazardly. Moira wondered if she should suggest making a catalogue like they had had at St Asaph's so that things could be found more easily. Perhaps it would be better not to; it might sound like a criticism, or even worse, it might sound as if she was asking for more work.

As the afternoon wore on she became absorbed. Ciaran had left a list of books he thought might be of help, and scribbled a quick note to say please to reach down anything else she wanted. It was nice that he had taken the trouble to do this. Moira thought it would be best to take the books down one at a time in as chronological an order as possible and scan them for musical references, making notes as she went. She would allot one page of her notebook to a century and see if that was enough.

It was fascinating work. You did not know where, or how far back you might find mention of the Ambrosian plainchant, which was earlier than the better known Gregorian chant, but which the monks here always used. There were the different versions of the Mass: the *missa dominicalis* with the chants from as far back as the fifteenth century, and then the *missa brevis* which was a short Mass with Lutheran elements in it which had been prevalent in the seventeenth and eighteenth centuries. There were the Good Friday 'reproach' chants, sometimes called *Improperia*.

Moira began to think there was enough material here for something far more exciting than a flimsy leaflet which would be stuck in a church display with a dozen others, and for which tourists would pay 50p in the belief they were helping church funds, and then never read. Was it being naive to wonder about writing a proper book on religious music? How learned would you need to be? It did not need to be a huge dry tome: it could be informative but chatty, so that it would appeal to all kinds of people who liked music and history and found religious pageantry interesting. You could have illustrations to jazz it up a bit.

Seated in the Abbey library, making notes, plundering the monks' manuscripts and folios and finding such a wealth of information, the idea seemed not only possible, but within her capability.

Ciaran had looked up a transcription of their Founder's chronicles: Brother Simon's himself, which Moira suspected was going to be the most interesting thing of all. The original was probably under glass somewhere, but this was a translation made around the seventeenth century, so that it was fragile but fairly easy to read. Simon had travelled widely before coming to Curran Glen, and there were accounts of his journey through Italy, and his stay in the little town of Cremona. Moira bent over, liking the fusty smell of the old paper and the sensation that you were opening up a door into the past. She would have to be extremely careful, because although the manuscript was not the original, it was still very old and precious and valuable.

There was a passage on how Simon had visited the house of a Cosimo Amati whom he referred to as a lute-maker, and there was a description of how Cosimo had sought Simon out one night in a panic, running under cover of darkness to the monks' house in Cremona's oldest part.

'The man was very distressed,' Moira read, 'and together we hurried through the night streets, our footsteps ringing out on the cobbled pavements, he turning every few steps

114

as if to make sure that nothing came after us.'

Moira went on reading, feeling a bit guilty because she was supposed to be researching the Abbey's musical history, not giving herself shivers by uncovering somebody's twelfth-century horror story. She allowed herself the excuse that a lute-maker might have something to contribute to the Order's musical history.

The account was extraordinarily evocative. Moira could almost see the monk and the lute-maker going together through the dark streets – 'the shadows clung to the sides of the houses, and my companion started at every movement'.

It was second-hand reporting, of course, and would have to be regarded with due suspicion. Brother – what was his name? Moira looked to see – Brother John Joseph, that was it, had been translating Simon's own story for the benefit of the seventeenth-century monks, six hundred years after the events. Monks were supposed to be eminently truthful, but most of the monks here were Irish and you couldn't trust the Irish not to embroider a good story. John Joseph had better be taken with a pinch of salt.

Simon had given a description of the Amati house, which John Joseph had probably not tampered with at all. It was, 'larger than that of most artisans and plainly quite prosperous, with the upper storeys overhanging the street a little, and embellished with corbels. At a lower level than the street were the workrooms, and a dull red light emanated from them . . .'

You could see it as plainly as if you were there. You could hear the ringing out of the footsteps, and the frightened scurrying of the man Cosimo Amati. What had he been frightened of? Moira read on, scarcely aware of the thickening dusk outside the library, or the shadows creeping across the quadrangle beneath the window.

'As we passed through the doorway, Amati's lady came to meet us. She was clad only in a thin bedgown, and her hair streamed over her shoulders, the colour of molten copper . . . She had a remarkable beauty, and I heard later – although not from Cosimo – that she was known to be something liberal of her favours . . .'

As twelfth-century bodice-rippers went, this was terrific stuff. 'Something liberal of her favours.' Moira grinned and wondered had Ciaran read this bit. Imagine that: old Simon, the monks' revered and holy Founder, dashing through the cobbled streets of Cremona, probably bearing a crucifix with him and solemnly anticipating the performance of some kind of religious rite or maybe a deathbed, and then finding a red-haired hussy undulating towards him in a nightie.

The bit about their footsteps ringing out on the pavements and Cosimo Amati turning to see if they were being followed was amazingly descriptive. You could very nearly see it: you could very nearly hear it as well . . .

Cosimo had not waited to see the creature that cast its sinister shadow over his workroom floor; he had flung down the bone-lyre and scrambled out of the workroom, using not the door that led to the street and was barred by the creature, but going up the little winding stair that led back into the main part of the house, and tumbling into the street outside.

Shadows lay thickly everywhere – yes, and what crouched within those shadows! – but he had gone on, running blindly through the town, heedless of the noise he made, terrified lest the thing should be following him, making for the narrow tall stone building on the outskirts of the town.

Because I have called to the devil tonight and the devil

has answered and I need God's help to vanquish him!

The door of the monks' house was opened almost immediately by the young dark-haired Englishman – Cosimo thought his name was Simon – who had been travelling through Italy but was staying here for a time. He remembered with relief that Brother Simon spoke Italian.

Simon listened to the gasped-out story, really listened, thought Cosimo gratefully, because even to his own ears, it sounded remarkably far-fetched. The ancient chant, the ritual that Isabella's family had guarded for so many centuries, and that Cosimo himself had pronounced tonight in a moment of weakness, well, all right, in a prideful attempt to sweep the plague from Cremona! He would admit to the sin of pride, said Cosimo, struggling to regain some of his lost dignity. But it had been a worthy and selfless act, he said, tucking his chins righteously into his neck, and it could have rid them all of the wretched plague. The trouble now—

'The trouble now, Brother, is that there is something in my house— Something has entered it that I think might be—' Here he faltered, because you could not tell this lean-faced, rather austere young man that you thought you had summoned the devil and that the devil might even now be sitting in your home.

Simon was not unaccustomed to troubled people requesting help at all hours of the day and night. Usually it was prayers for dying children or parents or family. It was remarkable how even the most hardened sinners panicked at the end. But this appeared to be a bit different. This appeared to be a deliberate attempt to seek not God, but one of God's adversaries. And to have succeeded.

'The Nameless One,' Amati called him, dribbling a bit in terror, his plump unhealthy-looking face white and his eyes bolting from his head. Simon thought him disgusting, and then reproved himself. One of God's children, no matter what he had done.

He scooped up a crucifix and took Cosimo's arm firmly as they went back through the night streets. It was a pity that these manifestations always had to take place by night, but they nearly always did. Why could people not summon the devil in the middle of the day when you had everything to hand and you could see what you were doing? Quench this ill-placed humour, Brother!

Simon made a quick survey of his pack as they rushed through the streets. Bible and crucifix. Stoppered flagon of holy water. All there. It was a pity they had not been able to bring a fragment of the consecrated Host, but it would have meant waking Father Abbot and Simon would prefer to see first if the story was genuine.

Cosimo Amati's house was unexpectedly large and prosperous-looking, and there was a little painted sign hanging outside, depicting a musical instrument – a lyre, was it? A respectable trade. A respectable man, as far as Simon could tell. Had Amati's imagination simply run away with him? Had he been drinking or – this was nasty – was he in the first stages of plague himself? Sometimes it began with a fever.

Cosimo pushed open the street door, and on the stair, looking down at them, was the most beautiful woman Simon had ever seen.

The minute Ahasuerus saw Isabella Amati he recognised her.

Susannah. Here in the underground room, standing on the stair, one hand going fearfully to her throat. Her skin was as white and as translucent as he remembered, the spill of copper hair falling about her face exactly as it had done in the Temple that last day.

For an instant the recognition was so absolute, that the shadowy workroom with its odd unfamiliar scents wavered and blurred, and he was back in Jerusalem, Susannah was slipping through the little side door into the Temple and standing before the altar waiting for him. Naked beneath the concealing cloak . . .

This was Susannah cast in a slightly different mould; a little younger, a little more rounded of face. But the curve of her cheek and the look in her eyes was unmistakable. The eyes of a saint but the mouth of a sinner.

The woman moved down the narrow wooden staircase towards him, and at that minute, Cosimo Amati burst back into the house, with the monk, Simon, at his heels.

Simon experienced his own instant of shocked recognition as well, but it was an instant filled with such cold horror that he felt his vitals slither with fear.

The Nameless One, Cosimo had gabbled in terror, the Nameless One answering the music's summons. But to Simon, the creature standing in the candlelit underground workroom, looking over its shoulder at them, was not nameless.

Ahasuerus. Ahasuerus the murdered High Priest of the Temple of Jerusalem. The renegade and the rebel; the butchered Scribe who had betrayed his vows and dishonoured the Sacred Altar and been stripped of every honour before being put to death.

Simon's mind was reeling, but he struggled to formulate some kind of physical or mental attack on the silent figure before him. He knew that he was confronting the very one whose body the founders of his Order had brought out of Jerusalem centuries earlier. He knew how the *Fratres Cruciferi* had bargained with the Temple Elders for the High Priest's body and how they had carried it out of the Holy City with the blessings of the people ringing about their heads. And, thought Simon cynically, with the payment of the Temple Elders weighing down their packs.

The monks had travelled slowly and apparently haphazardly, but at last they had come to the little town of Cremona, with its history stretching back to the Romans, the Roman wall which still stood firm and the mosaic pavements. And the catacombs winding deep into the hillside . . .

They had not precisely been searching for catacombs, but the catacombs had served their purpose very well indeed. As night fell they had lit torches and carried their grisly burden deep into the tunnels. They had buried Ahasuerus's stone coffin far below the surface and they had sealed the openings.

Because towards the end, when he had been almost beyond speech, Ahasuerus had looked down from the execution gibbet to where his Judges stood and made again the anguished threat.

I shall return . . .

And although no one had quite believed him, no one had quite dared disbelieve either . . .

And now it had happened; somehow he had risen from the coffin and found his way out of the catacombs.

Ahasuerus, the murdered High Priest, who had defiled the Temple of Jerusalem with his harlot, had returned.

Ahasuerus shrank into the shadows and wrapped the concealing cloak about him the instant he saw Susannah. She would not recognise him, of course she would not recognise him . . .

The monk was standing before him, and when he spoke, he did so in Latin: not the old pure language they had used in the Temple but a coarser more clipped form. But it was understandable.

'Why are you here? What do you want?'

'You called to me. I answered.'

It amused Ahasuerus to see the fear go through them and a portion of his mind noted the words and tucked them away for future use. He waited to see what they would do next, his mind absorbing details: how they spoke, how they behaved. Because I may have to blend with this unknown world; I may have to live here for some time. The woman he recognised as Susannah – Isabella, had they called her? – had not spoken but Ahasuerus knew she was watching him. She did not know yet, not quite, but she nearly did.

Cosimo Amati was feeling better. He could see that he had been a touch foolhardy – well, he had been very foolhardy indeed – but it was beginning to seem as if this cloaked stranger might not be the menace he had feared, and he thought it was time he took an active part in things. He puffed out his chest a little, and copying Simon and using his best Latin, he said,

'We want you to rid the city of plague. That's why I called to you.' And saw you obey, said his manner. Ahasuerus thought him a ridiculous little man. 'We have plague here in Cremona,' said Cosimo, tucking his chins into his neck and looking solemn at the enormity of the thing that had come to his town.

Ahasuerus said, 'What manner of plague?'

'What manner? What do you—'

'Locusts? Pestilence? Death of the first-born—?'

There was a sudden silence. A shiver of purest awe went through the two men and then Simon, staring at the motionless Ahasuerus, said very softly, 'The Ten Plagues of Egypt. That's what you mean, isn't it?'

Ahasuerus said courteously, 'I know of no other.'

'But that was— Brother Simon, he can't possibly— Oh dear me, do *something*!' cried Cosimo, wringing his hands and lapsing into his native tongue in his distress. Ahasuerus listened closely, noting the inflections, thinking he could almost guess at the meanings.

There was a movement from the stair, and the three men turned at once. Isabella moved lightly down to the floor of the workshop, her little bare feet scarcely touching the polished oak as she came. Ahasuerus, his every instinct alive, felt her mind brush his, and when she spoke, he experienced a swift surge of purest delight. Oh yes, that is exactly how her voice sounded.

Isabella Amati looked towards him and said, in Latin fully as good as Simon's, 'The plague that my husband summoned you to fight is pestilence.'

'Disease?'

'Yes. Brought in largely by rats.' And as Cosimo and Simon turned to look at her, she smiled the three-cornered smile that several of her admirers had likened to a cat, but that her detractors said showed her true nature.

'We want you to rid the city of rats for us.' She smiled again, and Ahasuerus felt time splinter and re-form in a different pattern, because it was exactly the way that Susannah had smiled in the Temple that afternoon.

That afternoon . . . Silent, drowsy, the entire city bathed in a shimmer of heat haze, no one knowing quite where anyone was . . .

Susannah's thin concealing cloak sliding to the ground . . . His own body betraying him instantly because she was naked under it, and she was dazzlingly beautiful. And that was the moment when I forgot who I was and I forgot what I was. That had been the moment when his mind had spun out of control, and he had pulled her to him, his body so violently aroused that he had cried out with the pain.

I took her there, he thought, staring at Isabella Amati in the little candlelit workroom. I laid her down on the floor of the Temple – actually the sacred High Temple – and I tore open my robe and entered her body with mine. Her thighs closed about me and her body was purest silk, drawing out the seed . . . And I was helpless before her. I am helpless before her now.

Aloud he said, still speaking in the Latin he had used so long ago, 'I will do what you ask, Master Lute Maker.'

Simon said abruptly, 'Can you do it?' and Ahasuerus looked at him coldly.

'I can.'

'How?'

'You must trust that. First, though, there is a condition.'

'So I assumed,' said Simon, his expression unreadable, and Ahasuerus said coolly,

'If you trade with the devil, you will find there is always a condition.' Take it or leave it, said his tone. And all the while, he was aware of a current of amused power ebbing and flowing within his mind, because they were believing him, the fools were cringing before him, they truly believed they had somehow raised the devil . . .

Just as the devil raised me that afternoon in the Temple, body and mind and soul.

Simon waved the babbling Cosimo to silence and said, 'What is the condition?'

Silence. Then Ahasuerus said, 'If I am to do what you ask, I must live among you for a short time. And therefore, I must learn a little of your world. Customs and speech and manners.'

'Yes?'

'To do that, I would ask to spend some time with your lady, Master Lute Maker. Only long enough,' said Ahasuerus politely, 'for her to teach me about your people and your ways.'

'Well, I hardly think—'

'A night would be sufficient.'

'A night?' Cosimo stared stupidly, and Ahasuerus smiled and looked across at Isabella.

'A night with your lady,' he said softly.

Chapter Twelve

Moira came out of the twelfth century and back into the twentieth as if she was walking off a lighted stage set.

The account was a bit sparse and it was couched in the rather florid style of the seventeenth century, but it had been remarkably easy to see the fearful Cosimo and his dazzling lady, and to visualise Simon holding up a crucifix to dismiss the stranger. Moira thought she would finish reading this tomorrow, because it was getting dark in the library and deciphering the thin spidery writing was beginning to make her head ache. But she would like to know a bit more about it all and she would certainly like to know the outcome. How complete was John Joseph's transcription? It might be worth asking could she see the original.

She poured herself another cup of tea from the tray brought earlier by Matthew. There were no casual saucerless mugs with sugar ready stirred in for Abbey guests: the Brothers lived fairly austerely but they had their own code for visitors and the tray held a flowered teapot with matching milk jug and sugar bowl and a plate of freshly baked biscuits. The monks did not have afternoon tea themselves, but they thought people in the outside world did.

She turned back to the manuscript, thinking she would just make a few final notes, and as she did so, she heard footsteps coming along the corridor outside. For an instant her heart bounded, in case it might be Ciaran – *Brother* Ciaran – coming to see how she was getting on. If he had time, perhaps they could have a cup of tea together and she could tell him what she had found and discuss Simon's manuscript with him. She was just framing a welcoming sentence, when the door was pushed open, and her father stood in the doorway.

'I've come to take you home, my dear,' he said.

Edward had not liked to see his Moire Silk so completely absorbed in something he had no part of and he picked up the transcript of Simon's journeys, frowning a little, hoping to find it shallow, trivial nonsense that could be indulgently dismissed. He flipped the pages over, picking out a sentence here and there. It was almost as he had thought but it was not quite as trivial as he had hoped. There was a good deal of rubbishy story-telling about the Abbey's founder and there was some preposterous tale in flowery language about Brother Simon and some Italian woman. Edward was surprised to find such gossip in a monastery library.

The brief description of the Italian creature – Isabella, was it? – struck an unexpected nerve.

A thin bedgown, and hair streaming over her shoulders, the colour of molten copper . . . He glanced up to where Moira was seated at the desk, the little electric wall lamp directly above shining on her hair. Lending it the appearance of molten copper . . .

There had been a moment when Edward had stood in the library doorway, and seen Moira look up, startled, and in that moment it had not been his little girl at all, it had been a stranger looking up with the reflex annoyance of someone disturbed from some deeply interesting task.

Someone with hair the colour of molten copper . . .

And then she had smiled and of course it was Moira,

dressed neatly in the way Edward himself had advised over breakfast.

'If I were you, I should wear your nice navy skirt and a plain blouse today,' he had said, and Mary had said to be sure to take a cardigan as well because it would be chilly later on. 'And it would be better to tie your hair back,' Edward had added.

There had been a moment when Moira had looked as if she was going to argue, which had surprised Edward, but then she had smiled and said, Yes, it was as well to be conventional with the monks, and had put on the navy skirt and a white blouse and tied her hair back with a navy ribbon, and Edward had smiled his approval and said, There! Now she was her daddy's pretty little girl again.

But as he had stood in the doorway, he had seen that the neatly confined hair had escaped from its ribbon and was tumbling about her shoulders—

Curling over her small firm breasts—

And of course, the last thing a respectable father did, the last thing a good Catholic husband did was to look at that spilling silken hair or at the neat white blouse which was in fact a shirt of thin soft lawn, tailored like a man's dress shirt and unexpectedly seductive. Edward would make sure that Mary told Moira that the blouse did not become her. It was remarkable how uncomfortable it was making him feel. Edward was naturally aware of his Church's ruling on the harbouring of impure thoughts and he was scrupulous about confessing them, unless it was Father Kane on confession duty, in which case he waited until it was old Father Dougal's turn, because Dougal was getting a bit deaf and could be counted on to miss most of what you said.

Mallow, seen by the light of the morning, was as

tumbledown as it had looked on Isarel's arrival.

He winced as he drew the faded curtains back and felt a stab of pain above one eye – sunlight! Death to a wine-induced headache! – but managed to set a kettle to boil on the Aga which was still warm from last evening. He swallowed two aspirin, giving himself the option of a third, foraged for the bread bought a hundred years ago on the way here, and managed to make toast by propping an old-fashioned toasting fork in front of the Aga. The creamy Irish butter melted into the thick bread, sunlight filtered in from outside and there was a scent of something sweet and nostalgic drifting in from the garden. Insensibly, Isarel's spirits lifted and although it was probably only the aspirin working, he felt so much better that he got up to pour a second cup of tea and toast another slice of bread. He remembered adding a jar of honey to the provisions and hunted it out. Tea and buttered toast and honey. Very English. It pleased him to be so English out here on the edge of the wild Irish coast. He spread the honey thickly and tilted his chair back to look through the window, thinking hard.

Clearly his midnight visitor had been in the later stages of madness and equally clearly, Isarel had been mad with him. Had they really walked through the copse to the Abbey with that thing – what was its name? Ahasuerus? – following, and had they really pushed it down into the noisome tomb?

At one o'clock in the morning, after two bottles of wine, it had been an intriguing tale and a bizarre adventure, but in the cold light of day it was plainly nonsense and it had probably not really happened. Isarel began to wonder whether Ciaran had been a monk at all, and whether his first assumption that he was entertaining an escaped madman might not have been correct.

128

But if he was mad last night, then so was I. And the music was there to give the lie to the madness. Jude's music. I don't dare think about it. I certainly don't dare believe it.

Isarel got up from the table and put his cup and plate and knife in the sink before starting on a tour of exploration. If Mallow was really falling to pieces it would be as well to find out which bits were likely to drop off first. It would certainly be more to the point than brooding over ancient entombed beings and devil-inspired music. He supposed he would have to walk or drive round to the Abbey later – or maybe Ciaran would come to Mallow – but it could be put off for a few hours yet.

He made notes as he went, expecting to find it depressing, but in the event not finding it any such thing. Mallow was neglected and battered, but beneath the decay and the dirt the fabric was very good indeed. Isarel was no architect or building surveyor, but even he could see that the damp patches on the walls had been caused by nothing worse than leaking and blocked roof gutters and that although the window frames were rotten, the beautiful sandstone lintels surrounding them were sound. And seen by the morning light the brickwork was lovely: soft mellow red. The mortar had crumbled here and there, but not to any alarming extent. It could be – what did builders call it? – re-pointing, wasn't it?

He went back inside and up to the first floor landing where light slanted across the bare floorboards, making the dust motes dance in and out, and where a small secondary stair wound rather precariously up to the attics. This would be the crunch: you could repair or replace window frames and you could renew crumbling mortar, but if roof joists had collapsed you were in severe trouble.

But the roof was dry and sweet, and the trusses and

joists were as solid and as strong as the day Mallow was built. A few tiles were missing and the roofing felt was torn, but he thought it was nothing that a good builder could not put right in an afternoon. Jude, you may have been an evil, faithless bastard and you may have died that shameful death, but your house is the most beautiful thing that has happened to me for a very long time. He stood looking through the little windows of the attic room, seeing the smudge of blue and green to the west that was the wild, beautiful Irish rim. This had been Jude's bolt-hole, this was where he had come when he wanted to run away from the world, to work, to study a score, to create. Or to be with one of his women.

There were one or two brief, tantalisingly vague accounts in the many biographies written about Jude, suggesting that he had had a number of mistresses before he married Isarel's grandmother in Vienna just before the war. Isarel remembered one account by a lady who had stayed here in the Thirties and who related how her host would sit at the head of the polished, mahogany dining table, drinking Chateau Yquem and dining off *foie gras* and quails by candlelight – 'Looking like a cross between a devil and a satyr.' Even if they dined late, Jude often got up at dawn and went down to the music room to pour music – occasionally his own, sometimes other people's – into the cool daybreak. 'He had the same remarkable gifts as the maestro, Arthur Nikisch, who in the Eighteen Nineties held his audiences and orchestra both completely spell-bound,' she had said, thus revealing that she was at least a decade older than she had previously admitted.

Another one, living as a *grande dame* in America, an unashamed seventy-something, had related how she used to go to Jude's apartment in one of the tall old houses in the Augustiner Strasse in Vienna, and how she would sit entranced as he played Schumann and Greig until the air sizzled with vibrancy and the room was bathed in a fiery blaze from the sun setting behind the Cathedral. How there had always been a silver wine cooler containing champagne in the bedroom and silk sheets on the bed. Decadent in only the way that Vienna before the war could be decadent, she was reported as saying. Certainly there had been more than a trace of what her generation had called the 'cad' about Jude Weissman. But when he sat down at the piano you ceased to care, because you would have followed him anywhere he cared to invite you.

Isarel thought that even allowing for the bias of these memories, Jude must have been a killer with the women. If you did not know better you would almost see him as a kind of demi-god, instead of the cold, calculating traitor he had really been.

All that, he thought, staring through the grimed windowpanes of Mallow's attics; all those women and all that adulation, and I never once suspected that Jude might have uncovered the *Black Chant*.

He frowned, shaking his head to dislodge the blurred shreds of memory and went downstairs again to continue with his list of repairs. Electricity was a priority, of course. What about plumbing? The bathroom was functional although that was about all you could say for it, and at least there was a bathroom and not a grisly little hut at the bottom of the garden. The pipework looked as if it was lead, which was impractical and probably dangerous; the bath was a massive iron affair on clawed feet and the loo was enclosed in a square mahogany box.

He surveyed the kitchen as the kettle boiled for a mug of coffee. He would like to keep the huge old dresser and the red tiles on the floor would polish up rather attractively. He could have a rag rug on them if such a thing could still be found, and a wooden rocking chair in the corner by the Aga. The Aga was proving unexpectedly efficient now that he had fathomed how it worked and discovered that you had to keep it burning more or less permanently. He thought he might keep it. But an electric hob and a few more cupboards would not hurt and it would be nice to have a fridge and instant hot water. Could he afford central heating? It would probably be economical in the long run, but it might be expensive to install. He drank the coffee and went on with his plans, resolutely ignoring the shofar which lay on the piano where he had put it after returning to Mallow in the early hours of the morning.

I'm not looking at you, said Isarel to it, silently. I'm not seeing you. In fact I've forgotten you're there.

He concentrated on exploring the house, clinging to practicalities, and all the while a part of his mind was busy repudiating what had happened in the Abbey's crypt and overlaying it with other, more believable things. Roof tiles and electrical wiring and woodworm. As the day wore on, he found it possible to relegate Ciaran O'Connor and his eerie story of immortal creatures who crawled up out of coffins to a kind of mental limbo. By the time he had assembled a scratch lunch of bread and tuna fish and tomatoes, with an apple and cheese to round it off, Ahasuerus was beginning to take on the quality of a bad dream. After lunch he drove into Curran Glen and discovered that one small firm could handle building, electrical wiring and plumbing, and that although the premises appeared haphazard and the bright-eyed, bow-legged proprietor was happy-go-lucky, the initial suggestions for the work were surprisingly efficient and unexpectedly imaginative, and the tentatively discussed figures not as high as he had been fearing.

But as the late-afternoon twilight stole across Mallow's

tangled gardens, he found himself back in the music room. It was absurd to want to play the music again and in view of last night it was probably dangerous, always supposing that last night had existed outside of a dream. It was not beyond possibility that some of his students had laced his toothpaste with LSD or Ecstasy or whatever disgusting drug was currently in fashion.

Beyond the windows, the lilac and purple dusk was stealing over the tangled gardens, and without warning a fragment of a half-remembered poem – Coleridge? – slid into Isarel's mind. Something about a man dreaming he had died and gone to Paradise, where he had plucked a rose. Only when he awoke, he found that he was still holding the rose . . . It was a shivery notion, but it was a seductive one, as well.

Did I travel to the centre of a dream last night? thought Isarel. Only it wasn't Coleridge's rose-tinted Paradise, it was a dark and ancient dream, someone else's nightmare, a drifting flotsam – or do I mean jetsam? – of something primeval and death-ridden.

Did I bring the rose back with me? He looked at the shofar again and at the sheets of musical notation on the Bluthner's stand.

There was only one way to find out. There was only one way to lay the lingering ghost, and that was to deliberately go back into the dark rose-scented nightmare.

The thought: Jude would do it, closed about his mind.

Isarel sat down at the piano and reached for the shofar.

Father seemed to think that the brief afternoon's work in the Abbey library had tired Moira. He walked unnecessarily close as they went down from the Abbey, taking her arm firmly. He would not, of course, have realised that Moira found this embarrassing because of the back of his hand touching her breast; he would be being protective. He was protective as they crossed a rough bit of path, even though Moira was perfectly able to walk over it unaided.

He asked about her work and said, nonsense, of course he would not think it boring, he wanted to know everything she had done, she was to omit no details. They should discuss it over a cosy supper, and then it must be an early bed. Moira thought of several responses to this, none of which were utterable. She tried not to mind about having her walk spoiled. They were in sight of Mallow House now, and this was the part she had been looking forward to. She could just hear the thin squeak of a bat somewhere overhead, and it was the half-light when you sometimes saw owls swooping across the sky. Lovely. In summer, you heard the dry chirrup of grasshoppers and crickets.

Father was talking about her afternoon as if it had been a ten-mile marathon for heaven's sake, and berating himself for not having driven the car up to the Abbey. Moira had felt uncomfortable about the breast-brushing part earlier, but now she began to feel angry.

Without the least warning, as much a part of the night as the bats and the owls, thin clear music drifted across the air, weaving itself into the magical twilight, so gentle and insidious that you could not be entirely sure whether you were imagining it.

At her side, Edward drew in a sharp breath and said he did not know what things were coming to when people were thoughtless enough to fling wide their windows and impose their cacophony on half the countryside. Clearly it was coming from Mallow, and equally clearly it was that insolent young man, Jude Weissman's grandson, who was playing it. Edward would have a few words to say to Isarel West in the morning.

The music had an odd quality to it. It was not loud but

it was difficult to hear anything over it. Moira found it difficult to hear what Father was saying. It was filled with achingly sweet promise and there was a beckoning, mocking quality. It reminded you of all the other worlds that existed – not fantasy, beyond-the-skies worlds, but ordinary ones where people had interesting jobs and friends and travelled and married and had children. The music gave you tantalising glimpses of other lives; like a thickthorn hedge parting for a minute. Like the lovely Bible line about In my Father's house are many mansions.

And then the music quickened and became sharper, and Moira half turned towards it and stumbled over a tree root, catching her sound foot and tumbling headlong on the ground. She was not in the least hurt – only a sudden jolt to her foot – but she felt silly and undignified in the way you feel silly and undignified if you do not look where you are going and end up flat on the ground.

Edward bent over her at once, saying she must not move, they would fetch help, putting his arms round her and smothering her against his tweed coat, making it difficult for her to breathe.

This was all ridiculous. Moira said firmly, 'I'm not in the least hurt – except I've ruined a new pair of tights,' but Edward was not having this. A terrible thing had happened to his Moire Silk, his dear one, but her daddy would get her home. They were near to the house anyway and she should be carried – no, he insisted. He put his right arm about her body and bent down to slide his left under her thighs and Moira experienced a jolt of repulsion.

She struggled to get out of his grasp and stand up. 'Father, please— I'm not hurt and I'd really much rather walk home.' It would not do any good: he would tell her that Father knew best, and wave aside her protests and in the end she would give in.

Letting the thickthorn hedge close again and letting the doors to all those mansions close . . .

He was hugging her against him; one hand was imprisoning her waist and there was the hot press of masculinity. Moira struggled to get free and as she did so, the music pouring out from Mallow swooped and spun all about them, and there was a moment – dreadful! sick-making! – when she was jammed up against Edward's groin and he was thrusting forward in horrid, rhythmic movements and Moira could feel the hard lump of flesh between his thighs and a sudden radiating heat. Revulsion scudded across her skin again.

Without warning, the music stopped, as if the musician had flung it away impatiently, and Edward stepped back, putting up a hand to his forehead as if suddenly dizzy or confused.

They went down to the house in uncomfortable silence.

It was pointless to argue against his ministrations once they were home: Moira did not bother to try, even though it was completely ridiculous to be carried up to her room and laid on the bed. The odd, confused look had vanished from Father's eyes; his face was jowly with possessiveness and he was calling for aspirin and hot milk, elbowing Mother out of the way, making a ridiculous fuss about a small fall. He patted pillows into place and drew the curtains completely instead of leaving the gap which let the moonlight shine on to the end of the bed.

'A light supper, I think,' he said, standing up and frowning down at the bed. 'A little fish perhaps, or an omelette.'

Mary said, 'We'd shepherds pie tonight—' and Moira started to say that would be great, because she was actually very hungry after her afternoon's work. Mother made a good shepherds pie, with the mashed potatoes crisp and brown on top of the minced lamb.

'Fish cooked in milk,' said Edward firmly, waving away the suggestion that fish would smell out the bedroom for twenty-four hours. 'Perhaps a little stewed fruit to follow. A thimbleful of brandy in warm milk afterwards. I shall sit with you while you have your supper.'

Mother had switched on the little bedside lamp after taking away the supper trays, and it cast a soft pool of light over the pillows. There was a bowl of dried lavender on the little bureau under the window, and a faint breeze from outside stirred it, taking away the fish smell. Nice, thought Moira, drowsy from the unaccustomed brandy. Mother made the dried lavender from the bush outside the dining room window and sewed it into little cotton sachets for tucking into dressing table drawers. Poor Mother, who led such a boring life. Poor Moira who will lead a similar one if I'm not careful. Push back the thickthorn hedge, thought Moira hazily. Is there any way I could do that? And what about that really dreadful moment outside Mallow? Will he do that again? And what on earth do I do if he does?

You did not, of course, fall asleep at this time in the evening – it could not be much later than half past eight or nine o'clock – but the unaccustomed brandy coupled with the aspirin, made her feel sleepy. Father had tiptoed out of the room after fluffing up the pillows and adjusting everything in the room that could be adjusted. Irritating. Moira closed her eyes and waited for him to go and after what seemed a very long time, she heard the door of her room open and close again. Good.

She closed her eyes and sank in a comfortable half-dream, the kind of drifting daydream where you floated

137

drowsily beneath warm sun-dappled beech trees and where you were not quite awake, but not so much asleep that you could not direct the dream. The thin sweet sound of the monks' Vespers' bell drifted across her dreaming. It was a pity she had not seen Ciaran this afternoon. Ciaran . . .

How might it have been if it had been Ciaran with her when she fell? How would it feel to be picked up and carried by him? Moira turned on to her back, smiling, feeling his arms, imagining him bending over her, brushing her cheek with his lips . . . He was an odd example of celibacy. He never looked at women with any kind of sexual edge, but Moira had often received an impression of some immensely strong emotion being banked down. She thought he had probably known a great many women before he became a monk.

It was very wrong to wish that that strong self-control would give way in her company, but it was immensely exciting to imagine it. He would be gentle and strong and his hands would fold back her nightgown and slide over her naked body, cupping her breasts, and then going lower. Even when you were drifting through a misty green-and-gold world of half-sleep it was possible to feel it all very clearly indeed. Moira could feel her breasts tingling with delight. She could feel the sudden startling intrusion of a hand between her thighs, of a thick warm masculine finger stroking her . . . Someone was breathing harshly with pleasure. Someone was bending over her . . .

The half-guilty pleasure vanished abruptly and Moira was aware that something very frightening was hovering about her. Panic flooded her mind and alarm bells pounded against her senses. Wake up. Wake up before the half-dream crosses over into a nightmare.

Moira opened her eyes and looked up into the hot eyes of the man leaving over her. Not Ciaran. Oh God, not

Ciaran. Not the celibate monk about whom she had sometimes fantasised.

Her nightgown was drawn up to her shoulders and her father was standing over her with a look of concentration on his face. One hand was stroking her naked body, pushing between her legs.

The other hand was fumbling inside his unzipped trousers.

The horror and the revulsion she had felt earlier, outside Mallow, swept over her, so that it seemed as if the little lavender-scented bedroom was filling up with it.

And I shall drown, I shall drown in the smothering lavender nightmare, I shall suffocate . . .

Moira clutched at sanity. Edward had gone from the room – it was impossible to think of him as Father any longer – he had gone stumblingly, clutching a hand to his groin, oh God, unbearable! – his face averted.

Moira wrenched her pillows into place and switched on the bedside lamp. Light. Yes, that was better. You could think better with light, you could feel more normal. She hugged the covers around her for warmth and comfort and forced herself to think.

The idea of running away, of escaping the stifling protectiveness, the looming boredom of the years ahead, had tugged at the edges of her mind for a very long time. Now it bubbled up and boiled over, swamping her in a huge, fizzy froth. Could it be done? How could it be done? Money in the post office, a dark night to creep out into . . . It was like seeing a crack appear in the skies that was only a thin sliver of light at present, but that you could, if you had sufficient courage, force open so that you could climb through into the shining worlds beyond.

Yes, but could she do it? Leave Mother and the twins,

139

leave Curran Glen which was the only place she had ever known in all her nineteen years and a bit? Even thinking about it made her feel sick and cold inside, but behind the sick and the cold feeling her mind was already considering practicalities.

Could she walk to the railway station a mile or so beyond the town and get on the first train that came along? Into the unknown . . . Yes, but climbing through into those beckoning worlds. Setting foot at last on the path that widened as it went, and the path that wound excitingly past all those mansions with their doors to the other worlds half open . . . I'll do it, thought Moira, and the shining, fizzing champagne fountain cascaded over her mind again, sprinkling it with delight, sweeping aside the guilt about leaving Mother and the twins. They would be all right. She would write to them as soon as she could, telling them that she was fine, not telling them where she was, but reassuring them. Maybe later on, the twins could come to stay with her. Extravagant visions of having her own little flat – well, maybe a nice bedsitter at first – rose up. Dublin University might even be a possibility, still. Did you have to have parental permission?

She had known since she was approximately fourteen that she would run away one day; the only thing she had not been sure of was when it would happen.

Now she did know. She had known the minute she opened her eyes and saw him with lust making his eyes bloodshot and with his left hand plucking rhythmically at his groin.

She was going tonight.

Chapter Thirteen

Moira waited until the house was silent and then slid out of bed. It took a long time to get dressed because of the need for silence, but she managed it. She put on dark trousers and a sweater, with a jacket and black sou'wester, and laid out a couple of cotton shirts and a skirt. She eased the dressing table drawers open, wincing when they scraped, and took a selection of underthings, folding everything into her old school satchel. It was a bit freaky to be running away from home with your things in a leather satchel – well, it was very freaky indeed – but the suitcases were all away up in the attic and impossible to reach without being heard.

The satchel was quite spacious. She tucked away her hairbrush and comb, and took her savings book from the bureau. Five hundred punts, saved from odd birthday presents sent by aunts and her godmother over the years, all of it diligently tucked away against the day when home should become unbearable, and occasionally added to by Edward who said smilingly that he knew ladies liked to have a certain amount of independence these days; Moire Silk should have a little money of her own to fritter. He had sounded like somebody's father in *Pride and Prejudice*. Moira suddenly wondered with panic if there was any way in which he could stop her from drawing the money. She had no idea if that was possible but, trying to cover every

141

contingency, she took her birth certificate out of the bureau and folded it into the satchel's zipped pocket. Proof of identity. She took her passport as well, obtained for a short holiday in France just after she had left school. Moira suspected that the holiday had been a way of driving a wedge between her and her schoolfriends who had all been taken up with going to colleges to learn to be teachers or nurses or physiotherapists. Several had got secretarial jobs and one was starting as a very junior reporter with the local newspaper which would be hard work but great fun. Two were going to Dublin University – Mother Bernadette and the nuns had been very pleased about that. God did not give you intelligence just for you to waste it, they said.

Moira would have settled for any job where she could have gone out each day and met people and done something interesting, or even something boring, but this had been waved aside. A little jaunt to France, said Edward. His Moira was not to be drudging in an office or spoiling her looks by studying in a college. They would be off to Paris, and they would see the sights together.

Moira had liked Paris, it was interesting and beautiful, but Edward had not cared for it. Nasty messed-up food, he said. Too much garlic. Cars hooting all the time, and had Moira noted the *cost* of things! Absolutely disgraceful, and he would like to know how people had the cheek to charge such inflated prices! Mother had been nervous and timid throughout, thanking waiters and hotel people too effusively. It had all been a disaster, but the one thing it had done was provide Moira with a passport.

She would leave a note, not saying where she had gone or why, but simply telling them she had left. The Victorian flavour of this pleased her, because her father had behaved like a modern version of Mr Barrett for years and it served him right if she fled into the night like Elizabeth. She wrote the note and propped it against the tea caddy where it would be one of the first things found in the morning. It was a good thing she had not a spaniel for her father to vent his wrath on like Mr Barrett with Flush, although it was a pity there was no sexy, poetical Robert waiting to carry her off to a romantic wedding in Italy. Had it been Italy? Well, anywhere at all.

She had no idea how far five hundred punts would take her. It seemed a very great deal but it might be a very small amount indeed out in the world. There would be such things as travelling, and the renting of a room of some kind until she found a job. This ought to have been daunting but it suddenly all seemed so exciting – the crack in the sky widening – that Moira did not care if she had to sleep in a Salvation Army Hostel. She did not care if she had to sleep on a park bench.

For more immediate needs she had just on ten punts in her handbag, which would do to buy things like a toothbrush and flannel and soap which she would have to do on account of the bathroom door squeaking badly and not daring to open it to get her sponge bag.

The side door squeaked as well, but it was on the other side of the house and it was pretty certain that it would not be heard. Holding her breath and praying to every saint in the calendar, Moira went down the garden path and out into the night.

It was not quite the classic flight through the storm, but it was not far off. Clouds were massing overhead, and the trees surrounding the Abbey and Mallow House were being whipped into contorted shapes against the darkness. Like reaching arms, like long-fingered hands clutching at you. There was a flurry of rain and the wind tore her hat away and sent it bowling into the dark night, snatching her hair away from her face like a huge angry hand. Moira gasped and turned resolutely towards the main street.

The Abbey clock was chiming softly as she approached the old stone arch. Two o'clock. There could not possibly be anyone abroad at this hour. Even the late-night travellers at Murphy's would long since have wrapped up their revels. Curran Glen would be sleeping.

Curran Glen was not sleeping. Lights burned in Mallow House – Moira could see the steady glow clearly, and she hesitated. It looked rather welcoming.

A dark figure loomed out of the shadows and grabbed her.

Moira had the breath almost knocked out of her, but the person who had grabbed her was female which was reassuring. A harsh voice said, 'What the devil are you doing? And who on earth are you?'

'I'm— I don't see what that's got to do with you!' said Moira, pushing her assailant's hands away and glaring. 'If it comes to that, who are you and what are you doing?'

The girl regarded her and an unexpected glint of amusement showed. Moira's eyes were adjusting to the darkness now, and she could see that the girl was a few years older than Moira herself: probably she was about thirty. She was tall and thin and she was wearing dark trousers and what looked like a man's donkey jacket. Her hair swung out like black watered silk, and her eyes slanted above high cheekbones. Her voice was English, with a cool, faintly arrogant edge to it.

'I'm robbing a grave,' said the girl. 'But since you've put paid to that for tonight, you'd better come back to the caravan and tell me who you are.'

The small caravan in the Abbey field was not quite what Moira had expected. It was sleek and modern, with bright curtains at the windows and a scarlet geranium in a pot on one sill. An estate car was tidily parked.

'I'm not a gypsy,' said the girl, glancing at Moira with amusement as if divining her thoughts. 'No strings of wet washing or scraggy dogs or nose-picking children. Come in.'

Inside, it was larger than it looked and very clean, and although it was untidy it was a rather nice books-and-music untidiness, with the books spilling on to the floor and tapes and records strewn over one window sill. A small CD player stood in the corner. There were two bunk beds, each one covered with a silk fringed counterpane with vividly coloured silk cushions scattered across the pillows. Most unexpected of all was what Moira recognised as a lap-top computer on the fold-down table at the centre.

The minuscule kitchen had things like garlic presses hanging up, and a mortar and pestle and a row of little jars labelled with different spices. There was a tiny cooker with a lidded iron casserole on it.

The girl stood in the kitchen, her arms folded, studying Moira. 'Now,' she said. 'Let's establish some credentials.'

Moira looked at her warily. 'You said you were grave-robbing—'

'Yes. But it's all right,' said the girl. 'I'm on the side of the angels. Never mind that for the moment. Oh, and I'm not gay, in case you were wondering about my motives. Far from it. There's no need to look so startled, it would have been a fair enough assumption. Now. I've got permission to be on Abbey land, although not, perhaps at this time of— You do know it's two o'clock in the morning, do you?' she said suddenly.

'Yes. I'm running away,' said Moira, matching bluntness with bluntness, and waited for shock or disapproval.

The girl said, 'Are you indeed? I ran away myself when

I was about your age. D'you want some tea? You can have coffee if you like but I always think it's too much of a stimulant at this time of night.'

'Did it work?' This was an incredibly unreal conversation to be having in the middle of the night with someone you had only just met.

'What?' The girl had been setting a small kettle to boil and reaching down two pottery mugs.

'Running away,' said Moira. 'Did it work?'

'Yes, of course it worked. I made it work. I suppose you're running away because of a man.'

'Well, it— Yes,' said Moira with resolution. 'Yes, I am.'

'It's what most of us do.' She studied Moira for a moment. 'You're very young. How old are you? Seventeen?'

'Nineteen,' said Moira indignantly. 'Almost twenty.'

'You don't look it. You know, you can't go roaming around the countryside in the middle of the night.'

'Why? I mean why should you bother about me?'

'Let's say I've got a soft spot for waifs. I was one myself once and somebody helped me. I'm passing on the favour. By the way, my name's Kate Kendal. You don't need to tell me your name if you don't want to, but it would make it easier to have something to call you. You can make up a name if you like. I shan't mind. I probably shan't know.'

Moira toyed with the idea of giving herself an exotic new name for her startling new life which appeared to be already beginning. Margot de Medici? Camellia Dumas? Roberta Barratt Browning? Don't be silly. Also, there was her birth certificate, carefully folded into the zipped section of her bag. You could not conjure up a new identity for yourself out of mid-air these days. She said, 'I'm Moira Mahoney. The man I'm running away from is my father.'

146

'Why?' said Kate and again Moira found herself answering truthfully.

'He came to my bedroom. I woke up and he was— His hands were all over me and there was— He had—'

'I see,' said Kate, and Moira had the feeling she really did see. 'Very nasty indeed. The bastard. Unzipped and nicely aroused, I suppose? Yes, I thought that was what you meant. We'll hope it withers and drops off. Did you get away in time?'

'Yes.'

'Good for you. Would you like something to eat?'

This rather off-beat sympathy was the last reaction Moira had expected and the offer of food threw her completely. She stared, and Kate said, 'When I ran away from home I was eighteen and I was so keyed up that I hadn't eaten for two days. When I got clear – to London – I passed out with hunger on Waterloo Station. There's some of tonight's supper left if you want it. Chilli con carne. I made it myself and it was very good. It'll only take five minutes to heat.'

'I—' Moira stopped and remembered the steamed fish. She said, 'Do you know, you're right. I'm absolutely starving.'

The chilli was very good indeed. Moira had never had anything like it – she could hear Father saying, 'Foreign rubbish,' – but she thought it was delicious and she ate a huge bowlful. There was a wedge of French bread to go with it.

'Could I wash up?' she asked tentatively, unsure of the codes obtaining here, but Kate said,

'Sure. Go ahead,' and curled up on one of the beds drinking her tea while Moira washed everything up carefully in the tiny sink.

'I think you'd better stay here tonight,' she said as Moira put the plates away. 'You can get on a train or something in the morning if you want. Did you bring a toothbrush?'

'No, it—'

'Would have meant making too much noise,' finished Kate. 'It's what everyone thinks when they run away. I think there's an unused toothbrush somewhere, however. Underclothes? Night things?'

'Yes, I did manage those,' said Moira, and added firmly, 'also some money.'

'Good for you.' Kate regarded her, and then said thoughtfully, 'I suppose I'd better tell you what I was doing out there.'

'Grave-robbing.'

Kate smiled unexpectedly. 'Have you ever heard of a piece of music called the *Black Chant*?' she said. 'Or of a cult called Serse's People?'

'I – no. I don't think so. What is it?'

'The *Black Chant* is an ancient piece of music that I've been trying to track down for three years.

'And Serse's People are its acolytes.'

Chapter Fourteen

'Four years ago,' said Kate, 'my husband started gathering material for a book. He was an anthropologist, and he'd just been awarded a research fellowship. The book was to be about music worshipping. I mean, literally, music worshipping: ancient fertility dances and rain dances. Mating rituals compared with present day cults: New Age Travellers and the Notting Hill Carnival and Woodstock. You wouldn't remember Woodstock,' Kate added. 'I can only just remember it myself. But it was a pop festival in America in the late Sixties.'

'It's a bit of a legend, isn't it?' said Moira. 'I've heard of it.'

'The idea was a good one,' said Kate. 'It wasn't wildly original, but Richard would have made it seem original. He'd have unearthed new material and he would have made it interesting and different.' She stopped. It was extraordinary how much it still hurt to think what Richard had been like. It was even more extraordinary to find herself talking so easily about him to this unknown waif.

'It sounds fascinating,' said Moira, who thought it did. 'Did you— were you working with him?'

'What?' Kate appeared to have relapsed into the past. 'God, no,' she answered. 'I haven't the intelligence. Or the application. I'm just a middle-man. Middle-woman. An agent. My partner and I have a small PR company, for musical promotions. Publicity for events – orchestral concerts and festivals. Sometimes finding publishers or record companies for new composers. Undertaking PR for orchestral seasons.' She grinned suddenly. 'Not modern music, or not very often. The pop boys have their own network.'

'Good music,' said Moira, nodding. 'Real music.'

'Yes.' Kate smiled properly for the first time. 'We never managed to get as far as Covent Garden or the Royal Festival Hall, but we did well enough. We'd discovered a couple of string quartets who were becoming fairly well known – we'd got them on to the Stately Homes concert circuit. And we set up some stuff with Classic FM – that's a commercial radio station in the UK, solely for classical music.'

'Yes. I know about it.' Father would have said this was no job for a woman and talked about parasites on society and layabout musicians who never did an honest day's work, but Moira thought it sounded interesting. She could imagine Kate being good at it.

'Quite early on in the research, Richard became fascinated by the ancient legends about Pan and the Pied Piper and Orpheus,' said Kate. 'He didn't become obsessional, but he began to talk about a piece of music – something very ancient indeed – that he said had existed in the world for thousands of years, and that was lost for most of the time, but occasionally surfaced. Later I found it referred to as the *Black Chant*, but at the time Richard called it "The Beckoning".' Kate paused, drinking her tea, cupping her hands around the mug as if for warmth. 'He was tracing it further and further back,' she said. 'I remember he said there was an oblique mention of it in the Old Testament, and that it even went as far back as Solomon and the Temple Scribes ten centuries before Christ. He said the Magi who attended Christ's birth had known about it as well.'

'Magi's a kind of short-form for high divine, isn't it?'

'Yes. Thank God for someone with an unblinkered mind,' said Kate unexpectedly. 'It sounds a bit far-fetched, telling it cold like this, and of course Richard didn't find it out all in one go. It took months of research and piecing together of odd fragments.'

She stopped again and Moira said, 'Please go on.'

'Just over three years ago he decided to attend a kind of rock concert to study the followers,' said Kate. 'Part of the general field research. He called them disciples, but he wasn't being patronising. He genuinely saw them as followers of a modern-day cult, exactly as he saw the Mayas or the Incas or the Bush tribesmen following a cult. I decided to go with him,' she said. 'I thought it might be interesting, and we planned that I would help him – circulate a bit and record a few interviews on my own account. That way we'd get double the material.' Her eyes were inward looking. 'We took portable recorders and cameras,' she said. 'And I remember buying new clothes to blend in. A long Indian cotton skirt and string sandals and a loose top. Richard just wore jeans and a shirt, of course.'

Moira said, 'Where was the concert?'

'Hampstead Heath. That's a huge open area on the north side of London,' Kate explained. 'A public common.'

'Yes, I've heard of it. Highwaymen's inns and gallows,' said Moira. 'Tyburn?'

Kate grinned. 'Well done, waif,' she said. 'Yes, loads of ancient inns and ghosts and public hangings and masses of history. Now people just walk dogs there or make love in the bushes and leave used condoms and hamburger wrappings everywhere.' She set down the empty mug. 'So we went to Hampstead for the concert,' she said.

It was as vivid as if it had been yesterday. Kate could remember the warmth of the weekend – it had been the end of June and blazingly hot.

'Midsummer's Day,' she had said. 'There'll be latter-day Druids and reincarnations of King Arthur six deep.'

But Richard had laughed and said that at Midsummer the Druids flocked to Glastonbury but in fact he'd enjoy meeting a few modern Druids to compare them with the original lot. It was twentieth century music worshippers he was after today.

'A part of the Heath had been cordoned off for parking,' said Kate, curled on to the bunk, her eyes staring back into the past. 'Although most of it was free for the concert. There were no formal sleeping arrangements, of course. Probably not knowing whose sleeping bag you'd share that night was part of it for a lot of them. It started off by being rather fun.'

The journey had not been fun: there had been the usual flow of people leaving the city and Kate, who always got impatient in traffic jams, had begun to get angry but Richard had said, 'Think of them as pilgrims. Like the Canterbury Tales.' He had started to make up Chaucerian limericks, trying to find a rhyme for the Hampstead Monk who became very drunk, and an unbawdy last line for the Pardoner from Wapping who went wife-swapping. Kate had joined in until finally they had both been laughing so much that they had not noticed the traffic starting to move again, and all the drivers behind had hooted and made rude gestures.

There would probably be a number of impromptu performances during the two-day concert, but there were six groups who would be playing from lunchtime each day until whatever hour of the night everyone wanted. By the time Kate and Richard arrived, people were already setting up little circles of territory. Beer and cider and wine was being consumed.

'And there were drugs,' Kate said. 'I have to admit that there were drugs. Mostly marijuana and cannabis, but I suspect that there were heroin pushers in the crowd and Ecstasy dealers, because there usually are, although I didn't see anyone dealing and I didn't see anyone actually shooting up either.' She paused. 'Richard never took anything stronger than an aspirin in his life,' she said. 'That's something else I should make clear. He didn't need anything to make him high. He was one of those people who think life is so good and so absorbing that artificial stimulants simply never occurred to him.'

One of the hardest of the memories was how much Richard had enjoyed life, how he had found humour in everything, how he had found interest in everyone. People never bored him; he liked to listen to them and he found them endlessly absorbing. Kate had sometimes thought he would have made a good psychiatrist or even a Catholic priest. 'And do without sex?' he had said in horrified amusement.

'No, maybe not. Unless you could have been a wicked cardinal in Henry VIII's day, or a Borgia pope.'

'Decadent and dissolute,' Richard replied, pleased with the small fantasy.

He had approached the pop festival with optimistic anticipation and had fallen into discussion with several people almost straight away. By then it was two o'clock and most people had eaten their lunch and had a few drinks. Anybody who had been smoking anything a bit questionable had finished it and put it out of sight. The concert was kicking into life.

Kate lost sight of Richard midway through the afternoon,

but they had expected this. They were going to meet outside their car at six anyway, and decide what to do about an evening meal. There would probably be a few of Richard's students around and there might be people Kate knew as well: journalists and feature writers and people from the music world. Somebody might ask them to supper, or they might decide to walk across to the 'Spaniards', where you could get very good fresh trout. Anyway, the plan was to circulate and soak up local colour and talk to as many people as possible and find out their motives and their motivations.

Kate had begun to enjoy herself by this time; they had shared a half bottle of wine over lunch, and the opening group had started off with some Sixties stuff so that everyone was feeling happily nostalgic, even those who had not been born in the Sixties, which applied to almost everyone there. Most people were flattered to be approached for a brief interview, and nobody minded enlarging on why they were there or what their beliefs were. Quite a few had simply come to find somebody new to sleep with, of course, and as many again were there to get drunk or high on drugs. Kate tried to avoid these. But a good number were there because they liked the music. It had meaning for them and they felt as if they were belonging to a great club, didn't Kate feel that? And wasn't the music terrific? Kate taped discussions to a pounding background of the Beatles and Buddy Holly and Elvis, and made copious notes to the soul music of Tina Turner.

There was some jazz which was shouted down – nobody wanted jazz by then – and people were drinking coke or beer from cans. Here and there they were brewing tea within their defined little areas. Kate was offered a cup by a group from Bexleyheath who all wore Greenpeace and Save the Whales badges. The tea turned out to be pale green and flavoured with camomile but it was unexpectedly refreshing and Kate had two cups. They exchanged thoughts on pacifism and animal rights and Kate was cordially invited to share a vegan meal later, which she managed to get out of by saying that her husband had already made arrangements.

She recognised one or two people from the music world who might be useful and spent some time talking to them. All grist to the mill. You never knew who you might need to ring up next week or next month or next year.

The sun was beginning to slip behind the horizon in a blaze of fiery splendour, and Kate was just thinking that she should start to make her way back to the car to meet Richard, when music that was totally and utterly different to anything played so far began to trickle out of the speakers. Kate turned back, and saw for the first time the group standing just below the stage, watching the audience.

The radiance from the sunset lit them to eerie life and the sight affected Kate as unpleasantly as if someone had dealt her a blow or as if she had fallen into a cold, greasy pond. She stood very still, studying them, trying to see what was so sinister. Just a group of youngsters enjoying the music, surely?

There were easily fifty or sixty of them; the youngest ones probably no more than sixteen, the oldest mid-twenties at the most. They were standing close to the wooden stage, and they were dressed like everyone else in jeans and T-shirts, flowing cotton or cheesecloth skirts and skimpy tops. One or two wore black leather bomber jackets, and some of the girls had Twenties-style velour hats crammed over flowing, Pre-Raphaelite hair. They should have been no different to anyone else at the concert but they were very different indeed. Kate thought it was not just that they were watching the audience so intently, although that was peculiar in itself; she thought there was a look about them, as if they had been stamped with something that set them apart, and as if they were very aware of it. A smugness, was it? Yes, they looked smug and secretive, as if they belonged to an exclusive club or as if they knew something everyone else did not. Kate had sometimes seen the same look on the spoiled children of the very rich and found it intensely irritating. We're better than you, we live on a higher plane.

Unlike most of the others they remained closely together. Kate edged nearer, trying to see more, noticing now that they all wore a silver chain with a heavy medallion on it, carved into the shape of some kind of ikon. It was like nothing she had ever come across before, although it was vaguely reminiscent of several things: the Celtic and Pictish crosses; even the Aryan swastika – or was it the Nazi one? Which way did the arms bend for the Aryans and which way for the Nazis? Encircling the ikon were engraved words which she could not read from this distance.

The music poured out in earnest then, and Kate stopped and turned to stare at the long wooden stage with the acoustic speakers and the trailing leads and microphones. This was music she knew, surely. Or was it? Recognition wavered.

The group playing it looked ordinary enough. They were dressed in the uniform of most pop groups these days: black vests and leather trousers and satin waistcoats. Two of the men had shaven hair with skull and crossbones tattooed on their scalps and two had long hair which could have had a Restoration appearance if it had been cleaner. One of the girls was determinedly butch and the other was a Madonna-lookalike. To Kate's eyes they were no different from any other group of today.

But the music was very different indeed. The music was haunting and compelling and it was worlds and light years from the normal pounding beat you heard at rock concerts. It cascaded from the speakers and poured out in a torrent. Frightening, Kate thought, caught between fascination and repulsion. *And it's alive, slithering across the grass, I can almost feel it lapping around my ankles.* For a minute this grisly image was so strong that she looked down at the ground.

Before the music began, people had been starting to think about their evening meal, as Kate had. They had been setting out primus stoves or unpacking sandwiches and the hamburger stands were doing a roaring trade. The scent of fried onions and hot chips drifted across the Heath.

But within minutes of the music beginning, the food was forgotten. People turned to the stage, transfixed and Kate thought: what on earth is happening? Why is the music affecting them so strongly? And then without warning, a cold hand gripped her stomach, and she thought: this is Richard's Beckoning. God yes, it really is. Despite the warmth of the early evening she began to feel cold and rather frightened. The music was like a summoning, it was like a command . . . *Follow me and obey me . . . Do what I tell you* . . . A Beckoning. Yes, Richard had been absolutely right.

By now everyone was staring at the very ordinary group playing the very extraordinary music, and Kate forced her mind to analyse it. She thought it was a tritone, repeated several times with a slightly different variation each time but although she had a reasonable working knowledge of music, the finer points of much of the theory were a closed book. And most modern music followed its own path without regard to the traditional constructions anyway. This appeared to follow the conventional patterns of loud insistent beat, but beyond that was the writhing coiling melody. A beckoning, thought Kate, feeling the fear increase. She looked round for Richard but he was nowhere to be seen, and she looked back at the group by the stage. And there, in their midst, silhouetted against the blazing radiance of the setting sun, was a thin-faced man with close-cropped hair and the coldest eyes Kate had ever seen. He was dressed in cords with a shirt like a lot of the men, and he wore the silver medallion of the watching group. But there was a look of such triumph on his face that Kate felt as if someone had driven a clenched fist into her ribs. She moved nearer, trying to see more.

To begin with she thought he had the look of someone who has unexpectedly discovered something tremendous, and then she thought that this was not quite right: it was much greedier, far more lusting than that. Someone getting a kick out of power – maybe even a sexual kick. Someone presenting a smooth polished façade but with evil beneath. I can *feel* that he's evil, thought Kate, torn between horrified disbelief and a spiralling fear. Cold-eyed and merciless. But urbane. Socially adept. The smiler with the knife under his cloak . . . Chaucer again. The Knight's Tale, isn't it? I wish I could see Richard.

The music was rising and falling all about them, and the silver medallion people were chanting in exact time to it. Kate thought they were not chanting any words: it was more like the Eastern mantras where you hummed a sequence of notes over and over until the humming reverberated all around you and enfolded you. A mantra – a real mantra – was soothing and filled with strength and goodness and light, but there was nothing in the least soothing about this sound. It was hypnotic, but it was hypnotic in the wrong way. It was frightening and strongly sensual and very powerful indeed. Kate remembered the drug dealers again. Could they have been spiking people's drinks without anyone noticing?

Behind her, on the Heath, people were beginning to join in the chanting, and to link hands and sway to and fro. Several couples were reaching for their partners, groping beneath clothing with avid, hot eyes, sinking to the ground and writhing against one another. Kate glanced back at the man, and saw his eyes flicker over the squirming couples, and a smile lift the corners of his lips.

The chanting was increasing, it was spreading to all parts of the audience, and those who were not openly copulating on the ground were pressing closer to the stage, holding up their hands. The silver ikon group were facing them, holding their hands out as if to receive benisons, their eyes shining, their lips slightly parted. The thick sexual groanings blended with the rhythmic chanting.

Kate's head began to spin and she was feeling sick, as if her mind was dislocating. There was anticipation in the music now: a huge tense apprehension that churned up your stomach so that you began to feel the kind of lurching fearfulness you felt when something nasty was getting close. Something's happening, thought Kate, looking about her. Something's approaching . . . The tension's winding tighter and tighter . . . Like an abscess about to burst. Like a thunderstorm piling up. Her head throbbed.

And then without the least warning, there was the violent report of a shotgun from somewhere behind the crowd: a shocking splintering sound that tore across the music and the chanting. The music shut off abruptly and the climbing tension ebbed instantly. There was a nerve-scraping whine of sound from one of the speakers and the audience turned to look confusedly at one another, spreading their hands in bewilderment. People who had been writhing on the ground sat up and fumbled embarrassedly with zips and buttons, and the group by the stage looked suddenly bewildered. They huddled close to the stage and Kate could see the cold-eyed man talking to them, and then indicating that they should leave.

Everywhere else people were screaming and some were crying. Panic and confusion replaced the slow mesmerised languor and people were crying. Like at a disaster, thought Kate, staring about here. Like when a bomb goes off or a fire breaks out in an enclosed space. But what on earth's happened to break the spell?

And then from the other side of the Heath came the blare of an ambulance siren.

Kate lifted her head and looked at Moira. 'The ambulance was for Richard,' she said. 'He'd been talking with some people near to the stage when the music started. They said afterwards that he seemed to respond to it like a puppet being jerked.'

Again the pause and after a moment, Moira said, 'What happened?'

'I never found out the exact details,' said Kate. 'Apparently he had been quite normal until then. Enjoying the Sixties music, recording interviews. He'd managed to talk to two of the Serse People – the group with the silver ikons. And then—' She stopped and took a deep breath. 'They said afterwards – the people nearest – that it was as if he'd suddenly been given a command. An order.'

She stopped again, and Moira waited. 'He took a gun out of the back of a parked jeep,' said Kate. 'God knows why anyone would bring a shotgun to a pop concert, but it was licensed and the owner turned out to be the son of someone who had a shoot in Kent. The jeep wasn't locked and the gun was under some sacking. A bit irresponsible, but not illegal.

'Richard put the shotgun under his jaw,' said Kate, her voice devoid of all expression. 'He pulled the trigger and blew away his face.'

Chapter Fifteen

There was such a complete silence in the caravan, that for a moment Moira could not think how to break it. At last, she said, 'The shooting was caused by the music.'

'Yes.' Kate looked at her defensively, and then said, 'At the beginning it seemed like the maddest kind of fantasy to think it, of course; I had only Richard's notes and his hunch, and my own vague suspicions to go on, and for ages I didn't believe it. I thought: I'm bitter and angry, and I'm looking for something to blame and I'm fastening on to Richard's weird premise. But when I thought properly, I couldn't remember Richard ever having been wrong when his own subject was involved. Academics do fall in love with their own theories but he was very level-headed, and he had too much of a sense of humour to let a theory get out of proportion. So then I thought: if he was right, there might have been other tragedies. I'll just dig a bit.'

'How?'

Moira could not imagine where you would start, but Kate said, 'I employed a press agency to send me all the reports of suicides and attempted suicides connected with musical events during that year. That was where I got the first shock, because there were far more than I'd expected. The second shock was when I found that almost every time the music I heard at Hampstead had been played, at least one person in the audience had committed suicide, or tried

162

to, either during the actual concert, or more usually just afterwards. The music went under various names, but I was sure it was the same.'

'The *Black Chant*. The Beckoning.'

'Yes. So then,' said Kate, 'I began to look at it the other way up – on the premise that Richard might have been right. That there really was an ancient piece of music that could influence people's minds. And that opened up a whole range of terrifying possibilities, of course.'

'Serse's People,' said Moira.

'Yes. I was already beginning to see them as acolytes of the music, and that wasn't so bizarre a view either; young people do follow trends in music to astonishing degrees, and odd religions and cults have flourished since the world started. There've been the Moonies and the Flower Children, and the Hare Krishna Movement in the Sixties. But there've also been the Hitler Youth and that group of fanatics a few years back in Texas, where some of the followers burned to death. I began to suspect there could be something very sinister about Serse's People, and after I'd talked to the families of some of the suicides, I was convinced of it.' She leaned forward, her eyes eager. 'All of the people who committed suicide were young, and most of them had been clever or creative. That's not so surprising, because it's mostly young people who go to those concerts and there's often a large proportion of students. But the really odd thing was that every suicide seemed to be balanced by a disappearance. Clever, bright young people simply dropping out and vanishing without trace. All doing so within days – sometimes hours – of one of the concerts.' She got up to pour fresh tea, and Moira thought about this.

'It sounds,' Moira said, after a moment, 'almost as if there was some kind of test. If they accepted the music they

163

were admitted to the fold. Made part of the— the chosen ones. But those that resisted, cracked mentally, or maybe were made to crack . . . I'm sorry – your husband – I didn't mean that to sound hurtful.'

'Oh, that's all right,' said Kate, shrugging it aside. 'It's actually quite refreshing to talk to someone who sees it the same way and doesn't make stupid scoffing comments.' She frowned, and said, 'D'you know, I haven't talked like this to anyone for ages. I can't imagine why I'm unloading it all on to you.'

'It's something to do with it being the middle of the night,' said Moira, blushing at the unexpected compliment. 'And because I'm running away, maybe.'

'Maybe it is. Of course, for all I know I might be simply turning into a crank.'

'Please tell me what happened next.'

'What happened next,' said Kate, 'was that I came to a full stop. I hadn't a clue where to go from there, although by then I'd tracked down the man I'd seen at Hampstead. His name's Conrad Vogel and he operates from one of the warehouses at St Katharine's Dock in London. Music publishing, music promotions – not unlike my own set-up. But he appeared to operate quite legitimately and there's nothing to prevent people from starting up their own churches and religions. I had nothing you could call solid evidence against him. So for a time I was stuck.'

'Didn't the police—' began Moira tentatively, but Kate shook her head.

'The police were one of the crowd who thought I was a crank. They were very polite but they were dismissive. Very sad, madam, but of course, there's a high rate of suicides among students. Which,' said Kate, 'there is. So I was still on my own.

'Until a couple of months ago when I heard a piece of

music called the *Devil's Piper* on Radio Three.' She stopped and Moira stared at her.

'Jude Weissman. Judas.'

'Yes, Judas. He wrote the music in the early Nineteen Thirties and although I'd heard of him in a general way, I'd never heard the music in my life. But I recognised it at once.'

'The Hampstead music,' said Moira. 'The *Chant*.'

'Yes. It was superficially different and unless you were looking for it, you mightn't have known. But I was looking and I did know,' said Kate. 'I was in the car at the time, but I had to stop and pull in. I couldn't drive, I couldn't do anything. I sat in a lay-by, staring at the radio, feeling sick and dizzy.'

'I've heard of the *Devil's Piper*,' said Moira. 'But I've never actually heard it played.'

'I've got a recording,' said Kate. 'You can hear it sometime. It took ages to find, because it's deleted now – that's the same as a book being out of print – but in the end I got one. It's the most extraordinary music I've ever heard.' She paused again and then said in a hard voice, 'Jude knew about the music all right, the *Black Chant*. He got his *Piper* from it and I believe Vogel got the Hampstead music from it as well. I could have concentrated on Vogel but I decided to work backwards. That's why I came here. To the place where Jude wrote the *Devil's Piper*.'

'Mallow House,' said Moira.

'Mallow was my original idea,' said Kate, 'but then I read up Curran Glen's history in Galway, and I found that its main claim to fame was a very old Abbey with a rather unusual tradition for early liturgical music. It set a few signals ringing. It's unusual to find such very old plainsong these days – most churches use the Gregorian chant which came later. It was a very long shot indeed, but it was just possible that the three things tied up: Jude Weissman, the *Black Chant* and the Abbey.'

She paused and then said, 'And so I came to Curran Glen, and that was when I discovered that deep in the Abbey's foundations is an ancient tomb, and that inside that tomb is something the monks have guarded for almost a thousand years since their founder brought it from North Italy.'

She stopped and Moira, her mind whirling, said, 'Simon of Cremona's devil. The Nameless One that Cosimo Amati called up from beyond the grave. That's what you mean, isn't it?'

'Yes it is. How on earth did you know?'

'We've both read the same transcript, I think,' said Moira. 'Simon's journal. But I didn't get to the end.'

'I did,' said Kate. 'And at the end, the thing that Cosimo summoned isn't nameless at all. Simon refers to him as the Devil's Music Maker once or twice, but his name was Ahasuerus.'

Ahasuerus . . . There was absolutely no reason why the name should strike against Moira's consciousness with eerie familiarity, but it did.

'Ahasuerus is at the heart of the entire thing, Moira,' said Kate softly. 'He's the core and the matrix. Amati believed the music had power over Ahasuerus, and that Ahasuerus himself could somehow control the music. At the end, Simon believed it as well. That's why he created an order of monks that would guard the tomb for as long as they endured.'

Moira felt the fear prickling the nape of her neck again, but she asked, 'Do the monks know about all this – I mean the present ones? Do they really know and do they really do it, or do they just pay some kind of lip-service to an old tradition?'

'That's quite a shrewd thing to ask,' said Kate. 'But yes, they do know.' She saw again the lurching faceless thing that had been drawn inexorably across the dark countryside, and driven down into the crypt, and pushed the grisly image away because there was no point in frightening this nice child more than absolutely necessary. She said, 'The monks do know. That silver-voiced creature who has no business being inside a monastery at all certainly knows.'

'Brother Ciaran?' said Moira tentatively.

'Brother Ciaran,' affirmed Kate. 'I suspect he could tell me a whole lot more about this than he's so far chosen to do. It's a pity Catholic monks aren't open to seduction,' she said, without thinking, and Moira looked up, startled.

'It's all right,' said Kate, grinning, 'I do know that an Irish monastery isn't the place for disreputable adventures.'

'Wouldn't you consider talking to him? He'd be completely trustworthy—'

'I'm sure he would. But it isn't that,' Kate replied. 'I don't dare talk to him.'

'Why not?'

'Because I'm going to steal the coffin.' She grinned, and said, 'I'm going to bring the Devil's Piper out into the world, Moira, and I'm going to confront Conrad Vogel with it – publicly and resoundingly – and then I'm going to destroy them both once and for all.'

'How?'

'If I can once get the thing out of the crypt, I'm going to do what Vogel did at Hampstead,' said Kate. 'I'm going to set up a concert – very public, very hyped. It's what I do for a living, after all, and I'm quite good at it. I'll have TV coverage, radio, video, press— Everything and everyone. And then we'll play the *Devil's Piper* and see what happens.' She set down her empty tea-mug. 'When you ran into me, I was trying to break into the Abbey crypt only there isn't a way to do it. And so tomorrow I'm going to find a way of stealing the tower key and break in after dark.'

At last Moira said, 'I'll come with you.'

'I don't think that's a good idea at all.'

'It's a very good idea indeed,' said Moira. 'For one thing you'll never lift the coffin on your own. And for another—' For the first time for what felt like several hours, she smiled. 'For another,' said Moira, 'you don't have to wait until tomorrow night. We can do it now. I've got the library key.'

She had almost forgotten being given it and she had almost forgotten thrusting it absently into the side pocket of her satchel when she left.

Kate said, 'But if it only fits the library—'

'There's a door from the library that leads to the turn,' said Moira. 'That's the porter's room just behind the main front door,' she added, realising that Irish and English could sometimes be two different languages. 'And in the porter's room—'

'—are the keys to the rest of the Abbey!' finished Kate. She stood up and the excitement was back in her eyes. 'What time is it? Three o'clock. The monks should all be devoutly asleep and if any of them are about at this hour, then they're up to no good and we'll blackmail them into silence.' She paused and Moira started to say something and then stopped, because she was by no means sure how serious Kate had been. 'I'm perfectly serious,' said Kate at once. 'I'll get into Brother Ciaran's bed if necessary and swear on the Bible that he raped me.' A reckless glint showed in her eyes. 'And once in his bed I don't think I'd be too quick to call for rescue, either,' she said. 'Ready?

Come on then. We can be out of the tower and out of the Abbey and halfway across Ireland before they go up to ring for Lauds!'

As Moira stole into the dark silent library, and out into the huge dark stillness of the main Abbey, her heart was pounding.

The unmistakable monastic silence was like a veil, and the indefinable scents of a religious house were very noticeable. St Asaph's had the same scents. Floor polish and lye soap and drifting incense and the ghost of whatever had been the day's mid-day dinner.

The door to the turn was open and there was sufficient light to see the large wooden notice board which the monks, typically orderly, had lined with green baize and set with neat black cup hooks. The keys were not only labelled, they were in alphabetical order with the Abbot's study on the top at the left, and the Vestry at the bottom right. There was what looked like a master key for the cells; Moira touched it with guilty longing. If she knew which was Ciaran's she could creep in. How would it feel to be in bed with him? The idea sent a shaft of delight through her because what had been disgusting and repulsive with Edward Mahoney would not be with Ciaran.

Kate had said something about blackmailing Ciaran into silence by getting into his bed and swearing he had raped her. She had clearly found him attractive. Would it have been mutual? Yes, of course it would be. Monks were not supposed to eye females with physical interest, but Moira suspected that Ciaran did. She hoped the jolt of emotion she had felt when Kate talked about him had not been jealousy. In any case, she was leaving Curran Glen and she would not see Ciaran again. She pushed the bleakness of this away and concentrated on what she was meant to be doing. Would the tower be under T for Tower or B for Belfry? B for Bell Tower, of course, yes, there it was! Moira unhooked the key, and went back to the library for Kate.

The quadrangle was drenched in grey and silver as they stole across it, keeping in the shadows as much as possible. An owl hooted softly and went soaring across the night sky above them in pursuit of a ragged-winged bat, and once they pressed back into the shadows as something pattered out of the bushes and scurried into the darkness beyond. Kate let out a breath of relief and Moira said in a whisper, 'Probably a badger or a fox.'

'As long as it isn't the ghost of some long-dead Father Abbot I don't care what it is.'

'There's the tower.'

'Yes. Where's the key? All right, here we go. Ready? You know what we agreed: I'll go down and spy out the land while you keep watch up here. If you hear me yell, beat it, understood?'

'Understood.' Moira would not beat it if Kate yelled, but it was not the moment to argue. She took a deep breath and unlocked the tower door.

It was cold in the crypt and very dark, but Kate did not want to switch on the torch until she was actually in the crypt because even a wavering torchlight might be seen from outside. The trouble was that when you were stealing down a dark stair you found yourself imagining that things were creeping up to meet you . . . Or even that undead creatures were crawling up out of coffins . . . No, he's shut away, I heard Ciaran and the other man do it. I'm safe, thought Kate firmly. She reached the foot of the stairs, took a deep breath, and switched on the torch.

The crypt was larger than she had expected, although she was not sure what she had expected. No real experience of crypts. It was cold and dank, which accorded with the best horror stories, but for all its apparent space and for all the far-reaching shadows, there was a feeling of being hemmed-in; a sensation that the walls were inching towards her and that the roof was closing down. Some kind of medieval torture chamber that slowly crushed you. Don't be ridiculous. Yes, but this place is older than medieval, and it's inhabited by monks, and monks and nuns can be very ruthless.

The sarcophagus was directly in front of her, and although it was menacing and awesome, Kate saw with relief that it was above ground. She walked round it, shining the torch. A large stone slab. Heavy and awkward, but not impossible to push aside.

It was important to remain very cool and very sensible, even though what she was about to do was drenched in superstitions of the bloodiest kind. Premature burials and living dead and resurrected corpses. But scores of people robbed graves and lived to tell the tale; it was not as if she was Burke and Hare digging up still-fresh corpses to sell to anatomists, or as if she was a greedy Egyptologist – Carnarvon or Howard Carter – plundering pharaohs' tombs wholesale and incurring the wrath of the gods.

Tomb robbers had never enjoyed the best of fates, of course. Burke had ended on the gibbet and Hare had been flung into a lime pit which had burned out his eyes. Howard Carter had not lived to a ripe old age either, and everyone knew the legend of Lord Carnarvon, dead of blood-poisoning from being bitten by a scorpion or a tsetse-fly or something at the entrance to Tutankhamun's death chamber.

It would be better not to think about curses or death-wishes at all. If you were about to plunder an ancient tomb, the last thing you ought to think about was curses. But it would be remarkable if this tomb of all tombs did not have a curse attached to it. Kate thought she should be prepared to find that something very nasty and very admonishing was carved into the coffin. 'Curst be he who moves my bones . . .' No, that's Shakespeare's grave, you fool. Nothing to do with this. If this tomb had a curse at all, it would be something much older than a piece of pseudo-Elizabethan doggerel of questionable merit and doubtful origin. I don't care if it's got fifty curses and a hundred direful admonishments, I'm going ahead. She moved purposefully forward.

Standing up against the tomb was the worst yet. It felt eerily alive. If you wanted to give yourself nightmares for the next ten years, you could easily think you were hearing sounds from within. Not breathing, which would be absurd through the stone, but little murmurings.

Ahasuerus whispering to himself inside the coffin . . .

Kate swallowed a gasp and set the torch down carefully so that its light fell across the tomb's surface. Her heart was pounding so frantically that she thought for a moment she might die of a heart attack. How ironic it would be to expire when you were opening a grave. She took a deep breath and grasped the edge of the stone, throwing her whole strength behind it. Could she do it alone? She had not wanted to involve Moira until they were ready to carry the coffin out, because it seemed important to have a look-out. It was important to give Moira the chance to get away as well, in case anyone came along and caught them.

The stone was stubbornly immobile. Kate gave a sobbing gasp and paused to wipe the sweat from her forehead, and then pushed again, this time bending her body at the waist, so that her shoulders were level with the tomb's rim. Push harder, Kate . . . Did it move then? Just a half inch? Yes!

The slab grated harshly, but it was unmistakably moving. Kate threw her shoulder against it, and felt it give a little more. With every second she expected to hear footsteps tumbling down the stair and shouts of alarm, but nothing disturbed the dark crypt and the only sound down here was her own ragged breathing.

Nearly there. God, what a noise it's making! Surely someone will hear. But Moira would warn me if anyone was approaching. Odd how I trusted her so completely, so instantly. I'd like to help her if I could. How am I doing? I'm almost there, I think. One more push . . .? Yes, it's coming. If I wanted to be sure of those nightmares, I could nearly believe that someone was helping from beneath. Ahasuerus coming out of the grave. Opening the coffin and climbing out . . . No!

One more thrust – yes, there it goes! I've done it!

The stone slab, dragged so frantically into place barely twenty-four hours earlier by Ciaran and Isarel, moved back with a harsh scraping sound that tore at Kate's shredded nerves. She stood back, her muscles trembling, and tipped the beam of the torch into the gaping tomb.

Within the ancient stone tomb lay a smaller coffin made of wood. Kate, her heart pounding but her hands steady, reached down. The lid lifted with unexpected ease and there within the coffin . . . Her heart lurched. Whatever she had expected – mouldering bones, gruesome bloated corpse – she had not expected this.

Lying in the coffin was the slender figure of a man, wearing a robe not dissimilar to that of the present-day monks here. But the cowl was pulled over his face and his hands were hidden by the robe's long full sleeves.

The Devil's Piper. Ahasuerus. Kate stared down at him and felt the strength drain from her, and if she had not been leaning against the tomb's side she would have fallen to the ground. Dear God, it's *true*. The legend, the scrap of gossip in Simon's journal, Richard's suspicions, are all true.

She reached for the coffin lid thinking she could wedge it back in place before calling Moira down to help her lift the whole thing out of the tomb, and it was then that she caught a movement from the coffin. Her heart leapt again and she gripped the wooden lid so tightly that the edge cut into her hands. She nerved herself to look down.

Kate heard her own strangled gasp as if it came from a great distance. The creature in the coffin was turning its head. Ciaran and the other man forced him back last night, but they had not sent him back into his strange deathless sleep. I should have been prepared for it, thought Kate. I should have been prepared to find Ahasuerus *alive* in the tomb. But panic swept through her and she fought for control, seeing through a blur, a confused impression of a pale clinging mask covering most of the creature's face. But the mask had eyeholes cut in it, and behind the eyeholes, were open eyes, glittering eyes, *living eyes* . . . He was looking straight at her.

Kate's mind tilted with terror, and she flinched, and as she did so, Ahasuerus reached up out of the tomb and the long deep sleeves fell back, revealing clawed hands – oh God, mutilated, nightmare hands – He's trying to get out—

Kate fell back, slipping on the smooth stone of the floor, throwing up both hands to protect her face, her eyes fixed on the open tomb, jarringly aware of the noise she had made. Would the monks hear and come running? I'd almost welcome it if they did. He's climbing out of the coffin . . . His hands are clutching the sides . . . His *hands* . . .

As the cowled, hooded head rose up over the edge of the tomb, there was the sound of scrambling feet on the stair, and Moira, her hair whipped into disarray, half fell into the crypt, and then stopped short, her eyes distending with terror as she saw the open tomb and the rearing shape of Ahasuerus. Kate clutched the coffin lid, ready to strike. Because any kind of weapon . . .

And then Ahasuerus turned his masked face to where Moira stood, and a terrible cry – the cry of someone whose mouth is spoiled and whose throat is mutilated – broke from him. He threw up his hands as if to shield his face from a blow, and cringed.

Kate moved at once, springing forward, bringing the coffin lid down on his head. There was a dreadful sound: the dull thud of wood on bone, and Ahasuerus gave another of the blurred moans, and fell back. Kate, gasping and shuddering, thrust the coffin lid down into the tomb after him. Don't look down, don't even think about looking down, and certainly don't think about what you're doing. She jammed the lid roughly into place, forcing it on to the coffin, dreadfully aware of the dank stench of the tomb gusting upwards, and then straightened up, shuddering and sick.

At her side, Moira said, shakily, 'All right? Did you force him – it – back?'

'I— yes, I think so.' Kate took a deep breath and stepped back, her eyes still on the tomb. But the iron vice had loosened its grip on her chest a little, and when she spoke again, it was in what was very nearly a normal voice. 'So far so good. But we've got to get him out of here as fast as possible. At least a coffin's easier to carry than an inert body.'

'Is it?'

'I don't know. But we'll say it is. What's the time?

Half-past three, is it? Then we can still give ourselves a good start.'

'Do we think anyone will come after us?' said Moira, looking about her nervously. 'If Ciaran knows so much about this creature, won't he follow us?'

Unexpectedly something warm brushed Kate's mind. Ciaran. That sharp intuitive mind. That held-in-check sexual glamour. Might Ciaran really come after them to reclaim the brothers' immortal devil? Come off it, Kate, monks are forbidden in any culture. I could probably be burned at the stake even for thinking about it. Yes, and I'm probably toppling into madness for thinking about it down here as well. But the thought of Ciaran steadied her, and when she spoke again her voice sounded normal.

She said, 'I haven't the least idea if he'll follow us, but I should think it's unlikely. But let's put as many miles between ourselves and Curran Glen as we can. Are you ready? Good girl. I think it looks heavier than it is. And there're handles at each end – see there? We'll lift it out and we'll carry it up the stairs and out to the caravan.'

Moira, leaning over, trying not to think too deeply about what this was and what she had seen, said, 'And then? Once we reach the caravan?'

Kate looked at Moira, and in the light from the torch, a smile of reckless delight spread over her thin face.

'And then,' she said, 'we're going to take the Devil's Piper to England.'

Chapter Sixteen

'Of course she's going to take Ahasuerus to England,' said Ciaran, facing Isarel in the music room of Mallow House, the morning sun striking red glints in his hair.

'Why should she? Why should she take the coffin at all?' demanded Isarel. 'It sounds like a completely motiveless crime to me. Unless she's discovered the legend and she's going to cash in on it – I suppose that's a possibility. Would you like some coffee, by the way?'

Ciaran accepted the coffee and sat down, looking about him. Isarel's builders had apparently arrived at the crack of dawn, and Mallow House was already shedding its air of neglect and damp and decay. There was the scent of plaster dust everywhere and the hot dryness of wood being sawed. A cheerful whistling drifted down from the upper floors, and from the cellars came the clanging of hammers and spanners against pipework. A small satisfied smile creased the corners of his eyes, but he said nothing.

'Electricians in the cellar and plumbers in the attic,' said Isarel coming to perch on the half-stripped window seat, his back to the garden. 'Or it might be the other way round. Don't ask me because I don't know. I'm hoping that at some point there will be light and that at another point there will be heat and instant hot water, and that somewhere along the way the woodworm will raise a flag of surrender and beat a retreat down the path. But nobody seems to have any time scale and as far as I can make out it could all happen anywhere between the millennium and next Tuesday. What makes you think that girl's gone to England?'

'Well, largely because she was English herself,' said Ciaran. 'And I suspect that the entire thing is the culmination of a long-standing plan.'

'Not your average Burke and Hare, then.'

'Far from it. She was a very smooth-talking lady,' said Ciaran thoughtfully. 'The sort with no chinks in the armour anywhere. In my disreputable pre-monastic days, I'd have called her a ball-shriveller.'

'Would you really?' said Isarel, staring at him.

'I would. And I'd have taken great pleasure in puncturing her armour,' said Ciaran grinning.

'You astound me.'

'No I don't. If I'd said I'd have taken pleasure in pricking her armour, that might have astounded you.'

Isarel grinned too and said, 'You gave her permission to camp on Abbey land?'

'I did indeed. She'd a perfectly believable explanation about research into early Church music. Mind you, if she has taken Ahasuerus's tomb, she told nothing less than the truth,' added Ciaran. 'D'you know, Isarel, I'm beginning to think she's a very clever lady, that Kate Kendal. I think she stuck to the truth as much as possible because she knew it was the easiest way not to trip herself up.'

'Oughtn't you to be advocating truth for its own sake, Brother Ciaran?'

'Yes, but I'm playing devil's advocate just now. I agreed to let her have the field for a modest rent and I told Brother Matthew to let her into the library for a couple of hours. And then I almost forgot about her until we found the tomb empty this morning.'

'"Almost" forgot about her?' Isarel had caught the

faintest change of expression in Ciaran's voice, and he watched the other man through narrowed eyes.

'Oh,' said Ciaran in an off-hand voice, 'I suppose if I was going to have forbidden fantasies about anyone, I might very well have had them about Kate Kendal.'

'Are fantasies forbidden to you? I've never been quite sure—'

'Absolutely forbidden,' said Ciaran, and although his tone was light Isarel heard the barriers click into place.

He said in an ordinary voice, 'And so the bird has flown. I suppose it couldn't be coincidence? No, of course it couldn't.'

'It's a pretty large coincidence if it is,' said Ciaran. 'No, it fits too well. I think she was after the tomb all the time.' He drank his coffee. 'She was very intelligent and she was rather coldly efficient. I think she'd be ruthless if something mattered enough to her.' He grinned at Isarel and then said, 'I'll have to go after her of course.'

'Really?' said Isarel in an expressionless voice.

'To get Ahasuerus back. Not for any other reason.'

'It didn't occur to me that there could be any other reason.' And, thought Isarel, I know, of course, what's coming next. But I'll damn well make you sweat for this one, Brother Ciaran. He leaned back on the window seat and waited.

Ciaran glanced round the room again and then said pensively, 'I've heard that it's like living in a beleaguered city when you have a house restored. Most people prefer to move out during the worst of it.' He looked about him. 'A shocking mess workmen make, don't they? I daresay they'll be here for some time, as well. What a nuisance for you.'

Isarel set down his coffee and regarded his guest. 'Let's drag it into the open, shall we? You want me to come with you on a ridiculous chase across Ireland after a female

179

grave robber.' And maybe a lady you're harbouring a bit of a yen for as well, said his mind. 'Well, you can save the sweetness and light,' he said. 'And you can charm never so wisely, because the answer's no and it'll go on being no.'

'Wouldn't it be better – wouldn't it be more comfortable than staying here?'

'No it wouldn't. I'd rather stay here with the woodworm and the dry rot than suffer your Church's idea of comfort.'

'As a matter of fact, we can stay in the guest house of some of the other abbeys along the way,' said Ciaran. 'The hospitality's surprisingly good. If you've never tasted proper Irish soda bread baked in a monastery kitchen, you've never lived. Or Dublin Bay prawns who were swimming in the sea an hour before they're on your plate.'

'I'm allergic to shellfish.'

'What a pity. Still, failing the abbeys, it'll be hotels. I can draw on Abbey funds for whatever's needed.'

'I'm sure you can,' said Isarel. 'The only thing that surprises me is that you've bothered to get Father Abbot's permission to leave Curran Glen. You have got it, have you?'

'Oh yes. And his blessing. We'd rather not draw attention to the tomb, but we've got to regain Ahasuerus's body.'

'Back into the tomb before daybreak,' said Isarel, half to himself.

'Yes. Also,' said Ciaran, 'that girl will never control Ahasuerus, Isarel. You saw him, you must know that.'

There was a sudden silence. Then Isarel said firmly, 'I'm not coming with you. I don't care if you've got the blessing of the Pope and the Chief Rabbi and the Dalai Lama all together. You can find your own stolen corpse.'

Ciaran leaned forward and said, 'But to recapture Ahasuerus we have to have the music. We have to lure him back.

'And you're the only one who can play it.'

'I should have gone on saying no. I'll regret this.'

'You're sounding like a deflowered virgin. Reach over the map till I see if we're on the right road for Dublin. I think they'll make for Dun Laoghaire and the ferry to Anglesey, don't you?'

'How should I know?' said Isarel disagreeably, foraging for the map and unfolding it.

'I think it's likeliest,' said Ciaran, accelerating along the road Isarel had taken four days earlier. 'It's what any sensible person would do, and Kate Kendal struck me as being eminently sensible. A straight drive across the waist of Ireland and then over to Holyhead. Wasn't it a fine thing we could hang on to your hire car?'

'It was even finer that Father Abbot agreed to pay for it,' said Isarel. 'Mallow House is leeching away any money I had left. Irish builders have no mercy on Jews, Turks, Infidels or Heretics.'

'Which are you?' said Ciaran at once, and Isarel turned to stare at him. Ciaran took his eyes briefly from the road and directed a very level look at Isarel.

After a moment, Isarel said in his harshest voice, 'Oh, a Jew, every time. One of the circumcis'd dogs, one of the screwing money lenders—'

'Don't forget the line about spitting on your Jewish gabardine,' said Ciaran promptly. 'That's one of the best.'

'It's no use,' said Isarel, after a struggle not to laugh. 'I can't quarrel with you. I don't know why I can't. I certainly don't subscribe to your faith—'

'I'm not sure I subscribe to it myself, sometimes.'

'—and I don't think much of your methods, either. I can't imagine why I'm here, or what we're going to do if we catch up with Kate Kendal. Ciaran, did we really lure

181

Ahasuerus back into the tomb the other night?'

'We did.'

'Using Jude's shofar?'

'Using Jude's shofar,' affirmed Ciaran.

'I was hoping it was a dream,' said Isarel. 'I almost persuaded myself that some of my students laced my toothpaste with LSD.'

'Well, it wasn't a dream and you weren't doped. Listen, I'm liking driving, but maybe we should swop over after we've eaten a bite of lunch somewhere because I'm a bit out of practice.'

'I didn't think monks were supposed to know about driving cars or reading maps. You're very worldly for a monk,' said Isarel.

'Would you believe I was once very worldly indeed?' said Ciaran.

'Readily. What were you? I mean what did you do for a living?'

'I was a lawyer.'

'Were you, by God,' said Isarel, staring at him.

'A barrister.'

'Highly suitable. You could argue your way out of anything.'

'Believe me, I've argued my way out of a good many tight corners in my time. And,' said Ciaran thoughtfully, 'into a few of them as well. Would you believe I was a very good barrister?'

'Easily. You've got all the necessary qualities. Disregard for truth's only one of them.'

'Oh, truth-telling's not always compatible with the defence of an innocent man.' Ciaran grinned and looked across at Isarel again.

Isarel said, 'That sounds like Oscar Wilde.'

'You're close. Bernard Shaw.'

'I knew only an Irishman could have said it. You're completely lacking in monastic humility, aren't you? Why on earth did you become a monk?'

'I've often wondered that myself,' said Ciaran and his voice held the note of reserve Isarel had caught before when Ciaran talked about Kate Kendal.

He sent him a covert look but only said dryly, 'Did you have much trouble coaxing funds for this trip out of your – what do I call it? – Treasurer? Bursar?'

'Treasurer will do. No,' said Ciaran, swinging the car into the by-pass. 'No trouble in the least.'

'I suppose coaxing Abbots and Treasurers is child's play after the Law Courts of – where was it? Dublin?'

'Well, I moved about a bit,' said Ciaran. 'Dublin and Galway and Waterford. I was in England for a time.'

'It's just as I thought, you're no better than a gypsy,' said Isarel. 'I can't imagine how I'm going to cope with you once we reach London. I can't imagine how anyone ever copes with you. You've got as much respect for the truth as Ananias, you manipulate people until their heads spin, and you drink nearly as much as I do, which is saying a good deal! And,' said Isarel, torn between exasperation and amusement, 'I can't begin to guess what you're doing inside a monastery.'

'At times,' said Ciaran a bit grimly, 'neither can I.'

Chapter Seventeen

The dawn was breaking over the narrow streets of Cremona as the four people in the underground workroom looked at one another.

A night with your lady . . . The words lay on the air, intrusive and startling.

Cosimo Amati had never been so shocked in the whole of his life. This enigmatic creature, this *servant* whom he had summoned from God only knew what dark crevice of hell for the sole purpose of obeying his command – *his* command, mark you! – had the arrogance to cast lascivious eyes on Isabella! It was no good wrapping the thing up: Cosimo knew perfectly well what the stranger meant.

Well, Cosimo was certainly not going to permit his wife – his dear, innocent Isabella – to be bartered over as if she was no more than a bushel of corn or a firkin of wine. It was not to be thought of, and that was all there was to be said, and the stranger was please to leave at once. Some other way would be found to rid Cremona of the plague, in fact now that Cosimo came to think of it, it was very likely not being brought in by the rats anyway.

Ahasuerus said softly, 'But how are you to banish me, Lute Maker?'

How? This was now not only preposterous, it was absurd. If an honest lute maker could not politely request an unwanted visitor to leave his home, and see that request courteously obeyed, Cosimo did not know what things were coming to!

'But I am not unwanted,' said Ahasuerus. 'You invited me in.'

It was then that Isabella moved forward and said quietly, 'Cosimo, I do not think we have any choice about this. There is always a price to be paid for—' A quick glance at Ahasuerus, 'for the devil's services,' she said demurely. 'We should remember that this may be the way to deliver Cremona from the scourge.' Isabella sent Ahasuerus another sidelong glance and then laid a hand on Cosimo's arm. 'If this could happen – if it could *succeed* – you would be remembered as the man who drove out the plague,' said Isabella. 'You would be revered for a very long time in Cremona's history.'

Cosimo pulled down his brows and said suspiciously, that that was as maybe.

'And,' said Isabella, her mouth a guileless curve, but mischief trickling from the corners of her long sensuous eyes, 'all that is intended is discourse about Cremona's customs and ways.' She looked fully at Ahasuerus for the first time. 'I have your meaning correctly, sir?'

Ahasuerus returned the look and saw the mischief and the sensuous sideways glance, and thought: Susannah, you faithless bitch! You know exactly what my meaning is – we both know what it is! – and you'll betray this fat, stupid, little creature without so much as a backward thought! I wonder how many times you've betrayed him already! But beneath his smooth cool manner, his heart was beginning to pound in furious anticipation.

He said in a disinterested voice, 'You have my meaning correctly, Lady.'

It was the monk who said, 'But you can't possibly— We have no idea of who this might be.'

'They do say,' murmured Isabella, 'that the devil, in many of his guises, is a gentleman. If I cannot – place myself in the hands of a gentleman for a few short hours to save Cremona, I should think myself wholly devoid of—'

'Public spirit?' asked Simon sarcastically.

'Lacking in regard for the good of all the town,' amended Isabella, and lowered her eyes but not before Simon had seen the amused glint in them. Cat! he thought, but was aware of a ripple of sensuality brushing over his skin, as if she had reached out a velvet-covered paw and stroked the inside of his thigh. A cat, but a very alluring cat. How on earth did fat little Amati keep her from straying? thought Simon, and at once knew the answer: fat little Amati did not keep her from straying at all, simply he did not know – or maybe simply did not acknowledge – that she strayed in the first place. The cat was a clever cat but she was discreet and perhaps she was not wholly devoid of feeling. He looked across at Ahasuerus and thought: and this cool-eyed, enigmatic stranger is going to have her for a night! He felt a sudden surge of arousal, shameful and hot and crude, immediately followed by a wash of jealousy. When he spoke, his voice was cold and harsh, 'Supposing we agreed to your condition?' said Simon. 'How would you do it? How would you rid Cremona of plague-rats?'

Ahasuerus had been more or less aware of Simon's thoughts and they had amused him. This monk was astute and he was probably devout, but he was also still very vulnerable to the sins of the flesh. He had looked at Susannah and he had suddenly wanted her very much indeed and then had hated Ahasuerus himself for what they all knew was ahead. This was all very interesting. As for Susannah, she had not changed at all. Sensual and mischievous and as manipulative as ever.

He said, 'The night is ending and it is nearly sunrise. I

am right? Then tonight at sunset I will play the music you played earlier, Lute Maker. I will play it on the lyre you used to call me and I will walk through your streets sprinkling the music everywhere. And the rats will follow me out of the city.'

'Are you sure of that?'

'I am sure. They will follow me because I know they will follow me.'

Amati said, 'If the power is in the music, why can't I—'

'You could not control it,' said Ahasuerus politely. 'You barely controlled it earlier.'

'Can you control it?'

'Oh yes,' said Ahasuerus softly. 'Yes, I can control it. We are old friends, the music and I.' He looked at them. 'I will draw the creatures to the catacombs on the outskirts of Cremona,' he said, and saw Amati and the monk exchange a look, as if saying: yes, that would be a practical solution.

Simon said, 'How do we know we can trust you?'

'You have my word,' said Ahasuerus, sounding bored.

'The devil is a gentleman?'

'I have no idea. But I—' He tapped his breast, 'I will make a solemn pact.' Did they understand his meaning? Was this a word in use here? He sought for a translation, but then saw that they understood him. 'I shall keep my part of the pact, and I shall not harm your lady,' said Ahasuerus.

Isabella Amati had always known that her morals had nothing in common with the morals of the respectable Cremonan ladies and she knew perfectly well the things that were said about her behind her back. Cat. Wanton. Quite a few people said she had no morals at all, which probably came closest to the truth.

But it was such fun to take a lover – it was even more

fun to take two or three together – and so long as you were discreet and the young men were discreet as well, there was no harm done. She had been very discreet indeed.

But faced with the dark cloaked stranger who had the most beautiful voice Isabella had ever heard, and who spoke in the purest, most golden Latin imaginable, Isabella was aware of a deep dark sensual hunger stirring and a wish to fling aside the stupid stifling codes and morals and tumble headlong into something thrilling and unknown and dangerous.

When the stranger said, 'A night with your lady, Master Lute Maker,' a bolt of desire sliced through her body and she thought: oh yes! A fleeting vision touched her mind: something about a pale lovely building washed in cool aqua-tints, and an altar soaked in solemnity and immense scholarly devotion. And beyond it all, a passion so intense you would die for it . . .

Nobody in Cremona really believed that Cosimo Amati had found a way to drive out the plague-rats, but nobody was going to miss the opportunity of seeing him try to do it. Quite aside from the spectacle it would provide, (especially if he failed), there was a very serious aspect to it. By this time, nearly every family in the town had lost someone to the plague and there had already been talk of opening up the old catacombs in order to bury the dead. There were a great many difficulties with plague, and one of them was the burying of all the corpses. The townspeople – overwhelmed by grief and frantic with fear – had already sealed Cremona by closing the city gates against travellers, which was common humanity, and had diligently dug a burial pit on the city's outskirts, which was common sense.

The closing of the city gates had thrown them in on themselves a bit, and a few moribund quarrels had flared into life, which you had to expect. There might be a problem with food if things lasted much longer, even though most people had good stocks of wheat and corn and barrels of herrings and salt pork, but this was something that they could probably overcome.

The real problem was the rats.

Several nights ago, the two old men who trundled the death carts through the streets each evening at dusk, giving their grisly call to bring out the dead, had come shrieking and wild-eyed into the town. Falling over each other and their own feet in their haste, they yelled that the bodies were moving, the corpses were coming to life. Resurrection Day! they screamed, and them with all their sins on them, and tottered into the tavern to be revived with copious draughts of ale, and to describe in horrid detail how they had seen the corpses moving as they tipped the newest batch of victims into the pit. They had stood horror-struck, they said, and then the corpse plagues had got up from the pit, climbed out, and pursued them through the night, their winding sheets unravelling, the stench of their putrescence borne with them on the wind. Oh, a terrible sight it had been; they had seen it with their own eyes as clear as they saw that empty tankard on the table there. They indicated the empty tankards rather explicitly at this point and several people leapt with alacrity to re-fill them because this was too good a story to leave unfinished.

Well! said the carters quaffing appreciatively, they had abandoned the tilt cart at that point and they had bolted back to the town for safety, which was only what you would expect of any man. They cast fearful glances over their shoulders in the direction of the door and prophesied that at any minute the rotting corpses would come shambling into the town in search of those who had put them there. At any minute the whole of Cremona might find itself over-run by decaying bodies searching for the ones who had buried them alive, out for vengeance, which was a thing to give you a shuddering grue, and speaking of grue, if there was a tankard more ale to be had, it would be very gratefully received.

Nobody had entirely believed any of this, but everyone had spent a very nasty couple of hours visualising the possibility of live bodies being buried in the pit, which was not altogether unheard of. Most people knew someone who knew someone who had an aunt or a cousin . . . Very unpleasant indeed.

And then in the end, of course, when a party had ventured out to the burial pit, they had found that the heaving of the corpses was not due to premature burial at all, but to the rats, horrid scavenging things, gnawing and nibbling at decomposing flesh and then scuttling back into Cremona's streets, carrying the loathsome disease with them. Small wonder the plague continued to rampage! said the townspeople, torn between disgust and fury. They burned torches constantly at the pit's rim, and after every new burial spadefuls of lime were sprinkled over the bodies. The two carters, pot-valiant old fools, had been told to keep off the ale while they were about their grotesque work because while it was understandable that they should take a mug or two of an evening, there was such a thing as moderation and everyone had had a very bad scare.

They all congregated in the Campo Santo, which was a good central point, and waited to discover what Cosimo Amati was going to do. Stories circulated. He was going to cast the plague out by means of an ancient Druidic ceremony handed down by his ancestors. No, he was going to call up the half-man, half-skeletal creature, the Maccaber, who lived in a windowless doorless black tower in the heart of the mountains, and possessed power over all pestilence. One rumour which ran amongst the more literate members of the population suggested that Amati had been dabbling in the art of alchemy and had uncovered the secrets of the Greek philosophers. Ah, people might laugh, but stranger things had been known, said these wise souls, and removed themselves to the far end of the square where it was easier to look as if you were discussing learned and weighty matters, instead of speculating on whether Isabella Amati's bed-hopping might be due to her husband's impotence.

The sun was bathing the old part of Cremona in a fiery glow and streaking the western sky with great swathes of gold and lilac and rose, when Cosimo Amati together with his lady and the young English monk, Brother Simon, walked up from the Contrada dei Coltellai and took their places in the centre of the Campo Santo.

Isabella had chosen a gown of palest ivory lawn, threaded with silver and scattered with tiny seed pearls. Her coppery hair was loose, but she had twined a thin silver thread in it, with a narrow headband at the front. Every woman present would know that she was overdressed for the occasion, which of course she was, and most women would speculate on who had paid for the seed pearls and the silver thread, and more to the point, why.

She was aware of the eyes upon her as she entered the Campo Santo. It was always a good moment when you came into a gathering – any gathering – and felt everyone turn to watch you. People spoke of her as beautiful, but she knew that she was very far from beautiful. What she had was something quite different from beauty. When the stranger said last night, 'The rats will follow me because I know they will follow me,' Isabella had had a blinding flare of understanding. That is how *I* feel! People will admire me because I know they will admire me. How remarkable.

Her whole body was strung as tightly as the strings on Cosimo's lyres. *I am waiting for him . . . The time until he is here is running away like sand trickling between my fingers. It's getting nearer. He is getting nearer.*

Her heart was racing and she felt as if huge weights were pressing down on her. *Supposing he did not come? Supposing it had been a dream?*

There was tension in the watchers now. Isabella could feel the waves of anticipation, laced with nervous fear and she thought that if you could reach out and pluck the atmosphere, it would be like plucking a musical instrument and the sound would vibrate on the air long after you had ceased to hear it. *They aren't precisely afraid but they know that something very strange is going to happen,* thought Isabella, looking around. *They know that something powerful and something outside their comprehension is drawing near. Coming through the deserted old town with scraps of mosaic pavements left by the Romans . . . Coming along the town outskirts where the city wall still stood . . . Through the dying day he was coming . . .*

Yes, but supposing he did not?

He would come. He would come because she knew he would. In another few minutes he would be here. In a very short time – perhaps no more than an hour – she would be keeping the tryst. Would he come to her, or would he summon her with that extraordinary blend of arrogance and directness? Isabella thought she would refuse to go obediently to him like a supplicant, and then she thought she would walk across white-hot cinders to get to him if she had to.

In just another minute the sun would be below the

horizon and the silhouette of the old Roman wall built hundreds of years ago would be nothing more than a black outline. Her heart was beating so fast she thought it would burst from her breast and she was finding it difficult to breathe – it would be the final irony if she died from passion now! thought Isabella wryly. At her side, Cosimo and Simon were both scanning the darkening square, not speaking. Isabella thought that of the two of them it was Simon who was the more tense and she sent him a covert look. Rather attractive, this monk, but then celibates could be immensely attractive; you had the impression of passion consciously banked down, and Simon gave that impression very strongly indeed. He's had to do battle with his appetites, thought Isabella. Would it be amusing to lure him into bed? She considered this and came to the conclusion that it would be very amusing indeed. But it would have to be after tonight was over. She could not think beyond tonight.

She had been straining her eyes to see every corner of the old square, and she had thought she would feel his presence before she saw him, but without any warning at all he was there, walking softly towards them, coming from between the two buildings at the far end of the Campo Santo. The cloak was still drawn about him, and there was the same indefinable air of other-worldliness.

He paid her no attention. He walked up to Cosimo and wordlessly held out his hand for the bone lyre.

Turning his back on the silent watchers, he began to play. It was certain that out of all the people present, aside from Cosimo only Isabella recognised the music. Isabella had grown up with the legend of the devil's music, the *diabolus in musica*; it had been part of her childhood, handed down by her grandmother and her grandmother's grandmother, and back and back through the women of her family.

She knew the music and once or twice, just for fun, she had sung it softly. But it was something to be very wary of, she understood that. She had sung it to Cosimo on their wedding night, poorest Cosimo, with his fat, uncomely body and his drooping manhood. He had heaved and grunted between her thighs for what had felt like an eternity, red-faced and sweaty and he had been so soft that he had not even been able to enter her. Three times he had rolled off and turning his back had frantically manipulated his wilting body to a semblance of stiffness with his hand. It had been unspeakably embarrassing but it had also been rather sad and at last, Isabella, by then wanting nothing more than to be left in peace to sleep, had started to sing the sweet soft music. Her grandmother, smiling the slant-eyed smile, had once said that it never failed. Burnt-out lovers, wrung-dry husbands always responded, said her grandmother. Cosimo had responded, grateful and delighted, and for days after achieving his puny trickling climax, he had gone about with his chest puffed out like a pouter pigeon.

The music was filling the square now, and Isabella thought every single person must hear its promise and its lure.

Follow me into the fire-drenched caverns of hell and beyond . . . Follow me through the frozen mountains and across the baked deserts and into the fast flowing rivers of the world . . .

Come out and follow me . . . Come out and obey me . . . COME OUT AND DIE . . .

But the strong sexual pull was there as well, like a dark swirling undertow. Isabella saw with faint amusement that several people were reaching for others' hands; that cheeks were becoming flushed and eyes bright. Men slid their arms about the waists of the serving girls from the tavern and the wine shop, pressing against them, thrusting their hands furtively into the low bodices. Does Ahasuerus see that? thought Isabella. Does he know about the music's fierce passionate side. Yes, of course he knows, fool!

But Ahasuerus paid no attention to anything other than the pouring out of the music. He was beginning to walk through the ancient city, the fiery glow of the setting sun directly behind him, so that the watchers saw him illuminated against the light: a black lone figure. But he is deflecting the light, thought Isabella, unable to look away. The light is not touching him, it is streaming off him like a blazing cloak, like a river of molten fire.

But behind him, the light fell in little sprinklings, as if quicksilver had been scattered, as if the music had taken on substance and then splintered . . . For an incredible moment, Isabella actually saw it: a thin silvery trail, a sticky spider's web, a narrow glistening ribbon unwinding over the cobbled streets . . .

Follow me . . .

From beyond the city centre they came, like a sable river erupting from out of the sewers and the cellars and the river banks. Cremona's dark underside vomiting forth its filth. Rats streaming down to fall into the musician's wake; no longer repulsive, corpse-fattened things bloated with their grisly battenings, but sleek furry creatures; pattering, woodland animals with pricked ears and twitching whiskers and bright, intelligent eyes . . .

Ahasuerus walked into the dimming glow of the sunset, towards the catacomb entrance, the light still streaming from him, the music pouring effortlessly out of the lyre.

And the rats following him unquestioningly.

Chapter Eighteen

The sun had disappeared beneath the western horizon and a silvery radiance was illuminating the countryside when Isabella reached the entrance to the catacombs. *So after all, I was obedient to his summoning. The catacombs at dusk, he had said. And here I am, as subservient and as grateful as if I had never taken a lover before.*

He had watched her approach, standing motionless at the catacomb entrance, and now that she was actually alone with him, Isabella was bereft of speech. As a rule on these occasions you knew where you were, but this could hardly be described as a normal occasion. What on earth did you say when you were about to spend the night with one of hell's emissaries? Perhaps it would be better to let him speak first. They had agreed in Cosimo's workroom that the devil was a gentleman. Or had they?

In the end she said, 'Well, stranger, as you see, I keep my word. You did what we asked. You delivered us from all evil—'

Lead us not into temptation, but deliver us from evil— Oh no, I didn't mean that bit!

'You purged the city of the plague-rats,' said Isabella. 'And so I am here as you requested.' But even then she was unable to resist the frivolous touch. 'I am your payment,' said Isabella demurely, although to her credit managed not to say: *and so take me.*

196

'My payment,' said Ahasuerus softly, looking at her.

His voice was precisely as Isabella remembered it: soft and very beautiful. Like thin silk being drawn over your naked skin. She forgot about being frivolous and she forgot about attempting to make polite conversation. Polite was the last thing she wanted to be. I could drown in his voice. I could sink fathoms deep in it and never want to surface . . .

Ahasuerus raised his hands and very slowly folded back the deep hood. The moonlight fell across his face. Every shred of half-bravado and half-fearful flippancy vanished at once; because of all the things Isabella had been expecting to see – fleshless features, horned head, red glaring eyes; anything had seemed possible – she had not expected to see this.

Pure, unspoiled beauty. *Pure.* Beauty so dazzling, so remarkable that you could not stop looking at it, and once you had looked you would never want to look away.

He is the most beautiful creature I have ever seen . . . The fear came uppermost again, because wasn't the devil said to be fair: the fairest of all the angels, bright as the sun, until he over-reached and under-estimated, and fell . . . This is how he might have looked, thought Isabella, half tranced, half frightened. Lucifer before the Fall. Satan riding out against God and His armies . . .

He was paler than the Cremona men, with a thin, translucent pallor, so that you could almost believe that if you looked closely, you would see the bones beneath the skin and the warm coursing blood . . . His hair was black and silky, worn longer than Isabella was used to seeing, and for some reason this, more than anything, heightened his air of having come from another world. His lips had the paradoxical quality of being thin and at the same time sensual, and the bone structure of his face formed a perfect

197

oval, the cheek-bones slightly slanting. And his eyes are grey, thought Isabella: clear and cool and rimmed with black. Eyes to drown in. A voice to die to . . .

And then Ahasuerus reached out and pulled her against him, and he might be a devil or a demon, but his body's response was that of an ordinary human man: he was hard and aroused and burning with sexual heat. The dark night blurred and Isabella felt consciousness waver and self-control slip its leash. As if I had been drinking poppy syrup, or mandragora, the sleep juice, the love juice . . .

She had half expected violence and she certainly knew the stories, half ribald, half believed, that the devil's phallus was icy cold and fletched like an arrow. Supposing . . . No, I can't think like that. If he doesn't do something in a minute I shall die of wanting.

Ahasuerus peeled the thin silver gown from her body and stood looking down at her, his eyes unreadable. At last his hands came out to caress her skin – like silk, like warm wine – and he sank to his knees before her, the soft black hair brushing the inside of her thighs. Oh God, this is indescribable. I have never felt like this before. I shall never feel like this again. I think I might faint from desire.

Isabella knelt as well then, so that they were on a level, their bodies so close they felt as if they were blurring into one. She cupped his face between her hands, and saw the black-rimmed eyes darken with passion. A low groan broke from him and he tightened his hold and said very softly, 'Susannah.'

The catacombs were cool and dry and there was a faint sad drift of dust and age. Bone-dust, thought Isabella, looking about her. I'm in here with corpses – probably hundreds of them. Through the shadows she could just make out the shelves of rock, and on the shelves, the gleam of fleshless bones . . . Empty eyeless skulls . . . Here and there was the outline of something shrivelled and yellow.

Ahasuerus pulled her back into his arms, and the poor shrunken bodies and the grinning skeletal heads faded. The surroundings no longer mattered because the two of them were clutching and clawing at one another in helpless need, and there was a whirling tumble of sensations: tongues and hands and lips, tasting his mouth, feeling the desperate longing, no longer able to tell who was who . . . Rolling in the bone-dust on the floor – sorry, sorry, sorry, poor dead, crumbled things . . . Forgive me . . . Blending into one, yes of course, this was the real meaning of being one.

When he entered her his groan was that of a creature driven beyond its farthest limits, and Isabella cried out and could not tell whether it was with pain because this could only be transient, or whether it was with delight because there had been nothing like it anywhere in the world, ever . . . She was sobbing with emotion, and as she pulled him deeper and as he began to move against her, hard, insistent, barely able to contain his passion, the world began to tilt and then to turn upside-down in a maelstrom of burning stars and erupting sunbursts, and there was a fusion somewhere – his mind into mine . . . Beyond the bursting stars in her vision, there was the impression of something like a deep, dark velvety curtain tearing . . . The walls of Time rupturing so that you could see through and you could see beyond and you were in a place you had never been to, only that you knew it very well . . .

I'm lying on the sacred altar with the High Priest of the Temple, thought Isabella, her mind snapping its restraints and soaring up and beyond the torn blue skies. I'm there with him and there is such white-hot passion raging through him, that he can no longer control it.

When your wife was being taken in blatant and wanton adultery, there was only one thing that would alleviate your anger and restore your loss of face.

Revenge. The death of the offender.

Cosimo Amati, speechless with indignation and beside himself with righteous rage, absolved Isabella from all guilt. Isabella was an innocent unaware soul who had had absolutely no idea of what she had agreed to do, but anyone of any experience – Cosimo himself, for instance – could see with half an eye that the stranger's talk about learning Cremona's ways was so much eyewash. What was even worse was that all of Cremona appeared to have seen it as well, and was now sniggering behind Cosimo's back about it.

Isabella was such an innocent. Cosimo liked this quality and had tried to preserve it. But of course, the dear child had no idea of the kind of raging lusts that men could harbour. Cosimo did not himself harbour particularly raging lusts but if he had he would not have dreamed of venting them on Isabella. A once-a-week indulgence in Isabella's bed was all Cosimo permitted himself and he only did that because the Church taught that a man should be one with his wife. Being one once a week was in fact as much as Cosimo could manage, and in fact he found even that a bit of a struggle but it was not the point.

Isabella had been bewitched and bemused by the creature who had answered the music: Cosimo had seen it instantly. His dear girl would have to be pampered and cosseted for a very long time to help her forget the terrible ordeal she was even now suffering. But for the creature who was so— so *besmirching* her, nothing was too severe. What should be done?

The use of the word ordeal struck a chord. Cosimo dug into his memory and remembered that a very long time ago, certainly as far back as the ancient Greeks, there had been something called the *per Dei judicium*, which even people of minor learning knew meant judgement by God. Trial by ordeal. If the miscreant survived the ordeal he could be judged innocent.

Cosimo Amati thought he was an amiable, reasonable man, but even amiable, reasonable men had their limits. He remembered that he was an important member of the community in Cremona – yes, *and* the one who had found a way to rid them of plague-rats! – and he clenched his fists and thought he would have his vengeance and by God it would be a public vengeance at that! He began to feel very much better, and he betook himself to the tavern, where a hasty discussion was going on as to what should be done with the stranger in the morning.

Cosimo, listening, was shocked to his toes to hear several people actually suggesting that the stranger should be let go, or at least handed over to the monks, and he was appalled when an unruly contingent led by the two carters spoke out in favour of reviving the ancient practice of stoning an adulteress and driving her from the town to the sound of rough music. This could certainly not be permitted: Isabella was not an adulteress, or not in the true sense of the word. In any case, the people of Cremona had not stoned an adulteress to death for years and if they were going to resurrect the nasty practice now, they were not going to resurrect it with Isabella.

He got to his feet, somebody banged a table for silence, and Cosimo looked very solemn and said it was all very well to talk about what to do with the stranger, but they should all remember the likely origins of beings who appeared to transcend the grave. He waited, and heard the words 'devil' and 'demon' murmur around the tavern, and plunged on.

Why should they not allow God to decide? asked Cosimo, looking fatly responsible and serious. Why should they not revive the ancient honourable practice of the *per Dei judicium* and see what God thought about the stranger?

He looked so fierce and so stern, even with the fatness, that everyone present remembered that after all Cremona had been purged of the plague-rats more or less at Cosimo's hand, and also that it had been Cosimo's lady who had been sacrificed last night. If that didn't give him the best right of all to decide what to do with the stranger then nothing did, they said firmly and refrained from remarking that Isabella had probably not taken much sacrificing.

It was the tavern keeper himself who asked what form the trial should take, and Cosimo, who had been waiting for somebody to ask this, said, 'Well, there are several possibilities.'

Isabella came out of a deep, pleasurable sleep, vaguely aware that she was lying on hard ground and dimly wondering why, but strongly aware that there was a familiar soreness between her thighs. For a moment, caught in the drifting, half-drugged world between sleep and waking, she smiled. Ah, have I been doing *that* for most of the night . . .?

And then memory rushed in, and she sat up abruptly. I am in the catacombs. And with me— She turned her head and saw him still at her side, the dark hair tumbled over his pale brow, a sheen of moisture on his closed eyelids, the sensual, sensitive mouth relaxed in sleep. Something fastened about her heart – *O, Ahasuerus!* – but then the mischievous smile lifted her lips into the cat-smile as memory peeled back a little further. How many times?

Dear God, I lost count. But over and over, as if we were both thirsting, as if we could never have enough of one another. Clutching, clawing, biting, scratching. And then, after the first hungers had been assuaged, gentler, slower, infinitely loving. Remarkable.

She propped herself up on one elbow and looked down at him. He had tossed aside the dark robe last night, and in the dim light in the caves, he had appeared to her only as slender and pale, with a faint luminous glow to his skin.

Now, with the cold grey dawnlight sliding into the cave, Isabella could see the things that the moonlight and the sensuality and the hungry passion had hidden.

Scars. Great ploughed weals and knotted furrows around the upper part of his body. He turned slightly in sleep, and Isabella saw that the scars furrowed his back, latticing in places. Her heart twisted again, and she reached out a hand and traced the scars lightly, as if to smooth them away. Without warning, Ahasuerus opened his eyes and looked straight at her with his level, disconcerting gaze.

Isabella said, in a whisper, 'Your back— Ahasuerus, what did that to your back?'

There was a moment of the most profound silence she had ever known, and then Ahasuerus said in a voice devoid of all emotion, 'It was part of a punishment. I was sentenced to suffer what my people called the Triple Death. The Three Agonies.' He touched the scars lightly. 'Those are the marks of the first of those agonies.'

And as Isabella waited, her eyes never leaving him, he said, 'Scourging. I was scourged at the pillar.'

It was as clear as if it had only just happened. The words of the sentence were as plain as if they had only just been pronounced.

'You will be scourged at the pillar while the sun

203

passes from the east to the west side of Jerusalem ... The next evening at sunset, you will be nailed to the Cruciferum ... The evening after that, again at sunset, fires will be lit around the foot of the Cruciferum, and your body will burn ...'

He could still see his grim prison beneath the cool lovely Temple and he could still smell it; the low-ceilinged, windowless cellar that reeked of the fear and the despairing agony of countless other prisoners.

He had been kept there for several days, lying in the dark, grim place, chained and manacled and given only a few mouthfuls of bread and water. There had been a pile of straw nearby which he supposed was for the relieving of bladder and bowels, and he had felt fastidious disgust. A High Priest to lie in his own ordure? He thought he would rather die and then he remembered that he would die anyway and it ceased to matter.

Scourged at the pillar, nailed to the Cruciferum, and then burned alive ... . Fear tore through him in great shuddering waves, but he held on to the thought of Susannah: Susannah who had lain with him and who had promised him that there would be the return ... Susannah would not let him die in screaming torment.

When they finally brought him up out of the underground room, he was so weak that the brightness of the day struck across his eyes like a blow, and he staggered and almost fell. But somehow he forced himself to stand straight and he surveyed the watchers with cold authority. Pride – that overweening pride that had contributed to his downfall! – came to his rescue, and he vowed that no matter how deep the agony and no matter how searing the torment, he would not show weakness or fear. He still wore the white robe of his calling and the cool silken folds gave him unexpected courage. I die, but I die as a High Priest of the Temple. I die as a Scribe and a Scholar of Jerusalem and you cannot take that from me. As the guards pulled him roughly to the immense stone pillar, he shook off their hands angrily, and deliberately stood for a moment studying the instruments for the first part of the execution. Yes, the *flagellum* was there: the whip made of several strands of square-sectioned leather and with it the *flagrum*, the lengths of cord with human knuckle bones knotted along them at intervals. He eyed the grisly things with complete calm, and then turned back courteously to the guards and held out his hands, as if saying: now I am ready.

The guards moved at once, chaining him to the stone pillar that was part of the Temple's kingpost and that was used for the punishment of those who defiled the altar. His back was towards the crowd but he caught, on the edge of his vision, the Elders silently watching, and he knew that if there was to be any kind of rescue, it would be hard won. The Elders were too anxious to show how renegades were dealt with in Jerusalem. He thought it not unlikely that some of them were even enjoying his downfall. Because they had been jealous? Because he had been clever and successful and because the women had been drawn to him? That hubristic arrogance again! Yes, but there was probably some truth in the notion.

The first blow from the *flagrum* was so much worse than he had been expecting that it almost broke his resolve. The hard knuckle bones jarred sickeningly against flesh and muscle, bruising his ribs agonisingly and he bit down a groan. Remain silent. Whatever they do, whatever the depth of the agony, remain silent. He concentrated his mind until it was focused on a single flame of glowing light and on the silvery call of Susannah's music.

Shut out the pain. Shut out the agony and the tearing brutality of the *flagrum*. Let me keep the light in my sight and let me keep the music in my mind, and let neither of them waver . . .

The scourges fell again and again: Ahasuerus heard them singing through the air before each blow, and when the blows came they tore at his flesh, lacerating it into bloodied tatters. Behind him, he was aware of the second guard reaching for the leather *flagellum*.

The *flagellum* was agony of a different texture. Subtler. Where the thongs met and tangled as they struck him, the pain was so fierce that the single shard of light blurred and the music faded. He felt salt tears mingle with sweat and sting his lip and he felt the tumbled hair glued to his brow.

But when the guards finally laid down the scourges and stepped up to free the chains and the fetters, he lifted his head and turned to face the crowd and with his last reserves of strength, he forced into his eyes the light that had beckoned and promised, and that had enthralled the women. His body was streaked with blood and the white robe was torn and draggled with gore. But I kept the light and I kept the music, he thought with sudden triumph. And if I can only hold on to those two things, I believe I can walk to the Cruciferum with the same courage as the Nazarene Himself . . .

'The light and the music bore me with them,' he said to Isabella in the cool dawnlight that filtered into the catacombs. 'They bore me forward and they took me through the scourging to what was waiting beyond it.' He stopped, and Isabella thought: the music! This is the source! This is the long-ago source of my family's ancient, handed-down secret! She waited, hardly daring to breathe, wanting him to go on, wanting to hear of his agonies, knowing in the same breathspace that hearing would tear apart her own flesh.

But Ahasuerus had turned his head to the entrance to the catacombs. 'Listen,' he said.

'What—' And then Isabella heard it as well.

Marching feet. People coming up the dry, dusty road towards them.

Isabella pulled her cloak about her and pushing her tumbled hair back with one hand, crawled cautiously out on to the ledge to see what was happening.

It was still very early. The light was pure and clear and there was a glistening newness everywhere. She narrowed her eyes and looked out along the road that wound from Cremona. Yes, there they were, a little band of people coming purposefully towards the catacombs. Travellers of some kind? But travellers were not usually about so early, and in any case they had closed the city gates soon after the plague broke out.

And then she recognised the man leading the little procession. Cosimo. At his side was the monk, Simon.

Chapter Nineteen

Cosimo had been overwhelmed with relief at finding Isabella safe. He had carried her back to the house himself, over-ruling her protests saying, Nonsense, of course she was not too heavy for him.

She must rest in her bedchamber, he said, finally setting her down on their threshold, somewhat empurpled as to face and short as to breath. He insisted on it and there was to be no argument. A terrible ordeal, said Cosimo, busily preparing a dainty little tray for his poor, dear girl, brushing aside the stupid sloven who was babbling about mulled wine and freshly made chicken broth, and who was all right so far as cooking and cleaning went, but could not be trusted with the care of his precious one.

He set the tray with a clean linen cloth, and put out a bowl of the broth which the sloven had made early that morning. There were sweet biscuits and sugared fruits: Cosimo arranged these on a plate and uncorked a bottle of the rich dark wine which Isabella liked and which it was his pleasure to buy for her.

He perched anxiously on the edge of the bed watching to be sure she ate and drank everything, furrowing his brow at the sight of the red marks on her white neck and shoulders, and at the faintly bruised look of her mouth. But when Isabella asked what was happening to Ahasuerus, Cosimo patted her hand and said they would not talk of it: she was to put the entire thing from her mind. The evil creature had been locked in the monks' cells, and justice was going to be done to him – at noon that very day if they were to be exact – but Isabella was not to be distressed by the details.

He patted her hand again, smoothed the bedsheets and went off to witness the downfall of the creature who had seduced his lady.

In the Campo Santo, an atmosphere of subdued excitement had reigned since daybreak.

The tavern keeper had been up betimes, and had made an expedition to his cellar to bring up several casks of October ale and small beer, along with the wine which he had been storing for the monks, but from which a couple of casks would not be missed. He would say that Father Abbot had miscounted if anyone challenged him.

His wife spent the morning baking some onion and vegetable pasties and a batch of little honey cakes which could be sold quite cheaply but which, since the spectacle had been set for noon, would do very nicely for people to eat by way of a mid-day repast. She had consulted anxiously with her spouse as to whether they should kill the last of the fowl and offer bowls of chicken broth as well. You could get quite chilled watching a judgement of a February morning, said the tavern keeper's lady seriously and, more to the point, they could charge for the use of the bowls. But in the event, there had not been time for chicken-killing or broth-making.

Cosimo had a bad moment when Brother Simon and a couple of his fellow monks approached him and asked whether Cosimo would not leave Ahasuerus in their keeping: there was something about an ancient vow, and an open sarcophagus brought up from the catacombs, all of which sounded so absurd as to be hardly worth answering.

Cosimo, in fact, was secretly looking forward to the *per Dei judicium* which would serve a two-pronged purpose: not only would it punish Ahasuerus, it would act as a warning to the impudent young men of Cremona whom he so often caught eyeing Isabella with covert lust. It would be a warning to Isabella herself as well, although Cosimo knew perfectly well that this was not needed.

But looked at from all aspects, the *per Dei judicium* was going to serve all of Cosimo's interests very nicely indeed.

He glanced up at the monks' clock tower and saw that there was only an hour to go.

Isabella had not argued against Cosimo because it would be pointless. She waited until he had gone, allowing him enough time to be well beyond the house, and then thrust the hateful tray aside and swung her legs out of bed. Across the rooftops the monks' bell was chiming the half hour: Cosimo had said noon and it was almost that now. She pulled a plain gown more or less at random from the lavender-scented cupboard and covered it with her dark cloak before slipping out of the house.

The streets were deserted and many of the houses still bore the grisly red plague cross. Cremona felt like a city of the dead. Isabella shivered and made her way to the Campo Santo, glancing over her shoulder every few minutes, imagining stealthy footsteps creeping along behind her.

But nothing stirred in the empty streets and Isabella understood with sudden anger that everyone was congregating in the square to witness whatever was being done to Ahasuerus. As she drew nearer she heard the monks' bell tower chiming the quarter.

The Campo Santo was Cremona's heart: it was a large square meeting place, bounded on all sides by buildings:

the Exchange and the smith's forge and several smaller buildings. A wall of the monks' house ran along the western side and the small clock tower rose above it. Half a dozen tiny side streets led off the square, all of them narrow and shadowy and cobbled. You could stand in any one of them and see everything that happened in the Campo Santo and no one would know you were there. Isabella positioned herself in the deep shadow cast by the monks' tower and scanned the crowd.

They were all there. All the townspeople and the tavern keeper and the artisans. Several of the monks – Brother Simon among them. Isabella had time to see that Simon was looking very sombre.

Cosimo was at the centre of it all, bustling importantly to and fro, talking to this person and that, and from her shadowy corner, Isabella saw the spring to his step and the unusual flush touching his normally pallid jowls and she understood that whatever was going to be done to Ahasuerus, Cosimo was behind it. Because Cosimo had known – everyone had known – Ahasuerus's intention. *Ahasuerus beckoned to me and I went*, thought Isabella.

At the centre of the square, directly outside of the forge where the smith did a roaring trade from the pilgrims and the travellers who passed through Cremona in normal times, a thick squat brazier had been set up and for a moment Isabella stared at it, puzzled. The two carters were engaged in feeding it with wood and charcoal, and as one of them bent to lift fresh wood from a basket of logs nearby, sick dread flooded Isabella's mind.

Across the top of the brazier, nearly white-hot with heat, lay long iron-handled tongs.

As the monks brought Ahasuerus out, the clock tower chimed the clear notes of noon.

* * *

211

Ahasuerus's black hair was tumbled and dishevelled and his skin was so pale that it was almost translucent. But his eyes glowed with a clear grey light, and he regarded Cosimo and the rest with icy disdain. Isabella dug her nails into her palms, praying for him to escape. But if he cannot escape, then let him not break. Please let him not show fear or pain.

Ahasuerus appeared to be listening to Cosimo with thinly concealed boredom and when Cosimo said, 'We require you to grasp in both hands the white-hot tongs from the brazier, one in each hand,' he merely nodded as if to indicate that he understood.

But Isabella, crouching in the shadowy alley, felt cold horror flood her mind.

Trial by ordeal. Trial by burning. Oh God, no. One of the oldest, one of the most barbaric forms of deciding justice. If the victim escaped unscathed it was decreed that God had intervened to prove his innocence. If he did not escape, God had left him to suffer his fate and guilt was assumed. Some form of burning or branding was almost always utilised, and in the past the grisly practice had been made just about credible by the fact that a handful of extremely holy men and women had managed to exert the force of their wills to escape being mutilated.

She stared at the brazier, seeing the shimmer of heat rising on the air, and seeing people backing away from it. The words of that other sentence, exactly as Ahasuerus had repeated them to her last night, wrenched at her mind.

'You will be scourged at the pillar while the sun passes from the east to the west side of Jerusalem . . . The next evening at sunset, you will be nailed to the Cruciferum . . . The evening after that, again at sunset, fires will be lit around the foot of the Cruciferum, and your body will burn . . .'

And now we're doing it to him again, we're burning him again.

The brazier was glowing white-hot, and Cosimo was importantly explaining what would happen. 'If you are unhurt and unscarred by the tongs from the brazier, we shall know that God has judged you innocent and—'

Ahasuerus said coldly, 'I am aware of the custom, fool. It is barbaric and brutal and it is the last resort of the weak.' His eyes raked Amati. 'Or even,' he said, deliberately, 'of the impotent,' and a murmur of delighted horror went through the watchers. Cosimo's face darkened to angry crimson and he clenched his fists. 'But,' said Ahasuerus coolly, 'if this is your wish—' He shook off the two men holding him and walking to the centre of the square, stood for a moment, apparently studying the brazier and the fiercely hot iron tongs. Then he turned away, and to Isabella, it was as if his eyes were looking at some unseen landscape: as if he knew he could not escape the torment devised, and as if he was simply concentrating his vision inwards, on to some marvellous dawn-drenched, music-filled horizon that no one else could see and no one else could hear.

As he did the last time . . .

When he turned back to the brazier, a tiny wind was ruffling the quiet square and the scent of hot iron and burning charcoal and wood was borne to where Isabella huddled, helpless and anguished. The shimmer of heat-haze rose strongly up again and people backed away once more. Ahasuerus glanced at them and his lips curved upwards in amusement.

And then he reached down and grasped the tongs.

The worst part was the stench of burning flesh. Like roasting meat, thought Isabella, shuddering and nauseated. She wrapped her arms about her body as if for warmth, rocking to and fro, her entire mind thrown forward into the square, trying to share his agony.

As his fingers closed over the glowing irons, Ahasuerus's face drained of all colour and sweat sprang out on his brow, soaking into his black hair. He staggered back, half falling, but then somehow righting himself. He had dropped the burning tongs almost as soon as he had grasped them, but Isabella could see that they had done their work. Ahasuerus's clear eyes were blurred with agony, and he was moving as if he was in a trance.

He held out his hands and a gasp went through the watchers and Isabella felt an icy hand clutch at her stomach, because his hands, his hands . . .

The skin and the flesh had melted and bubbled with the heat so that fat was running down and dripping on to the ground – greasy, colourless, exactly like fat runs out of cooking pork! – oh God, no! Sickness rose up in Isabella's throat and she swallowed convulsively and dug her nails into the palms of her hands. Mustn't be sick. Mustn't give way. Control it.

The four fingers of each of Ahasuerus's hands were fusing in the furious heat, the nails shrivelling and cracking. The tongs had fallen from his grasp and they lay at his feet, shreds of shrivelled skin adhering to them.

Let him not break, prayed Isabella in silent agony: let him hold on to whatever inner vision he has, let him continue to look beyond the agony to his far-flung horizon . . .

For a moment she thought consciousness was sliding from him, and he half fell again, sinking to his knees in the hot, dusty square. But then he raised his head and directed a look of such arrogance and such exultant triumph at Cosimo that something that was very nearly delight surged up in Isabella's mind.

Ahasuerus said, 'Well? Is this what you wished to see?' His voice was splintered with pain, but the pride was unmistakable. Isabella thought if she had not loved him before she would have done so then. But his hands, oh dear God, his hands.

It was as if half-charred lumps of meat, bleeding scarlet claws protruded from the sleeves of his robe. Raw bleeding flesh . . . Blackened finger-ends . . . Ahasuerus turned slowly, holding them out, palms uppermost, and as he faced the shaded side street, Isabella saw the agony of it, and the sickness lurched in her stomach again, so violently that this time she could not hold it back. She doubled over, retching and gasping, vomiting the sparse breakfast she had eaten on to the ground, her insides scoured, her eyes streaming.

When she finally straightened up, shuddering and wiping her mouth, it was to hear her husband saying, 'Maimed and wounded. Sufficient proof of guilt.' And then, looking round at the silent crowd, 'God did not protect him,' he said sententiously. 'And so we must count him guilty.'

It was then that Ahasuerus staggered and fell to the ground, and it was then that Simon and the monks moved.

Simon had never wholly believed in the legend of the immortal High Priest: the Scribe and the Scholar who had defiled the ancient Temple of Jerusalem with his harlot and whose name the Sanhedrin had tried to strike from history. But he had taken the vow and he had meant the words he had said, even while he was making private reservations. Now, staring at the helpless mutilated creature with the astonishing beauty and the remarkable, luminous eyes, the reservations melted and knew it had all been true. This is the creature my Order vanquished in first century Jerusalem, and this is the being I swore before God to shut away from the world for ever.

They had brought the stone sarcophagus out of the catacombs early that morning. It had taken eight of them to carry it up, and although it had been heavy it had not been as difficult as they had feared. But Simon, standing in the dim catacombs and looking down at the ancient elaborate tomb, had felt icy fingers brush the nape of his neck. So that is where they interred him. That is where they sealed his body after the sentence of the Triple Death and that is where he lay for ten centuries.

The Sanhedrin's sentence had been a travesty of Christ's own torments of course, intended to mock the heretic Priest. Simon touched the litany of Christ's sufferings in his mind, familiar from a dozen Easter vigils: the agony in the Garden . . . the Scourging at the Pillar . . . the Crowning with Thorns . . . the Carrying of the Cross . . . the Crucifixion . . . Had Ahasuerus suffered his own agonies in the same way? What about the final part of his sentence — the burning alive? How was he unmarked from that?

He looked back at the sarcophagus and thought: he didn't die then and he hasn't died now. But what happened all those centuries ago to ensure that sleep that was neither quite death nor quite life? Did the music create it? Or the grisly death sentence? And what do I do to ensure it now? Shut him into the tomb, alive and aware and slam down the lid? It was a harrowing thought.

They had brought the sarcophagus back to their own house in the Campo Santo and three of the monks had worked through the night in the carpenters' shop, fashioning a wooden inner coffin. It was plain by most standards and almost wholly unadorned, but Simon thought it would serve its purpose. The stone tomb was cumbersome and awkward, but a wooden coffin could be placed unobtrusively

216

in the shadows of the Campo Santo. Waiting for the re-interment.

Simon had been genuinely appalled at the burning of Ahasuerus's hands. He had seen the exultation in Cosimo Amati's face; he had felt the ugly sexual jealousy within the man and he had seen for the first time that this whole thing was little more than the revenge of a cuckolded husband. He has manipulated us all! thought Simon, staring across the square with its pall of grisly smoke and the stench of charred flesh in his nostrils.

The realisation was unpleasant and unwelcome, but for all that, the punishment would further Simon's own task. This was Ahasuerus, the rebel High Priest, the renegade who had threatened to return; this was the one whose Simon's Order had been formed to guard. No matter that after so long a time the vow had become perfunctory, and no matter that most of the monks in the Order had forgotten how and where Ahasuerus's body lay. Simon had taken the vow, and the vow had been to God and to his own Father Abbot, and you did not qualify a vow.

As Ahasuerus turned, Simon leapt on to him, forcing him backwards, aware that behind him the other monks were closing in. There was a moment when Ahasuerus resisted with all his strength, and when he fought back at Simon like a wild beast. Simon was unexpectedly aware of pity and admiration, because even like this, even mutilated and in screaming agony, Ahasuerus could fight.

As Ahasuerus fell back into the waiting coffin, Simon felt a tremendous surge of exultation that was so violent it was nearly sexual. He moved forward, his muscles tense, ready to meet Ahasuerus a second time, certainly expecting him to resist again.

But Ahasuerus did not resist. He lay where he had fallen, the long silky lashes fanning his cheeks, and Simon stood looking down, his thoughts chaotic, torn between triumph at having succeeded and pity and a half-fearful curiosity.

He's gone back, he thought. I don't understand how or why, but he's somehow slipped beyond us. The essence, the living, breathing thing that was the High Priest has eluded us. He glanced around the square. Something to do with the travesty of a trial that had mirrored the trial in first century Jerusalem? Something to do with the fire, even?

I don't know. I can't begin to understand. I can only thank God that it has happened. He bent to help the other monks wedge the coffin lid into place.

Isabella had crouched shivering and wretched in the little side street off the Campo Santo, rocking to and fro with agony and despair, still trembling from the violent nausea. After a time she wrapped the cloak about her, turning up the hood to hide her face, and went out into the streets again. No one gave her a second glance and for the first time ever she was glad of anonymity.

She was still reeling from what had happened: deaf and sightless and uncaring of where she went or what she did. But people were flocking into the streets to discuss what had happened, and little by little, the excited curiosity and conjecture began to pierce the shell of misery.

No one was entirely sure what had happened, save that the strange enigmatic being had been sent back into the eerie half-world he had come from, and that he had been re-interred in the stone sepulchre and the sepulchre sealed.

And now a little band of monks, led by the English Brother Simon himself, would travel out of Cremona and out of Italy, bearing the tomb with them. A better resting place, Brother Simon had said, sombrely. A safer resting place. The people of Cremona, going in rather cursory fashion about their work, told one another that while it was certainly true that the stranger had rid the city of rats, it was also being whispered that Amati had called him out of some dim and distant past and if that was so, he was better away from Cremona altogether.

Isabella, trying to listen without being recognised, managed to be drawn into one of these discussions inside the wine-shop, and interspersed a question about the monks' destination.

Well now, that was the oddest thing of all, said the wine-shop keeper, whose trade had been brisk on account of the excitement but who was not so busy that he could not pause for a word or two with a lady who looked as if she might be very comely beneath her enveloping cloak. That was the surprising part of it all.

It appeared that Brother Simon, along with eleven other monks, was returning to his homeland; the wine-shop keeper could even give a touch of verisimilitude to this snippet by adding that Father Abbot had ordered a cask of best mead for the monks to take with them on their journey.

And they were going not to England as most people seemed to think, said the wine-shop owner, but to some outlandish-named place on England's western side – an island or some such. It was nowhere the wine-shop keeper had ever heard of and nowhere he particularly wanted to hear of again, always assuming that he ever received payment for the mead, because a religious way of life did not necessarily guarantee payment of bills.

Dawn was again breaking over the little town as Isabella made her way towards the monastery.

She wondered how the strange episode would be woven

219

into the fabric of Cremona's history and into the history of the Amati family. Would Ahasuerus be a martyr or a sinner or even a devil?

But it no longer mattered, because Isabella would no longer be here. With the knowledge that Ahasuerus was being taken to Simon's homeland – an island on the west side of England, the wine-shop keeper had said – she had known that she must follow him, even though leaving Cremona would be the hardest thing she had ever done. But she could not stay. She could not bear to remain here to witness Cosimo's exultation. He would recount the story half a dozen times a day and he would gloat more and more about the part he had played, until in the end it would sound as if Cosimo had fought Ahasuerus single-handed and triumphed. The worse part would be that Cosimo would end in believing it himself.

It would be necessary to travel alone but that did not trouble her. The cat-like smile curved her lips suddenly, because there were any number of adventures that could befall you if you were travelling alone. And she would not really be alone, because she would be in the monks' shadow all the time. They would not know she was there because she would have to keep a few hours – even a few days – behind them, but if there should be a real danger, Isabella thought she could probably call on their help.

She was taking only the barest necessities. Some changes of linen; food until she should be clear of Cremona and able to buy provisions without being recognised. She had rifled Cosimo's private cupboard for money, uncaring of whether she would be branded a thief after she had gone, and she had packed all of her jewellery which she thought she could sell on the way and which should provide for her for quite a long time.

She paused as she slipped through the silent house,

looking down the stair to the workroom, and something stirred in her mind. The lyre. The old bone-lyre Cosimo had used to summon Ahasuerus from the catacombs. There was no reason to take it, and there was certainly no reason to imbue it with any magical qualities of its own. It was nothing more than wood and bone and catgut; the force was inside the music. But it was a link.

As she stood waiting in the shadow of the monastery tower, with the daybreak Office of Lauds chiming within, her mind went back to the remarkable night in the catacombs and this time the smile was no longer the cat-smile, but a real smile; the smile of the Isabella that Cosimo had never suspected existed, and that hardly anyone had suspected existed. The Isabella who had loved Ahasuerus, and who had experienced that eerie recognition, and who would one day love him again.

But she must follow him. They had shut him into the tomb, and they thought that had ended the matter. But supposing it had not? Supposing that he only slept, and that within the sarcophagus he was still alive and still aware? Sealed into the grave until the music should call him again? Like Simon, Isabella had no idea of what had sent Ahasuerus back into the death-sleep, but the thought of Ahasuerus alive and aware in the grim tomb fashioned a thousand years earlier, was unbearable.

There was only one thing to do and that was to stay close to him. To go wherever he was taken and to remain within sight and within hearing of the tomb.

And to hand down the knowledge and the music, as it had been handed down to Isabella herself, so that in some distant future, a future she could not imagine, Ahasuerus would walk in the world once more.

The secret smile curved her lips again and she slid one hand beneath the cloak and placed it on her still-flat

221

stomach. Hand down the knowledge . . .

It might be that the bone-lyre would not be the only link she would have with her High Priest.

Chapter Twenty

Moira thought she was acquitting herself fairly well so far.

The ferry crossing to Holyhead with the caravan had been uneventful and in fact a bit tedious, and Moira, who had been keyed up to expect questions or suspicious looks or even a search of their belongings, had almost felt cheated. There was no point in adventures if you could not experience a few threads of melodrama on the way. And then she remembered the dreadful thing that had happened to Kate's husband, and she remembered the coffin with its eerie occupant, and reality asserted itself. There was melodrama to spare in all this, and there was torment and danger as well.

The ferry had docked at what had seemed an unearthly hour of the morning – Moira had lost count of the days – and they had driven across Wales and down to London.

'Do you drive, Moira?' Kate had said as they were leaving Curran Glen behind.

'Well, no—'

'Oh, you mean your foot. But that wouldn't stop you driving an automatic, would it? This one's automatic – they're the easiest cars in the world to drive. We could get you a provisional licence and you could have a go sometime.'

Moira stared at Kate, caught between delight and

astonishment. Another gap in that thickthorn hedge. She managed to say thank you.

They stopped at a couple of motorway restaurants on the way which were not like anything Moira had ever encountered. It appeared that you could get petrol for your car and a bed for the night for yourself at some places, and you could order any kind of meal at any hour of the day or night. Father would have said that the motorway restaurants were filled with common loud people, and would have driven off the motorway into a town to find a nice old-fashioned dining room that could provide a cut off the joint and two veg, but Moira was fascinated by the classless service stations and the hybrid food. She liked looking at the other travellers and wondering what their journeys were about. There were families with children, mostly wearing jeans or tracksuits, talking excitedly about seeing Grandma or Auntie or friends, and there were businessmen in sharp, dark suits who discussed next month's board meeting or the extrapolated figures for the finance review and the new trade order from Japan. Sometimes there were women with them, dressed just as formally, with glossy, well-cut hair and briefcases of their own, drinking austere cups of black coffee. At adjoining tables lorry drivers ate huge platefuls of sausages and baked beans and chips at three o'clock in the afternoon, and smothered their food in tomato ketchup and sucked their teeth with automatic lasciviousness at every female under forty.

They made a detour off the motorway shortly before they got into London – it was a place called High Wycombe – to buy provisions because Kate said it would be easier to park here than in London which was always a nightmare. There was a General Post Office and a National Westminster Bank, and Moira took out some of her hoarded money. The man at the desk asked for identification, and she produced her passport and there was absolutely no problem at all. A hundred and fifty English pounds there and then, and another fifty-five to be added to the total.

'It's accumulated interest,' the cashier explained.

'How lovely.'

On her way back to the car-park Moira went into a large Waitrose supermarket and bought some food on her own account, because she had not really contributed anything to this expedition yet. It was rather fun to choose two fresh lean steaks and weigh out half a pound of mushrooms to go with them, and add a crusty French loaf and butter and cheese and tomatoes. She would cook supper for Kate that evening because Kate had been driving for what felt like half a lifetime. Moira was not very used to cooking, but anyone could grill steak and slice up mushrooms. She hesitated at the wine section, but there was a bewildering array of names and Moira had absolutely no idea what to buy. It might be worse to buy the wrong thing than to buy nothing at all. She would wait to find out what was correct to drink with steak and remember for another time.

Kate lived in a wide street in North London, with a mixture of brick or stucco-fronted houses and unexpected little restaurants and antique shops dotted along it at intervals. Some of the houses had basements with area steps and some had three or four different names against bell-pushes as if they had been divided into flats. Kate's house was a red-brick Edwardian building behind a tiny paved garden with a black spiked railing. A small patch of wasteland adjoined it.

'Very useful indeed,' said Kate, parking with the off-hand efficiency that Moira was coming to recognise. 'There was a garage at the side as you see, but the last owner turned it into a tiny flat. I'm lucky to have the bit of wasteland, because land in London's ruinously expensive.'

Moira loved the house. It was light and spacious with pale stripped-oak furniture and deep comfortable sofas and chairs and lots of books and tapes and records. The walls were plain, unpapered cream plaster, with Japanese prints hanging on them and Victorian cartoons, and framed newspaper cuttings of things that had happened in the area in the nineteenth century. Moira thought you could spend a week reading them. The downstairs cloakroom had a framed theatre poster of a sexy dark-haired man called John Martin Harvey who had played Sydney Carton in 1899 at the Lyceum Theatre, and Moira's tiny bedroom had one of Sir Henry Irving in The Bells. The rooms smelt fresh and aired and not at all like a house that had been empty for a month. There was a faint drift of lavender furniture polish.

'I have a cleaning lady,' said Kate a bit absently.

'Oh, I see.' Moira went to help Kate bring the box of groceries in. 'What about the—'

'The coffin? I think we'd better wait a bit. People in London aren't wildly curious about their neighbours, but two women lugging a coffin into a house might cause some comment. We'll wait until it gets dark.'

'Do you suppose he – it – is still asleep?' It sounded ridiculous saying it, but Kate took it dead straight.

'If he wasn't we'd have heard sounds. I think he wakes to the music, which means that as long as no one plays it we're all right. In any case, we knocked him out. Let's have something to eat before we start coffin shifting. What— Oh, fillet steak and mushrooms, how nice of you. Listen, can you manage the cooker, because if you can I'll fling a few things into the washing machine.'

In Curran Glen the whole of every Monday had been set aside for washing because Father must have a clean shirt every day, and towels and sheets had to be sorted and dealt with separately. If the world had been due to end on

Wednesday, Mother would still have had Monday's washing day and Tuesday's ironing morning.

Kate simply tipped everything in, pressed a couple of switches and left the machine to it. 'And if you can manage down here, Moira, I'm going to soak in a hot bath for half an hour with a large drink. I'm a bit stiff from driving. There's a little shower room just off the bedroom I've given you, but if you want a bath you can go after me. All right?'

Moira showered and changed quickly, and went back down to the kitchen. It was astonishing how at home she was feeling. It was even more astonishing how easy it was to be with Kate.

She grilled the steaks carefully, brushing them with melted butter, adding the mushrooms and tomatoes, and feeling very daring about sprinkling chopped garlic in the grill pan. Father said garlic was nasty foreign rubbish, but Moira was discovering it to be rather good. It was as well she had not risked buying wine because Kate had a wooden criss-cross rack filled with bottles in a tiny half-room just off the kitchen. Kate came padding downstairs, barefoot, but wearing jeans and a loose shirt like a man's, and opened a bottle of something called Rioja Reserva which was completely delicious. They washed up without any of the fuss Moira was used to where you had a separate cloth for glassware and put knives to soak with the handles out of the water, and then they sat drinking the remainder of the wine in the sitting room overlooking the garden. Night was falling and Moira remembered about bringing in the coffin, and shivered.

Kate said, 'I'll have to go into the office tomorrow, Moira. My partner's amazingly patient, but I've overstayed the leave of absence a bit this time.' She refilled her wine glass. 'And now I've got Ahasuerus, I'll set up a meeting with Vogel.' Her voice was cool and brusque, but Moira had the impression that she was squaring her shoulders as if she was about to assume an immense burden.

'Will Vogel know you? I mean – is he likely to recognise you?'

'He might. But I don't see how he can do any more than recognise me as Richard's wife or as one half of my own company,' said Kate. She leaned back, thinking. 'There's no reason why he should see anything suspicious about setting up a concert, because I've been setting up concerts for nearly eight years.'

'But this time you're involving Vogel and Serse's People,' said Moira.

'Yes. And this time I'm going to hype the thing until it squeaks,' said Kate. 'I hate hype normally, but it's meat and drink to my partner, and I'll get her in on it.'

'Does she know about all this?'

'Some of it,' said Kate. 'She's kept the business going through it all which is fortunate for me. And she'll love the idea of using the legend for publicity.' She drained the wine in her glass. 'There've been quite a number of versions of the music over the centuries,' she said. 'Jude Weissman wasn't the only one who discovered it. The eighteenth century composer Guiseppe Tartini wrote a violin sonata called the *Devil's Trill* that uses the music in the final movement, and there's a bit in Saint-Saens' *Danse Macabre* that touches it.' She paused. 'And Mozart, of course, has always been credited with knowing more about the *Black Chant* than was ever revealed.'

Moira stared at her. 'All those composers knew about it? *Mozart* knew about it?'

'Mozart almost certainly knew. There're one or two odd rumours about the company he kept towards the end of his life – when he was writing *The Magic Flute* – and he wove some very odd things into that work. It's supposed to have several Masonic rituals inside it, in fact, and there're so many other allusions that it wouldn't surprise me if somebody made out a case for the *Chant* being in there as well.' She smiled unexpectedly. 'And then there's that story about Paganini being in league with the devil to the extent that when he died in the mid-Eighteen-Hundreds he was refused Christian burial and his coffin was stored in an underground cellar for years.' She grinned. 'Grisly, isn't it? I can't think why writers of pulp horror need to think up fictional plots; there're enough real ones littering the world.'

'But – did the creature in the coffin wake each time the music was discovered or played?' asked Moira. 'Surely he couldn't have—'

'No, he can't possibly have done. I think that for one thing the music has to be exact and for another Ahasuerus has to be within reasonable distance. He was safe in that crypt, of course, and the monks were guarding him. The problem was that the music was still out in the world. Still able to cause harm. That's why it's got to be exposed.' She paused again and Moira was aware of the strength of her belief. 'I've been thinking about the format for the concert,' said Kate, 'and I think that if we use the legend for publicity, we can have a kind of pastiche of the music: jazz, baroque, heavy rock, symphonic, psalmodic, choral – we can bill it as a satanic day of music or something. That ought to bring the crowds in, people love anything tinged with the supernatural.'

'But,' Moria asked, 'can the music be transposed into all of those?'

'Yes, according to Richard's notes it seems to have a chameleon quality,' said Kate. 'It's adapted itself over the centuries – you could almost call it protective camouflage

– and it can be played in almost any form— What's the matter?'

'I think that's the most sinister thing you've said yet,' said Moira. 'You'll have the coffin at the concert of course?'

'Oh yes,' said Kate softly, and there was a sudden silence.

'Will it work?' said Moria, at last.

'Yes,' Kate replied. 'It'll work because I'll make it work. It might take more than once concert; it might take three or four. But in the end, I'll expose Conrad Vogel and I'll put an end to the Serse cult.'

Moira said tentatively, 'And Ahasuerus?'

'We'll destroy him,' said Kate.

'How?' said Moira. 'And why do you have to wait for the music to wake him before you destroy him?'

'Because,' Kate answered, 'to expose Vogel and the music, we need the full impact. And that means Ahasuerus emerging from the coffin.' She paused, and Moira felt a cold breath of fear brush her face. Ahasuerus fumbling blindly out of the tomb in the Abbey . . .

'Also I don't think Ahasuerus can be killed in a – a conventional way,' Kate added. 'Remember the mask? And the way he cried out – as if his mouth might be ruined. I think he's been mutilated – disfigured. Probably by people trying to kill him. Only they couldn't.' She made a quick gesture. 'I know it sounds absurd. Horror-film stuff at its most way-out. The Undead, the immortal creature, the amaranthine . . .'

'Boris Karloff coming up out of the swamp with the mummy-bands unwrapping,' said Moria without thinking, and Kate grinned.

'There'll be a way to destroy Ahasuerus,' she said. 'I don't know what it is because I don't know enough about him yet. But I'll find the way to do it. Only before that happens, I'm going to destroy Conrad Vogel.' She stood up. 'And now let's start coffin-moving,' she said.

Moira had been expecting to feel fear and repulsion at the sight of the coffin again, but there was a curious sense of familiarity. The brass handles at each end were smooth and cool and easy to use, and she and Kate simply lifted the coffin out of the caravan and carried it through to the back of the house.

'Down into the cellar,' said Kate. 'It's the traditional place to hide bodies, isn't it?'

'Like Paganini.'

'Yes.' She grinned. 'There's no electricity, but there's a good lock on the door.'

Kate propped the door open so that the kitchen light shone through into the cellar, and set two electric torches on the floor where they would illuminate the stair. The beams sliced through the darkness, showing up the cobwebs and the household junk: old kitchen chairs with broken backs and mangles and an ancient cabin trunk plastered with faded labels with exotic place names. It was rather cold and sad.

The steps were awkward and narrow and twice they nearly dropped the coffin. The second time Moira felt her heart lurch in panic, because surely there had been a movement from within. Had there? She stopped, listening intently.

'Nothing,' said Kate, understanding. 'I've been listening as well. If he was in the least bit aware in there, he'd have been snarling and clawing to get out long since.'

Snarling and clawing . . . I won't think about it, thought Moira firmly. They set the coffin down on the floor and straightened up. 'Easy,' said Kate. 'Who needs men? Where did I put the hammer?'

231

'What—'

'I think we should nail the lid down,' said Kate in an expressionless voice, and Moira repressed a shiver and then remembered the figure they had seen emerging from the stone tomb. 'He isn't awake, but – well, just, but.'

'Can I help?'

'Yes, hand me the nails one at a time, and ignore the Anglo-Saxon curses when I hit my thumb.'

Moira had not expected to be so upset by the hammering down of the coffin lid, but when Kate laid down the hammer she discovered that she was trembling all over.

Kate said, 'At least we know he's still unaware. I made enough noise to wake the— No, I won't say it. Are you all right?'

'Yes.'

'You don't look it. Come back upstairs and we'll have a large brandy each, we've earned it.'

'If I stay with you much longer I'll turn into a raving alcoholic.'

'Strong coffee, then.'

Moira hesitated, looking back at the coffin resting in the middle of the cellar floor. It looked rather forlorn and it suddenly seemed dreadful to be leaving it down here like this. How must it feel to be sealed alive into a coffin and abandoned?

But Kate was right, of course: Ahasuerus could not possibly be aware.

Chapter Twenty-One

Moira rather enjoyed being on her own after Kate left for her office.

She peeped into Kate's books, which ranged from Agatha Christie to Stephen King and Jane Austen, and back again via Rider Haggard and Susan Howatch, and which included a great many about music. There was a shelf of musical biographies, not just on people like Mozart and Beethoven, but more modern composers as well: Aaron Copland and Janácek and Gershwin. There were several about conductors: Henry Wood whom Moira knew about because of the Proms in London, and Arthur Nikisch whom she had never heard of but who had apparently been called the last of the romantic conductors. And there was one titled 'A Traitor of Genius', with a black and white photograph of a young man on the cover, dressed in the sharp formality of evening clothes of the Thirties. Jude Weissman. Moira reached the book down, intrigued. He was much younger than she had imagined and he was much better-looking as well if the photograph could be believed. Would Kate mind if she curled up with this for an hour or so? She thought she would not. She poured a cup of coffee from the pot made at breakfast and took it into the little sitting room at the back of the house.

The house was quiet, but in the not-completely-silent way of most houses. There were little creaks and clicks.

The ticking of the central heating clock in the kitchen. The whir of the fridge switching itself on and off. Houses always had a secret life of their own. Kate's house was not quite silent in the way that houses never were quite silent but the small sounds were friendly. It was a friendly house. Moira thought Kate and her husband would have been happy here; having friends call, Kate cooking her lovely meals for them.

Father had not liked visitors: he always said, What do they want to come calling for, poking and prying? Or: I'm not spending my money on feeding a lot of strangers. Mother's two sisters came to stay sometimes, and Mother Bernadette occasionally looked in to enlist help for church events. Father could not say much about Mother Bernadette, who seldom even accepted a cup of tea, but he always grumbled about Mother's sisters, saying it was a waste of good money, and: I suppose this means extra food to be bought. Moira thought they had not been wildly rich, but they had been what a good many people would call comfortable. You had reluctantly to conclude that Father had been rather mean. This was rather a dreadful thing to discover, although it was not as dreadful as what he had done that last night, of course – well, almost done. Didn't it say somewhere that meanness of mind indicated meanness of spirit? Father was a mean-spirited man and being free of him was as heady as – well, as heady as the wine that Kate drank. Moira thought that in time she would manage to forget the sight of him standing over her bed and the feel of his hands on her, but she would not forget the meanness and the stifling atmosphere he had built up around her.

Tumbling straight into this strange quest – the Devil's Piper and Serse's People and the music – had made running away easier; you could not be anguishing over leaving home when you had been plunged into a desperate adventure, or when you had fallen in with someone like Kate. Kate was so different from anyone Moira had ever known that she might almost be from another planet. She was certainly from another world, but that was good, because it was a world that Moira had yearned after for years. I suppose I do believe her, thought Moira suddenly, I suppose this isn't all a wild plot? But she could see no motive behind it; nobody appeared to be out for gain, in fact most of the players sounded more like victims.

She made a sandwich and a cup of tea at one o'clock. Kate had said to help herself to whatever she wanted to eat and drink. She took the sandwich and the tea back to the sitting room and the book about Jude Weissman, which was proving rather interesting. A whole chapter was devoted to his last major public performance which had been in a medieval part of Eastern Germany, near to Weimar on the outskirts of the ancient Forest of Thuringia. It seemed to be one of those lovely fairytale jumbles of dynasties and petty dukedoms, with any number of vaguely sinister legends woven into its history. After the War it had become part of the Russian zone of occupation, which Moira thought added to its remoteness. Hadn't Russian states been like another world then? Beyond the Iron Curtain.

The performance had been at Eisenach Castle which was on Thuringia's outskirts. There had been photographs of castellated battlements and a jagged-toothed yett at the centre, and circular towers and turrets. All the standard things, thought Moira. The book listed the titled and famous people who had attended the concert, most of whom Moira had never heard of, and there was a description of the evening by someone called Angelika von Drumm, who sounded racy and rather fun, and who apparently had some kind of proprietorial rights in the Castle because she referred to the concert as the most glittering night in all the history of her family's home.

Moira put the book down reluctantly, wondering if that had been the famous concert at which Jude had played the *Devil's Piper*. Kate thought he had only performed it once in public and the dates would fit. It would be interesting to read on and find out, but Moira had promised herself that she would write to Mother and the twins before Kate returned. It would not be an easy letter to write, but it was important to let them know she was all right. She could be reassuring but vague about her whereabouts: the envelope would show the London postal area but that could not be helped, and surely to goodness it was anonymous enough.

It was odd how the scratching of a pen ran so exactly in time with the scratchings and rustlings of the house. The scratching would be the kitchen noises again, or maybe the plumbing in the little half-room beyond the kitchen which led down to the cellar.

Unless the sounds were coming from the cellar itself . . .

Moira laid down her pen, listening. Was it someone outside? Or – this was far worse – someone inside? A prickle of fear brushed the nape of her neck and she sat very still, listening. It was not being fanciful to just listen; in view of what was in the cellar, it was probably quite sensible, in fact. Nobody with the smallest shred of imagination could sit in an empty house with a coffin and not hear a few creepy sounds. There would not be anything to worry about: Kate had been sure that Ahasuerus would only wake again if the music was played, and this seemed logical.

The trouble was that the sounds could no longer quite be classified as the fridge humming, or the central heating switching itself on or off. There was a faint scraping. Like wood splintering . . .? Like nails being torn out of coffin lids . . .?

The bolt to the cellar door was quite definitely drawn; Kate had done it and Moira had watched. So there was no need to keep visualising the three steps leading down from the half-room with the wine, and then the whitewashed wall with the deeply set oak door of the cellar itself. Moira could remember the faint scratch of sound the bolt had made.

Like the faint scratchings she was hearing now . . .?

This is ridiculous, thought Moira crossly. I'm suffering from did-I-switch-off-the-iron?-syndrome, that's all. I know the cellar door is bolted. I know the sounds can't be coming from the cellar. But just as you finally had to check to see had you really switched off the iron, Moira knew that she would have to go and check the bolt. She would do it now and then she would feel safe and she could finish her letter.

She went through to the kitchen and into the little half-room. And there it was: the thick heavy iron bolt, firmly and unmistakably drawn across. Relief flooded through Moira's mind, along with annoyance at her stupid nervousness. She placed both hands, palms flat, on the door just to prove how solid and how firmly bolted the door was.

She had turned to go when she caught, faintly at first, a rasp of sound from the door. Moira turned back. Was it a noise from the cellar? Wasn't it something outside, or even a mouse scuttering behind the skirting board in the quiet?

She waited and the sound came again, and fear flooded in, in huge suffocating waves.

From within the dark cellar came the sound of slow dragging footsteps coming up the stairs.

Moira jerked back from the door as if it had scalded her and stood staring at it, trembling all over, the breath catching in her throat.

Ahasuerus had broken out of the coffin! He had broken out and he was on the other side of that door! Only he can't be! thought Moira, in panic. He needs the music, he can't wake without it . . .

Even as the thought formed, the black, old-fashioned latch-handle started to move, in a blind fumbling way at first and then with more assurance. Ahasuerus, unfamiliar with modern-day door fastenings, feeling his way in the dark . . . Lifting the latch of his cellar prison . . . The door shuddered in its frame as if someone was pushing against it from the other side, and Moira shrank against the far wall. The latch clicked up and down again, and the door-frame shivered, the hinges straining outwards.

Moira tumbled out of the kitchen and stopped abruptly at the doorway into the wide hall. What to do? What was quickest? Police – yes, phone the police and also Kate. And then get out of the house and wait in the safe, friendly street where there were cars and shops and passers-by. But as she made for the hall table with the phone, there was a blur of movement from beyond the front door. Moira's heart leapt and then started to thud painfully.

Whoever had renovated the large old house had kept as a feature the Victorian red and blue glass in the upper half of the front door; Moira had rather liked the way the glass cast harlequin patterns across the plain, polished floor of the hall last evening.

But at four o'clock in the afternoon, there was no gentle dusk to cast diamond-shapes. There was thin, London sunlight filtering through the glass, sparkling on the small panes and showing up every detail clearly.

Showing up the dark bulk of a man standing outside.

Someone was standing furtively in the shelter of the

porch, looking in. And whoever the someone was, he was whistling, very softly, a sequence of notes over and over again. Moira had never, to her sure knowledge, heard the music, but she knew at once what it was.

The ancient music, the *Black Chant,* Jude Weissman's dark seductive *Devil's Piper.*

Beckoning Ahasuerus back into the world.

Moira was caught in the most complete terror she had ever known. She dared not go forward because it meant going nearer to the door and the intruder would see her through the glass panels. And she could not go back because of Ahasuerus. She stood very still and dug her nails into the palms of her hands.

The whistling was still trickling into the house, cold and silvery and insidious. There was a hypnotic quality to it, and Moira felt the hairs on the back of her neck prickle.

She looked towards the stair. Could she reach it without being seen? Yes, it was set back from the front door, just about beyond the sight-line. Keeping her back to the wall, Moira began to inch forward. She would have to be slow because the man outside would see any sudden movement. But if she could get upstairs, she could get to the phone in Kate's bedroom. She inched her way down the hall, and felt with relief the first step of the carpeted stairs. Her heart was thumping so furiously she thought the intruder would hear it, but she crouched low, going up the stairs on all fours, looking behind over her shoulder as she went.

She stopped on the first landing. This was where the main bedrooms were and the bathroom, and a tiny slip of a room that had once been a dressing room. At the far end was the little secondary stair that wound up to the attic. Moira stopped and looked down into the hall.

The music was still pouring in and even through her

panic, she could feel the sensual pull. *Follow me and do what I tell you . . .*

This is what Kate's husband heard, thought Moira, staring at the motionless figure beyond the glass. This is what all those others heard. Do what I tell you. Shoot out your brains, go home and turn on the gas, swallow a hundred aspirin and wash them down with a bottle of gin . . . Prove I am your master. Is that what this is about? Mastery over people's minds? And is that Conrad Vogel standing outside, peering in through the glass, calling to Ahasuerus? Vogel . . . It's a cold name, a shivery name, midway between an ogre and a vulture.

The man was standing perfectly still in the porch, but the light was behind him so that Moira could only see him as an outline. She thought he could not see her up here and she thought she could get to the phone extension in Kate's bedroom and ring the police emergency number. What should she say? Come and rescue me. Why, madam? Well, because somebody is standing in the porch outside whistling and there's this corpse in the cellar that's come to life . . . Would it really sound as far-fetched as that? She hesitated and as she did so, an articulated lorry rumbled past, shaking the ground as it went. Under cover of the sound, the man outside lifted something small and hard and brought it smashing into the small pane of glass nearest to the lock. As Moira froze into horrified disbelief, he knocked out the shards of glass with a black-gloved hand, and reached through to the inside latch.

The door swung open and he was in the house.

Moira sank into a frightened little huddle on the carpeted floor of the landing, staring down into the hall. As the man moved forward she saw him quite plainly. Thin-faced, grey hair. If this was Conrad Vogel he was older than she had visualised. He was at least forty and probably nearer fifty and he had the coldest eyes Moira had ever seen.

He did not look up the stairs. He crossed the hall and Moira was aware of him standing very still, listening. For Ahasuerus? And then he moved again, going purposefully towards the kitchen. He's located him, thought Moira. Either he knows where Ahasuerus is or he can hear him. He's going to let him out. Oh God, what do I do? He's drawing the bolt on the cellar door. There's the music again.

Come out into the world, Piper . . .

Moira began to crawl towards Kate's bedroom. Into the room, close the door – with luck there might even be a key – and then dial 999. This was a tangible emergency – it was no longer a matter of walking corpses or vague menaces. An intruder had broken in and Moira was hiding upstairs, frightened for her life. But would Vogel hear her? She remembered with horror that if you lifted an extension phone, the other extensions usually pinged. The main phone was in the hall, but there was another extension in the kitchen.

She paused again, trying to hear sounds from below, trying to gauge where Vogel was and – this was more important – where Ahasuerus was. Vogel was still at the back of the house. Would it be better – would it be safer to run down the stairs and out into the street and yell for help? Would she get that far? Angry bitterness welled up, and she thought: even if I could run properly, he'd hear me. Damn being lame! If I could walk properly I could be out of the house in ten seconds flat!

As she hesitated, there was a sound from the attic stairs behind her and the sudden terrifying awareness of another human being creeping up behind her.

A hand came over her mouth and a man's voice said in a harsh whisper, 'Don't make a sound.'

His hand was like an iron clamp over her mouth. Moira struggled and felt the other arm come out to imprison her. There was a warm press of masculinity and the clean scent of soap or male deodorant. He was holding her so tightly that she could barely breathe.

And then Vogel appeared in the hall, and behind him, dragging its painful way in his wake, was something dark and sinister; something that wore a dark cloak and whose face was hidden by a deep hood. Moira struggled again and her captor tightened his grip.

'Keep quiet and keep still,' he said in her ear.

Vogel was standing in front of the street door, the coloured glass casting a red glow across his face. He was still whistling the music: it trickled through the hall, cold and inhumanly beautiful. It struck at your innermost being and it fastened a vice about your mind so that you could not think. I'm in the grip of an intruder – Vogel's accomplice? – and I can't *think*! cried Moira in silent anguish.

Ahasuerus was level with Vogel now, his stance one of rather terrible humility. His head was bowed and the deep hood hid his face.

Vogel reached in his pocket and Ahasuerus flinched as if fearing a blow. There was the glint of a hypodermic and as he crumpled to the floor, Vogel moved towards him.

The man finally loosened his hold on Moira. Keeping one hand over her mouth, with his free hand he grabbed her wrist and half dragged, half carried her up the attic stairs.

Once inside, he locked the door and, pocketing the key, crossed the room and stood looking down on the street through a narrow window.

Moira took a deep rather shaky breath and straightened up, looking about her.

The attic was a long, sloping-ceilinged room, dimly lit by a small lamp on a low table at the far end. Moira's scared eyes took in the fact that it was furnished with unexpected comfort, and that there were two or three rooms, apparently stretching out over the garage at the side of the house. Had Kate said something about a flat added on? At the far end, a door was half open, and Moira glimpsed a minuscule kitchen.

The man was still at the window, his back to her. He was tall but rather slender, and the light from the reading lamp fell across the lower part of his body. He was wearing dark corduroy trousers, a navy sweater and sneakers. Unremarkable. Only he isn't, thought Moira, the fear scudding across her mind, her heart pounding. I can *feel* that he isn't.

In a completely ordinary voice, without turning round, the man said softly, 'Listen. And trust me. Please trust me. We haven't very much time.'

Moira was standing with her back pressed against the locked door. She thought if she could have been sure of not alerting Vogel or Ahasuerus, she would have smashed the nearest window and yelled for help.

'I'm not going to hurt you,' said the man. He had still not moved. The shape of his head was silhouetted against the pale oblong of the window: a thatch of thick glossy gold. 'It's all right, Moira,' he said. 'It is Moira, isn't it? Yes, I thought I'd got it right. Moira, I promise you it's all right.'

It was probably illogical, but his use of her name made Moira feel suddenly safer.

'That was Conrad Vogel just now, wasn't it?' said the man. 'He broke in to get the – the creature we saw in the hall.'

Moira had no idea of what to say or what to do, but she said, 'Ahasuerus. Yes.'

'Ahasuerus.'

It came out softly and very thoughtfully, and Moira dredged up her courage and said, 'Would you mind telling me who you are, please?'

For a moment she thought he was not going to reply, and then he turned and walked into the circle of light cast by the table lamp, and the soft glow fell across his face.

Moira heard her own gasp of shock. One hand flew to her mouth, as if to force back a scream.

Terrible. *Terrible*. A face so mutilated and so grotesque that you could not believe it was a human face. A nightmare . . .

The skull beneath the thick corn-coloured hair was lopsided, so that you had the impression of a brain that was lumpish and distorted. The face was ugly beyond belief: spoiled, thought Moira. *Spoiled*. Where the nose would have been was a thin ridge of bone with two nostrils, and beneath them a flat mouth, pulled back into a shark's cruel enigmatic smile. The cheek-bones were lopsided, pushing the eyes up, giving a vicious idiot tweak to a face that must once have held intelligence and humour and all the ordinary things.

'Who are you?' whispered Moira, but even as she said it, she knew who this was.

The man said gently, 'My name is Richard Kendal. I'm Kate's husband.'

Chapter Twenty-Two

Richard was still looking through the window. His back was to the light so that Moira was aware only of the glossy thatch of hair. Like this the terrible face was no more than a blurred outline; in fact until you saw it, you would think you were about to see rather an attractive man. He had been firm and strong when he had grabbed her but he had not been ungentle. Had he actually saved her from Vogel and Ahasuerus? Yes, but why? A shudder went through her.

'You didn't die,' she said, still speaking in a whisper, but her mind in such turmoil that for a moment she even forgot why they dared not risk being overheard.

Richard glanced at her, and then said, 'No. I didn't die.' He turned his back again, and said, 'Although it might have been better for Kate if I had.'

The bitterness in his voice was so dreadful that Moira could not think of anything to say. And then Richard said, 'Hold on, Vogel's coming out again.'

'What's happening?' Moria was no longer mindlessly terrified, and although she was scared, she was beginning to focus on the other danger downstairs again.

'Vogel's unlocking the back of a Range Rover,' said Richard. 'It's parked blatantly in the drive as well, the cheek of the man— There's a damn great packing case in the back, exactly like a—'

'What?'

'Like a coffin,' said Richard slowly. And then, as Moira moved forward, 'Don't come too near the window,' he said. 'Vogel might look up and see movement—No, it's all right, he's come back into the house.' He turned around again, so that his back was against the light. 'That's the bastard who did this to me, you know. And Kate's trying to smoke him out, isn't she? To get evidence. Yes, I thought I'd got it right. I'll ring Kate the minute he goes but in the meantime, at least let's get the registration number of his car. I think I can just see it – yes, I can – would you jot it down, Moira, there's paper and pen on the desk over there.'

Moria scribbled the number and then went to stand beside Richard, looking out of the window cautiously. 'He's coming out,' she said. 'That was the scullery door closing, wasn't it? And he's got—'

'He's got Ahasuerus,' said Richard, staring down to the street. 'At least I suppose it's Ahasuerus. He's wrapped him in a bolt of old felt or a carpet or something. Clever. Even if anyone sees, there's nothing very remarkable about loading a rolled-up carpet into a car in broad daylight. Could you keep an eye on him while I phone Kate? Good girl. Don't let him see you.'

As he dialled the number, Moira felt him look across at her again. 'Kate didn't tell you about me, did she?' he said. 'No, I can see she didn't.'

'She did tell me,' said Moira carefully. 'But I might have misunderstood—'

'I keep a pretty low profile,' said Richard expressionlessly. 'You'll understand why.'

Moira said carefully, 'I know about the music. The *Chant*.'

'You're not one of Serse's People, are you? No, I can see you're not, I think I could still spot one of those poor sods at twenty paces, because – hold on a minute – Lauren?

246

It's Richard. Is Kate there? It's rather important—'

Moira, trying to be polite, concentrated on watching what was happening below. Vogel was still leaning into the back of the Range Rover's interior; he seemed to have loaded his gruesome burden inside the coffin-shaped box, and Moira thought he was arranging some pieces of green baize over it.

Behind her she heard Richard replace the receiver, but when she turned round, he had retreated into the shadows beyond the circle of lamplight again. But Moira caught the vivid blue of his eyes. They were the most expressive part of him.

'Did you get her?'

'I got her partner,' said Richard. 'Kate was out. She was out because she'd gone to keep a business appointment.'

He stopped, and Moira said horrified, 'Vogel. Wasn't it? She went to meet Vogel?'

'Yes. It was in her diary quite clearly. She was meeting him at twelve-thirty for lunch,' said Richard. 'And she hasn't got back.'

Moira stared at him. 'But – it's almost five.' Below them there was the sound of the Range Rover's boot slamming shut. They looked at one another, and then Richard crossed the room, and dragged a jacket and scarf out of a large wardrobe.

Moira said, 'You're going after him. Aren't you?'

'Yes.' Richard seemed to hesitate, and then said. 'He might have Kate or he might not. There might be a perfectly ordinary explanation. But I'll have to find out. And I'll have to move very, very fast.' He turned to face her and met her eyes. 'Moira, I don't think I can do it on my own.'

He stopped, and Moira thought: he wants me to go with him. After Vogel. He's afraid he won't be able to cope with the world after so long. Yes, but what he doesn't know is that I can't cope with the world either. Or can I? Oh, God what do I do? I don't know whether I can trust him. I don't even know if he's sane . . . He's been shut away up here . . . And Kate pretends he's dead. No, pretends is the wrong word, she implies it. He tried to shoot his face away and it isn't sane to do a thing like that . . . I could pretend I don't understand. Because he hasn't actually put it into words. I could let him go by himself and I could phone the police.

But she was not surprised when she heard her voice say, 'I'll come with you.'

The relief in his eyes was instant and unmistakable. It was as if his entire means of expressing emotion had been channelled into his eyes. 'Thank you, Moira,' he said.

'What do we do?' It was good to discover that she sounded perfectly calm and practical.

'The minute we hear him drive off,' said Richard, tumbling a bureau drawer open and scooping up a cheque book and credit card, 'we'll have to be down the stairs and after him. It'll take a minute or two for him to manoeuvre that thing into the traffic at this time of day, but it won't take that long. Kate left her car here, didn't she? – yes, I thought she had. Does she still keep the keys on the hook by the cooker? All right, I'll get the keys while you snatch up anything you want.' He sent her a twisted grin. 'I never knew a woman who'd go out of the house without her handbag,' he said, and then, without warning, 'have you got any cash?'

'Well, some—'

'Good. I'll pay you back afterwards but we don't know how far we might have to drive, and if we need petrol, cash is quicker than a cheque.' He stopped, and Moira heard the sound they had both been waiting for. The throaty growl of the Range Rover's engine firing.

They went down the stairs and across the hall to the

back of the house almost without thinking about it and as Richard grabbed the car keys, Moira dived into the hall for her handbag and the jacket that was thrown over the banisters.

As Richard unlocked Kate's car, he said suddenly, 'You're Irish, aren't you? That probably means Catholic? Then pray to every saint in heaven that I can still remember how to drive!'

He flinched as the fading daylight and the street sounds hit him, but he remembered perfectly well how to drive. He pushed Moira into the passenger seat and fired the engine, swinging the car into the stream of traffic.

'He's still in our sights,' he said pointing. 'See? Four cars ahead. At least a Range Rover is easy to follow. Flashy, but distinctive. Did you bring the note of the registration number—? Oh, well done. Hang on to it, we might need it.'

Moira glanced covertly at him. He had pulled on a plain black jacket in the attic and had jammed on to his bright hair a wide-brimmed hat, a bit like a jazzed-up homburg. From a distance he would look a bit eccentric but no more than a great many people Moira had seen since leaving Curran Glen. As they merged with a double line of traffic, he gestured to the glove compartment. 'I used to keep sunglasses in there. If Kate hasn't thrown them out they'll give me even better concealment.'

'They've still here,' said Moira, after a minute.

'Thanks. God, I'd forgotten how loud everything was and how people rush—' He put the glasses on and Moira thought he would pass as very nearly ordinary now. 'That,' said Richard, making her jump, 'is the idea. If we're to follow that monster without being spotted I can't chance being noticed. How much do you know about all this, by the way? You don't have to tell me anything you don't want to: I trust Kate's judgement completely – I always have.'

'I'll tell you when we're out of this,' said Moira. 'But I know about Ahasuerus and the music, and the Hampstead Concert.' She paused, and said, 'Kate said there had been a shotgun— You don't have to tell me either,' she said.

'I don't know much of it to tell,' said Richard, intent on driving. 'I tried to kill myself. No, that isn't at all what happened: I was *ordered* to kill myself. I can't put it any better than that, even after all this time. I certainly haven't an explanation. Suicide was the last thing in my mind that day. I was researching the Serse cult and the music – Kate told you about all that, did she? – yes, good. I was looking forward to talking to the Serse People, and I was enjoying the concert – dammit, I was enjoying life.' His voice changed suddenly and he said softly, 'I was married to Kate. Who would want to opt out of that?' He frowned and Moira waited. 'I ought to have died, of course,' said Richard. 'I only survived because the barrel of a shotgun's so long: apparently I jammed it under my chin and forced my head too far back. The bullet ploughed upwards. But Vogel intended me to die.'

'Because you resisted the music?'

Again the quick, sidelong glance. 'Yes. That's perceptive of you.'

'It was Kate's conclusion, not mine.'

'Kate,' said Richard, and the twisted smile touched his lips. 'She half bullied, half seduced me through all the operations: I lost count of the number. I lost track of time as well. There were repairs and bone surgery and skin grafts. But she wouldn't let me give up. She's a witch or a saint – maybe she's both. I hope she finds a bit of discreet consolation here and there,' he said unexpectedly. He glanced sideways, and Moira, unsure of how this ought to be answered, but hearing the desolation in his voice, suddenly understood what he must have been like before the music destroyed him. I believe it's all right, she thought. He's clever and nice and intuitive – all the things Kate said he was. He's bitter and sad as well, but what else would he be, for heaven's sake? I'll take him straight for the moment and I'll only worry if things change.

'Where's Vogel going?' she said, after a few bewildering turns through London. 'Do we know?'

'Not in the least. I'm just following blindly,' said Richard. 'This traffic's awful, isn't it? I'd truly forgotten how raucous and impatient the world was. I feel like a monk emerging from solitude and— What have I said?'

'Nothing.'

'Yes, I have. I've touched a nerve,' said Richard. 'Oh, there's the River – see? Over to your right. A whole world in itself, the Thames. Very interesting, River people. I once wrote a— Hold on, he's turning off. I don't think he knows he's being followed; this car's pretty anonymous.'

'Where's he going?' said Moira, as they shot forward. London seemed to be a huge confusing city, filled with traffic and people and cars all in a tearing hurry, and with bewilderingly complex road systems. Richard had flinched several times from the streams of cars, but he was coping.

'Docklands, by the look of it,' said Richard, and sent her another of the skewed smiles. 'We're going into the land of converted wharves, and millionaire teenagers from the City, Moira.'

'Millionaire teenagers—'

'They used to be called yuppies,' said Richard. 'At least they did the last I knew.' He gripped the steering wheel.

'I'm not sure what's going to be at the end of all this, Moira, but I've got a feeling that it wouldn't hurt to cross your fingers. And you could keep praying as well.'

Chapter Twenty-Three

Kate had left her office at twelve o'clock, picking up a taxi in Charing Cross Road, partly because she was unsure of the exact location of Vogel's office and partly because she wanted to present an unflurried appearance when she got there. It was not very likely that he would see her arrive because his office was at St Katharine's Docks which meant it would probably be too high up, but if he did look out, he must not see his twelve-thirty lunch appointment trundling up and down the street, windblown and dishevelled and squinting at numbers. He must see an efficient lady, emerging coolly from a taxi, attending an everyday business meeting. As she paid off the taxi, she glanced at her watch. Twelve-twenty-three. Exactly right. She should be entering his office at two minutes before the half hour.

It was impossible to pretend that this was a run-of-the-mill meeting. Her heart was racing, and she studied her reflection in the stainless steel wall of the lift. All right? She had scooped her hair into a silky twist on top of her head that morning and secured it with a thin thread of jade and she was wearing a calf-length black skirt with suede boots under it and a black shirt. Over this she had put a sleeveless green surcoat which had a vaguely medieval cut and which reached her ankles. The swish of the velvet surcoat was subtly reassuring. At the last minute she had wound a long jade and sapphire silk scarf about her neck.

All right? thought Kate again, and then with a spurt of anger: this is ridiculous! I'm about to beard the purveyor of the devil's music in his den – the monster who destroyed Richard – and I'm worrying what I look like.

The lift doors parted and Kate took a deep breath and stepped out.

Conrad Vogel met her in a large light room on the fourth floor, with huge windows and a view over the grey, mist-wreathed river. Kate, trying to take in everything at once, received the impression of cool austere furnishings – frosty-blues and whites – that formed a background for Vogel's own vibrancy. He sat behind a large glass-topped table, which held only a leather-bound notebook and a crystal sphere for holding pens. Kate was given a chair facing him.

They were in more or less the same kind of business, she and Conrad Vogel, but this up-market converted wharf was light years away from Kate's own office on a corner of Old Compton Street, where, once you had climbed the five gruelling flights up, you had a warm, friendly view of wine bars and bistros and Soho porn cinemas, and where the walls were lined with books and records and the old framed prints of London theatres which Kate's partner hunted out with the compulsion of an addict. Vogel's apartments had a hushed thick-carpeted aura which felt unreal compared to Kate's office, where phones rang incessantly and people were always calling in for a drink or a cup of tea on their way to somewhere else. Richard had once said that uncluttered austerity in a workplace was usually indicative either of immense activity or the complete lack of it.

The potent eyes she remembered from the Hampstead concert focused upon her and she felt a lurch of something that was half fear and half blazing excitement. This is it! thought Kate. This is the thing I've been building up to and waiting for and looking forward to for three years. I'm about to bait the trap.

Conrad Vogel was tall and thin as she remembered him, with close-cut grey hair and steely grey eyes and a narrow sensual mouth. But he was older than her recollection – probably in his late forties – and he was more urbane, as if he might have worn one mask for the Hampstead concert, an abrasive, aggressive, magnetism mask, but had donned another, smoother one for this meeting.

He was dressed in conventional modern fashion, with dark trousers and a buttoned-collar tie-less shirt, but it was discreetly expensive conventionalism. Kate thought that the shirt was probably Turnbull & Asser and that his shoes would be Italian leather. The villain was turning out to be a silk-lined villain behind his mask. She had expected this, however.

What she had not expected was smooth charm, or the impression of controlled force beneath the silk exterior, or – and this was disturbing – a strong sexual magnetism. He's attractive, thought Kate, momentarily taken aback. He's very attractive indeed. This is someone I'd be rather pleased to be seen with. And then, with horror: this is someone I could go to bed with. Appalled disgust scalded her mind, and for the first time since that night on the Heath three years ago, her confidence wavered. I can't do it! I can't possibly outwit someone like this! And then she remembered Richard – sweet, sensitive, brilliant Richard – and she thought of all those suicides – clever, creative youngsters – and she knew that somehow it had to be done.

Vogel was asking whether she would have something to drink – a cup of tea or coffee, or a glass of wine, even, before they left for the restaurant.

'There is a seafood restaurant near here that is very good. That would be acceptable to you?'

'Yes, certainly.'

He spoke almost perfect English, but Kate thought he was not English. Was he German or Austrian? This was something she had not picked up in their brief telephone conversation. It would be best to keep a clear head, and so she asked for coffee. Vogel poured it from a filter machine at the far side. It was very good coffee, plainly freshly ground, and it came in expensive-looking bone china cups. Silk-lined on all levels. She drank the coffee and kicked her mind back on course.

'Mr Vogel, thank you for seeing me.' Her voice was the voice of the professional who was known in her own circles as a sharp resourceful business lady. Good!

'Conrad, please.' His voice was as velvet as the rest of him, but Kate fancied she could hear the steel beneath. The razor under the silk. The knife under the cloak. Don't forget the knife, Kate. He was watching her, as if saying: and now it is your turn.

She said, 'And I am Kate.' A pause. She met the cool, grey eyes steadily. They were cold, precise eyes. They made you think of razors, of glinting axe blades, of sinister, triangular fins slicing through cold, murky water.

Kate said, 'I'm currently arranging several concerts – a mixture of straight classical and some modern music – and I think you control several young musicians who could be included in my programme. Assuming we could reach a sensible agreement about commission, and assuming my backers agree, it's more than possible that we could join forces on this promotion.' This was a not unstandard opening, and Vogel would recognise it as such.

He nodded, and reached for the notepad, flipping out the nib of a silver pen as he did so. Everything about him is cool and expensive, thought Kate. He said, 'Your backers are—'

'Anxious to remain nameless for the moment.'

Vogel smiled and leaned back. 'Tell me about your idea.'

It was easier than Kate had expected. She went into the presentation she had lain awake most of the night devising, explaining the plan for a series of concerts at historic houses, explaining how her backers were interested in using classical and modern music in the same itinerary. The idea was to mirror their settings in the music as much as possible: baroque music for the places built during the Restoration; folk music that echoed the countryside they were in at the time and so on. It was not a particularly new idea, but they hoped to treat it in a new way, said Kate. They would be playing modern music as well, of course. It was important to call to the followers of today's cults. She paused as she said this, trying to gauge his response.

But Vogel was listening with apparent interest, and Kate felt her confidence returning. She was on familiar ground; this was what she knew about, this was what she was good at. She began to enjoy explaining her ideas to him and painting her word-pictures, exactly as if this was an ordinary promotion.

But all the time, several layers beneath consciousness, ran the knowledge that she was face to face with Richard's destroyer, she was confronting the creature who had uncovered the devil's music and created Serse's People and destroyed people's minds and lives.

When she finished speaking, Vogel asked a number of questions and Kate realised at once that he had grasped almost all of the details instantly. He had a sharp, incisive mind and it would be difficult to fool him.

And then without warning, he smiled, and Kate felt a shiver of apprehension. The knife glinting.

Vogel said, 'And now we will stop playing games, Kate.' And produced from his desk drawer a revolver, and pointed it at her.

'I am not going to shoot you,' he said. 'But you are going to do exactly what I tell you.'

This was so ridiculous as to be absurd. This was the classic line: the German-accented voice saying, You will obey my orders . . .

Kate forced anger into her voice and said, 'I haven't the least idea what you mean.' Had that sounded sufficiently outraged? She reached for her shoulder bag and stood up.

Vogel said, 'Sit down, Kate. If you try to run away, I shall have to shoot you. I have no intention of killing you, but perhaps I will shoot you in the leg so that you cannot run away. A bullet in the kneecap is said to be extremely painful.' He smiled, and there at last was the villain, the shark who spun the beautiful, evil music that swallowed people's minds . . . Kate felt an icy lurch of fear. This is real.

She said, 'What are you going to do with me?' and was annoyed to find herself using such a hackneyed phrase.

The knife-smile showed again. 'First, I am going to make sure you cannot continue your troublesome investigations into my people,' he said. 'And secondly, I am going to use you as bait.'

There was a sudden silence, and Kate stared at him. 'Richard,' she said at last. 'It's Richard you want, isn't it?'

'I admit I should very much like to have Richard,' said Vogel, and a spasm of anger twisted his face. 'Richard was one of the very few who managed to resist the music and do you know, I found that immensely annoying.'

'I can believe it,' said Kate sarcastically. 'He eluded you.'

'Yes. He was getting too close to understanding the music's source and something had to be done. I could of course have disposed of him, but I prefer to keep inside the law. And so I marked him out as a—'

'Neophyte?' said Kate tartly, and Vogel said,

'Convert would be nearer. You understand about Serse's People do you—? Yes, I see you do. The *Black Chant* has been put to a number of uses over the centuries, but I think this is the first time it has been used to beckon to people's minds . . . And I have gathered in some extraordinary minds, Kate. Bright, clever, *young*— There is no power so great as having power over young, malleable minds. I think no one has ever before channelled the music in quite that way— That is what I have been doing,' said Vogel. 'But of course, you know that. Richard knew it as well.' He paused, and a look of sudden greed came into his eyes. 'Richard,' he said softly. 'All that intuitive brilliance and all those teaching gifts— He would have been a valuable recruit; the youngsters would have followed him and he could have been of very great use to me.'

Kate said very deliberately, 'What about the others you failed with? All those others who fought you like Richard did, and ended up dead or destroyed? If you go on littering your path with suicides, people will soon start getting suspicious. They'll ask awkward questions.' Like I did, said her mind suddenly, only nobody listened. I wonder if I'm going to get out of this. The light modern room was beginning to seem oddly blurred. She frowned, forcing her mind to focus.

'Once I have Ahasuerus the suicides will end,' said Vogel. 'The music is powerful and Ahasuerus is powerful as well – or so the legend tells. But combined they must be invincible. With them together, there is nothing I could not do, no one whose mind I could not reach—'

Kate heard for the first time the escalating note in his voice but then Vogel said in a prosaic tone, 'I am really very grateful to you for bringing Ahasuerus to England, Kate. It saved me a tedious task – that unpleasant Irish crypt – and also an irritating journey.' Kate looked up sharply, and he smiled. 'You are very easy to follow, my dear,' he said. 'And Serse's People can make themselves very unobtrusive if they have to. Who looks at a couple of youngsters or a handful of students? I kept tabs on you very nicely, Kate. You have brought Ahasuerus out of Curran Glen, and now I can present to my people the Master I promised them.'

Kate stared at him and thought: of course, he's mad. I heard it in his voice a minute ago, only he's quenched it now. Is that really what he's going to do? Present Ahasuerus to Serse's People as some kind of – of what? Messianic being? A Christ-figure? He won't be the first, of course and he certainly won't be the last. There've been charismatic leader-figures all through history, and some of them have wielded very great power indeed. And if he has Ahasuerus and the music . . .

She said, 'So you're going to make Ahasuerus your puppet, are you? I hope you aren't forgetting all those other power-mad men who created a monstrous servant and saw it get away from them?'

Vogel laughed. 'Frankenstein and the man-monster? We aren't in the pages of Gothic fiction, Kate.'

'Of course not. I was thinking,' said Kate coldly, 'more of Adolf Hitler and the fall of the Third Reich.'

There was an abrupt silence. That's hit a nerve, thought Kate. I've touched a core of anger, as well. Damn, I've over-reached!

Vogel had been standing behind the desk, but now he came around it, and stood over her, the gun resting against her head. It felt cold and very evil. Kate felt her courage draining, and sick waves of terror closed about her head, but she said, 'You do know, do you, that I left word of where I was coming. The appointment is recorded in my diary. This will be the first place Richard will look—' She stopped. 'That's what you want,' she said, staring up at him. 'You want Richard to follow me— Supposing I simply let you kill me?'

'I shan't kill you,' said Vogel. 'If you resist me, I shall first of all spoil your face, as I did your husband's.' He traced the outline of her cheek with the gun's muzzle, and smiled as she flinched. 'I should enjoy doing that,' he said softly. 'And afterwards I could turn my attention to your precious Richard, because make no mistake, Kate, there are still a good many things I can do that would hurt Richard very much indeed. One of your fingers in the post – perhaps with your wedding ring still on it. The next day your thumbs— He would soon come running into my net.'

'How dreadfully second-rate,' said Kate scoffingly. 'You're sounding like a bad horror film. Chopped-off bits of bodies sent through the mail— That went out with Jack the Ripper and the half-eaten kidney, Conrad. Is this the part where I recoil in terror and ask where you're taking me? Not,' added Kate, pleased that her voice was coming out so steady, 'that I wouldn't like to know, you understand.'

Vogel said, 'We're going to the place that I have made the centre and the focus of Serse's People. Hadn't you tracked that down, Kate? How lax of you.' He reached across the desk, and picked up a set of keys.

'Serse's People,' said Vogel, 'have their – I could almost say their headquarters – in a place deep within the old kingdom of Thuringia: today part of modern Germany. That's where we're going.'

Kate stared at him, her mind tumbling. She said, with

what she thought was a creditable attempt at scorn, 'You can't possibly hope to take me out of the country – I haven't my passport with me for starters. We'll be stopped at the first checkpoint we reach.'

'We shan't be stopped,' said Vogel. 'You won't need a passport, because you won't be visible, Kate. Stand up – move slowly.'

Kate stood, and at once the room tilted. She grabbed the back of the chair. *My God, he's drugged me!*

'In the basement garage here is my car,' said Vogel. 'And in the back of it is a long wooden packing case. You'll be travelling inside it, Kate – it bears a rather sinister resemblance to a coffin, I'm afraid, but perhaps you won't mind that. If you are lucky, you won't even be aware of it.'

He unlocked the door and motioned her through, and Kate glanced up and down the corridor outside, assessing her chances. *Could she call for help? Or spring on him when he locked the door behind them?* She found that she was forced to lean against the wall to stop her legs from buckling. *Damn. I believe he really did drug me, the bastard!*

'Yes, you are drugged,' said Vogel offhandedly. He pulled the door closed, and the Yale lock clicked of its own accord. Vogel took her arm, pulling her towards the lift. 'And yes, it was in the coffee,' he said. 'Chlorpromazine – very useful and astonishingly easy to obtain. Quite harmless – little more than a strong sedative – but it should render you unconscious for the journey.

'And if you're contemplating calling for help or trying to run, don't bother.' He pressed the button and the lift slid up, its doors opening smoothly. 'I'm the only tenant of this building now, unfortunate how many of the yuppies over-reached in the Eighties, wasn't it? Parts of Docklands are like a ghost town these days. But that serves my purpose very well this afternoon.' He pushed her into the lift, and Kate sagged against the wall, her senses blurring. There was a thin whine as the lift descended.

The Range Rover was parked almost directly outside the lift and the basement was deserted. It looked as if Vogel had told the truth about the building being empty.

Kate was barely keeping back the overpowering waves of unconsciousness, but she felt Vogel take her hands and loop thin rope or twine about her wrists. As he bent to open the Range Rover's boot, she saw, as if from a great distance, the long wooden box wedged in the back. A coffin. Dear God, he's going to put me inside it. The ground was tilting sickeningly, and awareness was sliding away down a long echoing tunnel. Even if I could run, I wouldn't get six feet, she thought bitterly. And anyway, he'd shoot me. Chlorpromazine. I suppose he did tell the truth about that? But she could dimly remember Richard being prescribed doses of it at the beginning, as a sedative.

Vogel was opening the coffin-box, but his free hand about her wrist was hard and strong. Kate thought even without it she would have stayed put, because she could not have run two steps now. When Vogel spoke again, she heard him through a rushing tunnel. He said, 'I believe I have judged the dosage of the drug accurately, Kate, and I believe you will be unconscious until we reach Eisenach.'

In a blurred voice, Kate managed to say, 'Eisenach—'

'Eisenach Castle,' said Vogel. 'The place where, over fifty years ago, Jude Weissman played the ancient beckoning that he called the *Devil's Piper*. The place that has become the base for Serse's People. As we speak, they will all be making their way to the Castle – some by foot, some by road, some by air or sea. It's a pilgrimage, Kate, a mass bringing-together of my people.' Again, the soaring note of madness. Kate shivered. 'They are coming to meet the One I promised them,' said Vogel. 'They are coming to pay homage to the Devil's Piper.' He pushed her forward. 'This is your travelling compartment,' he said. 'And in a little while, you will have a companion.'

He paused, and Kate, her mind being sucked down the whirling tunnel, was dimly aware of Vogel smiling down at her, and of his voice swooping about her head.

'When I have you stowed away, my dear, I shall be loading up everything for the concert. It will take some little time, I'm afraid, but you will be long beyond knowing about it.

'And then,' said Vogel, 'I am going to drive out to your house for Ahasuerus. There is room for the two of you in here.

'You will travel to Eisenach Castle in the arms of the Devil's Piper, Kate.'

The drug was closing in as Vogel lifted her into the car's interior, but there was still a vestige of dreadful awareness left.

A thick blanket or a rug lined the box: at least he has that much consideration! thought Kate hazily. She felt him bend over her, sliding one hand under her thighs, the other about her shoulders, and then he was lifting her easily. He's thin but he's wiry and strong, thought Kate, torn between wanting to hold on to consciousness and praying for oblivion.

But she was still hovering on the borders of awareness. She could smell that Vogel wore the same aftershave as an old boyfriend, someone from her university days . . . The scent touched her nostrils. Didn't they say that the sense of smell was the last one to go? No, that's hearing. I can still hear. I can hear that Vogel's breathing a bit fast because of the exertion. I wish I weighed eighteen stone and was six feet tall, so that he'd have had a heart attack or a hernia when he picked me up . . . He's laying me down now – it's like a travesty of being taken to bed – I'm going to bed with Ahasuerus, God, no . . .! I suppose this is the punishment for fooling the monks at Curran Glen. Ciaran . . . I fooled you, Ciaran – or did I – and I stole your immortal creature. But it looks as if there's a reckoning coming up. The punishment fitting the crime, no, that's not Christianity, or is it? I can't think . . . I don't want to think . . .

Vogel was levering the lid into place: Kate thought there was not a lock or a hinge, but that it wedged into a groove. At any minute the light will shut off and I shall be in the dark. It's not airless – I can see tiny bored holes for air – but it'll get stale. And once Ahasuerus is in here as well . . .

And then Vogel pushed the lid into place, and Kate shuddered. There was the sound of a chain going around the outside, and the snapping of a lock. Chained and padlocked in.

Before the final layer of unconsciousness closed in, she heard Vogel slam the boot closed.

Chapter Twenty-Four

'Have we got the remotest idea where Kate Kendal might be heading?' said Isarel, as the hire-car bucketed its way across North Wales through sheeting rain. 'Or are you simply trusting in heaven to point you in the right direction? Beyond the last blue mountain, across the angry and glimmering sea— There's a traffic island up ahead.'

'Even heaven would get confused by traffic islands,' said Ciaran. 'These are terrible roads, aren't they, it's taking all my concentration to keep—'

'On the straight and narrow?'

'In the right lane,' rejoined Ciaran equably. 'I always had difficulty with the straight and narrow, and I certainly couldn't find it in this rain. Is that our turning up ahead?'

Isarel peered through the rain. 'Yes. Siphoning us off to the left. Get in lane now.'

'Siphoning's the right word in this weather,' said Ciaran, swinging over. 'But I thought we'd find our way in the end.'

'O Faith, that meets ten thousand cheats, yet drops no jot of faith— You do know where you're going, do you?'

'I do indeed.'

'Well, could you share the information? Because this certainly isn't the Golden Road to Samarkand.'

'I thought that since Kate Kendal is headed for London we'd head there as well,' said Ciaran. 'The touch'd needle trembling to the pole and so on. Would you know is that meant pruriently, by the way, because I don't think Father Abbot would like me to say it if it is—'

Isarel had turned round in the passenger seat to stare at him. 'How the devil do you know she's going to London?'

'Because I paid the ferryman.'

There was a sudden silence, disturbed only by the rhythmic swish of the car's windscreen wipers. At length Isarel said, 'Have you any idea how extraordinarily sinister that sounds?'

'It was the Irish Sea, not the waters of the Styx—'

'Was it really as easy as that?' said Isarel curiously.

'It wasn't strictly speaking the ferryman. I only said that to provoke you—'

'Well, you succeeded.'

'But those dock officials can be surprisingly open to persuasion. I said we were discreetly following the lady, and implied that there was a divorce case involving child custody. If Ms Kendal doesn't want to be followed she shouldn't have such a memorable entourage. A caravan in tow and the lady herself—' Ciaran paused. 'The lady herself is the most memorable part of it,' he said softly. Isarel waited, but Ciaran said in an ordinary voice, 'It sounds as if she's only twenty-four hours ahead of us and my man heard her say something about reaching the motorway network quickly because of getting to London before dark.'

'I don't remember hearing anybody tell you any of that,' said Isarel suspiciously.

'No, you were in the bar at the time.'

'Is that a criticism? Listen, I'm here under protest, Brother Ciaran. I don't give a damn about your itinerant corpse!'

'Of course you don't,' said Ciaran. 'By the way, you did

pack Jude's shofar, didn't you? Yes, I recall seeing you wrap it in that sheepskin rug to protect it on the journey.' He sent Isarel a mischievous look. 'I didn't rely wholly on bribable dock officials, of course. Kate paid the rent of the field by cheque and her cheque had the name of a North London branch of Barclays. From which, my dear Watson—'

'You deduce she lives – or possibly works – in North London,' said Isarel. 'On the subject of cheques and rents, and speaking as a member of the oldest financial fraternity in the world—'

'How did I get the money out of Father Abbot for the journey?'

'I ask purely out of professional curiosity, you understand.'

'Very easily indeed,' said Ciaran. 'We're pledged to guard Ahasuerus and the tomb, and once we found he'd gone we hadn't much choice but to follow. Actually we're a reasonably well-off Abbey and the finance wasn't a problem. Our money's almost all invested – in fact we employ a stockbroker in Dublin to watch it for us. When a monk enters the Abbey, in theory he brings a dowry with him, I'm not sure what the present amount is, but it used to be something like four thousand Irish punts. That's more or less the same as four thousand English pounds, but I think a punt buys a bit less than a pound these days. In practice nobody with a true vocation is turned away of course, which sometimes means it's all output and no income.'

'But,' said Isarel, who was finding this deeply interesting, 'the Abbey is almost self-supporting, surely?'

'Almost's the operative word,' said Ciaran. 'We have a few projects going on most of the time – bottled fruit and honey, and dried lavender from a monastery garden – stuff which sells in Galway and Shannon. There's a book about religious music in the pipeline as well – that's quite a departure for us and it's an ambitious project, but we're very optimistic about it. One of the local girls is helping us, partly because we're trying to prise her away from her father – he's a bit unhealthily protective of her and Father Abbot was getting concerned – but largely because she's a bright, intelligent child and we really did want her help.'

Isarel said very tentatively, 'If you want any more help—'

'Oh, with you on the strength as well, we'd have a bestseller overnight,' said Ciaran at once. 'Or at least replenish the coffers for a time which would be good because there's a shortfall between income and expense most years. Inflation, the cost of maintaining a structure that's nearly a thousand years old . . . we do a lot of that ourselves, of course; between us we've got carpenters and stonemasons and electricians. And fortunately there've been no really major expenses since the eighteenth century when the Troubles ended. I believe the Father Abbot of the day pushed the boat out so enthusiastically then that it nearly bankrupted the Order.'

'It's quite difficult to imagine a monastery going bankrupt,' said Isarel.

'The story is that the Abbot-General made a visitation and found caches of empty brandy bottles and unpaid bills for venison and turkey. The monks were in disgrace for months,' said Ciaran, grinning. 'But even that wasn't as bad as the Fifteen Hundreds when not only did they refuse to take the Oath of Supremacy to Henry the Eighth, they actually cast a bell which they named after the exiled Catherine of Aragon. It was a gesture of loyalty to a discarded Catholic queen, of course, but unfortunately it

269

was also a very public and very blatant nose-thumbing at Henry Tudor. It took some time for Thomas Cromwell to hear about it because he was too busy dissolving English monasteries – he'd a whale of a time at that by all accounts, hadn't he? – but he did hear in the end, of course. And in the spring of 1539, a party of men from London, headed by the King's Commissioner, Sir Rodger Cheke, rode into Curran Glen to call the monastery to account.' He sent another grin across to Isarel. 'According to the reports handed down it was very nearly the end of the Abbey; Cheke found the monks celebrating the consecration of the Aragon bell, dancing on tables, most of them what in the parlance of the day was referred to as "myse-dronck", which today we'd call—'

'Thanks, I can translate for myself,' said Isarel.

'Well, it was regarded as a terrible thing, anyway. Can you imagine it, Isarel, men of God drinking and carousing and singing bawdy songs?'

'If they were anything like you, only too easily.'

'It's one of the great scandals in our history, because the Abbey nearly lost most of its revenue and some of the monks were executed for heresy.'

'That's terrible,' said Isarel.

'Isn't it? They were shockingly dissolute of course and flabby-minded as well. They say the only one who stood up to Cheke was Brother Martin, the sub-Prior.'

The monks had been very cheered at the idea of having a bit of a feast to celebrate the new bell cast in the poor spurned Queen's honour, even though Brother Martin, terrible spoilsport that he was, had said weren't they tempting Providence, leave aside drawing down the notice of Henry Tudor's eagle-eyed spies.

Nobody had paid this any attention, because you could

not be worrying about Henry Tudor's spies every minute of the day, and also they were far too busy preparing for the banquet which Father Abbot had said they might hold after the consecration ceremony. You could not consecrate a new bell without a bit of a supper to mark the event, and the King's long-nosed snoopers could pry somewhere else, they said cheerfully. In any case, Ireland's west coast was a long way from Greenwich Palace, and His Majesty far too absorbed in his search for another wife. Word of Henry's proxy wooings of half the princesses of Europe had even travelled as far as Curran Glen by this time, and the monks had been shocked to their toes to hear of an anointed King behaving in a way better suited to a licensed buffoon.

The entire Abbey had always held firmly by the true Queen, of course, Catherine of Aragon, and after her death the Princess Mary, and they were very glad indeed that Ireland had no princesses for Henry to wear out, or send to the block, or divorce – there did not seem to be anything to choose between the three as far as the King was concerned. Father Abbot had firmly declined to be party to the infamous Act of Supremacy, and although this was a grand thing to have done, most of the monks had suffered a few sleepless nights after hearing of the terrible sentences passed on English religious houses. Brother Wilfrid had regularly woken from nightmares in which he had been roasted over a fire with two Carthusian monks for company, and Thomas Cromwell himself turning the handle of the spit and saying evilly, 'A little *slower*, brother?' But in the end they had all ceased to worry, and only Martin had continued to warn against the possibility of a visit from the King's Commissioners.

The banquet was a very splendid affair indeed, although it was reported that Wilfrid was very nearly distracted with the task of having to provide it, and had told anyone who would listen that monastic life did not really fit a person for cooking banquets. Wilfrid was very reliable when it came to pease pudding and turnip pottage or stewed mutton, but you could not be serving turnip pottage at a banquet. He had baked and spit-roasted and stewed for an entire twenty-four hours beforehand, he said, and had barely had time for a mouthful of dinner, never mind taking his proper part in the normal round of services which made up the monastery's day.

It was Martin who said they should lock the doors during the Bell consecration, and it was Martin again who had insisted on sending poor young Edmund – the Abbey's newest novice and not a day over fifteen – to act as lookout. Exactly as if he believed that a party of the King's Commissioners would come riding up the hillside and fall on them that very night! said the monks, amused, and arranged amongst themselves to save some of the food for Edmund, poor soul.

Martin had also somehow bludgeoned Father Abbot into holding the consecration Mass by night on the premise that a nocturnal ceremony was less likely to be noticed than an ordinary daytime one. Most of the brothers had found this rather intriguing and had asked hopefully whether they might not have a candlelit procession through the cloisters, to which Father Abbot, who felt it time to assert his authority over Brother Martin, had said he did not see why not. It would lend an air of mystery to the whole thing, and they could as easily consecrate the Aragon bell at midnight as at mid-day. They would write a little piece of Abbey history, he said firmly.

'Be it on your head,' said Martin, but he added, 'Father,' with the scrupulous deference he always displayed, which meant that he could never quite be reprimanded for disrespect to his superior in God. Father Abbot found him very exhausting.

In the end there was baked carp and roast venison and beef for the feast, followed by a grand selection of sugared fruits which were a very great delicacy indeed, and a pudding made from sweetened chestnuts. Father Abbot thought it would not be unsuitable to bring up a cask or two of the good wine presented to the Abbey by no less a personage than the Earl of Kildare, because you could not be having inferior stuff at such an occasion, and anyway inferior wine always made Father Abbot bilious next morning.

The Mass was duly sung and the Aragon Bell duly sounded and pronounced very sweet and true. They could use it to ring Vespers said the monks, pleased, and beamed round the table at one another, flushed with wine and the unaccustomed rich food. Brother Wilfrid, whose life before God beckoned to him had been rather robust, and whose potations in the matter of the wine had been somewhat liberal, started a round of songs, most of which were highly unsuitable for monastic gatherings but which turned out to be known to most of the monks with the understandable exception of Father Abbot. It was as well that young Edmund had been sent out to keep watch after all, because the sentiments of 'A Cuckolding Cock' were not fit for an innocent lad of fifteen to be hearing; in fact they were not fit for monks to be singing in the first place. Father Abbot glanced nervously around and tried to frame a reprimand which would not spoil anyone's enjoyment of the occasion.

By this time Wilfrid had abandoned 'A Cuckolding Cock', and embarked on 'A Knight's Lusty Lance', which was even worse because it was a part-song, and Wilfrid insisted on acting out the part of the Knight and then one of the younger monks leapt up to take the part of the fair young maid who screamed at the seducer's evil advance and swooned at the sight of the knight's rampant lance. Father Abbot remembered he had always had misgivings about the proclivities of Brother Ralph and it looked as if he had been right.

It was into the sly, rollicking singing and dancing, and into the unmistakable stench of belched and farted wine, that Sir Rodger Cheke the King's Commissioner for the Dissolution of the Monasteries of Ireland came.

Rodger Cheke was genuinely horrified at the sight that met his eyes. Men of God – actually professed, supposedly devout monks – drinking and singing and dancing in such a lewd fashion that any decent man would think shame to see. Well, this would certainly shock Master Cromwell when Sir Rodger wrote his report, which he would do that very night on account of not wanting to forget any of the details. Not that any of them were in the least forgettable.

It was unfortunate that Wilfrid's back was to the door when Sir Rodger entered, and it was even more unfortunate that he carried on singing for an entire verse, unaware of the newcomer. It was absolutely disastrous that he continued with the song's actions. He had actually reached the part where the Knight had hoisted his lance in his hand and leapt on to the fair maid, shrieking out the chorus of, 'Trollop and frolic and lay bare the bums', before it dawned on him that his companions had trailed into horrified silence. He hesitated, forgot the next line, and turned to see himself regarded with a chilly eye that he later described as a fisheye and as nasty a thing as you could wish to see, particularly when you had hiked up your habit the better to play the lusty Knight.

Sir Rodger let his gaze travel over the now-speechless Wilfrid for a moment before looking round to select the oldest and most worried-looking of the monks. He was gambling (although not very much) that this was the Father Abbot. And he bowed his head in a cursory acknowledgement, before saying in his frosty English voice, 'I'd be obliged of a word in private, Father.'

It was wormwood and gall and it was black bitter bile to know that Martin had been right all along. Henry Tudor's wrath had descended about their heads, and if they escaped with their lives, never mind uncharred skins, it would be God's mercy, said the monks and remembered with horror the reports that had trickled across of the English Carthusian monks who had rejected the Oath of Supremacy and had not only lost their monasteries, but had been burned alive as heretics. Chastened and repentant, they filed humbly into the chapel and set about praying very earnestly indeed for God's mercy or Rodger Cheke's benevolence and preferably both. They closed and locked the chapel doors against the coarse-mannered men who had accompanied Sir Rodger and who appeared to be making an inventory of the monastery's entire contents – and very noisily too! – and reminded one another of the old English law of sanctuary. Wasn't it right that you could claim sanctuary for an entire month in a religious place? they demanded of one another, and there and then determined to remain in the chapel praying for a whole twenty-eight days non-stop if it would deliver them from Henry Tudor's wrath.

Sir Rodger Cheke eyed Father Abbot in the little study and glanced briefly at the dark-haired, thin-faced Brother Martin whom he took to be the sub-Prior.

'I presume,' he said coldly, 'that you keep proper records here?' All religious houses were supposed to do this of course, but in view of the scene Sir Rodger had witnessed earlier, nothing would have surprised him. He added, 'You are aware, I suppose, that an edict is in existence for the closure of all monasteries where income is less than two hundred pounds in a year.'

Father Abbot said in a voice that he managed to edge with quite as much frost as Rodger Cheke's, 'Certainly we keep proper records. You will find everything in perfect order.'

He cast an anguished eye at Brother Martin, who stepped forward and said smoothly, 'Our income far exceeds that sum, Sir Rodger. But you are welcome to inspect our rent rolls for yourself.' Since, said his tone, you clearly won't believe my word. He eyed the Englishman coolly and Cheke thought with irritation that this was precisely the kind of monk Cromwell's Commissioners had been instructed to pluck out. Arrogant, clever, given to the kind of slippery arguing that lawyers often employed and that was sometimes called specious.

Martin said, 'Would you wish to come along now to the scriptorium, Sir Rodger?' and turned to the door scarcely waiting for the affirmative.

The ledgers and the accounts were immaculate, of course. Cheke thought he should have guessed it. The entries were all meticulously made in the small precise script of the monks and there was an air of calm about them, as if whoever was responsible for the work carried it out efficiently and unhurriedly. There was nothing that was the smallest bit questionable and there was certainly nothing that could be used against this lax House! Sir Rodger was conscious of a slowly stirring anger. Had he come all this way – five days' hard riding to England's west coast and that dreadful sea crossing where he had been sick four times over the side of the boat, and then a further six days' journey – to find absolutely nothing of any value? Be damned to that, he thought. Let's see what can be done! He bent his mind to concentrate on the rent rolls and the records placed before him by the supercilious devil who was quite plainly the power here in all but name.

Most of the income appeared to derive from the usual sources of tithes and endowments, and rent from lands and farms. There was a not inconsiderable sum from tolls and bridges and it appeared that the monks also had the right to hold a market and a fair on their land which would probably bring them some very fat dues. The Abbey's income, in fact, was much higher than Sir Rodger had been expecting and if Thomas Cromwell's edict was to be followed to the letter, the Abbey could not be closed down on the basis of its low income – far from it. But that was only one avenue that was closed to him and there were more ways than one of skinning a stoat or depriving a monastery of some of its riches. What about that behaviour earlier tonight? Lewd, gluttonous frolicking and the singing of bawdy songs around a groaning board of an evening? This House of Curran Glen – this dissolute, disorderly House – was precisely the kind of place that ought to be closed down.

Rodger Cheke knew perfectly well that with so many of the lesser monasteries dissolved, Thomas Cromwell's sights were being set higher. The larger Houses now, he had said. Rich pickings for the King there. Rich pickings for the King's Commissioners as well if they are loyal, he had added slyly and Cheke had known that by 'loyal', Cromwell had meant 'discreet'. Cream off what you want but don't let anyone catch you doing it. You might almost call it a Tudor policy.

Curran Glen had some very rich pickings indeed. Could some of them possibly be creamed off here and now? How? More to the point, could he justify such an action? He set himself to think.

Ireland was not really part of Cromwell's overall scheme of dissolution; it was a long and wearisome journey from Greenwich – that dreadful heaving sea – and Sir Rodger would not have come here at all if it had not been for the reports of blatant flouting of the Oath of Supremacy and slavish and forbidden fidelity to Catherine of Aragon and the Lady Mary. Even without the shocking licentiousness these monks were very nearly behaving treasonably in fact. *Treason.* Treasonous people and especially treasonous monks needed to be punished. And now he had arrived at the conclusion he had wanted.

He allowed none of his thoughts to show. He went on studying the rent rolls, asking questions of Brother Martin, hoping to uncover mismanagement or impropriation, but not really expecting it. This arrogant Irish monk knew exactly what he was doing.

'You have half the usufruct of this land here and here?' He pointed to a small map which had been drawn on a piece of plain parchment with the usual loving monastic attention to detail, and then bound into the book which bore the legend Usufruct Rights.

'Yes, the east and south,' said Martin. 'A gift to the House in Thirteen Hundred. The Deed is bound into the book also as you see.'

'From Godfric of Liscannor.'

'Yes. The eastern land includes a shoot and a hide which yields game and fruit and vegetables, and the south takes in a stretch of river there—' he pointed on the map, 'which gives us the first thousand of each shad and herring shoal.'

This was perfectly clear and in accordance with normal monastic practice. The amounts from the usufruct rights alone were more than the rents from Sir Rodger's own small estate in Warwickshire, which increased his anger even more. What had become of the vow of Poverty here? Sir Rodger had been forced to mortgage a third of his lands to pay off his father's debts and unless he could find a rich wife he might have to mortgage another third soon. It was monstrous of these celibates to enjoy such fat secure lives, and now he came to think of it the celibacy could be called into question as well!

But when he spoke, his voice was calm and detached. 'Your income is certainly above the amount set by the Vicar-General,' he said. 'And therefore you are not—'

'Under sentence of death?'

Sir Rodger remembered with disapproval the colourful extravagant way the Irish sometimes had of speaking. He said coldly, 'Closure is not a consideration here.' Adding meaningfully, 'Not yet, that is. The present statute may soon be altered. But there is a degree of laxity which I must report to Master Cromwell.'

He paused, and Martin said, 'Unless?'

'Unless what?'

'You are about to make a condition, Sir Rodger. "Unless such-and-such is done, the behaviour witnessed earlier tonight will be reported to the King's Vicar-General." I suppose,' said Martin thoughtfully, 'that your condition will be a monetary one.' He sat down opposite Cheke and clasped his hands under his chin, regarding the other man levelly. 'Well, Sir Rodger? What do we have to give you to ensure your silence?'

Chapter Twenty-Five

'Brother Martin, you have done *what*?'

'Agreed to cede the King half the dues for ten years from the sheepfolds and the timber forest's charcoal.'

Father Abbot moaned and lay back in his chair, shading his eyes with one hand. He did not know when he had been so overcome, and he had in fact had to send Wilfrid to mull some wine by way of restorative.

'Also,' said Martin relentlessly, 'Cheke is to have the silver altar ornaments and the Italian chalices.'

'The Italian cha—? *Our Founder's jewelled chalices*?'

'Yes.'

'You have – let me get this clear – you have *given away* Simon of Cremona's ruby and topaz chalices, the ones we use for Easter Sunday Mass and to celebrate Our Blessed Lord's birth?'

'Yes.'

'Well, I shall never recover and that's all there is to it,' said Father Abbot, with decision. 'You have allowed that *English robber* to strip this Abbey of its most precious possessions, to say nothing of the sheepfold and afforestation income, and what I am to say to the community— Well, you'll have to tell them. I can't.'

Martin said, 'The rents are not so very much. And England is a long way from here. It wouldn't be the first time that returns had been adjusted.'

Father Abbot said aghast, 'You would *lie* to Thomas Cromwell?'

'If it meant the saving of our Abbey I would lie to Thomas Cromwell, Henry Tudor and the entire College of Cardinals,' Martin replied. 'I agreed to cede half the income for ten years,' he said. 'But I didn't specify which ten years.'

'Well, but—'

'Nor,' he continued, 'does the Agreement bear the word "consecutive" anywhere in it.' It was rare for the stern Brother Martin to smile, but he smiled now, his thin, stern face suddenly relaxing into mischievous delight. Father Abbot stared at him.

'But, Brother – that is surely – bless my soul, I'm not sure *what* it is, except that it sounds very *devious*.'

'It is devious,' Martin agreed, leaning forward. 'But Cheke was present at the writing of the Agreement – Ralph wrote it out for us and made two copies – and Cheke signed it and sealed it with Cromwell's seal. He didn't challenge the wording at all.'

'Of course he didn't challenge it,' said Father Abbot, who could not recall when he had last been so shocked. 'He didn't know he was dealing with a master of sophistry!'

'In England they call it being a lawyer,' responded Martin instantly, and Father Abbot threw up his hands in frustration.

'We aren't going to renege on the arrangement,' said Martin, adopting a more persuasive tone. 'We'll pay the dues, but we'll do one of two things. Either we'll pay only in the years we've had good returns – which could take a very long time indeed – or we'll defer the start of the payments, for fifty or a hundred years if we can. And I don't believe,' said Martin, 'that there's a thing that anyone can do about it. Thomas Cromwell's a lawyer and the

281

King himself has studied law. They'll both see the argument.'

'Henry Tudor's a rogue,' said Father Abbot at once. 'And Thomas Cromwell's a villain. They're already calling him *Malleus monarchorum* – hammer of the monks. And this is the man you think you can cheat!' He mopped his brow and gestured weakly to the mulled wine.

'Would you have preferred Rodger Cheke to carry tales of carousing and drunkenness back to Thomas Cromwell?' demanded Martin, replenishing the glass.

'See now,' said Father Abbot, rallying, 'you know as well as I do that that was an isolated incident. It was extremely unfortunate that Cheke and his men should choose that very minute—'

'Wilfrid is prostrate with remorse.'

'So I should hope,' said Father Abbot tartly. 'For you know quite well that we *never* carouse, not from one year's end to the next. We're a – a most abstemious House,' said Father Abbot, drinking his mulled wine, apparently unaware of irony. 'And it's very unfair if we're to be accused of laxity and forced to buy that frog-eyed Englishman's silence.' He looked at Martin from under his brows and added waspishly that if they were to be deprived of their Founder's chalices, it would be no more than God's justice on Rodger Cheke if every one of them was broken on the journey to England.

Martin said politely, 'Would you have preferred closure, Father? Disgrace and scandal and the community made homeless?'

'You're a hard man, Brother Martin,' said Father Abbot, glaring. 'I sometimes wonder if you've an ounce of feeling in your entire body, because—' He broke off as the sound of footsteps came pattering along the corridor. There was a cursory knock and the door was flung summarily open to reveal Brother Wilfrid, his plump face ashen, his hands clasped agitatedly.

'Forgive the interruption, Father but – oh, is it you as well, Brother Martin? – well, I'm very sorry to come bursting in on you if you're in conclave, but there's been a, well, a terrible thing—' Wilfrid paused to get his breath and reassemble his wits. 'A terrible thing,' he said again. 'I don't know how to say it—'

'What—?'

'It's the tomb,' said Wilfrid. 'Father Abbot, Brother Martin, Sir Rodger Cheke's men have forced the tomb of Ahasuerus open.'

Martin was on his feet, but Wilfrid, who had by now regained his breath, waved him back.

'It's no use you going down there,' he said. 'Because they've already left, they went early this morning, furtive as tomcats while we were all at Lauds, and if I'd *guessed* what they were up to while we were all thanking the good Lord for the new day—'

Martin and Father Abbot both said exactly together, '*What about the tomb*?'

'Gaping open like a hungering, black-mouthed beast,' said Wilfrid, with an unexpected note of poetical macabre, and Martin felt a cold hand brush the nape of his neck. 'The slab forced up with no more ado than if it had been one of my pastry crusts – *and* with no more consideration for damage to Abbey property than you'd expect from a drunken sailor! – and the coffin scooped out like a— a mussel from its shell! Quite gone! And if you'll kindly excuse the liberty, Father, I'd be very grateful for a mouthful of that mulled wine, because it's been the most dreadful shock—'

Martin ladled out a measure of wine and passed it across. He looked at Father Abbot, his eyes dark with anger, but when he spoke, his voice was quite steady.

'Cheke's men have clearly taken far more than the bargain,' he said. 'I suppose they saw the tomb as some kind of valuable historical relict to present to the King.'

'Yes, Brother, and hadn't we the silver coffin made some years back to replace Simon of Cremona's old one?' put in Wilfrid who was, truth to tell, beginning to rather relish the excitement of everything. 'It'd be valuable on its own, that coffin.'

'It would,' said Martin grimly. 'Very likely we'll find a few other things missing as well. The sacristan had better start making an inventory. That Englishman may have stripped the Abbey of everything precious it possesses.'

'I knew it,' wailed Father Abbot. 'It's the biter bit, it's retribution on us for being devious. God's mills grinding us into dust. He that diggeth a pit shall fall into it— I told you, Martin, I said: never trust an Englishman.'

'So you did.'

'The hiss of the viper and the smile of the Saxon with a knife beneath his cloak, dear me. I remember my father quoting that to me, not that Sir Rodger did smile, cold-eyed, fish-blooded creature, but he did wear a cloak— Ahasuerus's tomb plundered, the thing we've all vowed to guard with our lives— yes we have, Martin – our lives, leave aside our souls—'

'Souls don't come into it,' said Martin. 'Cheke and his men can't have got far if they only left at daybreak. And if they've got Ahasuerus's silver coffin, it'll slow them down considerably.'

'And then there're the chalices,' remarked Wilfrid.

'How did you know about that?' said Martin sharply, and Wilfrid turned fiery red with embarrassment and said that Brother Ralph had just mentioned—

'There's a sight too much gossiping goes on in this

monastery,' said Father Abbot crossly. 'Well, Martin? What are we to do?'

'Go after them,' said Martin, meeting his superior's eyes straightly. 'Follow them to England if necessary and bring Ahasuerus back.

'Return him to the tomb before he can walk in the world again.'

Sir Rodger was very glad indeed to reach England safely. He had endured five separate bouts of vomiting on the boat as well as the indignity of purging at the same time. And as anyone who had suffered it knew, there were certain awkward practicalities involved in simultaneous vomiting and fluxing. In the end, he had been forced to crouch over a pail in a sheltered corner of the deck, retching miserably into a pan. It was not at all the kind of thing that enabled you to exert a proper authority over your men, and Sir Rodger knew perfectly well that vulgar epithets – of which 'Tossguts' was the mildest – had hissed derogatorily around the boat, just out of his hearing.

But the journey was behind them now, God be thanked, and here was a very flattering invitation for a night or two's hospitality at the house of no less a personage than the Dowager Duchess of Norfolk. Quite aside from the honour, this would save Sir Rodger the price of a common lodging house before presenting himself at Greenwich and meant he would have a couple of nights' rest and a chance to plan exactly what he should say to Master Cromwell and the King. Really, the invitation was very timely.

The Duchess received him with offhand civility. She had heard good things of Sir Rodger from Thomas Cromwell, she said, and had wanted to meet him. Sir Rodger, no innocent when it came to Henry VIII's Court, thought: aha! the Howards trawling for likely spies to infiltrate Court again!

The wine proffered by Her Grace was so sour it nearly made him gag, but he downed it valiantly and heard that the Duchess had been acquainted with his maternal aunt.

'You will know of her of course,' stated Her Grace. 'For a time she was Lady in Waiting to my poor doomed granddaughter.'

'Granddaughter?'

'Anne Boleyn,' said Her Grace crossly and stumped off to tell her housekeeper that the small room on the second floor would do very well for this Warwickshire hobbledehoy; they need not bother to air it, and they were to place the gape-mouthed yokel exactly level with the salt at supper – no higher, mind! – and keep him out of the Duchess's way because he was no more suited to be recruited as a Howard spy than the stable-cat!

Sir Rodger eyed his allotted chamber with determined gratitude. It smelt of mildew and he would have preferred the sheets to have been fresher, to say nothing of the sweeping up of the mice-droppings in the corner, but he was not going to be finicky about it, because to be given a chamber to yourself was a luxury on its own, and to be noticed at all by the House of Howard was flattering beyond expectation. It was unfortunate he had not remembered his aunt's service with the disgraced Anne Boleyn, but doubtless it had gone unnoticed.

When he found himself allotted a place level with the salt he was sure of this. Really, things were turning out very well. The exquisite jewelled Italian chalices from Curran Glen Abbey were all safely stowed in saddle bags, along with the very good silver plate and the marble statuary. Several other things had found their way into the baggage as well: some very valuable gold candlesticks and bowls, which would adorn Sir Rodger's house in Warwickshire, and a number of twelfth-century illuminated manuscripts which could be presented to His Majesty. The King had a scholarly turn of mind – Sir Rodger had no time for people who said rudely that Henry was becoming a bloated old tyrant – and he would be very pleased with the gift. He would be very interested as well in the curious and remarkable silver tomb that Sir Rodger's men had carried up from the Abbey crypt under the most awkward of circumstances, and brought across the terrible Irish Sea. The silver coffin alone would be immensely valuable, leave aside what other artefacts they might find sealed inside it. He would instruct his men to lever it open but he would wait until tomorrow, because if you were opening up an ancient coffin you wanted daylight when you did it.

Sir Rodger Cheke, pleased with himself and with life, ate his dinner in this exalted house, drank the wine poured for him and prepared to enjoy the music of a travelling minstrel who was about to play for the company's pleasure, and who was eyeing the saucy-eyed, red-haired minx at the Duchess's side with undisguised interest. Sir Rodger, not to be caught out a second time, demanded of his near neighbour who was that pretty child, and learned that it was yet another of Her Grace's granddaughters.

'Edmund's girl,' said the neighbour. 'Catherine Howard.'

'Ah? Indeed?'

'Due to go to Court next week. I shouldn't be surprised,' said Sir Rodger's neighbour, 'if she didn't catch a few people's eye.'

Sir Rodger thought he would not be surprised either.

Catherine Howard had heard with pleasure the news that a travelling minstrel was at the gates, asking if he might entertain them at supper. Grandmother had given permission

– a little music would cheer them all up, she had said – and Catherine, who liked music, had been pleased. There might be a new song or two that she could learn and play at Court next week. It was an immense honour to go to Court to be in the Queen's household; Grandmother had said she was to hold her head as high as anyone, never mind that it was that great, ungainly Flanders mare whose service she would be in, and she must behave with the dignity suitable to her family, even when it was only Anne of Cleves who occupied the place alongside the King. Catherine was a bit light when it came to dignity, said Grandmother reprovingly, but providing she did not forget herself with any *unsuitable* young men at Court, there was no saying what might be ahead, said Her Grace with the cunning of one who fifteen-odd years earlier had seen one granddaughter rise to undreamed-of heights and did not see why a second could not do the same. It was unfortunate that the first granddaughter had met that ignominious end on Tower Hill, but the Duchess was inclined to blame the sire rather than the dam there: Anne's mother had been the Duchess's own beloved daughter and clearly blameless, while Tom Boleyn was the descendant of upstart Norfolk mercers and nobody that anyone had really heard of. What was in the meat came out in the gravy. Anyway so long as Catherine remembered not to mention her dead cousin, and especially not in the hearing of the King or the Queen, she would do very well, said the Duchess firmly.

Catherine quite saw that you did not, if you had the least shred of self-preservation, emphasise your kinship with a lady found guilty of adultery and incest against a King of England, particularly when the King was Henry VIII. There were rumours that he had never really got over Anne's wantonness and that he sometimes moaned her name in his sleep, but nobody believed this last, because whoever else Henry Tudor might call for in the night watches, it would certainly not be his faithless murdered Queen.

Grandmother had instructed the minstrel to play some of the good old tunes tonight; they did not want die-away dirges more fit for a funeral than for a Christian table, she said tartly, and they would have something to cheer them up.

'Whatever you wish, madam.' He had an odd way of speaking; English, but with a lilt at the ends of words. Italian, was it? The Italians were rather attractive. The minstrel was rather attractive. Catherine eyed him speculatively.

He played the most beautiful music she had ever heard. To begin with, he sang about the old days of England, when it had been called by other names, and travellers and mariners had seen it as an island of magic and enchantment. He sang of the days when men could talk to beasts and spirits lived in trees and magic stalked the earth. Lovely! thought Catherine. Lovely to hear about the world when it was sparkly new, when there were no bewildering changes of worship so that you were not sure if it was safe to admit to a Catholic upbringing, and when you did not have to worry about letting slip the name of a fascinating, disgraced cousin in the King's hearing, or even whether Grandmother might discover that you were not as chaste as you were supposed to be.

Catherine was not precisely surprised when the minstrel sought her out after everyone had gone to bed, although she was a bit taken aback that he should have done it so soon. In Catherine's experience you played a game of flirting first: you exchanged languishing looks, and then you progressed to hand-clasps, the apparently accidental brushing of a hand against a breast or a thigh. From there you went on to stolen meetings in shrubberies or music rooms where nobody ever went, or sweet-scented apple orchards in the drowsy heat of a summer's afternoon where you explored one another's bodies more intimately, and where there were any number of delicious conclusions that could be reached.

The minstrel had clearly surveyed the terrain before making the tryst, and Catherine, slipping through the door of the rather gloomy book-room where Howard ladies had occasionally retired to write a letter or nurse a headache or meet a lover, thought he had chosen well. Nobody was going to come in here at this time of the night.

The minstrel was standing beneath one of the burning wall brackets, and the flame fell across his hair, turning it into an aureole of radiance. His cheekbones slanted upwards, giving his face a three-cornered faintly feline look. And if I look hard enough, thought Catherine, with a sudden prickle of fear, I believe I might find that his ears are pointed.

She did not do so. She stood just inside the door and folded her hands and looked at him with the demure smile that was not demure at all, and waited.

The minstrel said in his soft beautiful voice, 'My lady, I am here to fulfil a promise made many years ago.'

'A promise?' This was intriguing, even if it was not quite what Catherine had been expecting. She said, 'What promise?'

He paused, studying her, and then said, 'That as soon as I judged you sufficiently mature, I should give to you this.' And held out a lute, worn smooth with age, polished to a deep mellow sheen with usage.

'It is very old indeed,' he said sitting on the deep window-seat, the shutters drawn against the night and the light from the wall sconces falling more directly across his face. Catherine could see now that he was older than she had thought. He would certainly not see thirty again, and he might not even see forty. By ordinary standards this was quite old, but old was not a word you could apply to him. Ordinary was certainly not a word you could apply either.

She said abruptly, 'I don't know your name.'

'Nicolas.' He gave it the Italian emphasis.

'Nicolas. You have – no other name?'

'Not one that matters.'

'I see.' Catherine did not see at all, and this whole thing was beginning to take on a dreamlike quality. She said, 'Please tell me about the lute.'

The minstrel said, 'Four hundred years ago the lute belonged to my ancestress, who brought it out of Cremona. She was a lady of very great beauty and courage and there is a tale that she bargained with the devil for his music and that the devil succumbed.'

'That is – a very unusual story.'

'She was a very unusual lady. Tales are told of how she travelled out of Italy and through many lands over many years, and how she played the music as she went.' A faraway look crept into his eyes. 'They say that at times during her lonely travels she sang into the still night, and it was so beautiful and so alluring a sound that men would wake from slumber and lie listening. They said she could call the dead out of their tombs with her songs, and also how at times she could ease the passing of the dying.' He paused, and then said, 'She is reputed to have had many lovers, that long-ago lady, but to her only son she bequeathed her lute and the devil's music that she swore must be handed on. This—' he touched the lute, 'comes in direct line from her.'

Catherine thought that the assignation was not turning

out quite as she had expected, but this was a fascinating story. She was unsure of precisely where Cremona was, but it would not do to say so. The lute was very beautiful. She turned it over in her hands and as she did so it gave the faintest shiver of sound. Sweet. What had he said? My ancestress bargained for the devil's music . . .

Catherine said, 'Why am I to have this?'

For a moment the minstrel did not speak. Catherine saw now that he was certainly nearer forty than thirty. There were lines at the corners of his eyes and about his mouth. And although his hair appeared to be a shiny cap of molten gold it was touched with silver gilt at the temples. She had the impression that he was unwrapping some fragile precious memory. But at last, he said, 'Almost twenty years ago I sold this lute to a lady of the English Court. I did not wish to do so, but I was very poor at the time and very hungry. The lady to whom I offered it was lovely and gay and generous. She gave me a very good sum for the lute and I—' A sudden smile so reckless and so filled with mischief that Catherine blinked. 'I was able to eat again and pay for a bed for the night and for many nights afterwards,' he said. 'I stayed in England then; I was grateful to the lady and I was interested in her. I watched her rise to prominence. And then, five years ago, I watched her fall as well.' He reached out to touch the lute's smooth surface, and as he did so, his hand brushed Catherine's bare wrist. A dozen white-hot wires seemed to pierce her skin, and she shivered.

'Before she died, she sent for me,' he said. 'She returned the lute to me and made me promise that it should be passed to you.'

'Why?'

'Because she understood its power,' said the minstrel. 'Because she wanted you to have it.'

'The lute? Or the power?' said Catherine in a whisper.

'The two go together.' The minstrel touched the lute again. 'My ancestress coaxed this out of the devil four centuries ago,' he said. 'And the devil taught her his music. Twenty years ago I taught that music to your cousin.

'Anne Boleyn.'

Chapter Twenty-Six

Nicolas could remember it as clearly as if it had been yesterday. How she had sent that imperious message via one of her trusted servants – 'You must come at once' – and how he had gone instantly, almost without thinking about it. He thought that anyone she beckoned to would do the same. Yes, but would they have done so before she had the lute and before he had taught her Isabella's music?

He had been taken in to the Tower by one of her women – there had been some jumbled plot about his having brought a message from her family – he could not remember the details, and he was not sure if he had ever known them. But he had been taken to her.

Even in prison she had been haughty. She had received him as arrogantly as if she had been still Henry's pampered, cossetted Queen, and Nicolas had thought: madame, you have come a very long way from that eager young girl who bought from me the devil's lute of my ancestress and who laughed when I warned of the music's force.

She indicated to him to be seated and regarded him composedly. When she spoke, her voice was exactly as he remembered it: low-pitched and faintly husky.

'You see, Minstrel, I have travelled a long road since we met.'

Nicolas jumped because her words had been uncannily in tune with his thoughts, and he remembered the vague rumours of witchcraft that had always surrounded her. But he said gently, 'So you have, madame, and I am sorry for it.'

'It does not matter now.' For a moment the dark eyes that no painter had ever been able to capture were inward-looking, and Nicolas thought: she is going to break. She is going to break now and I am going to be the one to witness it. She has resisted cardinals and chancellors and kings without fear, but the fear is very close to the surface. It's in her eyes. It's like staring into a black abyss . . . As if I am seeing into her soul . . . And then Anne turned away and when she spoke again, he knew the moment had passed. She would not break now and he was glad. For I should like to remember her as she would wish: imperious, aloof. Untouchable. *Touch me not, for Caesar's I am* . . . One of her admirers had written that to her, and Nicolas saw how true the words had been.

In her cool, low-pitched voice, she said, 'There is one thing I will ask of you.' The dark eyes flickered back to him. 'It is the request of a dying woman.' There was a glint of wry mischief.

Nicolas said, 'Yes?'

'The lute you sold to me so many years ago.'

'Well?'

'You remember it?'

'Oh yes.'

'I thought you would.' She paused, as if weighing up two courses of action, and then said, 'When she is old enough, I should wish the lute to be given to my cousin. Catherine – Edmund Howard's girl. You are the only one I can trust to do it. Teach her the music you taught me.' A pause. 'Tell her it failed me, but it may not fail her.' The dark eyes met his coolly, but Nicolas felt as if a velvet-covered feline paw had traced a caress down his spine. He remembered again the whispers of witchcraft and he remembered how, four hundred years earlier, Isabella Amati was believed to have trafficked with the devil. And for almost twenty years, this thin-faced, haunted-eyed woman had possessed Isabella's music, and for at least fifteen of those years she had held a King in such thrall that he had turned England upside-down for her and slaughtered monks wholesale to have her in his bed. *Touch me not, for Satan's I am.*

He said, 'You trust me to do that?'

'I do.' She studied him and after a moment she smiled. 'Yes, I do trust you,' she said. 'I have not travelled that long road without learning who to trust and who not. You will do what I ask.'

'Yes. But it seems an odd choice.'

She caught his meaning at once; she said, 'You think it should be my daughter who has it? But Elizabeth is too young.'

'Yes?'

'And I do not think she will need it,' said Anne.

'The devil's lute and the devil's music is to go to Catherine Howard. For I have no more need of it.'

Nicolas sat in the window-seat of Lambeth House and watched Catherine Howard turn the ancient lute over in her hands. Three years since he had accepted the odd secret task; three years since he had stood on the edges of the crowd on Tower Hill and watched that strange disconcerting woman go to her death.

He looked back at Catherine Howard. This one had not the elusive bewitchment of her dead cousin, but for all that, Nicolas was reminded of Anne. Something of the same quality in the eyes and in the expressive, graceful hands. And the slender, flower-stem neck.

A prickle of disquiet ruffled his mind, but after a moment, he said, 'Your cousin wished you to know the music that has come down with the lute. You permit?' He reached for the lute again and ran his hands across the strings.

Catherine, staring, thought: he is caressing the lute as if it was a lover. How would it feel . . .? No, he is twenty years older than I am, an old man, and I could never . . . Yes, but his hands are slender and soft and they would feel like silk on your skin . . .

It won't do, thought Catherine determinedly. Think of going to Court, think of the people there – men, *young* men. Listen to the sequence of notes he is playing. Cool, beckoning. Insistent. This is what *she* wanted me to know about – Anne. How very extraordinary.

And then Nicolas handed her the lute and said, 'You play it,' and Catherine, her mind tumbling with sensuous delight, stared at him and thought: it would not matter if he was forty or thirty or seventy.

She began to trace out the sequence of sweet, silvery notes that four centuries earlier had been played by another wilful wanton lady with red hair, and that a thousand years before that had seduced a High Priest from his sacred vows. The music drifted into the quiet room. Like quicksilver breaking up and running in tiny, glinting fragments, thought Catherine. Like icicles tapping against frosted glass. A beckoning. Follow me and do as I bid you.

The music was borne upwards, like swansdown, so that it trickled into the upper rooms of the great house.

In one of those rooms, within the silver coffin, Ahasuerus stirred.

Chapter Twenty-Seven

As Isarel and Ciaran came through the English Midlands and merged with the rushing motorway traffic, Isarel said,

'Ciaran, why did you really enter a monastery? You can tell me to mind my own business if you want, I'm only an ignorant Jew after all. But I'm curious.'

Ciaran who was driving, paused for so long that Isarel thought he was not going to answer. I've gone over the line this time, he thought.

But then Ciaran said, 'Well, do you know, I was called into God's service twelve years ago.'

'As long ago as that? Then,' said Isarel, 'you're older than I thought. Or are you?'

'You didn't quite ask,' said Ciaran. 'But since you're being so unusually polite, I'll say I was thirty when I rebelled against the world and the devil and all his works, and the rest of the circus.'

'How? I mean,' Isarel asked, 'what happened?'

Again there was the hesitation, as if Ciaran was weighing up his thoughts. Then he said, 'There'd been too many years in courtrooms manipulating the truth so that slippery criminals could walk free. And I was getting bored with telling half-truths and spinning specious lawyers' arguments. I had a sneaking suspicion I was getting too good at it as well. And,' he added wryly, 'there had

298

certainly been too many females in my life. I'd really have to say there were quite a lot of them.'

'That I do believe,' said Isarel.

'I woke up one morning – in a bed I shouldn't have been in in the first place – and thought: what in God's name am I doing here? And the answer, of course, was that it wasn't in God's name at all.' He glanced across at Isarel. 'I felt physically sick that morning. As if I'd surfeited on rich food for weeks on end. I suddenly found that what I really wanted was to drink clean, pure, spring water. Does that sound ridiculous?'

'No.'

'I was sick in the unfamiliar bathroom,' said Ciaran, his eyes intent on the roads which were shiny with rain in the gathering dusk. 'And I was half suffering with a migraine from too much wine and too much sex.'

'Too much wine,' said Isarel promptly. 'Nothing to do with sex.'

'I'll accept your judgement. Anyway, after I finished throwing up, I began to realise that the jagged light chiselling through my skull wasn't a migraine at all. The light was inside my mind.'

Isarel, staring, said, 'Paul on the road to Damascus.'

'Well, not literally. The idea of swapping over to a more worthwhile life had been stealthily creeping up on me for some time; I'd simply chosen to ignore it. But there were little threads and little shoots furtively unrolling in my mind. That morning was simply the moment when everything polarised. It was as if – as if a trapdoor or a skylight had opened up somewhere far above my head and light was pouring in.' Ciaran pulled into the middle lane to overtake a Mini. 'I bade farewell to the lady—' The mischievous glint that made him so very unmonkish showed unexpectedly. 'Actually there were two of them in the bed that morning,' he said with a reminiscent grin. 'Although I should point out that I hadn't made a habit of tripartite copulation.'

'No, quite.'

'Entering Curran Glen monastery didn't happen for a very long time,' said Ciaran, his eyes on the road. 'It took me ages to accept that moment for what it was. I resisted and I rebelled. Sometimes I'm still resisting and sometimes I'm certainly still rebelling.'

'But – it's still there? The light?'

'Yes. Warm and golden and incandescent. The light of the world, the burning and shining light . . . Evocative, those New Testament writers, weren't they?'

'"A lamp unto my feet, and a light unto my path,"' said Isarel, half to himself.

'So you do know parts of the Christian Bible? Yes, exactly.' He glanced at the clock on the dashboard, and when he spoke again, Isarel knew that the moment of confidence had gone.

'There's a good three hours yet before we'll reach London,' said Ciaran. 'Shall we stop somewhere for a bite of supper?'

'Yes, and then I'll take over the driving for a spell. Do we know where we're staying, by the way?'

'There's a smallish Franciscan House in London. Father Abbot was to phone ahead and ask could they offer hospitality for a time. You'll be sleeping in one of the bastions of Christianity tonight, my Hebrew friend.'

'That'll raise the price of pork,' said Isarel. 'Where exactly is this smallish Franciscan House?'

'As a matter of fact it's at Greenwich,' said Ciaran.

'On the site of the old Royal Palace by any chance? Yes, of course it would be,' said Isarel sarcastically. 'I daresay it's all of a piece with the rest of this madness. I should have guessed we'd end up following some ridiculous Irish will-o'-the-wisp legend.'

'Have you never heard that there are circles in Time, Isarel?'

'Oh, there are circles in Time and there are spirals and corkscrews as well, and if we're in anything at all, we're in a corkscrew,' said Isarel, at once. 'In fact, now I come to think about it, screw is the operative word here. I suppose you think Ahasuerus is tracing a circle out, do you? The next thing you'll do, you'll start talking about Wheels of Fortune and quoting Beothius.' He slid down in his seat and scowled out of the window.

Ciaran said, with perfect composure, 'The existence of the circle in Time is certainly something that can't be ignored.'

'Oh God, I knew you were about to wax philosophic. Well, let's go to the original site of Henry Tudor's Royal Palace, if we must. The place where – what did you call him – Brother Martin came in pursuit of Ahasuerus in Fifteen Hundred and something.'

'It feels odd to be in England and chasing Ahasuerus,' said Ciaran suddenly. 'I wonder are we going into a Time spiral after all.'

'I bet it'll turn out to be a corkscrew.'

Brother Martin thought it felt odd to be in England.

Sir Rodger Cheke would probably go straight to Greenwich, to lay before Thomas Cromwell and the King the spoils of his trip to Curran Glen, which meant that Martin might have to infiltrate the Court before the coffin could be regained. Therefore, certain practical matters had perforce to be considered. Martin could hardly appear at the palace wearing his monk's habit and expect to be asked in and given a favoured place at table; it was more likely that he would be hauled off to the dungeons and put in chains.

If he was to reach Ahasuerus, he would have to present an acceptable appearance, but it could not be an appearance that Cheke – if Martin should encounter him – would connect with the stern monk from Curran Glen. Martin would keep Cheke at a distance, but it was important to allow for every possibility.

He had deliberately not shaved during the journey, and a dark glossy beard now framed his face. His hair had already grown and thickened over the tonsure and he studied his appearance in a square of looking glass and thought he looked very unlike the man Cheke had met so briefly two weeks earlier. Suitably garbed, he could pass as a respectably landed squire, although it would have to be an Irish squire because the Irish accent was impossible to hide. He set himself to think which of the prominent Irish families had not offended the King, and decided on the buccaneering O'Neills. The O'Neills were one of the few Irish families still being regarded with approval by the Court, and it was rumoured that the rebellious chieftain, Con O'Neill, was to be created Earl of Tyrone. Martin thought he could use the O'Neills as a wedge to get into the Court. He would be deliberately vague about the exact degree of the relationship and even slightly embarrassed, so that a bastard connection would be assumed and awkward questions would not be asked. This was risky but not as risky as all that: Henry Tudor's Court would never tolerate a monk in their midst but the majority of them were in no position to look askance at a bastard.

It was easier than he had dared hope to keep Cheke's party in his sights as he crossed Ireland. Cheke's men were noisy and disruptive; they left a trail of drunken quarrelling and womanising, which Martin, deliberately keeping one village, one township behind, followed with ease. Once or twice he had to bribe an inn-keeper or a toll-keeper to pick up the trail, but he had been prepared for this. In any case he knew where Cheke was heading and he had no intention of trying to re-capture Ahasuerus on the journey.

He stopped at religious houses as he went, rather liking meeting other Orders; grateful for the unquestioning bed and board he was given, and the promises of prayers for his quest.

'We do not ask you to divulge any secrets, Brother,' said one bright-eyed Abbot on Ireland's east coast. 'But if you should be returning by this road it would be very interesting to hear your story – if,' he added scrupulously, 'it is a story you are permitted to tell. And, of more immediate moment, we have arranged for you to cross to England by fishing boat.'

Catherine Howard was having the time of her life.

From the moment of entering the great candle-lit, food-scented banqueting hall at Greenwich, she had been surrounded by young men, anxious to solicit her hand for the dancing after supper. It was lucky she had learnt how to dance gracefully at Grandmother's house, although it was better not to remember how Grandmother had come upon her in an intimate embrace with the young man who had taught her.

Catherine, blushing at the extravagant compliments being showered upon her, scattered promises amongst her admirers and occasionally stopped to marvel that this was actually her, this was Catherine Howard at the glittering Court of Greenwich; attracting admirers like honey attracted bees. She giggled when the young men said she was the prettiest thing to come to Court for years, and blushed in confusion when they prophesied that His Majesty would soon be casting his sights in Mistress Howard's direction.

The King *had* looked down the table at her, but this might only have been because there was such a crackle of life all round her. Naturally a King would like to know what was going on. Naturally he would look to see what was at the centre of the fun. She had found that look rather frightening, because the King was so massive, so loud and red-faced and overwhelming in his padded brocades and his jewels. Catherine, brought up on the legend of the golden-haired Tudor prince who had dazzled England and Catherine of Aragon alike in his precocious youth, was secretly disappointed in Henry and then rather sorry for him. Horrid to become old and bloated and have to be helped out of your chair, wheezing as you got up. Poor fat, old King, thought Catherine, dancing off to take her part in the pavane. Poor Anne of Cleves married to him! Could there be anything nastier than finding yourself in Henry Tudor's bed?

Martin had found it surprisingly easy to slip unnoticed into the glittering throng at the heart of this vast palace, and stand watching from a curtained alcove. The disguise seemed to be effective: Martin, accustomed to the austerity of Curran Glen, had wondered if it might be too noticeable, but one look at the Tudor Court dispelled his doubts. No one seeing this assembly tonight – any night – would ever worry about being noticeable, because every single person here was clearly engaged in a fierce struggle to be as noticeable as possible. Martin, surveying the cloth of silver and gold, the ruby brocades and the diamond-studded shoes, the ermines and martens, the dagged sleeves, padded doublets and jutting codpieces, was aware of sardonic amusement. Was this all they had? Posturing and dressing richly, intriguing and plotting? Surely they must become bored with such a vapid way of life?

It seemed they did not. They danced to what Martin thought rather jangling, discordant music, and one or two of the ladies sang in little, sweet voices, accompanying themselves on stringed instruments. Most of the songs seemed to be about love and about winning the loyalty of a golden prince. Each time the golden prince was referred to, everyone smiled and nodded in the direction of the great, heavy-jowled, red-faced man who presided at the far end of the hall and who slurped his wine from a jewelled chalice and eyed the ladies with small, rather mean eyes.

The King, thought Martin, caught between fear and fascination. Henry VIII of England, Defender of the Faith, murderer of Catholics. Nasty! Is that the once-golden Renaissance Prince, the Aragon Princess's 'Sir Loyal Heart', the vengeful lover of Anne Boleyn?

And then the King beckoned with a plump, beringed hand, and Martin saw that he was indicating a young pink-cheeked, chestnut-haired girl. There was a murmur of benevolent approval, and as the girl moved to the centre of the room and sat on the embroidered stool set out for the earlier performers Martin understood that this was a newcomer; a young girl at Court for the first time. He thought the girl was pretty but guessed the benevolence was assumed. Kindness had no part in Henry Tudor's Court.

Rodger Cheke, not quite at the centre of the Court, but padding alertly around its edges, thought that no one would dare to say aloud that the King was making a doting old fool of himself over this sauce-box Howard minx but that everyone was thinking it.

It was clear that those ambitious Howards were doing everything in their power to thrust their latest candidate for the Royal bedchamber into prominence. Any other family would have learned its lesson with Anne Boleyn, but not a bit of it: the Howards were flocking to Greenwich in triumphant droves and the sinister word 'divorce' was already hissing round the Palace. And anyone who could remember what had happened last time the word 'divorce' was mentioned – and the time before that as well – had cause to feel uneasy. It was all very well for the righteous to say that if people would intrigue and plot they must accept the consequences: this was Greenwich for heaven's sake, where you intrigued or died. Sometimes you intrigued *and* died, of course, you could never tell. And everyone knew that to utter the word 'divorce' was like dropping a stone into a pool; the ripples spread outwards and quite often they bore words like 'imprisonment'. And 'imprisonment' could ooze slimily into 'execution' and execution these days could mean anything: straightforward beheading, which was nasty, but mercifully swift; hanging, drawing and quartering, which was messy and neither merciful nor swift: while being burned alive at the stake was the grisliest, most agonising death of all.

Sir Rodger hoped he was not what men called a 'turncoat', but he thought it was impossible to help noticing that with the toppling or divorcing or death in childbed of each of Henry's queens, several leading statesmen had toppled at the same time. Was Thomas Cromwell, Cheke's own mentor, about to topple at the same time as Anne of Cleves?

The hissed word 'divorce' was already being subtly altered to 'non-consummation' which, said the Court, only went to show how determined Henry was to replace Anne from Cleves with Catherine from Norfolk, because no man – and certainly not a King – wanted *that* label hung on his codpiece. A few daring souls were already talking with epigrammatical wit about how the King could neither find, *NorFuck* the Queen, but the amusement surrounding this pleasantly bawdy jest had to be subdued. Henry VIII had not yet disembowelled any would-be jesters but there was no saying when he mightn't begin.

In such a climate you had to look out for yourself. Rodger Cheke, preparing to abandon Master Cromwell with rat-like speed, looked about him and decided that the present Bishop of Winchester, Stephen Gardiner, might do very nicely as a replacement. The King liked Gardiner. The story was that he liked him so much that he had already visited his house on the South Bank several times – quite informally. The story running alongside this was that that naughty chit Catherine Howard had visited the Bishop as well, just as informally. Nobody knew how often the visits of these two coincided but most people were prepared to lay and take wagers about it.

Rodger Cheke, keeping his eyes peeled for information and his ears pricked for useful gossip, decided to present himself at His Lordship's house. He would take along the silver coffin he had brought out of the Abbey at Curran Glen as well – yes, that was a master-stroke – because what had been intended as an offering for one master would serve equally well for another, and the Bishop was reportedly something of a collector of curiosities. Things were turning out very well indeed.

Catherine did not begin to feel afraid for what afterwards seemed to be a very long time.

It had been flattering to find herself singled out by the King, and it had been immense fun to discover that she was the centre of attention because of it. To begin with, the singling out was quite sedate and private, or as private as anything ever was at Court. There were little suppers at the house of the Bishop of Winchester, at which the Bishop never seemed to be present but at which the helpful young man newly attached to the household – Sir Rodger Cheke – was always present, waiting to escort her to the small panelled dining parlour, reminding her that a bedroom had been prepared for her should she like to accept His Lordship's hospitality for the night. Nasty and chilly to make the return journey after dark, even in May, said Sir Rodger, before discreetly withdrawing.

Catherine was expected to preside over the suppers, and afterwards she was nearly always required to play her lute and sing. She fell into the habit of using the minstrel's lute on these occasions: she thought she never played so well as when she used it and it was important to play her very best for the King. There was nothing to worry about in the King's interest: Henry was at least thirty years older than Catherine and therefore well beyond any kind of dalliance.

There was nothing to worry about but there was everything to worry about.

To begin with, the little evenings had not been alarming. It had even been rather fun to accept the Bishop's offer of a room for the night. Catherine had accepted it several times now, enjoying the unusual privacy of having a room to herself, liking the lavish breakfasts the next morning and the subtle deference accorded to her by Rodger Cheke and the rest of the Bishop's household.

The King was fatherly: he wanted to hear all about her, and he sat close at her side patting her hand – his huge meaty fist swallowed up her own small hand – and told her how pretty she was. Catherine had not minded this and she had rather enjoyed hearing the stories he had to tell: the splendid pageantry that had taken place before she was born; the famous meeting with Francois of France on the Field of Cloth of Gold; the marvellous joustings and hunts of Henry's youth, and of course the battles against France when he had taken part in the sieges on Therouanne and Tournai. She did not mind either when he brought her presents: ruby and pearl clusters; a square of table diamonds which could be worn as a hair ornament; the dearest little sable-lined muff to keep her hands warm. These were things that could be worn openly and defiantly.

The King was always so splendidly dressed, his hair and beard rubbed with scented oils and his jewels so dazzling, that Catherine was able to overlook the fatness and the fact that he puffed and wheezed when he got up from the table. She was even able to ignore how the fatness caused him to waddle when he walked across a room.

But none of it could be ignored on the night late in May, because when Catherine entered the panelled supper room there was Henry, clad in a fur-trimmed robe, partly open at the top to expose flesh and a sprinkling of coarse grey chest-hair, and so negligently tied at the waist it was obvious that he wore nothing beneath. His face was red and shiny and when he leaned over her, his breath was sour from the spiced wine he had been drinking.

The instant Catherine saw the furred robe and glimpsed the naked, not very wholesome flesh beneath, she felt cold and a bit fearful. When Henry invited her to sit on his lap she felt frightened, because it was hardly an invitation, it was more like a Royal command.

But she took a deep breath and did as she was bidden, but as she sat cautiously on Henry's mammoth thighs and felt his hand slide slyly into the bosom of her gown, she could not help remembering that this was the hand that had struck off her cousin Anne's head – not literally of course but as good as – and when she felt the fleshy thighs shift under her, she remembered the suppurating ulcers from which Henry suffered.

There was a stale, sickish smell from between his thighs as well – his male organs? – oh God and he's pulling my hand down to touch him! Her hand brushed the bandage over one thigh and she wondered in panic if a pus-filled leg was preferable to a sketchily washed prick. Royal prick. Royal or not, he's barely half-mast, thought Catherine, daring to glance down to where her hands were being guided into the most intimate of caressings.

The large red face swam nearer, and Catherine forced herself to smile, and prayed she would not sick up the mulled wine she had drunk ten minutes earlier. Was she seeming sufficiently inviting? Was she seeming dazzled and flattered?

It seemed she was. Henry reached eagerly beneath her skirts, and Catherine, feeling his thick fingers between her thighs, thought dizzily: I've misread the entire situation; he's intending to make me his mistress, after all. Is he? Yes, I believe he is. Can I do it? Can I let this bloated, red-faced, old man do that to me? Heaving and grunting, naked in a bed . . .? And which bed? Whose bed? Would she be expected to lead him to the room allotted her in this house? Was that why it had been set aside in the first place? Or would they do it here, on the floor or the settle? Not even Catherine's wildest imaginings had ever included being ravished on the floor by the King of England.

But all the time a little voice was beating insistently against her brain, and it was a little voice that said: I'm being a success! and a tiny core of ambition she had not known she possessed curled itself about her mind. She was successful! She was snaring the King! She was succeeding where all those curved-nail women who had looked down their noses at her had failed!

And under all that, buried very deeply beneath the insistent voice, a dark undercurrent of fear was swirling and eddying, because to excite the admiration of this particular King was courting danger with both hands.

It would be undignified to lie on the floor and open her legs for Henry, but it might be safer to do that than to marry him. Vague plans began to coil and uncoil in her mind, and half with the idea of teasing the King, but also to gain a breathing space, Catherine slid off the massive Royal lap, and reached for her lute. Should they not have a little music before matters progressed any further? she said, her eyes innocent, but her lips curving in a mischievous smile. Without waiting for the King's response, she picked up the minstrel's lute, running her hands over the smooth polished surface.

In the firelit supper parlour of the Bishop of Winchester, Catherine Howard played for Henry Tudor the ancient music taught to a renegade High Priest almost a millennium and a half earlier. The thin cool notes drifted out through the window in the scented May night, and in the upper room that the Bishop had utilised for the storing of the very interesting ancient coffin presented by the helpful Sir Rodger Cheke, Ahasuerus opened his eyes.

Chapter Twenty-Eight

The awakening was smoother and easier this time.

Ahasuerus lay for a while listening, waiting, absorbing the ambience of whatever world he was in. Cooler than Cremona. Farther north? Yes, possibly. Did Simon and the monks bring me here? Where is 'here'? There was the impression of vaguely stifling luxury, and beyond that an unease; the sense of corruption and inter-mingling intrigues. A frightened people. Yes, but a greedy people as well. Eager for power. And the music is here. Susannah's music. Isabella's music. A smile curved his lips. The warmth was flooding his body as it had done in the catacombs outside Cremona, and he could feel the familiar cramping pains in his calves and forearms. But beneath the pain was an undercurrent of excitement. I am going to do it again! I am going to answer the music, and walk in the world on the other side of the grave once more!

He had no means of knowing yet what kind of world it would be, or how many years had passed, but he knew the music was close. And this time he would be warier, more watchful. He would remember the lesson learned in Cremona and there would be no arrogant setting aside of plagues: no careless imperious sprinkling of the music at the feet of fools. No bargains involving red-haired seductresses.

He looked cautiously about him. At least he was in a room in a house, and not in stifling, decay-drenched catacombs. It was unfamiliarly furnished and there were a number of objects whose purpose Ahasuerus did not recognise, but there was a discernible resemblance to Cosimo Amati's little house. A bed stood at the room's centre, with wooden posts at each corner and a flat canopy over it. Someone had thrown down a silk-fringed shawl: Ahasuerus recognised it as an item of feminine apparel – Isabella Amati had worn something very similar around her shoulders that first night.

He padded across the room to a deep cupboard set into the chimney wall, and surveyed its contents thoughtfully, and then looked at his reflection in the long oval looking glass.

His hands bore the mutilations of Cosimo Amati's revenge. Burned maimed claws. So he was to bear those wounds just as his back bore the wounds of the scourging at the pillar in Jerusalem, was he? Bitterness welled up again, but he beat it down. Concentrate on blending with the people of this unknown world; think about how to talk to them if their language was unknown, as the Cremona language had been. Could he pass as a traveller of some kind? Surely travellers were normal in any world?

The cupboard yielded a number of unfamiliar items of dress, but there were several sets of what Ahasuerus saw to be gloves. Could they conceal the burned claw-hands? He tried them and thought they could.

The other clothes struck him as faintly ridiculous: odd thin woollen coverings for the legs and short breech-like garments of thick rather luxurious stuff for the body, but it was fairly easy to know what to wear on which part. And once on, the things were surprisingly comfortable: soft and subtly caressing. He discarded the dark cloak – no one would question an ordinary cloak hanging in what was clearly a place for garments – and looked back at his mirror-self. All right? A smile curved his lips. All right. I can do it! I can go out into this unknown world and blend with it! The rich, dark red, velvet cloak and the glowing emerald and silver brocades of the other garments had at first seemed over-elaborate and faintly absurd but now he saw that they gave him an exotic look.

He slipped out of the door and went as warily as a cat through the Bishop of Winchester's house, towards the music.

He saw the girl through the half-open door; a servant of some kind had carried in a flagon of wine, and failed to close it properly. Ahasuerus could see straight in. He could see how the candlelight cast a soft aureole of radiance about her head and he could see the curve of her cheek. His heart lurched and he thought: Susannah! And then: or is it? Am I wanting to see her so much that I allow my eyes to trick me? But she is playing the music.

Keeping to the shadows, he skirted the galleried landing, and managed to conceal himself in the recess of a deep curtained window.

This child was not quite Susannah, not in the way that Isabella Amati had been. This one had not Susannah's red hair, despite the chestnut lights glinting beneath the head-dress. But Ahasuerus saw now that there were more similarities than he had initially thought. She was young and ingenuous-looking, and although at first glance she was as innocent as a babe, she had Susannah's eyes and Susannah's ancient-wisdom smile. She had Susannah's deceptive guilelessness as well: the same virtuous eyes, belied by the mischief trickling from her sensual lips. Ahasuerus felt Time spiral backwards, so that for a moment he was in the Temple again, hearing the ancient beckoning for the first time.

And then he saw what he had not seen before: the coarse brutal-featured man in the loosely girdled robe sitting watching the girl – *his* girl, the present keeper of Susannah's music! The small hot eyes were blazing with possessive lust and the girl was struggling to conceal her repulsion.

The small private bedchamber set aside by the amiable Sir Rodger Cheke for Catherine's especial use had never seemed so welcoming. Get inside, close the door against any further importunities, and survey this haven gratefully. Yes, and give thanks that the King's fumblings stopped short of complete love-making.

She was so busy savouring her deliverance – was that too strong a word? no! – and thanking heaven that she had managed to hide her revulsion, that it was a moment before she realised that someone had been in her room while she was downstairs.

This should not have been sinister: it certainly should not have caused a cold trickle of fear. Maids and laundresses would presumably come in and out, and the Bishop's servants were probably not above snooping to see what latest trinket His Majesty had bestowed. And I wouldn't trust that unctuous Rodger Cheke either! thought Catherine fiercely.

There was something inexpressibly eerie about the feeling in the room. As if someone had come stealing in, glancing over his shoulder and had concealed himself. Catherine looked about her.

Her silk-fringed shawl was at the foot of the bed, instead of on the pillow, and she had certainly not left the casement window open. It swung to and fro a little in the night air, tapping against the mellow red brick outside. She leaned out to pull it to.

The clothes press was ajar, and a long dark cloak was

half spilling out. Catherine pushed the door firmly shut. Better. There was an unfamiliar smell in here as well – something old and dry and stale and rather sad. That might be what had made her uneasy. It was an uneasy kind of smell: it made you think of ancient tragedies and lost loves and – what did the priests say? – unhousell'd spirits. Only you did not talk about priests these days, not without first looking round to see who was within hearing. Probably the old, sad smell was nothing more than garden rubbish being burned below her window. She gave a stir to the bowl of lavender on the side table and then threw off her clothes and reached for the ewer of warm water and the geranium-scented soap put out for her. Whatever else Rodger Cheke might be, he was very thorough when it came to guests' comforts. She sluiced away the feeling of the King's hands on her body.

Lovely to slide between the lawn sheets of the tester bed. The room was faintly scented with lavender now. Luxury beyond imagining not to have to pretend pleasure at Henry VIII's clumsy fumblings and proddings. No wonder he has trouble siring children, thought Catherine, half defiant, half pitying. Imagine discovering that the King of England was so inadequate. It gave her an unexpected feeling of superiority to have seen the King's precise degree of potency. Hardly even half mast, thought Catherine, smiling sleepily into the pillow. Soft as a feather pillow, in fact. It was a pity it was not the kind of information you could make use of.

It was at this point that the door opened and Henry himself, still clad only in the fur-trimmed robe, entered the room and crossed to the bed.

Catherine gasped and shrank back against the pillows, and Henry lumbered on to the bed, his small eyes hot with lust, his hands reaching for her body.

The fumbling and the prodding was much more urgent and far more insistent than it had been earlier, and Catherine choked back shudders of disgust.

He pushed aside her thin bedgown impatiently, squeezing her small, high breasts and reaching lower. His hands were strong, the fingers like iron. Murderer's hands. I'm being raped by a murderer.

His body was coarser and grosser than it had seemed downstairs. Rolls of fat, thought Catherine, her mind spinning dizzily out of control. Mounds of blubber. And the bandages over that weeping sore. This was worlds and years worse than the half-respectful caressings downstairs: this was blind greedy lust. Clutching hands and hot fetid breath and thrusting groin. It's *repulsive*, cried her mind. Revolting.

In the end it was a heaving, struggling affair of hands and bodies, of stroking and prodding and then of being coaxed to take the flaccid lump of manhood in her hands and rub ceaselessly until her wrist was aflame with cramping agony. And even now, he's barely standing! thought Catherine, torn between pity and exasperation. I mustn't let him guess I'm comparing him with anybody. I certainly mustn't show disgust.

The really dreadful thing was that the King's struggling lust was stirring up feelings that she was not supposed to have, feelings she was supposed to have forgotten about. Grandmother had said very sternly that Catherine must put behind her those shameful nights in the Norfolk house when all manner of debauchery had apparently taken place – Her Grace had heard about it all and very unseemly it had all sounded!

Catherine, in a whirl of delighted gratitude at being brought to Court, had done her best. Part of a slightly regrettable youth. To be put firmly in the past.

The trouble was that once you had known what it felt like to be made love to – properly and fiercely and *satisfyingly* – you could not settle for anything else. Catherine, her body stirred by the King's flimsy love-making, thought angrily: what wouldn't I give to be in bed with a real man now!

And then, just as she thought her wrist would explode with pain, the King, red-faced, grunting and sweating, clutched her shoulders painfully and bellowed in triumph.

'Ha, sweetheart! Now you see how a proper man does! Now—'

The sad sparse drops of love-offerings splashed thinly on to her thighs, and he fell across her, gasping and wheezing.

'You'd get – nothing like that from the – primping boys of the Court!' gasped Henry.

'No, I am sure not, sire,' said Catherine obediently, and felt the wet stickiness on her body, and thought rebelliously: no, for *that* would scarcely fill half a thimble, never mind make a Tudor prince! She lay back, thankful that it was over, Henry still slumped heavily across her, pinning her to the bed.

It was at that instant that she caught a movement on the other side of the room. She turned her head and saw the door of the clothes press, slowly opening.

The figure of a tall, dark-haired man with the most beautiful clear grey eyes Catherine had ever seen bounded across the room and dragged the King from the bed with angry contempt, flinging him to the floor. Henry's head struck the corner of the bedpost and he slid gruntingly into an unconscious heap.

Catherine had always known that she possessed a good

deal of what some people called wantonness in her make-up. All those nights in Grandmother's house, all those young men—

She had absolutely no idea who the dark-haired stranger was, but he had dragged the King from her bed and shaken him as if Henry had been no more than a disobedient dog, before flinging him to the floor. There had been blazing anger in his face and in that instant, Catherine had felt a shaft of desire so violent slice through her, that for a moment the room tilted. She forced herself to look to where the King lay. Dead? No, don't let him be dead! At least not in my bedchamber! She was half horrified, half angry because self-preservation was the last emotion she should be feeling.

But Henry was not dead. He was certainly unconscious, and rather repulsively so: he was sprawled across the floor in bloated disarray, his legs open and that organ which reportedly had so assiduously tried to quicken four Queens' wombs was flopping over his left thigh in an ungainly fashion. His face was empurpled and spittle dribbled from his flaccid lips. Horrid! thought Catherine. But at least he's only stunned. This stranger hasn't killed him.

This stranger . . .

Ahasuerus turned his head towards her and his astonishing eyes seemed to blaze with life and to shine a dazzling, hurting light into the darkest, most secret corners of her mind.

Catherine felt as if she had been suddenly tossed from a high cliff into a black, boiling sea, and in the same moment there was a flash of something – she was not sure what – but it was somehow bound up with a brutish, glowering sunset and a tormented figure silhouetted against it, blood-streaked and dying in agony . . .

319

Susannah . . . The name spun dizzily about her head, but she had no idea if it had been spoken aloud or if it was part of that churning darkness and that lonely tortured figure . . .

And then the queer half-vision faded, and Catherine remembered that she was naked in the bed and then thought there was really no point in trying to hide it. It was a pity that the sheets still smelled of the King, but other than that— And Henry would surely be unconscious for a little while yet.

Because here was the real man, the proper man she had been longing for not ten minutes since. She smiled and said softly, 'I think you have tried to save me from what you believed to be a rape, sir. And I am very grateful to you indeed.'

It was the most shameful thing anyone could ever have done anywhere, ever. To have one lover lying in a snorting stupor at the foot of your bed, while the one who had put him there took you into his arms.

And this time there was no awkward embarrassing coaxing to be done: the man, whoever he was, felt like steel covered in purest silk against her body. Silk entering you, steel firing the embers so clumsily lit earlier. Catherine forgot about her erstwhile Royal partner, and drew him closer, feeling the purest ecstasy she had ever known unfold.

The fact that he did not undress lent an air of spiralling urgency to what he was doing: the feel of his silk-gloved hands briefly caressing her body and sliding under the lawn bedgown, was the most arousing sensation she had ever known. Like a cat's velvet paws, but with the hint of cruel claws beneath, ready to unsheath. It was a ridiculous thing to think at such a moment, but Catherine, spinning into ecstasy, did think it.

Silken claws and pleasure beyond imagining, and violent steely passion. There would never be any feeling in the world to equal this, not if she lived to be eighty, not if she lived for ever . . .

Ahasuerus moved against her, and the spinning rapture claimed them both.

Ahasuerus had attacked the grunting, red-faced creature because he had been hurting Susannah. An immense anger had flooded his mind so that he had been across the room and dragging the man off the bed almost before he had realised it. It had been *good* to feel the flabby creature cringe and struggle: it had been strong soaring joy to see him fall helplessly on the floor. *That's* for forcing your repulsive body on to Susannah! he had thought in triumph, and that's for spewing your seed over her body like an animal!

The exultant feeling had sent fierce longing through him, and when the girl had held out her arms, he had gone into them. It was the maddest, most dangerous thing ever, but he had always known that a very thin line separated violence from sexual arousal, and that an even thinner one could separate sexual arousal from insanity. As he went into Catherine Howard's bed, he was distantly aware that he was crossing that line.

Her body was the sweetest, most ardent thing imaginable. Ahasuerus felt it close about him, and he felt her delighted response. So the old man had managed to warm her a little, had he? Her lips opened under his, the most natural thing in the world, and the culmination, when it broke, shook them both with its force.

But he dared not allow himself the luxury of lying in her arms. The old man was stirring, making choking gasps where he lay. Ahasuerus moved from the bed towards the door, and in that moment, Henry opened his eyes and saw his attacker.

Chapter Twenty-Nine

The King sat in the apartments set aside for his use and regarded the Bishop of Winchester and Sir Rodger Cheke balefully.

He had never been so outraged in his entire life. It came to something if a King could not pay an innocent visit to his little protégée, solely for the purpose of bidding her a good night's repose – *solely* for that, said Henry, fixing Sir Rodger with so fierce an eye that Sir Rodger blenched – and then find himself set upon by a ruffian hiding in her room. Did the Bishop not give a proper eye to his guests' safety? demanded Henry, working himself up into a tantrum. Did Cheke himself not have a care to the life of his King? The intruder would certainly have murdered him where he stood, said Henry wrathfully, and even in his own chaotic state of mind, Sir Rodger noted that the King had been careful to say 'stood' and not 'lain'.

Murdered within call of dozens of people, said Henry furiously; brought within a pig's whisker of death, and the guards never even hearing until Henry himself had called out for them to come to his aid! Well, the creature who had been hiding in Mistress Howard's bedchamber was to be taken to the Tower forthwith – *forthwith*, Sir Rodger was to mind – and there left to rot in chains.

Rodger Cheke, brought up on the 'good laws of Edward the Confessor' and Magna Carta, murmured something about a fair trial before a just punishment but Henry was having none of this. If a King – and a King of England at that! – could not order imprisonment for a creature who had attempted not just plain murder but actual regicide, there was no justice in the world.

'Of course he daren't let it be known that he was found in Catherine Howard's bed,' said the Bishop of Winchester, approached for advice afterwards by the anxious Sir Rodger. 'We none of us dare let it get out. And the King certainly can't risk any kind of trial for the man— Who is he by the way, do we know yet?'

Sir Rodger, who was beginning to wonder if the game was worth the candle, explained that the assailant had been placed under temporary restraint in the Bishop's own wine cellars but that so far as anyone could tell he spoke no English, nor French nor Spanish.

'Try him in Latin,' said His Lordship. 'Explain to him that he's being taken to the Tower and that he'd better put his soul to rights with God in whatever way he chooses. Oh, and Cheke, if this ever does get out, for the sake of all our reputations make sure it's never known where we imprisoned the culprit last night. We don't want to find ourselves a laughing stock.'

Sir Rodger quite understood all of this. You could not be letting people know that the King of England was having clandestine and adulterous meetings with a chit of a girl thirty years younger; you certainly could not let people know that the Bishop of Winchester had lent his support to such sinful meetings, or that the arrangements made by Sir Rodger had been so inadequate that a murderous foreigner had gone on the rampage. Sir Rodger had been welcomed very pleasantly into the Bishop's household, and even though his duties had turned out to include acting as pander to Henry, a plump emolument had been offered by way of recompense. It was very important indeed to guard the King's reputation and the Bishop's but it was even more important to guard Sir Rodger's and he did not intend to go down in history as the man who had put Henry VIII's murderer in a wine cellar.

They would all keep the secret and Catherine Howard would keep it as well, because the King would tell her she must, and she would be too frightened to disobey him. It was not a secret that would need to be kept for long, because whoever this unknown man was, he would die inside the Tower before he was much older. Even if the cold and the disease and the sparse food did not kill him, Henry would arrange for one of his scuttling sycophants to finish him off. Poison in the food. A clean silent smothering. It would not be the first time that embarrassing prisoners had been discreetly killed inside those grim dungeons; Sir Rodger knew this and the Bishop would know it even better. It was not anything that needed to be put into words.

But since this foreigner had tried to murder Henry Tudor, death in some wretched dungeon was no more than he deserved and in fact a far kinder death than he had any right to expect.

Ahasuerus understood that he had been taken prisoner because the man he had attacked was a powerful ruler and everyone was frightened of him. This had been apparent the minute the guards had rushed in to the room at the man's summoning.

Fear of a ruler was something Ahasuerus could sympathise with, but the hasty interment in the sour-smelling wine cellar, the furtive scuffling into captivity was not. Were there no trials here, no justice?

It seemed there were not. Once in the cellar he was chained to the wall and his hands were restrained with iron manacles. The two men brought in to do this were coarse-featured, brutish-natured, and they jeered at his maimed hands, pretending to dodge out of their range as if Ahasuerus was a clawed wild beast. One had a lowering jutting forehead and the other a disfiguring squint. Ahasuerus received the impression of low intelligence in them both and all the old arrogance and rebelliousness surfaced. How dare these unknown people treat him like this! How dare they throw a High Priest into a dark, windowless, underground room, with keepers whose comprehension was that of brute-beasts! He held on to the fury, because it was a strong emotion, and strong emotions helped people survive in times of danger. He would not let these creatures cow him and he would certainly not show them any fear.

He did not try to talk to them. The greedy-featured man called *Cheke* had questioned him earlier, speaking in halting, very imprecise Latin. Ahasuerus had understood *Cheke*'s meaning but he had been wary; he had said only that he was a traveller from the East. He had been unable to tell how this had been received, or even if *Cheke* had properly understood him.

The two keepers apparently had sufficient intelligence to follow orders, because several hours after his capture – Ahasuerus had lost all sense of time in the dark cellar, but he thought it might be the next night – they dragged him out of the house and down a short flight of slippery steps to where a small boat was tied to a tiny landing stage, with below it a dark slow river flowing silently past. A low-lying mist wreathed the river's surface.

As Ahasuerus stared at the lapping waters and the waiting boat fear clutched at his throat. Where am I being taken? What are they going to do to me? And what happened to Susannah?

The two guards led him down into the boat, and

clambered in after him. As they rowed out into the expanse of dark water the mist shrouded them, muffling everything, so that the only sound was the rhythmic dip of the oars. Ahasuerus shivered and pulled his cloak more closely about him. A cold place, this. Lavish and splendid on the surface, but corrupt and selfish and grasping underneath. He thought that his first impression had not been far wrong: it was a little like Cremona had been, but it was a Cremona grown grander, grown greedier and shriller.

The river mist clung to them with dank, clammy fingers, making it difficult to see more than a yard or two ahead, but one of the guards had hung a horn lantern from the boat's prow and a smeary light showed their way. Ahasuerus made out tall, very splendid houses on their left and saw that almost all of them had flights of stone steps leading down to small landing stages where boats were tethered. Under any other circumstances he would have been interested in this custom of building houses on to a river so that you could use it for travelling, but he was chilled to the bone and more apprehensive than he had ever been in his life.

The two guards were peering through the mist, occasionally glancing furtively over their shoulders as if fearful of pursuit, once or twice exchanging low-voiced remarks. As the river curved to the left one of them nudged his companion and pointed to something ahead and fear closed about Ahasuerus's heart. Looming up out of the swirling fog was a huge dark fortress, a great brutish hulk of a building, so immense that for a moment sheer awe drove out the fear.

The dipping of the oars was muffled by the mist and a brooding silence seemed to lie over the river. As they drew nearer, Ahasuerus saw that the fortress was built of dark, rough stone, with jagged towers silhouetted menacingly against the night sky, and with mean slitted windows set high up in the turrets. Here and there flaring torches burned in twisted wall brackets, casting a wavering, reddish glow over the stones. An icy hand gripped his entrails. Whatever this place was it was grim and fearsome; it was soaked in human agonies and human despair. *And I am being taken inside.*

The walls were so close that Ahasuerus could see where the black stone was crumbling in places, and how there was a crusting of moss and lichen in the cracks. He shuddered, wondering what lay within this dark river prison. Ever since they had taken him from the cellar he had been trying to plan an escape, but this was not a place he could possibly escape from: this was a place so far removed from anything he had ever encountered that he could not even begin to assimilate any kind of plan. As they drew closer he could smell the stench of death and torment and fear.

The two men were rowing through a high stone entrance now, gouged out of the thick harsh stone and lit by flaring twists of wood thrust into iron wall brackets above the water. Where the light fell it cast hundreds of tiny dancing lights on the river's surface.

There was the fearsome sound of immense machinery over their heads, and in front of them a huge portcullis began to rise, with a screeching, clanking sound that made Ahasuerus think of snapping teeth and the gobbling jaws of leviathans. So their arrival had been expected, and someone had been watching out for them. As they passed under the yawning grille he looked up and saw the dozens of pointed iron teeth that guarded the entrance. Would they bite down after the boat had passed through?

The open stretches of river were behind them now and they were rowing along a narrow inlet, bounded on both sides by the ancient walls. The lantern cast a dull glow on the walls, and several times the boat bumped against them. From somewhere nearby was the steady drip of water, the sound magnified and echoing sinisterly.

The shadow of St Thomas's Tower fell across them as they entered the Tower of London through the legend-drenched Traitors' Gate.

Behind them there was the deafening clang of iron machinery as the terrible portcullis descended once more.

Chapter Thirty

The Greenwich monastery that Ciaran had referred to was much nearer to the Tower of London than Isarel had been expecting.

'In the shadow of old Henry the Eighth's butchery,' observed Ciaran, spreading out the *A to Z* to direct Isarel through the night streets. 'You can almost see Traitors' Gate from Father Abbot's study, I believe.'

To their left was the muted hum of London's never-still night traffic, but to the right was the unmistakable lapping of the Thames, muffled and subtle. Isarel had the sudden feeling that he was straddling two worlds: one the rushing importantly busy twentieth century, and the other a long-ago world where people had different fears and different stresses. Where you did not have to worry about nuclear wars and Third World starvation, or unemployment and inflation, but where, if you were caught practising the wrong religion at the wrong time, you could lose your head and your entrails in a grisly form of legalised murder. Were terrorist bombs preferable to being hanged, drawn and quartered? Isarel frowned and shook his head to clear the nightmare images. Perhaps it was the closeness of the Thames that was making him feel like this. Hadn't Tudor London – Henry VIII's London – used the Thames in the way people today used the M25? I wonder if it got as congested, he thought. Tudor rush hour. Tailbacks of barges for five miles.

The river had seen centuries of history and some of it had been very dark and very bloody history indeed. All those people who had been rowed by night to the Tower, and flung into some wretched, windowless dungeon to die of cold and hunger. A riverboat carrying prisoners intended for St Thomas's Tower shed its load earlier today, and passengers are advised to use alternative routes because the floating corpses are blocking two lanes . . .

He scowled and with a vague association of ideas, but also with the intention of bringing himself back into the present, reached for the switch of the car's radio.

'Do you mind, Ciaran? Just to keep me awake for the last stretch?' Just to keep me in the twentieth century, said his mind.

'Yes, sure.'

It was just after midnight, and as Isarel swung the car in the direction of Greenwich Observatory, the midnight news headlines were ending. The Economy, somebody's speech in the House of Commons, a plane crash somewhere . . .

And then the announcer said, 'The Metropolitan Police reported earlier that there is still no news of Kate Kendal who vanished from her North London home yesterday and that they have not ruled out the possibility of kidnapping. Kate Kendal has a music promotions agency in Central London, and is married to the anthropologist, Dr Richard Kendal, who published several books on his subject, before a severe injury three years ago forced him to live in semi-retirement.'

Isarel jerked the car to the side of the road and switched off the ignition. He and Ciaran sat in stunned silence, staring at the radio.

And then Isarel said, 'Ahasuerus. He's got Kate. It must

be that; it's too much of a coincidence to be anything else.' He glanced at Ciaran, silent and still at his side. 'If Kate took Ahasuerus to her house,' said Isarel, 'which is a reasonable assumption, and if Ahasuerus broke out, God alone knows what might have happened. They mention a husband – did we know she had a husband?'

'No, but it doesn't matter.' Ciaran's eyes were shadowed, but after a moment he said, 'I think you're right about Ahasuerus being involved. But I can't begin to think where he'd have taken Kate—'

'Or more to the point, why.'

'No, but we've got to find out.' He broke off, and Isarel said,

'You know, it's probably wholly illogical, but I haven't been seeing Ahasuerus as a killer.'

'According to the legends, he never was.'

'But you're no longer sure about it.'

'No. I believe he was appallingly mutilated by Henry the Eighth's men and it's possible that because of it he's no longer entirely sane—' He made an angry gesture. 'I hear what I'm saying, but I hardly believe I'm saying it. I'm talking as if he's an ordinary sentient being—'

'We're both doing that.'

'Yes. But God help me, Isarel,' said Ciaran, his voice filled with angry bitterness, 'I don't know what we do next. I don't even know where we start. I've been out of the world for too long. Twelve years of the cloister— I can't cope with practicalities any more—' He hit the dashboard angrily. 'Sod being in Curran Glen, it's equipped me for fuck-all—'

He broke off, and Isarel thought: it's not so much to do with the monastery as the girl – Kate. She's stirred up something in you that you thought you had under control, only I don't think you ever did have it under control, not properly. And I think you're in the wrong job, my friend.

After a moment, he said, 'When you let down the barriers you do it with a vengeance.' And without giving Ciaran time to reply, 'One thing at a time. First off, we'll find Kate's address.'

'That ought to be easy enough.' Ciaran's tone was noncommittal.

'And after that,' said Isarel, starting up the car again, 'we'll try to talk to people who knew her. We might get a lead there. Neighbours, or her business associates. His business associates, even.'

'Won't the police have done all that?'

Isarel said thoughtfully, 'They might. But I'd guess they aren't treating it too seriously yet. Unless there was any evidence of violence or force – or something unmistakable like a ransom note – they're probably being pretty perfunctory about it. "Your wife's vanished, has she, sir? Dear me, very worrying for you, but these things happen." The police are probably making mental reservations about lovers – yes, and remembering that this is a lady with a husband who's disabled in some way.'

'The radio said a severe injury that forced him into semi-retirement—'

'I'll bet,' said Isarel, 'that the only reason Kate's disappearance got into that news bulletin at all was because of her husband's tragedy, whatever it was. It's exactly the kind of thing today's press would pounce on. Journalists are ghouls and cannibals, although I'll admit there was probably some news value in Kendal's reputation. It sounded as if he was quite well known in his own circles. I wonder what happened to him three years ago? That might be another line of enquiry we could pursue.'

'I wonder,' said Ciaran, 'if it was anything to do with the music.'

'Now that I hadn't thought of.' Isarel put the car in gear and let out the clutch. 'Did you mean that about Curran Glen, by the way?'

'I've no idea. I think we turn left along there for Greenwich.'

The guest master welcomed them at the Greenwich Monastery, waved aside any suggestion that their extremely late arrival might have caused inconvenience, hunted out a telephone directory at Isarel's request, and padded off to make them a pot of tea.

Isarel drank the hot tea gratefully, and turned the pages of the directory.

'You've found her?'

'Yes. There's no private number, but there's a business one in Central London.' He passed the phone book over.

'Kate Kendal & Associates,' said Ciaran, reading the entry. 'And an address in Old Compton Street. "Music Promotions: publicity for all Orchestral and Sinfonia Concerts. National Trust Concerts arranged. Specialists in late baroque and chamber music."'

Ciaran looked across at Isarel, who said softly, 'I'm on home ground with the lady.' He set down his teacup and stood up, stretching to ease the stiffness of the long drive. 'It's one o'clock in the morning,' he said. 'Lead me to the cells before I fall asleep at this table. If there's a hair shirt laid out on my bed I shall tear it up and throw it out of the window.

'But in the morning we'll phone Kate Kendal's office.'

Kendal & Associates were housed in one of the old redbrick buildings near the Charing Cross Road end of Old Compton Street.

'Bang in the centre of Soho,' said Isarel, sending Ciaran

334

a malicious grin. 'You're falling among the thieves and robbers and the whores with a vengeance now, Brother Ciaran.'

'Christ rubbed shoulders with them all,' observed Ciaran.

'Well, so long as you don't start overturning the Money Lenders' Tables in the Temple.'

A bistro took up the entire ground floor of the building, and there were three or four floors above.

'And police and paparazzi everywhere,' said Isarel, surveying the crowds disgustedly. 'No wonder the bistro was suggested as the meeting place. Didn't I say that reporters were vultures? Let's go straight in, shall we? Those two females in black leather look as if they're staking us out.'

'What did he sound like?' asked Ciaran as they found a corner table of the smoky, garlic-scented bistro. 'The partner?'

'She. American. Energetic. And a kind of brusque efficiency mixed with unconventionality. She asked for a couple of phone numbers so that she could check our credentials beforehand.'

'What did you give her?'

'The Greenwich Monastery and Curran Glen Abbey,' said Isarel. 'What did you expect me to give her? The nearest hell fire club or a strip joint? Pass the wine list, for heaven's sake. I'll need at least half a bottle if I've got to cope with American dynamism.'

'Greenwich and Curran Glen will undoubtedly vouch for us,' said Ciaran. He sounded abstracted and Isarel looked up from the wine list.

'What's the matter?' He met Ciaran's eyes, and comprehension dawned. 'God, yes of course, it's all this, isn't it? You're out in the world again – I mean really out.

As you said last night, twelve years in a monastery didn't equip you for—'

'—you're bowdlerising what I actually said—'

'—didn't equip you for any of this,' said Isarel, ignoring the interruption. 'The journey here – motorways, the ferry – they didn't make much impact, because they were transitional things, and Greenwich Monastery's like an extension of Curran Glen. But this is different. Not just this bistro, but London, Soho, everything. People and shops and the tube and the rush hour. This is the real world again, and you've been rocketed back into it, and it's happened so abruptly that it must feel like a – a series of violent blows.' He looked at the crowded restaurant. In one corner, three men in their twenties wearing sharply-tailored suits discussed finance and answered mobile phones that rang intrusively. At another table, some kind of interview was clearly being given, and the table was strewn with a notebook and pens and a small portable recorder. Elsewhere people swapped office scandal or rehearsed sales presentations, or post-mortemed meetings.

Ciaran said quietly, 'I'd forgotten how loud the world was.' He gestured briefly about him. 'At first sight you'd think they were doing it to impress. Talking loudly, answering those mobile phones to show everyone how busy and important they are. It's hype – have I the right word?'

'Oh yes.'

'But they don't know they're doing it, do they? Even if they did it for effect at the beginning, they aren't now. They're like rats going round and round on a treadmill, but they're no longer aware of the treadmill.' His eyes went from one table to another. 'I thought I'd put it all behind me,' he said, half to himself. 'All that worldly allure. All those temptations.'

'But,' said Isarel softly, 'they're still there? The temptations?'

'Yes, they're still there.' Ciaran's eyes flickered over the crowded bistro, and then he made an impatient gesture and said in a much sharper voice, 'Well, one thing I do remember about temptation is that the only thing to do with it is yield to it. Have we a decent Hock on the wine list?'

Lauren Mayhew sat opposite to them and ate poached trout and salad niçoise with the brisk attention of one intent on nothing other than re-fuelling. She was a small, energetic lady of about thirty-five, with short fair hair cut in a glossy cap, and huge tinted spectacles which emphasised very striking blue eyes. The American accent was not as marked as it had been on the phone.

She talked in short, sharp bursts between mouthfuls, punctuating her story about Kate Kendal with frequent draughts of the sharp frosty Traminer which Isarel had ordered, and which she drank as if it was tap water.

'That's pretty much all I know about this crazy business,' she said, laying down her knife and fork and reaching for cigarettes. 'And it's not a whole lot more than you know. Do you mind if I smoke? Kate hated it in the office, but it helps me to think.' She arranged her cigarette packet squarely in line with the lighter. 'Kate was meeting the guy from the Hampstead Concert for lunch on the day she disappeared: and then Richard and Moira saw him break into the house and take the thing out of the coffin later the same day – around five.'

Ciaran leaned forward abruptly. 'You did say Moira Mahoney?' he said, and Isarel glanced at him.

'Yes. I guess you'd know her, of course. Kate picked her up in Curran Glen, or maybe she picked Kate up, I'm not sure which. I don't know too much about her yet.'

337

'Red hair and huge smoky eyes?'

'And a complexion I'd give my virtue to have,' agreed Lauren. 'Oh, and some kind of slightly damaged foot or twisted leg or something, although it's the last thing you notice about her.' She reached for her wine glass again. 'It's my bet she's run away from a man,' she said, shrewdly.

'Why?'

'With those eyes and that hair there'd be bound to be a man around somewhere.'

Ciaran said, 'There was, but not in the way you think.' And then, with a sudden pleased grin, 'So she finally got away, did she? Good for Moira.' He looked back at Lauren. 'She's at Kate's house now?'

'She sure is. She and Richard chased Conrad Vogel half across London, but they lost him in the end.' She sipped her wine. 'We didn't tell the police any of that part – the chase and Ahasuerus – they were sceptical enough as it was – and we figured that if we started to hold forth about undead creatures from beyond the grave we'd get even less co-operation. They were polite but—'

'Perfunctory?'

'Perfunctory will do. Their trouble is they haven't enough evidence to promote a large-scale search; our trouble was that the only evidence we'd got was so unbelievable we didn't dare disclose it. But the appointment with Vogel was written in Kate's diary, and she didn't return from it. We're sure that Vogel's got her but we can't prove he has.'

'What about his office?' said Ciaran. 'Or his home?'

'Both closed up with answerphones to take messages.'

'What did Kate think was behind this Serse set-up?' asked Isarel.

'I don't think she knew, not properly. But she knew the coffin-creature was connected with it, and she was going to try to use him to expose the whole thing. She was pretty

338

pleased at having got him out of your monastery,' said Lauren, grinning at Ciaran. 'And I remember that she laughed about locking the coffin in the cellar with him inside it. She said it felt as if she'd got on to the set of a schlock horror film and that if Moira hadn't been there to help, she'd have lost her nerve.' Lauren paused, and then said, 'She didn't know you two were following her, though, I'm pretty sure about that.'

'We weren't very efficient,' said Ciaran. 'We lost her crossing the Irish Sea.'

'I'm not surprised,' said Ms Mayhew promptly. 'I've lost all kinds of things crossing the Irish Sea. It's turbulent and very feisty.' She sent Ciaran an appraising look. 'But I'm rather partial to turbulent feisty Irishness. Should I call you Brother or Father, or what?'

'Just Ciaran.'

'Well then, tell me, Ciaran, do you take part in all those high-gloss Catholic ceremonies? High Mass and Evensong and so on?'

'I do.'

'Plainchant? What about plainchant? Do you sing that?'

'Certainly,' said Ciaran. 'But I'm a very indifferent performer.'

Lauren Mayhew blew a plume of smoke into the air and looked straight at him. 'I should think you perform rather well,' she said coolly.

There was a silence. Isarel thought: well, he asked for that one. How will he field it, I wonder?

But Ciaran showed not the least trace of embarrassment. At his most Irish, he said, 'Ah, it's a long time since I was at concert pitch, Ms Mayhew,' and infused his tone with such a note of regret that Lauren laughed.

'I guess I asked for that,' she said. 'Would you take it as

a *double entendre* if I said, Sorry and I hope there are no hard feelings?'

'Oh, that'd be an insult,' said Ciaran, at once.

Lauren blinked, and then leaned forward. 'Listen, Ciaran, you're an ascetic fighting to quench the man of the world, right? Well, if the ascetic ever loses the fight, remember I'm in the phone book.' She looked back at Isarel speculatively and said, 'That goes for you as well. You never know, you might get bored with Irish solitude in Jude Weissman's haunted house.'

There was a brief pause. Isarel looked at her. 'So you know who I am, do you?'

'Sure I do. Anyone in the music business would know. I don't mean rubbish music, which is what I mostly handle: I mean Kate's kind of music. The serious stuff.' She stubbed out her cigarette. 'You're Jude's grandson,' she said. 'I know the story and it isn't a very nice story, but it isn't your fault that your grandfather sold out to the Nazis.' She narrowed her eyes thoughtfully. 'You're very like him, aren't you? I mean you're like his photographs.'

'So I've been told.' Isarel reached for the wine bottle and re-filled their glasses. 'Tell us about this man on Hampstead Heath, Lauren.'

'Conrad Vogel.'

'Conrad Vogel,' said Isarel thoughtfully. 'Yes, I thought that was what you said.' At his side, Ciaran looked up.

Lauren said, 'The whole idea of bringing him to justice was like something out of a Thirties novel – *The Thirty-Nine Steps* or something. John Buchan and Bulldog Drummond, did you ever read those guys?'

'Yes,' said Isarel.

'It was like something out of one of those books. The wronged heroine chasing after the villain to wreak revenge. Corny, but it was something Kate had to do. She was wild

340

with anger and bitterness over what had happened to Richard – well, so we all were. But she believed in that music – the *Black Chant* – very strongly indeed.'

'That sounds as if you didn't,' said Isarel, and Lauren paused.

'I thought it was a little far-fetched if you want the truth,' she said, at last. 'I certainly believed her about the cult thing, because it's the kind of thing that kids – especially students – get involved in. But as for the music— I thought it was more likely that Vogel was using – what do you call it – that thing they do with computers that affects the mind?'

'Fractal,' said Isarel. 'Not dangerous by itself, but if it's used alongside drugs it's mind-blowing.'

'I thought he might be using something like that,' said Lauren. 'Or even drugs on their own, and either way he was going to get his come-uppance eventually. But I went along with Kate, because I thought that what she was doing might be cathartic, you know? Turning grief into positive action. The business was doing pretty well here – not making a fortune but doing pretty well – and for Kate to take a brief sabbatical wasn't going to ruin us. How it worked in the end was that Kate travelled about a bit but she made sure never to be away for more than two or three weeks at a stretch. And then she worked like a fiend when she got back. We aren't really in a nine to five set-up anyway and it pretty much balanced out.'

Ciaran asked carefully, 'Kate's husband— Is there any possibility that he could be connected with her disappearance?'

'God no,' said Lauren at once. 'Richard would never do anything that would hurt Kate. He wouldn't do anything that would hurt anyone. He's a humanist. Split up the word "gentleman" and you've got him. A gentle man. But fun.

341

Nice. He's smashed up physically, of course.'

'Were they happily married?' said Isarel. He caught the faintest flicker of movement from Ciaran.

'Ecstatic. Old fashioned, isn't it? Mind you,' said Lauren, 'I wouldn't like to take a Bible oath that Kate hasn't consoled herself once or twice in the last three years.'

'She's taken – lovers?'

'My, what a word.' Lauren regarded Ciaran with amusement. 'Yes, she's taken lovers. She didn't screw around, but I'm pretty sure that there've been one or two affairs— Listen, she's thirty-three and she's clever and attractive and normal. Richard wouldn't have known, because Kate wouldn't have let him. And although Kate never said it – too loyal – I'd guess that what happened to him was a bit of a—' She caught Ciaran's eye and grinned. 'It mentally emasculated him,' said Lauren. 'Which means Kate would need to blow off a little sexual steam from time to time, like all of us.' She sent Ciaran another of her mischievous looks. 'Like most of us,' she amended. 'You met her, didn't you?'

'I did.' Ciaran's voice was devoid of all expression.

Lauren reached for her bag and shrugged her shoulders into her jacket. 'I think you'd better come out to Kate's house,' she said. 'Richard's still there of course, and Moira.'

'I should like,' said Ciaran thoughtfully, 'to see Moira again.'

'Well, maybe between us we can figure something out,' said Lauren. She looked at them both. 'All right?'

Ciaran and Isarel exchanged a quick look. Then Isarel said, 'All right.'

Chapter Thirty-One

Rain lashed against the windows and by four o'clock it was almost dark, but inside Kate's house fires had been lit and lights burned and the central heating purred comfortingly in the radiators. Moira, who was still cold and numb at what had happened to Kate and filled with sick horror at what might be ahead, was grateful for the interlude of warmth and the feeling of safety.

When Kate's partner telephoned to ask could she bring over a couple of fellow collaborators, and then explained who they were, Moira merely said, 'What time will I expect you?' and went off to put a pot of coffee to percolate. She examined her lack of surprise and came to the conclusion that it was because there had been so many shocks and so many extraordinary things happening that she was incapable of feeling astonished at anything.

But setting out the cups and saucers, she was aware of the familiar, half-guilty spiral of pleasurable anticipation at the thought of seeing Ciaran. And I'll be seeing him on a different footing to the one we were on in Curran Glen, she thought. We'll be bound together in this bizarre adventure. Ahasuerus and the music and trying to find Kate.

Ciaran arrived first, entirely without ceremony, and sat at the kitchen table, explaining about the journey across to England, and the ancient vow to guard Ahasuerus's tomb.

'And this will be a council of war,' he said, sending her the remembered smile. 'We'll be pooling information and ideas.' A pause. 'It's good to see you, Moira.'

He was exactly as he had always been; the clear, grey eyes, the mobile, Irish mouth, emphasised rather than hidden by the short, chestnut beard. The strong, under-the-surface glamour was exactly as it had always been as well. It was the first time Moira had seen him wearing anything other than the dark, rather shapeless monastic robes, and she thought that dressed like this he was more masculine and much more authoritative. But he was watching her covertly, and Moira braced herself for the inevitable enquiry. It did not come quite as she had anticipated. Ciaran, helping with the coffee-making as naturally as if he had lived here for years, merely said, 'Listen now, did you finally run away from him, Moira?' and Moira, who had been wondering how on earth she was going to explain about running away, was jolted into a plain truthful answer, exactly as she had been with Kate.

'He came to my room one night—' She stopped, and Ciaran said,

'Ah. Yes, I understand,' and Moira had the feeling that he really did understand, and that he was not very surprised.

'I'm not going back,' she said, a bit too loudly.

'Do you really think we'd let you?' said Ciaran, and Moira suddenly felt warm and safe and surrounded by friends. "We" might have meant the monks at Curran Glen, or Ciaran and Kate, or Ciaran and any of the people mixed up in this extraordinary adventure, but whoever it meant, it was a good word.

But she said, 'I left a note for Mother and the twins – and I've written to them to say I'm all right. Only—'

'Yes?'

344

'I can't help wondering what Father will be feeling,' said Moira, in a rush. 'About what he'll say and do.'

Ciaran took a minute to answer. 'I think,' he said at last, 'that he'll come up with some story that puts him in a favourable light, and I think that in time he'll come to almost believe it himself. He's got a very flexible conscience, Edward Mahoney.' The sudden smile lifted his lips. 'He's a selfish man, Moira and a self-satisfied one as well, and those kind of people have their own armour. Tell me what happened when you left? You ran into Kate while she was robbing the crypt, I suppose?'

'More or less,' said Moira, and grinned.

'And the pair of you joined forces. What a combination,' said Ciaran, and Moira remembered that Ciaran had met Kate and started to ask about this, when the door knocker clattered again.

'That's probably Lauren and Isarel,' said Ciaran, standing up. 'They were going to Lauren's office to look up something about this Serse cult, and then coming here.'

Moira had met Lauren when Richard called in the police after they had chased, and lost, Conrad Vogel. They had all sat up until what had felt like dawn trying to persuade the police to search for Vogel, and Lauren had sat up with them and had been bracing and practical and very scathing indeed about the police's thinly veiled belief that Kate had gone off with a boyfriend. Moira had liked Lauren for that. But she said now, 'Isarel?'

'Isarel West,' said Ciaran. 'Jude's grandson. Aggressive and clever and temperamental. The charm of an angel and the temper of a devil. And an extraordinary musician. I'm beginning to think he's Jude's reincarnation.'

'Is he another collaborator?' asked Moira.

'He is. We're all chasing the same villain.'

'I hope the collaborators don't all need feeding,' said Moira, going to open the front door. 'Because we've almost run out of food.'

Moira had feared that Richard would retreat to his attic again, but although he had not answered the door, when Moira carried the coffee things in to the large sitting room he was seated with his back to the light, the dark glasses firmly in place.

There had been a curious flicker of something from Ciaran as he shook hands with Kate's husband: Moira had the oddest feeling that it was nothing to do with Richard's disfigurement, and she had looked up from pouring coffee. But Ciaran had merely said something about not wanting to intrude on an awkward or painful time, explaining that they believed they might be of some help, and then had sat down in a chair on the other side of the hearth, and the moment had passed. Moira handed round the coffee, and then curled on to one of the low seats, preparing to listen and studying Isarel West covertly.

Ciaran had said: The charm of an angel and the temper of a devil, and Moira thought that the temper could probably be very stormy indeed, but that charm was quite the wrong word. Charm suggested a calculating facility to be all things to all men, and Isarel West looked as if he would never trouble to be anything other than his exact self to anyone in the world. A kind of modern-day Sydney Carton, caring for no man, and not minding if no man cared for him. What Moira had been totally unprepared for was his astonishing likeness to Jude.

It was Ciaran who said, 'We're here to pool our information and see if we can discover where Conrad Vogel has gone,' but it was Isarel West who said, in his cool English voice,

346

'I know where he's gone. At least, I can make an educated guess.'

The others stared at him. Then Richard said, 'You can?'

'I think so. I guessed when Lauren first mentioned the name of the man behind the Serse Concert.'

'Conrad Vogel.'

'Yes.' Isarel took the coffee that Moira handed him, and stirred it, assembling his thoughts. After a moment, he said, 'Fifty years ago, in a place in Eastern Germany, my grandfather performed a piece of music he had written, and that he called the *Devil's Piper*.' He paused, and Moira suddenly knew with a queer little thrill what was coming.

Isarel said, 'The place was Eisenach Castle. That's somewhere on a border of what used to be called Thuringia, quite near Weimar, in one of those tiny, once-free states made up of dukedoms, all with names like Saxe or Schwarzburg. The concert is famous: it's described in all the books about Jude – what a glittering marvellous night it was, all the important people who attended.'

'Kate's book even mentions the music,' said Moira without thinking, and looked up to see amusement in Isarel's eyes. It was the first time he had smiled and Moira found herself hoping he would smile again.

'Yes,' said Isarel. 'As Moira says, one or two even mention the music, although most of them concentrate on how the women fainted because of Jude's magnetism, and how the *Devil's Piper* rocked them in the aisles. Probably the fainting women are an exaggeration—'

'Also rocking in the aisles in the Nineteen Thirties.' This, inevitably, was Lauren, who was seated opposite to Ciaran, a battered briefcase at the side of her chair. 'Is it true that he had a different mistress for every piece of music he played— Sorry, Brother Ciaran.' She looked at Moira over her glasses and winked, and Moira understood Lauren was as appalled as anyone at what had happened to Kate, but that she found Ciaran attractive and could not resist half-mischievously flirting with him.

Isarel said, 'Nothing would surprise me about Jude. But it was at Eisenach that he met the man who was Hitler's Special Envoy, and it was at Eisenach that he threw in his lot with the Nazis.' He paused, and Moira suddenly thought: he's hating this. He's hating having to talk about Jude being a traitor.

Richard was leaning forward, his eyes on Isarel. When he said, 'Go on,' Moira knew he had forgotten about being awkward and bitter, and knew that this was the real Richard, the one with whom she had shared that frantic abortive car-chase across London.

Isarel glanced at Richard and Moira saw that he looked at him precisely as he would have looked at anyone. He said, 'The name of that Special Envoy never got into any of the history books about the war, or about Jude himself. But my father knew his name, and I know it as well.' He paused. 'He was a man called Karl Vogel.'

There was a sudden silence. Ciaran said, 'Son – grandson?'

'Grandson, I should think.' Isarel was watching Richard, and after a moment, Richard said,

'You think that's where Conrad's gone, don't you?'

'Yes I do. I think he's taken Kate and Ahasuerus back to where the music last surfaced. Eisenach Castle.

'And I think we've got to follow him.'

This time it was Lauren who broke the silence.

She said, 'I hadn't credited the Serse cult with too much importance before, but when Isarel told me about Karl Vogel it felt like a pattern was beginning to emerge.'

'Not a very nice pattern,' murmured Ciaran.

'Hellish,' said Lauren cheerfully. 'But it began to sound as if Serse's People might be more of a force than I'd reckoned on, so I figured it was worth checking into my E-mail.' She glanced at Ciaran and Moira. 'That's a kind of computer mailing service. Electronic mail. It's largely junk-stuff which means I don't look at it as often as I should: circulars about forthcoming events, publicity releases by road managers or other agents. Ninety per cent dross, ten per cent gold.' A brusque shrug. 'But if anything was about to happen with Serse's People – a concert or an event, or something that linked Vogel with Eisenach – it was possible the details had been circulated.'

'And – had they?' Richard leaned forward eagerly.

'They had,' said Isarel, and grinned at Lauren suddenly. 'We nearly missed it, but it was there.'

'I got a little distracted during the search,' said Lauren, returning the smile, but handing round sheets of A4 paper. 'But it was there all right. And if this doesn't refer to Conrad Vogel, and if that isn't our missing Devil's Piper, then I'll enter a convent, or maybe a monastery.' This time the mischievous glance was at Ciaran. Moira, taking the print-out, thought Lauren was dividing the favours about equally.

The computer print-out was very clear. Sharp black lettering stood out at the top, and the layout looked professional, even to Moira's untrained eye.

'Two-day music festival at Eisenach Castle on the 9th and 10th of next month. Works by J S and C P E Bach, Berlioz's *Damnation of Faust*, and Goethe's *Wandering Jew* poem, set to music, and read by distinguished actor—' Here followed a name Moira did not recognise, '—on second day. The music of the masters in stunning, medieval castle, with ancient, historical associations. The pinnacle of the Festival will be the first ever public performance of the newly written symphonic piece: *Satan's Lute-Player*. The soloists will be—' More unrecognisable names. 'Ticket prices include admission, lunch on both days, and champagne buffet supper on second night. Overnight accommodation can be arranged in village.'

At the top of the poster, in thick bold type, was the heading: SERSE'S PEOPLE, and underneath it, a small logo that bore a resemblance to the Aryan Cross of Light.

As she laid down the print-out, Isarel said, 'The ninth and tenth. That means we've got three days to get there and get Ahasuerus.'

Lauren had commandeered the phone and was speaking into it. Moira caught the words, 'Lufthansa', and then, impatiently, 'No, Berlin *isn't* near enough – I'd have thought anyone could have— Well, of *course*, Frankfurt's more like it.' She began to feel unreal.

It was almost seven o'clock. Moira carried the coffee cups into the kitchen and dumped them in the sink. Ciaran and Richard were consulting maps and at any minute somebody was probably going to say something about eating. Moira had absolutely no idea what to do if that happened. Did you ask guests to help you cook a meal, especially when you were a guest yourself? Would Richard help? There was not very much food in the larder, and although there was a deep freeze and a microwave oven, Moira had never dealt with either appliance in her life. Father had regarded freezers as unwholesome and insisted on freshly prepared food, and Mother had thought microwaves dangerous. Moira felt exasperated with both her parents.

Maybe they would go out, which might be awkward on account of not knowing what was correct behaviour over paying the bill in this situation, and whether you shared it or let yourself be paid for. Also, she had only brought a skirt as well as the jeans she had worn to run away in, and she had no idea how much people dressed up to go out to dinner in London. She began to feel exasperated with herself now for not knowing quite ordinary things.

Isarel had followed her into the kitchen, and reached for a drying cloth without being asked, which Moira thought unexpected of him, but nice. He said, 'Lauren's booking seats with Lufthansa, but it's anybody's guess how soon she'll get them. Richard and Ciaran are poring over maps and looking up references to Eisenach. I wish we knew more about Vogel's motives. I don't mean why he wants Ahasuerus, because I think that's clear: he wants him to reinforce the music.'

'And he wants to reinforce the music so that he can gather in more people like Richard,' said Moira. It did not seem in the least odd to plunge straight into a conversation like this with someone you had only met two hours earlier. She said, 'Is it possible that Vogel wants to present Ahasuerus to Serse's People as some kind of Messianic figure?' This was an idea that had occurred to her earlier, but she had not said anything in front of everyone in case it sounded ridiculous.

But Isarel said at once, 'That's rather a shrewd idea, Moira. I believe I can almost see Ahasuerus as some kind of charismatic figurehead – Ciaran mightn't agree, but it's easy to see how Vogel could sell him to Serse's People in that guise. And whatever Ahasuerus looks like now, according to Ciaran, the original legends depict him as dazzling and persuasive and altogether irresistible.'

'The High Priest from the past,' said Moira thoughtfully.

'Yes. I wouldn't be surprised to find that Vogel's making him out to be the New Redeemer or the Risen

Christ or Buddha Reincarnated for those poor misled children.'

'Why are they called Serse's People?' asked Moira. 'I kept meaning to ask Kate if she knew, but I never got round to it.'

'I've been thinking about that,' said Isarel. 'And I talked to Richard just now – he's got a brilliant mind, hasn't he, that's a very great tragedy—' He stopped before continuing. 'Richard says that some sources equate the first Ahasuerus – the one in the Old Testament – with a Persian King dating back to around five hundred B.C. He was the son of Darius, but he was more usually known as Xerxes.'

'Xerxes – Serse.' Moira tried it out.

'Handel wrote an opera called *Serse*,' said Isarel. 'In it the character of Serse – more properly Xerxes I think – sings the aria most people know as Handel's Largo.'

'*Handel* knew about the *Black Chant*?' said Moira incredulously, and wondered how many more famous composers were going to emerge as having known about it.

'Not necessarily. But I'm beginning to wonder,' said Isarel, 'how many of the really great composers escaped its influence. In fact, I'm beginning to feel thoroughly cynical about every piece of music that purports to be an original composition at the moment.'

'What did you think of the concert poster?'

'I felt cynical about that as well,' said Isarel. 'And I thought it was a piece of monstrous cheek. "Satan's Lute-Player", my God, who does Vogel think he's fooling! *And* Goethe's *Wandering Jew.*'

'I didn't grasp the significance of that.'

'It's the very ancient legend of the doorkeeper or servant or something who was asked by Christ on His way to Calvary if He could rest there,' said Isarel.

'Oh, I do know it, then,' said Moira. 'The doorkeeper refused, didn't he, and Christ is supposed to have cursed him. Something like, "I will rest here, but thou will walk the world for ever." But I still don't see the connection—'

'Whatever name the Jew had to start with – if he existed outside of romantic myth – Goethe called him Ahasuerus,' said Isarel.

'The Wandering Jew was called Ahasuerus?'

'Well, according to Goethe he was.'

'There're a lot of legends, aren't there?' said Moira, after a moment. 'About Ahasuerus, I mean. Well, and the music. There're strands and bits here and there. And some of them mesh together.'

'Things filter down,' said Isarel. 'That's one of the fascinating things about—' He stopped, as Lauren came into the kitchen. 'Well?'

'Well, my dears,' said Lauren, sounding pleased with herself. 'It's all fixed. Midnight flight from Heathrow. And listen, I don't know about you, but I'm absolutely starving.'

These were the words Moira had been hoping nobody would say. She started to explain that there were only eggs and cheese in the fridge, and to ask would omelettes be acceptable, but Lauren said, 'So I guess I'll order pizzas if that's all right?'

'Fine,' said Isarel. 'Everything on mine except anchovies.'

'Moira?'

'I don't—' Moira stopped and then said firmly, 'Yes, the same for me, please.'

'OK. We've got plenty of time before you need to leave. It's Heathrow to Frankfurt, did I say? It's not as near to Eisenach as it might be, but it's the best I could get. You can take the hire-car to Heathrow and trade it for one at the other end. You ought to be able to reach Eisenach before the concert kicks off. I booked for the three of you, of course.'

'Three—'

'You two and Ciaran. I'd like to come with you, but somebody's got to mind the store. And it's out of the question for Richard.'

Moira, frantically calculating her money said, 'The tickets—'

But Lauren at once said, 'Hell, honey, I paid by credit card, it's no big deal. I'll put it down to expenses and get most of it back by tax.' A sudden smile. 'Ciaran thinks you shouldn't go,' she said.

'I don't,' said Ciaran, coming into the kitchen.

'He's remembering the conventions,' said Lauren wickedly.

'Blow the conventions,' said Ciaran, as Moira stared at him. 'I'm thinking about the danger. We don't know what we're going into. Moira ought to stay here.'

'With Richard? Now that's *really* unconventional—'

'We can't take Richard,' said Isarel, at once. 'No, it's nothing to do with him not coping, he'd cope perfectly well. But what if this is a ploy of Vogel's to get Richard into his hands?'

There was a sudden silence. Then Moira said, 'Yes, because if you think about it, Vogel's hardly bothered to cover his tracks, and if he'd really intended to get clear he could have done it easily – faked messages, false kidnap notes. We might spot the red herrings but the police would go straight after them.'

'And,' said Isarel, 'while all that was going on, Vogel could be getting himself beyond everybody's reach. Moira's right; it wouldn't be hard to lay a false trail, it wouldn't stand up for long, but it'd stand up for long enough for him to get clear with Ahasuerus, if that was what he really wanted. Maybe even into a country without an Extradition Treaty. You're right about the danger, Ciaran, but you're wrong about not taking Moira.' He sent Moira another of the sudden smiles. 'Moira ought to come with us,' he said. 'We're primarily concerned with Kate, that goes without saying. But we're also trying to get Ahasuerus.'

'What's that got to do with it?' demanded Ciaran. 'Getting Ahasuerus hasn't got anything to do with Moira coming with us.'

Lauren, who was leaning against the sink with her arms crossed and listening to this interchange with huge enjoyment, said, 'You're turning out to be a *femme fatale*, Moira. I'd kill to have these two fighting over me.'

Isarel was regarding Ciaran with exasperation. 'Either you've been spinning me a parcel of lies for the past week or the drink's befuddling your mind,' he said. 'Hasn't it occurred to you to wonder how we're going to lure Ahasuerus back?'

'The music—' began Ciaran. 'The shofar—', and Isarel made an angry dismissive gesture.

'We'll be competing against that accursed concert and from what I've heard about Conrad Vogel so far, it doesn't sound as if he does anything by halves!' He indicated the print-out impatiently. 'He's presenting Bach and Berlioz, and although you can get away with an organ and a couple of violins for a lot of the Bachs, you can't play *The Damnation of Faust* with anything less than a full-blown orchestra! And that, Brother Ciaran, can mean anything between forty and a hundred musicians! If you think Jude's shofar can compete against that, I don't!'

'If we can't use the shofar, what—'

'God give me strength, we have to take Moira as bait,' said Isarel. 'That's if she'll agree,' he said suddenly. 'Moira, what about it? Are you prepared to lure the Devil's

Piper into your arms, and then back into his coffin?' The sudden smile lifted his face, and Moira blinked. 'It's a hell of a thing to ask, but you won't be in any danger,' said Isarel. 'I won't let you be. We'll both be there with you, even this dissolute Irish monk who has to have a fact spelled out to him.'

He paused, and Moira stared at him and heard her voice say, 'All right.'

'You'll do it?'

'I'll do it.'

'Good girl.' Isarel looked back at Ciaran. 'Do you still not know why?' he said.

Ciaran was staring at Moira. 'Dear heaven, I do,' he said. 'It's because—'

He stopped, and Isarel said softy, 'It's because in all of the legends, Ahasuerus had ever a weakness for red hair.'

Chapter Thirty-Two

The small, stone dungeon in the Tower was dreadfully reminiscent of the underground cellar at the Temple, where Ahasuerus had lain in chains waiting for the Sanhedrin to pronounce sentence. As he lay in the cold, mean room now, shivering with cold and light-headed from hunger, his mind spun helplessly between the two worlds. Which one am I in? I must remember which world I am in.

But his mind was blurred with weakness, and all he could see was Susannah's enigmatic smile and all he could hear was Susannah's voice saying that the walls of Time were thinner than most people ever guessed, and that if you could control the music, you could control Time. The dungeon wavered, until it was as if he was seeing it under water, and he was back in Jerusalem, the world where once he had been powerful. Susannah's world, scented with olives and sun and sweet, resinous wine. The world where they had dragged him out to the plain behind the Temple, to suffer the second of his agonies.

Crucifixion . . .

He blinked and tried to thrust the searing images away, but this place, this evil river prison had raked cruelly at the long-ago memories and the terrible miasma of despair and pain that had soaked into the stones of this place was dragging the nightmares through Time's paper-thin walls and forcing them into the present.

He might have been lying helpless beneath the Temple again, listening for the light, quick footsteps that would mean Susannah had brought help.

She had not done so, of course: Ahasuerus thought he had been mad to have hoped for it. The Elders would never allow the renegade High Priest to escape the punishment; guards would be stationed everywhere and even Susannah would not get through them.

But he had continued to hope she would try. He had held on to the thought – Susannah and the ancient music – and it had carried him through the scourging, which had been the first of the agonies. It had carried him all through that last despairing night as well, when he had lain beneath the Temple, chained and helpless, hearing the sounds of hammering as they constructed the instrument of the second torture.

The cruciform . . .

It had been finished by the time they brought him up, and the instant he had seen it he thought he had never seen anything so sinister and so menacing. It was a towering structure of thick solid oak, the centre portion at least ten feet in height, the crosspiece nailed two thirds of the way up.

They had already driven it into the ground, and as the guards pushed him forward the sun was setting behind it, so that it stood out stark and black against the glowing red sky. As Ahasuerus approached it, its shadow fell over him, and he stood motionless for a moment staring upwards in sick dread. Soon I shall hang from that. Soon I shall be silhouetted against the sky, dying in agony.

The crowd stepped back, silent and fearful, and as the gaolers pushed him forward he scanned the watchers, searching for the tumble of red hair, the slanting cat-eyes.

During the scourging he had prayed that she should not witness his humiliation, but now he wanted her to be here, he ached for a last glimpse of her. Did she then care so little that she can not be here for me now! his mind cried in silent anguish. Am I to go into Death without seeing her for a last moment? Susannah, you bitch, are you deserting me?

They were hoisting him upwards, using wooden ladders propped against the centre-piece. Beyond the Temple, towards the western side of the valley, he could make out smoke rising from dozens of cooking fires and the faint, sweet tinkle of goat-bells was borne on the wind. A sudden desperate longing seized him for the ordinary things that he had known so well and that he would never know again. Because even if the music calls me back, it will not call me back into this world. I shall never see this Jerusalem again.

And then they were winding the chains around his arms and chest to keep him in place until the nails were driven home, and his mind rocked in horror as the nails were brought up, cruel iron spikes, each one the length of a man's forearm, sharpened to vicious points. As the guards placed them over his wrists his heart began to pound violently and sweat poured over his brow, half blinding him.

He fixed his eyes on the distant landscape again: the unseen horizon, far, far beyond the evil, red-streaked sky, worlds away from the plain that smelt of death and fear and betrayal and agony. Rose-tinted dawns and wine-dark seas ... Susannah's music and Susannah beside him, tasting of love and sweet sinless rapture ... Are you out there, you faithless cat? Perhaps standing with the black-robed Brotherhood, the *Fratres Cruciferi* who will take my body away and lose it in some bottomless pit when this is all over?

The guards brought the great, heavy-headed mallets

down and the nails plunged straight through his wrists and embedded in the wood behind, severing tendons, splintering bone, tearing muscle and flesh. Blind screaming agony ripped through his arms and Ahasuerus cried out, his whole body shuddering in spasms of torment. It was excruciating, it was a hundred, a thousand times worse than the scourging. Pain undreamed-of. He felt the blood streaming over his arms, dripping off the cruciform, on to the ground beneath.

I'm dying, he thought. Nobody could suffer this torture and live. Yes, but what of the Nazarene who had hung like this for three harrowing days? And what of the final part of Ahasuerus's own sentence? He looked down and saw that the guards were already bringing the braziers to the foot of the cross, and that a pile of wooden faggots stood ready.

Panic engulfed him and despair scalded his mind, mingling with the raw agony of his body. *Let me die before they light the fires.*

Because once they ajudged him near to death, they would revive him with vinegar-soaked sponges and young sour wine. And then they would set light to the funeral pyre at his feet.

Ahasuerus the renegade High Priest, the scholar and the lover and the poet, would die in screaming torment while the sun set behind the cross.

He would burn alive.

'He'll burn alive,' said Nicolas, facing Martin in the low-ceilinged room of the Rose and Crown tavern in Fetter Lane. The room was crowded, thick with the greasy scents of food and human sweat and with the sourness of spilled wine and ale.

When the message had come to Martin's lodgings that a friend awaited him in the tavern, he had not been unduly

360

alarmed. It was not unlikely that his own Father Abbot had sent someone after him, or that one of the enquiries he had set afoot in the teeming City about Rodger Cheke and his arrival from Ireland, had returned bearing fruit.

He had thanked the street urchin who had brought the message, given the boy a coin, and made his way to Fetter Lane, threading his way through the streets. He had thought he was growing comfortable with Martin O'Neill, landed Irish gentleman, but as he entered the Rose and Crown, he felt suddenly vulnerable, and he saw that one or two people looked questioningly in his direction. He was relieved when the slenderly built, dark-eyed man came up to him and led him to a table in the corner. A goblet of malmsey was placed at his hand, and Nicolas, introducing himself brusquely, said without preamble, 'I know who you are, Brother Martin, and I know why you are here.'

'What—'

'There is no time for lengthy explanations, and if there were, this would not be the place for them.' Nicolas lifted his own wine, and for a moment the golden glow spilled upwards, giving his eyes a curious cat-like quality. Martin blinked.

Nicolas sent a covert glance about him, and then said very softly, 'The one you are here to find is inside the Tower.'

'How do you know what I am here to find? What is all this?'

'I know because I am on the edges of everything,' said Nicolas. 'Particularly I am on the edges of the Court. I listen and I look and no one realises it, because no one pays much attention to a minstrel. I am a vagabond, you understand, a gypsy; I am outside of the intrigues and the spiders' webs that are spun at such places, and so I hear many things that were never meant to be heard.' A sudden

361

smile softened his face, and Martin thought: after all, he's remarkably good-looking, and after all, he's much younger than I first thought. Or is he?

'Also,' said Nicolas, speaking rapidly and softly, 'I know the story of that one you seek.'

That one . . .

'How?' said Martin tersely. 'How do you know it?'

'It is a legend handed down in my family. I know of the vow the people of your Brotherhood make to guard Ahasuerus, and I know that you are pledged to forfeit your life to that end if necessary.' He drank deeply of the wine again. 'How strongly would you honour that pledge, Martin?'

Martin was not precisely thrown off balance, but he was certainly disconcerted by this strange creature who spoke in soft, lilting cadences and who had the most extraordinary eyes Martin had ever seen. The suspicion that someone might be setting a trap or playing an elaborate hoax flickered on his mind, but he could think of no reason why anyone should do such a thing. If anyone had discovered that Martin O'Neill was really Brother Martin, surely he would simply be taken prisoner without these complicated manoeuvres?

And so he said, 'I take the vow to guard Ahasuerus very seriously.'

'You would honour it even unto death if necessary?'

Martin paused, but again he could see no reason not to be truthful, and so he said, 'Yes.'

'Very well. It should not be necessary, but there is a chance that if things go wrong one of us may not live. Listen, there is a plan.'

He spoke for a moment, and Martin, listening carefully, thought: this is a very astute gentleman. Do I believe him about Ahasuerus being in the Tower? I think I do. And his

362

plan is very simple, simple enough to work. Would I die for Ahasuerus? I would die for Christ, certainly. A tiny traitorous voice said: yes, but would you *burn*, Brother Martin? Would you endure hanging, drawing and quartering? Half-strangled, and then cut down to have your bowels gouged out? And then your head severed? He shivered and reached for the wine again.

Nicolas, watching him, said, 'Well? You agree?'

Martin set down the empty goblet. 'I agree,' he said slowly. 'But I should like to understand your part in all this.' He waited, his eyes on Nicolas, and now it was no longer a richly clad, Irish landowner, the bastard connection of the roistering O'Neills, but the real Martin. The austere, implacable sub-Prior who had been prepared to deceive Thomas Cromwell, and who had come unhesitatingly out of seclusion to honour a long-ago pledge. 'Who are you?' he said sharply. 'Where do you come from?'

Nicolas studied him for a moment, and then said very gently, 'Your founder was in Cremona five hundred years ago. And so was mine.' He regarded Martin with a glint of amusement, and Martin, staring at him, thought: Ahasuerus's son. He's Ahasuerus's son. Not literally, of course, five hundred years separate him from that first waking. That first waking . . . Ahasuerus walking through the old walled city, sprinkling the ancient music about him, luring away the plague rats, and seducing Isabella Amati into the bargain, if our records speak the truth. Nicolas is the descendant of those two. Is it possible? I don't believe it, because I don't dare believe it. Aloud, he said, 'Even if it is true, why should you risk your life?'

'Oh, for many reasons,' said Nicolas, and now it was the flippant, touch-me-not tone of the wanderer, the true gypsy who cared for no man.

'But let us say that it is a little because there is a lady

363

caught up in this particular spider's web, and that lady has red hair.

'And,' Nicolas continued smoothly, 'like my ancestor, I have something of a weakness for red hair. Will you have more wine? No? Then I think we should leave now.'

Chapter Thirty-Three

Guarding the water entrance of the Tower was a nasty, cold kind of job of a night. The four guards on duty took it in turns to go in to the gate-house for a bit of a warm by the gate-keeper's fire and a nip of mulled wine with a dash of ginger. It kept out the chill a treat, mulled wine, and the gate-keeper wasn't ungenerous in his portions, either!

Not that you dared be drunk on duty. You never knew when you might be called on to challenge an intruder: some nasty plot hatched by Papists or Spaniards, there was not a lot to choose between the two, or some sneaky rescue attempt by somebody's mother or sister or daughter. There was a saying about the female of the species being deadlier than the male, said the guards, quaffing their warm spicy wine with pleasure, and it was remarkable what ladies desperate to rescue their husbands or fathers or brothers would do. And while it was a mite cold and draughty just inside St Thomas's Tower, not to say eerie what with the Thames lapping against the walls, better people than Tower guards had pumped their manhood dry up against a stone wall! they said, nudging each other. They swapped stories and told how you could satisfy yourself and have your hose re-buttoned between one sentry change and the next and no one the wiser. It did not get the stupid women inside the Tower, of course, but they did not need to be told that until afterwards. And on a cold night there was nothing better to

365

warm your cock robin than to get it between a pair of firm plump thighs.

They finished the gate-keeper's mulled wine, wiped their mouths with the backs of their hands, and flipped a coin to see who should take the next two-hour turn at the gate. A filthy, wet evening it was, just the kind of weather when you'd expect plotters to come rowing stealthily down the river, armed with ridiculous stories about bringing food and warm blankets for the prisoners.

The two who came rowing along the river entrance did not have a story about food and blankets, but the guard who had lost the coin-tossing was wary. Some tale about being here on the orders of Sir Rodger Cheke and the Bishop of Winchester it was, and orders to shrive the soul of the prisoner brought in two nights ago.

'Shrive?' said the guard suspiciously. He walked along the narrow ledge, holding up his horn lantern, his footsteps echoing hollowly. As he drew alongside the small row-boat, the wavering light from the stub of tallow inside the lantern fell across the water. 'Priests, are you?' said the guard, peering down.

'Priests?' said the cool voice from the boat. The guard noticed that it was tinged with Irish and that there was a faintly mocking quality to it. 'Now that's a nasty, old-fashioned word to be using, and us here to save a man's soul before he meets his maker. You'll know of the burning at noon tomorrow? Yes, of course you will.'

'Of course I know about it,' said the guard, who knew no such thing, but was not going to admit it. 'Burning him at noon they are,' he said firmly.

'Then,' said Martin, 'you'll have had the orders from the Lieutenant of the Tower to take us to the man's cell.' Despite the dankness in here, sweat was sliding between his shoulder blades, but he heard with relief that his voice

366

still held the cool note of authority. 'Raise the portcullis and be sharp about it now,' he said. 'What? No orders? I shall have something to say about that to Sir William tomorrow, yes, and the Bishop! Hold that lantern up till I see your face, man – ah, yes. And your name?'

The guard was alert – of course he was – to all the ploys and all the deceptions, and he was certainly not going to allow this unknown pair through the portcullis without he had first made a few enquiries. He bade them wait here and betook himself off to the gate-house because if anyone was going to take the responsibility for letting a pair of strangers in through Traitors' Gate, it was not going to be him!

Sir William Kingston, Lieutenant of the Tower, woken abruptly from his bed, listened with furrowed brow to the tale brought to him of a priest apparently sent by Rodger Cheke and the Bishop of Winchester to hear the confession of the mysterious man placed in his care two nights earlier. He sighed as he clambered out of bed, because he foresaw an awkward decision.

There were always awkward decisions when you had in your charge gentlemen who had made enemies at Court, but knowing what was expected of you before you were told about it, did not get any easier with practice.

'The thing is,' said Sir William to his lady, who was sitting up in bed, beet-red with annoyance and her nightcap awry, 'the thing is, if His Majesty was wanting to be rid of this foreigner *discreetly*, he'd choose just this way, d'ye see? A respectable priest, purporting to have come to hear the prisoner's confession, and then a drop of poison slipped into the water jug, or a dagger slipped between his ribs, I dare say there isn't much to choose between the two. And I shouldn't want to ruin any plot that might come from the King, he wouldn't be best pleased, what do you think?'

What Lady Kingston thought was that any plot so obscure that even the people supposed to perpetrate it did not know about it, was doomed to failure from the outset. She also pointed out, a bit tartly, that discretion and Henry Tudor's name were not two things that occurred to you in the same breath, and that at this stage of his reign the King was not very likely to bother about being circumspect. If he wanted to remove somebody who was likely to be an embarrassment or a nuisance he would simply order beheading or hanging, or, if he was feeling especially peevish, burning.

'Let the two men in and double the guard,' said Lady Kingston, and having delivered herself of this pithy judgement, re-tied her nightcap and composed herself for sleep again. If you were to properly fulfil your duties as the wife of the Tower Lieutenant, squeamishness in your nature was not something you could afford.

Sir William, not precisely squeamish but anxious to be loyal to his King and conscientious in his work, conferred with his head guard again and could not see the harm in allowing the young Irish priest in to hear the prisoner's confession. As his lady had said, the guard outside the cell could be doubled or even tripled for the night, and the priest and his companion could be searched before and after the event because it would not be the first time that knives and daggers or poison had been smuggled into cells.

Sir William was having none of any rescue nonsense. If the King had decreed that the prisoner should burn on the morrow, then burn he would!

Martin looked with horror at the winding stone corridors, each one seeming to branch off into half a dozen others, each one lit at sparse intervals by flaring wall torches which showed up the moisture running down the walls and the sickly, green phosphorescence that clung everywhere. How many people were imprisoned in here? How many poor ordinary creatures had been flung into one of these miserable cells and locked away in the dark, and forgotten? All for offending the King, or for serving God in a different way to that ordered by Henry VIII? Sick dread churned the pit of his stomach. How close am I to being thrown into one of those dungeons myself?

As they went past the low doors with pointed Norman archways over them, there was the most overpowering stench of human despair and human excrement and human terror Martin had ever encountered and his throat closed with nausea.

The guards were leading them farther in and with every step they were going deeper into the most appalling danger. This was the Tower of London, the grim prison of legend, the place where people were torn into bloody tatters on the rack. This was the ancient fortress built by William the Conqueror's bishop-architect: the great, sprawling, blood-soaked world within a world, where there were underground dungeons and torture chambers, and where there were little enclosed courtyards where butchered remains could be discreetly buried and charred bones quietly interred. Martin, feeling the huge, sombre prison close about him, had never felt so completely shut away from God. At his side, Nicolas padded silently along, apparently unnoticing – or maybe uncaring – of the stifling atmosphere. Once or twice he turned his head, and Martin saw his eyes catch the light. Like a cat's. He thought: I suppose it's all right to trust him. I suppose he isn't leading me into a trap.

There were five guards with them: two leading the way and carrying lanterns and three more bringing up the rear, and Martin saw how watchful they were and how swords hung ready at their sides. They would never trick these men. Panic replaced the fear.

The cell was at the farthest end of a narrow, dank passage, and the tallest guard was forced to duck his head as they went under a low arch. Martin shivered. No natural daylight would penetrate down here, even on the sunniest of summer's afternoons. The cell is the last one, he thought, trying to get his bearings. The farthest, deepest dungeon ... And inside it is Ahasuerus.

Beyond the end cell was a blind, blank wall. Was the river on the other side of that wall? It was a chilling thought. A single torch burned outside the cell, and the leading guard stood under it, fumbling with a huge iron ring of keys. As he reached down to unlock the door, there was the screech of hinges unused and unoiled, rasping on Martin's already-raw nerve-endings.

But he was already pushing wide the thick, oaken door, seeing how the greasy light showed up the wretched cell with the wisps of straw on the floor and the deal table with the water pitcher and a pannikin of coarse meal. Behind the door was a narrow pallet bed and seated on the bed . . .

It was important not to show any emotion. Martin waited until the guards closed the door on them and then said very softly, 'I am Brother Martin, and I am come to rescue you.' And then, as the figure on the bed stared, uncomprehending, he heard Nicolas's cool voice behind him, speaking in soft, smooth Latin, and he remembered with a thrill that Ahasuerus came from a world that had probably never encountered English speech.

Ahasuerus seemed to understand Nicolas. He reached for a thick, dark cloak and Martin had time to see that he was younger than he had been expecting – what had he been expecting, anyway? – and he had time to note Ahasuerus's startling, luminous beauty.

As Nicolas began to strip off his clothing, Martin felt his heart pounding, but with exhilaration this time, because they were going to do it, they were going to succeed. Escape from the impregnable fortress. Simply by exchanging places. Two men had gone in and presently, two men would go out. And by and by Nicolas would call for the guards, and tell them the agreed story about being set on, being knocked out and left in the dungeon. Martin's heart was pounding with fear and anticipation and dread.

Along the passage, filling it with the light of burning torches and the sound of running feet, came Rodger Cheke, Sir William Kingston, and a dozen of the Tower guards. The cell door was flung open with such force that it crashed against the stone wall and the guards fell on Martin, knocking him to the floor.

Sick blackness closed about him and he knew no more.

The thin disguise that was to have fooled the Court and had certainly fooled the Tower guards, was no disguise in William Kingston's inner sanctum with Sir Rodger Cheke at the Lieutenant's side. Martin eyed Cheke in disgust and then looked away.

Rodger Cheke, in fact, was congratulating himself on the way things had turned out. It would have been uncharitable to exult over the wholly unexpected capture of the cold arrogant monk who had tried to make a fool of him at Curran Glen, and since the Chekes were not, as a rule, uncharitable, he did not do so. But in the eyes of the King and his Commissioners it must appear that Sir Rodger had adroitly handled an awkward business very neatly indeed. Rodger Cheke thought he might be pardoned for feeling – not smug, a nasty word – but a trifle complacent.

Sir William Kingston, arranging his papers preparatory to writing down whatever statement they could wring from this young Irish monk, recognised the steady light in the Martin's eyes and sighed inwardly. Heretics and martyrs and fanatics: no matter the name you put to them, once they had given you that look you knew what the end was going to be. And say what you would: the torturing of a human creature was a nasty business.

But he knew his duty; he had questioned more men – and an occasional woman – suspected of treason and heresy than he could remember, and he had encountered varying degrees of fear and obstinacy and courage. But this stony-faced Irish monk made him uncomfortable. Brother Martin showed not the smallest trace of fear; he eyed his interlocutors arrogantly, and he refused, absolutely and completely, to tell them anything about Ahasuerus.

Sir William found himself remembering the astonishing endurance shown by those two remarkable men, Thomas More and John Fisher, and he thought that Brother Martin had something of the same quality. Steadfastness. An unswerving faith, an unshakeable trust and a belief in something so strong, something that swept aside the pettiness of the world so overwhelmingly that once you had discovered it, you would face torture and an agonising death rather than deny its existence.

He questioned Martin exactly as he would have questioned anyone about the escape of a prisoner: courteously to begin with and then sternly, and finally threateningly. Martin defeated him at every turn. He knew nothing, he would say nothing, he would tell nothing, and eventually, Sir William, knowing what his King expected of him, nodded to the four guards who stood sentinel at the door.

'Take him down,' he said.

Martin was convinced that Kingston and Rodger Cheke

would not have questioned him so fiercely unless Nicolas and Ahasuerus had escaped. He was holding on to the thought, and he was praying for strength to endure what was ahead. Help me to suffer it, God. Let me not break, and let me not betray Ahasuerus. Above all, God, let me not betray You.

He was taken into the Tower's most sinister chamber by the impassive guards, and he began to feel as if he was descending into hell. Hell, where the red-eyed demons tear at the sinner's flesh with white-hot pitchforks . . . Where there is nothing save everlasting torment . . . But God is still with me.

The guards pushed open the door of a long, low-ceilinged room, filled with leaping firelight and twisting shadows, and as Martin entered, the stench rose up to hit him. It was like walking into a solid wall of terror and pain and blood. Stale sweat and fear-expelled urine and the raw echoes of men screaming in torment.

The guards thrust him roughly forward, and there was the grim sound of the door closing and of the key turning in the lock. Locked in with the torturers. He looked about him, forcing his mind to calm, but his senses were still reeling and for several minutes all he could see was a blurred mass of crimson firelight and the glint of machinery in the shadows.

A circular iron frame, studded with evil-smelling tallow candles hung from the ceiling, swinging slightly in the warmth. At the far end a fire burned in a low wide stone hearth, causing the twisting shadows to leap and prance across the stone walls, so that to Martin's fevered sight, this was truly hell's fire-drenched cavern.

As his senses steadied, he saw that standing before the fire were four of the most brutish men he had ever seen. They had massive muscular arms and shoulders, and they were stripped to the waist, in the manner of scaffold executioners. Their faces were impassive, but the firelight gave their eyes a crimson glint and washed over their rippling muscles.

Kingston and Rodger Cheke had followed the guards and they were seating themselves at a small table near the fire, with writing things set out. At a sign from Sir William, the guards moved, thrusting their prisoner towards a low, coffin-shaped frame at the room's centre, and Martin's stomach lurched in fear and panic. The rack. He thought he had never before seen an inanimate structure imbued with such silent menace.

The guards were forcing him to lie facing upwards. So that they can watch my expressions, thought Martin. So that they can gauge the exact degree of torment. Directly over the rack, the circular iron candle-holder swung gently to and fro.

The ropes were being secured about his wrists and ankles – there was a stench of unwashed flesh and onion-tainted breath as the guards bent over him – and the ropes themselves were greasy against his skin. As the winches were wound tight and the ropes stretched taut, there was a thin, teeth-wincing screech of machinery. They're ready, thought Martin, his heart pounding, sweat breaking out all over his body. They're ready to begin.

From his place behind the table, Sir William Kingston said in a calm, detached voice, 'You see what will be done if you persist in your obstinacy. And so once more, I ask you to tell us the identity of the prisoner known as Ahasuerus.'

Martin thought: if I don't speak they can't do anything. Can they? Didn't Sir Thomas More 'stand on his silence'? Yes, but More was Henry's Chancellor, beloved, powerful, extraordinary, and I am nothing and no one by comparison.

And even More went to the block in the end. He compressed his lips and waited. How many minutes would they give him before the torture began?

Several eternities slipped past before Kingston said, 'You won't speak?' There was the ghost of a weary sigh. 'Very well.' He nodded to the guards, and Martin heard the terrible creak of the machinery again and with it—

Oh God, oh sweet Jesus, there was never such pain in the world! His entire body was stretched taut and every joint was wrenched in its socket. Sweat ran into his eyes and he tasted the blood of his bitten tongue.

'Answer!' It was the implacable voice of the King's Lieutenant of the Tower now. The detached voice of the inquisitor. 'Who and what is Ahasuerus?' And then, as if beseeching, 'Tell us, man, and save yourself further pain!'

Through a red mist, Martin saw the not unkindly face of Kingston, and next to him Rodger Cheke, his plump, jowly face red with obscene excitement. His tongue came out to lick his lips, and Martin understood that Cheke was enjoying this, he was relishing Martin's downfall. But he shan't see me break!

The questions came again, cutting through the pain. Who is Ahasuerus? Why were you trying to take him out of the Tower? What was the plot? Who was behind it? You won't answer? Then again! There was a plot, and we will know of it!

This time he felt his wrist-joints dislocate with screaming, tearing agony, and as the winches loosened, he sagged, a red mist obscuring his vision. Someone nearby was groaning, terrible sobbing cries of anguish. Someone was lying with him in this grisly coffin-like box, and it was someone whose sweat he could smell and whose blood and pain he could taste. But he was not breaking, he was holding on to all the good things, the safe, sane things:

plainchant in the Abbey chapel, and autumn rain, and the mist over the Wicklow Hills and the sun setting on Ireland's wild, beautiful west coast . . .

Again the pulleys turned and again the ropes wrenched at his body, and again the pain swept mercilessly through him. His wrists were helplessly, bonelessly out of their sockets, but now searing cramps were clutching his legs, and gristle and bone was scraping in his shoulders as both arms were twisted from their sockets.

Firelight and God's mercy and prayer . . . Hold on to it, oh God, let me hold on to it . . . His lips formed a silent prayer, but as the guards bent to their work again he felt his mind splinter and divide, and on one side of the schism was the real Martin, devout and austere, and able to cling to the shreds of truth and courage, but on the other was a poor weak creature who could not bear this pain, and who was within a hairsbreadth of telling them whatever they wanted to know.

His whole body was a mass of screaming agony, and the creak of the pulleys was inextricably blended with it. At any minute he would give way. In four more heartbeats he would speak . . . In three, two . . . He would betray Ahasuerus, he would betray God . . .

There was a final jolting wrench and Martin heard himself scream. Impossible pain, unbelievable agony. It soared to an excruciating climax, and then a thick blessed unconsciousness swooped down on him.

He did not hear Kingston say, 'He's not going to talk. Untie him.'

'And then?'

Sir William hesitated and then said, 'We must await orders.' He glanced at Sir Rodger. 'But I think there can be only one sentence.'

Chapter Thirty-Four

As they brought him out of the Tower, Martin was dazzled by the brightness and bewildered by the noise. How much time had passed since his racking? He had no idea, for time had become meaningless in the dim cell where he had lain, his mind blunted by pain.

He had managed to drag himself across the floor to gulp thankfully at the water left for him and he had managed to bring his hands together in prayer. But when they came for him, he could not walk and he could not stand, and the guards had to carry his poor mutilated body out into the sunlight. As they set him down on the ground he felt sick and dizzy, but for the first time since his racking, his mind cleared and he could think: I kept faith!

There had been some kind of deputation to his cell; something about the Oath of Supremacy, something about Ahasuerus again but he had turned his head to the wall and at last they had left him alone.

A crowd had gathered, and as he was brought up there was a murmur of half-eager, half-pitying excitement. The guards were looping a rope about his neck, and he thought: am I then to be hanged? But he saw the glint of finely honed steel in their hands and he saw the way they avoided his eyes. Nothing so merciful as hanging. Certainly nothing so merciful as beheading.

'No, Brother Martin,' said Sir William, ascending the

scaffold and standing over him. 'No, there is to be nothing so merciful as beheading. Hanging, drawing and quartering.' He pointed to the far side of the square. 'And if you look to your left – yes, prop him up, guard – you can see the stake that is being prepared, no, not for you. But can you see the faggots being piled up? And now can you see the prisoner being brought out?'

Martin, dizzy with pain and weakness and fear, felt sick despair close about him. Ahasuerus. It had all been for nothing. Ahasuerus was being brought out to be burned.

As the guards tied Ahasuerus to the stake he scanned the crowd, searching for a familiar face. Absurd of course, no one here could know him. A desolate agony flooded his mind as they secured the gyves, and kicked the piled-up faggots into place. Then it is to end here, exactly as the Sanhedrin in Jerusalem intended. The final stage of the Triple Death. Burning alive. His mind spun out of control and for a moment he felt again the excruciating pain of his nailed hands and the searing cramps in his chest and shoulders as he hung in torment.

Scourged at the pillar while the sun passes from the east to the west side of Jerusalem . . . The next evening at sunset you will be nailed to the Cruciferum . . . The evening after that, again at sunset, fires will be lit at the foot of the Cruciferum and your body will burn . . .

He had searched the crowd frantically then as well, but that time he had been looking for Susannah, because he had been so sure she would not leave him to die. They had already been bending to light the fire and the heat had started to rise. Impossible not to struggle. Impossible not to writhe and try to break free, even though every movement was agony.

And then she had been there. Between one breathspace

and the next, she was there. Susannah, the harlot, the sorceress. She had come running into the square, her hair streaming wildly about her shoulders, a gaggle of armed men running in her wake. Ahasuerus had been almost beyond thought then, but he had recognised them as mercenaries: hardened, tough creatures who would give allegiance to anyone who paid them enough and who would fight for any cause if it was made worth their while. Delight poured through his mind, because she was coming to his aid, she had rounded up this raff and skaff army, and she was risking her own life to reach him.

The music came with them; it spiralled and twisted about the square, pouring down on to the heads of the guards and the Sanhedrin and the black-cowled monks on the crowd's edge. Despite the curling flames and the choking, black smoke, triumphant delight coursed through him. Susannah coming to rescue me! Running straight at the Temple Guards leading her ruffian army. Singing the music as she comes and forcing her scurrilous soldiers to sing with her. The music was like a great curling wave, and it reared up and hit him with such relentless force that for a moment the agony and the fear was washed aside.

The Temple Guard had been almost overcome by Susannah's unexpected attack, and the music had not precisely overpowered them, but it had certainly disconcerted them.

Now! thought Ahasuerus. This is the moment, Susannah – now, when they are bemused and dazed! The flames had not reached him, but the skin of his feet was already splitting and blistering. My love, my love, if you ever possessed any powers, use them now for the guards' confusion won't last! Get me down, Susannah!

But she was already running towards him, and with her ran three of her ragamuffins, hurling blows and imprecations at the crowd as they came. The crowd were falling back, as bewildered and as dazzled by the sudden onslaught and the music as the guards, and Susannah had a clear path. As they reached the foot of the cross the men flung thick cloaks and blankets on to the flames, stamping at them, grinning up at one another showing blackened, stump-like teeth in their delight at outwitting the Temple Elders and the Sanhedrin.

As Susannah began to swarm up to where Ahasuerus hung helplessly, there was a rush of movement on the outskirts of the crowd, and the black-robed monks who had bargained for the High Priest's body, bounded forward and knocked Susannah to the ground.

They cut me down before the flames could reach me, thought Ahasuerus, staring about him at the grim bulk of the Tower and the guards. The accursed black monks cut me down and forced me into the elaborate tomb and they sealed the lid. I went down into the abyss and the last thing I heard was the music and the last thing I remembered was Susannah trying to save me. Did I die there? Am I about to die again now?

Fires lit and your body will burn . . .

But this time there is no Susannah to rescue me.

Catherine Howard had examined and impatiently discarded a number of plans for Ahasuerus's rescue: forged pardons from the King, guards ordered out on orders purporting to be Henry's, some kind of diversion to distract the executioner. There were tales of how relatives or loved ones – even executioners themselves if they were paid sufficiently well – sometimes crept up behind the burning prisoner and strangled him under cover of the smoke. Could the executioner be bribed on this occasion?

But any of these plans needed an accomplice – several accomplices – and there was no longer anyone Catherine dared trust.

Coming to Tower Hill today was the most tremendous risk she had ever taken, but not to be there was unthinkable. And supposing a chance to reach Ahasuerus did occur? I must be there, thought Catherine determinedly. I'll have nightmares for the rest of my life, and I'll never forget any of this, but I have to be there.

She was hooded and cloaked, her bright hair bound beneath a kerchief to avoid recognition. The King's ardour was becoming known, and Catherine was accorded a wary admiration when she went abroad these days. There had been endless instructions issued by Grandmother and even her Uncle, the Duke of Norfolk himself. Do this. Be sure not to do that. And, once, when she had rebelled: But don't you *want* to be Queen? they had said incredulously, staring at her as if she was an imbecile. She had thought: not if it means having Henry Tudor in my bed! but the words could not be said, not even to her own family. Especially not to her own family.

Today it had ceased to matter, because today at noon Ahasuerus, her enigmatic, beautiful lover, would burn. And there was nothing Catherine could do to prevent it.

The crowd was larger than she had expected – did they enjoy watching a burning, these people? Catherine shuddered and flattened herself against the wall on the side of the square. The stake had been built higher than usual – to ensure that there was no stealthy merciful strangling? – and it jutted upwards, a grisly, black outline against the bright sky. A small brazier was being dragged out, the charcoal already white-hot. Catherine stared at it fearfully.

As the guards brought Ahasuerus out, a ragged cheer went through the watchers, and people began to push closer. Catherine was thrust back against the wall, but she could see everything. She looked at the people and wondered how they would tell Ahasuerus's story after this was over. Would this execution be woven into the fabric and the weft of the Tower's bloody history? Would Ahasuerus be a martyr or a sinner? Or would he simply be one more heretic who had opposed Henry Tudor? She had asked Sir Rodger about him, and Sir Rodger had said, oh, she was not to worry; they had discovered the creature to be some kind of Papist spy. And they all knew what happened to Papist spies, said Sir Rodger, as comfortable as if he had never crossed Smithfield Square by mistake on the morning after a burning, and had never smelled the too-rich, too-greasy smoke that lay on the air like a pall, or had to run into a side street to vomit his breakfast on to the ground because of it.

Ahasuerus was walking arrogantly between the guards, but Catherine saw him flinch from the bright sunlight and once he brought up a hand to shield his eyes. Bitter fury rose in her because they must have kept him in some dim, underground dungeon; not troubling – probably not caring – to make his last days comfortable.

But as he approached the rearing outline of the stake he seemed to gain strength. He straightened up and looked at the crowd, authority and defiance streaming from him, and even at this distance, Catherine could see his clear grey eyes shining. She was suddenly deeply grateful to him for maintaining the enigma and the strange allure, even facing death.

The guards were binding him to the stake, using thin snaking chains, but he seemed scarcely to notice. His head was turned to the far side of the square, and Catherine, looking in the same direction, saw that a scaffold had been erected, and that some other poor prisoner was being dragged up the steps. A monk, was it? The block was there, black and grim, and the guards were sprinkling sawdust. Catherine shivered but turned back to Ahasuerus. I can't spare any pity for the unknown monk, she thought. I'll pray for him later – I promise I'll pray for him, whoever he is – but I can't think of anything other than Ahasuerus. They're locking the chains in place now. Oh God, this is going to be unbearable.

Without warning, the brilliant May sunshine slid behind a cloud and the sky darkened abruptly, almost as if an unnatural night was descending. Huge black clouds massed overhead and a wind scurried across the square, catching at the women's hair and stirring up the litter and the dust. People squealed and clapped their hats firmly on to their heads, laughing and pointing to where one man's cloak had gone flapping away from him so that he had to go chasing after it. They cheered him on, enjoying the small diversion, and Catherine hated them.

Ahasuerus was looking about him with a confused air, almost as if he had forgotten where he was. His eyes slid over the watching crowd and then away, as if they were not worthy of notice. He looked almost bored and Catherine thought if she had not loved him before she would have done so in that moment.

But the guards had moved in and they were lighting torches from the brazier, and orange and scarlet flames leapt into the air. The scent of hot metal from the brazier drifted on the wind, and then, at a signal, the guards thrust the burning torches into the piled faggots, firing them in four places.

Catherine could not look away. She was beyond thought; she was beyond everything in the world but the helpless figure chained to the stake. The flames caught instantly: they licked hungrily at the wood and tore upwards, trickles of fire catching at the hem of Ahasuerus's robe. Clouds of dark smoke belched out, partly obscuring Ahasuerus's body and Catherine gasped and thrust a clenched fist into her mouth.

In another few minutes, the whole stake would be blazing and his entire body would be alight. He would burn: his flesh would singe and blister, and the blood would boil in his veins. And his eyes – unbearable thought – his sweet, lovely eyes would burn, he would be blinded, he would be sightless long before the end.

The scudding clouds were rolling in in earnest now, blotting out the sun, and with them came the feeling that something was stirring: something immeasurably ancient and something vast beyond belief and awesome beyond imagining. They're harbingers, those storm clouds, thought Catherine, glancing up. Death's heralds. Is Death creeping across the square now, wielding his immense, ebony scythe as he comes? If I looked round would I see him stealing up on me? She glanced across at the other scaffold, at the crouching bulk of the block, and for a moment a different fear brushed her mind – how close are any of us to death?

From overhead came the first brutish growl of thunder, and Catherine drew her cloak about her. Absurd to feel cold when in front of her a man was burning alive . . .

There were other sounds beyond the low snarl of the thunder now and Catherine frowned and half turned her head. Music, sly, rollicking music, and the sound of voices – several of them – singing. Strolling players of some kind? Troubadors? The word *minstrels* formed in her mind and her heart gave a great leap of hope. But did I hear it in truth or was it a trick of sound? She looked back at the burning pyre, her mind spinning.

Ahasuerus was struggling against the fetters, his head thrown back, his face contorted in agony. Catherine saw his hair catch fire and his hands come up to his face –

terrible hands! clawed! Those were the hands that caressed me! Memory spiralled back to the sensuous feel of sheathed claws roaming across her body and drawing forth that astonishing response. There was no revulsion at the pitiful mutilated hands: there was only deep aching agony for whatever had happened to him in the past and for what was happening to him now, and there was pain at the memory of his arms about her and of his skin like velvet against her body, and of strength and silk-over-steel passion.

Ahasuerus's dreadful hands were vainly trying to shield his face, they were clawing outwards and clutching at the air as if the flames were solid things that could be grasped and pushed away. But his face was starting to burn: Catherine could see it blistering and bubbling with the heat.

The thunder came again, much nearer now and the underside of the storm clouds was becoming suffused with angry crimson. To Catherine, huddled wretchedly in her corner, it was as if the tormented figure was already dying, bleeding and burning into the skies. Jagged lightning tore across the heavens and huge drops of rain began to fall, spattering on to the ground. The blazing pyre faltered and black, evil-smelling smoke gusted across the square. Catherine drew in a huge breath – if ever there is a chance to rescue him this is it – and clutching her cloak about her, sped across the square.

In the same moment, from the western side there streamed into the square not the guards or soldiers she had thought of, but a tumbling, dancing, cartwheeling troupe of travelling entertainers: minstrels and gypsy dancers and a shambling performing bear, and acrobats and jugglers. The tootling music of the minstrels and the rattling tambourines of the girls was shocking in that agony-filled place, but impossibly there was laughter and shouting blotting out the murmuring of the crowd and the grim crackling of the fire. As the rainbow colours of the dancers spun and whirled, Catherine stopped in mid-flight and scanned them eagerly and thought: Nicolas? Could it be? Delight exploded within her, because he was there: not bringing an army or soldiers or fighting brigands to rescue Ahasuerus, but bringing his own people: the vagabond brotherhood who roamed the countryside, performing in barns and meadows and tilt yards and inns. Troubadors and gleemen and puppet-makers and bards. Gnome-faced freaks, barely four feet high. Dancing dogs and wild-eyed Romanies with streaming hair and brown skins.

The music altered course suddenly, it took on the strange elusive beauty of the melody Nicolas had taught her that night and that she had played to the King. Catherine could see Nicolas clearly, at the centre of it all, leading his people into the fire-drenched square, scattering his marvellous, irresistible music like quicksilver over the cobblestones of Henry Tudor's torture yard.

The guards were shouting and pushing the entertainers out of the way, and Catherine fought her way forward, trying to see the best way to help. Because all the while he was burning, Ahasuerus was still burning . . . A hand closed about her wrist, and Nicolas's soft voice said in her ear, 'Keep back if you value your life, mistress, and leave this to us!'

Catherine felt her heart give a great lurch, but without taking her eyes from the blazing pyre, she said, 'You can save him?'

'If we are not too late – the King's men brought forward the time of death! But we will do our best!' And then he was gone, darting forward, caught in the whirling confusion again.

As the fire burned up, fighting the quenching rain,

Catherine saw the bright figure with its cap of red-gold hair vanish into the heart of the billowing black smoke.

Martin had seen Nicolas through the smoke and the shouting: he had seen the minstrel moving forward to the terrible blazing prisoner. The descendant of Ahasuerus and Isabella Amati, he thought; the seed of the Devil's Piper going into the flames to reach the immortal High Priest.

He fell back on the floor of the scaffold, almost gratefully. Nicolas knows what must be done. It will be all right. And I kept faith. I kept the vow. Now I can keep faith with God.

He caught the sound of furious shouts from beyond the blazing pyre, and then of mocking laughter followed by hoofbeats. There was the pounding of running feet, and Martin's lips curved in a painful smile. He's got him. Nicolas has got him away.

He felt the guards' hands on him, rough and impatient, as if they might be saying: this one at least won't escape, and he cried out with the pain of his dislocated limbs. As the shadow of the gibbet fell across him, the noose slid about his neck and tightened as he was jerked upwards. Upwards into the dark sky with its bloodied storm clouds, he thought wildly.

There was vicious pain again as he fought the hanging, and the rope bit into his neck, strangling him, choking him . . . He felt himself treading air, knowing it to be useless to fight, but fighting all the same. Sweat mingled with rain poured down his face, and a red mist obscured his vision. Knife-like pains sliced into his lungs and he knew himself to be slowly strangling.

As the red mist turned to black and blessed unconsciousness closed in, they cut him free, and air rushed into his lungs. He fell gasping and choking, hitting the floor in a sickening crunch that jarred his mutilated bones, so that he hunched over in agony, sobbing for breath.

He barely heard the soft footfall of the executioners as they moved forward, but they were there, bending over him, straightening him up from his foetal crouch. There was a moment of obscene intimacy as they removed his robe and drew down the cotton under-drawers. Their hands were calloused with jagged nails that rasped his skin, and they breathed noisily as if they might be aroused by what they were doing.

He was aware of his own voice screaming as they gouged out his bowels, and of pain that clawed scorchingly up through his throat, so that he retched and vomited into the sawdust beneath him. Almost immediately there was the terrible stench of his own entrails being burned. But I am almost there, he thought. I kept the vow and Ahasuerus is safe. And now, finally and at last, I can feel God's love. God's mercy descending about me.

As they dragged him to the block, one of the guards slipped in the blood and vomit on the ground and let out a curse, but Martin scarcely noticed. He was concentrating on God's love and God's mercy, and somewhere just beyond his vision, a light was beginning to shine on the horizon he could barely see.

Only a very little way to go now, he thought, and his mind reached for God, not the narrow vengeful God of Henry Tudor and his sycophants, but the real God; the God of love and light and compassion. Even though Martin's body was suffering almost beyond endurance, his mind was beginning to unfold to receive that beckoning light, and his heart was singing with the sweet promise of Heaven. The golden beckoning of the New Testament pledge was bearing him up and taking him forward into the light; it was the air beneath his wings . . .

'*For eye hath not seen, nor ear heard, neither hath it entered into the heart of man, the things which God hath prepared for them that love Him . . .*'

I'm nearly there, thought Martin, laying his cheek against the smooth hollowed-out shape of the block.

As the axe came down, severing his head, he was still smiling.

The sun was setting in a blaze of crimson and gold behind Curran Glen, as Nicolas seated himself in Father Abbot's study and regarded the elderly monk levelly.

'We are greatly indebted to you.' Father Abbot thought it was difficult to know quite what to call this odd man, who was neither young nor old, and who had simply introduced himself as 'Nicolas'. It was even more difficult to thank him sufficiently for what he had done. Father Abbot had come across most kinds of men – and women as well – but he had never before encountered anyone quite like this Italian minstrel.

Nicolas said, 'It is not necessary to thank me, Father. I did not succeed in all I set myself: Brother Martin died at the hands of Henry Tudor's butchers and I had hoped to rescue him. I am sorry I did not do so. But he died as a man of God should – you and your people will be pleased to know that. He died bravely and calmly and he kept faith to the end. The burial was of necessity inside the Tower,' he said. 'There was nothing I or my people could do about it. But the other one—' He made a brief gesture to the un-curtained window, through which they could see the small horse-drawn cart with its burden standing on the quadrangle. 'The other I have returned to you, in accordance with your vow and my own,' said Nicolas. 'The coffin was made by two journeymen in Cheapside; it is plain and makeshift, but I dared not stay in England any longer.'

'Goodness me, of course not,' said Father Abbot, at once.

'Your devil's music-maker is bound by the grave once again.'

Father Abbot said carefully, 'How did you— That is, I have never quite understood—'

'How he is re-captured? How he is sent tumbling down into the dreamless sleep until the music wakes him again?'

Father Abbot thought you might trust a ballad-maker – and an Italian at that! – to put it in a flowery way, but in fact it was precisely what he had meant.

Nicolas said, 'Father, I do not know. I do not think your founder, Simon, knew, either.'

He glanced to the window, and Father Abbot, cold fear brushing his spine, said, 'He is – forgive me, but you are sure that he is – not awake?'

'Awake and sealed into his coffin? Yes, it would be a gruesome thought, that,' said Nicolas. 'One could not sleep at nights for thinking of it. But he is not awake, Father.' For the first time, he hesitated. Then he said, 'I know of Ahasuerus from my mother, who had it from her father, and he from his father— Many, many generations back. And although I know the story of the renegade High Priest who was condemned for heresy and who claimed immortality, and although I know, as you know, what wakes him—'

'You do not know what it is that sends him back?'

'No. But,' said Nicolas, 'I have thought about it.' He paused as if arranging his thoughts, and then said, 'Three times now Ahasuerus has been sent into the grave. In Jerusalem, in Cremona, and this last time in England. And each time a particular sequence of events was present. A trial, agony by fire, the music, and—' He paused, and a smile curved his lips. 'And the presence of a certain lady,' said Nicolas.

'In Jerusalem he was tried for defiling the Temple with Susannah,' said Father Abbot thoughtfully.

'And the Triple Death was pronounced.'

'The extreme penalty,' said Father Abbot, with a shudder. 'But we know of it from Brother Simon's journal.'

'And I from my ancestress,' said Nicolas. 'Also from my ancestress I know that in Cremona Ahasuerus was put to the *per Dei judicium*—'

'Trial by ordeal and God's judgement,' said Father Abbot.

'Yes. His hands were badly burned and they withered into claws, although he escaped death.'

'And now in England he was again sentenced to burn,' said Father Abbot, staring at his unusual guest.

'Yes. There was no trial, but there is something known as the *auto-da-fé*. The passing of sentence on one regarded as a heretic and the public burning of the heretic. Used during the Spanish Inquisition. And,' said Nicolas, 'Ahasuerus had already been branded as a heretic once.'

'Yes, I understand. And,' said Father Abbot, 'the lady?'

Nicolas paused, and then said softly, 'I believe the lady was there each time.' He glanced through the window to the silent coffin again, and then said, in a different voice, 'You understand that he is burned? They brought forward the time of the execution – perhaps they heard of the rescue plan – and we could not get to him in time. The flames burned his legs very severely. And his face was mutilated—'

'Dear God,' Father Abbot sketched a small cross on his breast.

'We covered it,' said Nicolas softly. 'A thin dun-coloured mask with eyelets. It does not really matter, but I could not let him lie in his coffin without some semblance of dignity.'

'That was considerate. So,' said Father Abbot, half to himself, 'Ahasuerus has become a hideous outcast in addition to everything else he has suffered.'

Nicolas said gently, 'Without the mask he is a distressing sight,' and into the warm study with its splendour of sunset beyond the latticed windows, a little sighing breath gusted.

Both men looked uneasily over their shoulders, and then Father Abbot said briskly, 'It does not, of course, matter, because we shall ensure that he does not escape again.

'Ahasuerus will not rise again. No one will ever look on his face.'

Chapter Thirty-Five

Moira was beginning to feel as if she had fallen into a Fifties thriller film: the kind where Dana Andrews fought back the walking corpses or Janette Scott fled from triffids, and where everything was set against one of those perilously shaky backdrops so that you could tell that the swamp or the smoke-wreathed graveyard was painted-on, and the car chases all had the give-away rims of light denoting back-projection. Father had indulgently dubbed them rubbish and had wondered that his clever girl could find entertainment in such flimsy nonsense, but Moira had derived a kind of comforting nostalgia in watching the TV re-runs and getting glimpses of how the world had been before she was born, although presumably grappling with carnivorous plants or passing death-bringing runes on to enemies had not been an everyday occurrence in those days.

Heathrow Airport had been a seething mass of people, even at eleven o'clock at night, and Moira, trying to look as if she was used to all this, was secretly very glad indeed that Isarel and Ciaran were familiar with the procedure about collecting tickets and boarding passes and surrendering luggage. She managed to cash some more money at the Bureau de Change, and went into one of the airport shops to buy an extra shirt and a spare pair of jeans or cords, and some more underthings. Lauren, who had accompanied them to the airport, came with her, and watched her thoughtfully for a moment, before taking from the rack a vivid turquoise-green silk shirt and an ankle-length mohair skirt the colour of moss. 'Because, my ewe lamb, you can't go off with those two without something halfway decent to wear in the evening.'

'It's not that sort of journey,' said Moira. 'It's—'

'It's a journey with two of the sexiest guys I've come across in ages and you've got to grab every opportunity you can in this life.' Lauren winked at the assistant, who was listening, round-eyed, and turned to survey the rest of the tiny shop.

'And I think you should have a daytime jacket as well, don't you – oh look, how about one of those green waxed things, you'll be a Sloane abroad in that, very British, you'll look terrific.'

The waxed jacket was the kind you saw being worn by the Queen and Princess Anne at horse shows and the silk shirt was Italian with a designer label, and Moira nearly passed out at the prices. They had quite an argument in the shop because Lauren had produced her American Express card to pay for everything and Moira was determined to be independent, even though neither the silk shirt nor the mohair skirt, and certainly not the waxed jacket had entered into her careful calculations. In the end, Lauren said, 'Listen, kid, you got into this by mistake, and you're doing Kate and Richard a very big favour by going to Eisenach. If it makes you feel better I'll bill the firm – legitimate business expenses,' and then clinched the matter by scribbling a signature.

She had been right about the things looking terrific. Moira regarded her reflection in the changing cubicle and remembered how last autumn Father had picked out for her a tweed coat with a self-belt and velvet collar, and a navy linen two-piece with a pleated skirt. And even though it really wasn't that kind of a journey, and even though Moira was frantic every time she thought about Kate in Vogel's hands, she thought you would have to be very nearly inhuman not to feel pleasure at being given such marvellous things.

She sat by Isarel on the plane, and with the idea of finding out a bit more about what they were going into, asked him about Jude.

'That's if you don't mind talking about him?'

'God, no,' said Isarel, at once. 'Jude's haunted me all my life, Moira. When I was very small, I dreamed about him – night after night. I used to wake up terrified, expecting to see him standing in a corner of the bedroom watching me. I dreamed about this place we're going to as well—'

'Eisenach Castle?' It increased the feeling of unreality to be seated here with someone who looked like the photograph of Jude come to life. Lauren had said these were two of the sexiest men she had met for ages, and Lauren probably thought most men under the age of ninety were sexy, but even so— 'Tell me about Eisenach,' said Moira.

'I don't know where to begin. But it's grim and stark,' said Isarel. 'A mountain fortress. There's a central hall where Jude's last concert was held: a huge, glittering place with chandeliers and stone pillars and a marble and gilt stairway— He came down that to confront his audience that night.'

'When he played the *Devil's Piper*?'

'Yes. And there's a dining room with faded tapestries lining the walls, and sombre bedchambers above, and a turret on the eastern side—'

He broke off abruptly, and Moira said thoughtfully, 'Did you ever read any of those stories about a traveller who dreams of a place night after night, and then comes upon it unexpectedly years later, and is told that it's haunted?'

'And is recognised as actually being the ghost who haunts it,' said Isarel. He smiled suddenly, 'I did indeed.'

Moira said, 'I wonder if you're going to be recognised when we get to Eisenach?'

'So do I.'

Lauren had been efficient about the arrangements, which Moira thought she should have expected. The rental car was reserved for them at Frankfurt, and Isarel, after consultation with Ciaran, took the wheel.

'I'm out of practice at driving on the right,' said Ciaran.

'And if you're not driving, you can go to sleep in the back,' rejoined Isarel.

'Certainly not, I'll point out the sights to Moira as we go.'

'You don't know any of the sights.'

'That won't stop me,' said Ciaran.

As they neared Eisenach, they began to get tantalising glimpses of the old romantic Germany: the Germany that had once been sprinkled with names like Bohemia and Bavaria and Saxony and Mecklenburg, and that had been a patchwork of petty dukedoms, ruled by palatines and margraves.

I'm going into a fairytale, thought Moira, entranced. I'm going into the Black Forest – I mean the place not the pudding – the ancient Forest of the Kingdom of Thuringia. This is the land where wood-cutters change into prowling wolves when there's a full moon, and princesses get shut away in doorless towers and have to make a rope from their hair and climb down it through a window. It's a pity about the motorways and fly-overs and whatnot, but I suppose

396

the journey would have been a lot more difficult without them.

We're going to Eisenach Castle, she thought; we're going to the place where Isarel dreamed he walked as a child, and where Jude Weissman performed the *Devil's Piper*. And now it's going to be performed again, only Conrad Vogel's calling it by another name. Satan's Lute-Player, that poster said. I suppose it is the music. Yes, of course it is. Vogel's simply re-hashing it, and giving it another name, the rat. There's a word for that – I don't mean plagiarism, or do I? Palimpsest? Yes, that's what I mean. New writing on an old manuscript. How remarkable. I wish we knew if Kate was all right.

Ciaran had taken over the wheel for the last stretch, and they were driving down a long winding road with scented pine forests on both sides. Directly ahead, the sun was sinking behind the trees, setting the skies ablaze with great swathes of scarlet and crimson and lilac. Oriflammes streaming across the sky, thought Moira, entranced.

Isarel said suddenly, 'We're nearly there. In a minute there'll be a break in the trees on the left, and you'll see it.'

'Are you sure? According to the map—'

'Yes, I'm sure.'

And then it was there, exactly as Isarel had said, suddenly in their view between the trees.

A stark mountain fortress, set amidst the sprawling pine forests of ancient Bavaria and Bohemia, at the heart of the dark fairytale Forest of Thuringia, the lost kingdom of the Franks and the Saxons. Turrets rose on all sides, and even from this distance, Moira could see the jagged castellations, and the slit-windows of the Middle Ages and earlier, and the dark band of shadow circling it that indicated a moat.

Eisenach Castle.

* * *

397

Kate opened her eyes and winced as light sliced into her brain.

She was lying on something hard and uncomfortable – wood? – and she was stiff and bruised and cold. She moved cautiously, and banged her arms against the wooden sides. A box? Panic nudged at her mind, and then memory began to return in painful strings: herself seated in Conrad Vogel's office and Vogel himself smiling the smile of the knight with the knife under his cloak . . .

Drugged coffee, thought Kate, struggling to force back the thick folds of unconsciousness. How long ago was it? It felt as if it could have been several hours. Another strand unravelled and she thought: he was going to bring me to Eisenach Castle with Ahasuerus! Is that where I am now?

She moved her hands and feet again, and met rough wood on all sides. No ropes. Is this the packing case? I think it must be. At least the lid's not on and I can see out.

The absolute nightmare would be if Ahasuerus was still here with her. But even as the thought formed, Kate knew he was not. There was no longer the indefinable sense of another presence. She had shared this wooden case with the Devil's Piper, but he was no longer here. This discovery was such a relief that she thought she might be equal to climbing out and exploring. In any case, to lie here wondering where she was and what might be waiting for her, was unthinkable. She pushed herself up on one elbow, flinching from the pain in her head again.

The light was not so very bright after all, in fact what light there was was extremely dim. It was just that after the drugged unconsciousness her eyes were sensitive. Where the devil am I? thought Kate. Somewhere cold and dank and cavernous. Could it really be Eisenach Castle? A cellar? A dungeon? Don't be ridiculous.

It was important not to give way to panic. It was even

more important not to listen to the insidious little voice whispering that she was shut away in a dark underground place and that Conrad Vogel might be waiting for her and – what was far worse – that Ahasuerus might be waiting for her as well.

She clambered out, wincing afresh as her cramped arms and legs protested, but finally standing upright. She was numb and stiff and she spent a few minutes massaging her calves and arms. Agonising cramp-pains clutched her muscles as the blood began to flow again, but her sight was adjusting to the dimness and she was feeling better. She was crumpled, she felt vaguely stale, and the green surcoat she had donned in London about a hundred years ago was badly creased. None of this could be helped and none of it mattered.

She thought her first impression of being underground had been accurate. The packing case was lying in what appeared to be some kind of earth tunnel, about fifteen feet wide, with a low ceiling. There was a vaguely claustrophobic feel, and Kate thought the tunnel walls and ceiling were hard-packed soil or rock. There was a dank earthy smell as well, which she associated with subterranean mounds and ancient excavations. Or even cemeteries with freshly dug graves – no, not that.

The idea of being in an underground tunnel was rather nasty. You could not help thinking about all the things that lived underground. Blind wriggling worms and slugs and the horrid scuttling things you sometimes saw when you turned up a clod of earth in your garden. Kate shivered, half with repulsion, half with cold.

The first thing to do was find out how far the tunnel stretched and how to get out. The entrance would probably be locked or barred, but this was something else not to think about yet. And I've done this before, thought Kate. I was locked into the Abbey bell tower at Curran Glen, and I got out all right. I'll get out of this, as well. I'm an old hand at escapes and I'll *insist* that I'll get out.

There was sufficient light to see a few yards in each direction and she inspected the walls cautiously. Yes, hard-packed earth, veined here and there with pale gristly jointed tree roots. So I was right about being under the ground. At some time someone dug down – or maybe dug into a hill or an escarpment – to make this. Is it some kind of Roman hill fort or a pre-Christian barrow? No, it's more modern. I wish there was more light. If I smoked I'd have matches or a lighter. I never thought I'd regret not smoking. Her partner smoked constantly and they had had a few battles about it before agreeing on demarcation lines and smoke-free hours in the office. Kate would have given a very large sum of money for one of Lauren's boxes of matches just now.

The earth tunnel curved slightly to the right, and Kate went forward warily. It was important to remember about not being frightened and although it was rather horrid down here, so far nothing had actually happened to her. She was certainly wrought up and angry, which was probably a good way to feel, because of the adrenalin, but nothing had happened.

Ahead was a faint ingress of light, and the faint cold gleam of steel. Doors? She stopped, listening intently, but if anything prowled behind her in the dark, it prowled soundlessly. I think I'm alone, thought Kate, torn between thankfulness and terror.

She looked back at the doors. Were they some kind of trap? Was Vogel – or whoever might be working with him or for him? – expecting her to walk through those doors? What was on the other side?

The doors were huge double oblongs, each one ten feet

high, with massive iron bolts across them, rusting and pitted with age. The doors might lead anywhere or they might lead nowhere. Vogel or Ahasuerus himself might be standing on the other side, waiting for her. But she was damned if she would go back into the tunnel.

The doors yielded to her touch, but the hinges shrieked with a high-pitched squeal that set her already taut nerves jangling. But beyond them it was perceptibly lighter, and Kate could see into a large, brick-lined room. It v s huge and echoing, but as she entered the breath caught in her throat and for several minutes she had to fight against a feeling of physical suffocation. And there was pain lingering here, and the most appalling terror.

She advanced cautiously to the centre of the chamber, which was immense, at least eighty feet long and probably twenty feet wide. It was no gouged-out affair of earth and rock: this was a proper room, the walls lined with dark red brick, crumbling in places with the dryness of age but mostly sound. The floor was cold, hard concrete and her footsteps echoed hollowly. The ceiling was lower than the tunnel, but near the top where wall and ceiling met, were steel vents of some kind, each one about a foot in diameter, placed at regular intervals. Kate stared at them, trying to understand their purpose. They were like yawning mouths. Black and cavernous and rather sinister. There was absolutely nothing else in the room, but it was so full of agony and panic that it was nearly choking her.

At the far end was a small, low door, half sunk into the wall, surrounded by more of the dark, old brick. Might it be a way out? As she walked across the concrete, the thick terror surged up again. Dear God, what is this place?

But comprehension was already flooding her mind, and fragments of memory – things heard, things read – were forming a grim pattern. This dark underground cavern, this

401

brick-lined room with steel doors and steel vents . . .

She had been brought to Eisenach Castle – Conrad Vogel had said it was where he was taking her – and until very recently indeed, Eisenach had been in Soviet-ruled territory, in the Eastern Bloc. Behind the Iron Curtain, in fact. Remote and impenetrable. Anything might have gone on there. Anything might still go on. Serse's People. Conrad Vogel presenting his travesty of a Messianic creature to the gullible youngsters who followed the music's lure.

Eisenach, of course, had been the glittering background for Jude Weissman's famous concert, but it had also been rumoured that it was one of Hitler's most secret bastions. One or two of the history books had suggested that it was there that Jude had entered into that terrible pact.

None of the books had ever suggested that the castle had been more than a meeting place for high-ranking Gestapo and SS officers, however, and there had never been so much as a hint that it could have been a death camp. But Kate, looking around her, understood with blinding clarity the purpose of the underground room and she knew at last where she was.

Conrad Vogel had carried her into one of the Nazis' disused gas chambers and sealed all the exits.

Chapter Thirty-Six

Kate knew that if she was to escape, she must try to think clearly again, and she must force back the horror and the agony and the clustering ghosts.

She moved swiftly across the hard concrete floor, resolutely not looking up at the gaping vents, concentrating on reaching the small sunken door at the far end. Shut out everything except the thought of survival, Kate. She pushed open the low brick door on the room's far side and went in.

To begin with, she thought this was better and then she thought it was a hundred times worse. The light was better here and she could see that there was the same concrete floor and the same red brick walls.

But set into the wall facing the door, about halfway up, were six or eight immense holes, each one three or four feet across, and roughly semi-circular. They looked like the mouths of tunnels and each one was surrounded by thick steel plating and framed by a jutting parapet. Circular steel doors were still attached to two of the openings, huge bolts holding them in place, but their hinges rusting and their edges pitted and blackened. They were exactly like rather old-fashioned bakers' ovens. They would be fired and there would be long-handled implements to thrust deep inside to test the heat and to test the baking bread.

For a minute, Kate stared at the openings, grappling with the bizarre notion of finding bakers' ovens down here, and then the juxtaposition of the room with the grisly outer chamber struck her with dreadful clarity.

The outer chamber had been the gas chamber, and it was fearsome and pitiful and soaked in the long-ago agonies of the poor doomed creatures forced into the underground chambers and murdered. But after the gas had dispersed the bodies were dragged through into this room. Because the yawning tunnels were exactly what she had seen them to be: ovens.

They were human ovens.

This was the crematorium.

As Kate's senses reeled, footsteps crossed the floor of the outer room, and she spun round.

Conrad Vogel was standing in the doorway, his thin lips smiling, a small black revolver levelled at her.

'So you have recovered from the chlorpromazine, have you, Kate?' he said, and walked forward until he was standing in front of her. 'You are a trifle dishevelled and pale,' he said, 'but on the whole it is not unattractive.'

He put out a hand to touch her face and Kate said very clearly, 'If you lay a hand – or anything else – on me, I shall gouge out your eyes.' She glared at him. 'And then I shall twist your balls off – very slowly and using my fingernails.' God, I'm descending into profanity with a vengeance, she thought. But if that's the only weapon I've got at the moment I might as well use it. And I'm damned if I'll let him see how frightened I am!

But Vogel said, 'Physical violence can be very arousing. Don't under-estimate my tastes, Kate. You might find that I like it.' He leaned against the wall, the gun still levelled, his eyes never leaving her. 'And I can think of worse fates than taking you to bed,' he said.

Kate replied in a strong, clear voice, 'I would rather be

fucked by Ahasuerus.' And thought: well, you've hit gutter-level now, Kate. I don't care. I *would* rather be fucked by Ahasuerus.

Vogel studied her for a moment. 'Your husband did not follow you,' he said. 'He is still in London,' and Kate felt such a rush of relief that for a moment she forgot about her own danger and Vogel's sly insinuations. Richard had not taken the bait! He was still safe! Then I've only got to worry about myself!

'Which means,' said Vogel, 'that we shall have to lure him a little.'

'How?'

'I'm going to make a phone call to him,' he said, regarding her thoughtfully. 'Suggesting that he comes out here for you. And so that we can be sure of it, you are going to add your persuasions to mine.'

'Am I indeed?'

'You are. You're going to make a tape recording, begging him to come for you. A brief message that I can relay over the phone.'

Kate managed a scornful laugh. 'Losing Richard's really upset you, hasn't it?' she said. 'You'll go to any lengths to get him. Well, you can screw your tape recording, Conrad, because I won't do it. Did you honestly think I would help you to drag Richard into your nasty little cult? If you really thought it, you're either very naive or merely mad.'

'Oh, I'm not mad, Kate. Simply I intend to do what my grandfather's master failed to do more than half a century ago. But where he failed, I will succeed.'

My grandfather's master . . . The silence closed down, menacing, filled with creeping evil.

At last, Kate, scarcely believing her ears, said, 'Hitler?'

'Hitler,' affirmed Vogel. 'My grandfather was one of his most trusted confidential aides. How quick you are,

Kate.' He sounded pleased, as if he was complimenting a particularly apt pupil. 'Karl tried many times to find Ahasuerus and to raise him, but he never succeeded. He managed to acquire Ahasuerus's music, but never Ahasuerus himself. But now I have done so. And in a very short time, I shall bring the two together. Ahasuerus will walk to the music's bidding, and I shall have absolute mastery over the young minds I have spent so many years in drawing about me.'

Kate said, 'We're in Eisenach Castle, aren't we? Yes, I thought so. Complete with gas chamber and crematorium.'

She glanced about her, and Vogel agreed. 'Yes, Eisenach had the machinery for disposing of some of the subhumans.'

'Subhumans?'

'Jews,' said Vogel, and Kate felt as if something had traced a cold, slimy path down her spine.

She said, 'At least you told me the truth about our destination. This is where Hitler's people coerced Jude Weissman to work for them, isn't it?'

'Oh, Weissman needed no coercing,' said Vogel at once. 'He liked money and he liked women. He was very vulnerable to bedroom persuasions and easy riches.'

For some illogical reason this careless dismissiveness angered Kate. Had Jude really bartered his marvellous shining gift for sexual gratification and wealth? But she only said, 'If you want Richard, you can get him for yourself. I'm not going to make any fake recordings. In any case, phone calls can be traced, had you thought about that? Richard could have the police on to you within an hour of making the call.'

'Not if he was told that to call in the police would be dangerous to you.'

'Death threats?' said Kate contemptuously. 'You've

missed your vocation, Conrad. You ought to be writing cheap thrillers.'

'I've already said I shan't kill you,' said Vogel. 'There are far more interesting things that I can do to you. And a short while ago you expressed a preference for being – dealt with by Ahasuerus.'

'What about it?' Kate glared at him, but a dreadful suspicion was beginning to form.

'It's a very intriguing idea,' said Vogel. 'The more I think about it, the more intriguing it gets. Ahasuerus is in here with us, you know. Or didn't you know? Haven't you heard him creeping along the unlit tunnels, dragging his mutilated body nearer and nearer?'

'No. And I don't believe you.'

'The mutilations would certainly not prevent him from – finding you attractive,' said Vogel, as if Kate had not spoken. 'And women were Ahasuerus's downfall more than once, if the legend speaks truly. He had a weakness for red hair, but I think he would find you attractive, Kate. And I think that after a night shut in here with him, you would feel very differently about sending that message to Richard. Assuming that is, you retained your sanity. If you didn't, I should be forced to send for Richard on my own account – or perhaps the doctors would do it for me.' He began to move back to the steel doors, still keeping the gun levelled.

'Tomorrow,' said Vogel, 'my concert will be starting, and my musicians will play the music that has gone by so many names, but that you and I know as the *Devil's Piper*.' He paused, regarding her. 'Once that begins, Ahasuerus will be forced to obey it. And so once it begins, he must be inside the castle. He must be within reach of the music.'

'You're really going to present him to Serse's People as their Messiah?'

'Yes,' said Vogel softly. 'Yes, I am. But before that

happens, there is a whole day. And a whole night, Kate. And so I am going to leave Ahasuerus in here with you. He will take a little time to drag himself through the dark tunnels towards you, but he will find you, Kate.

'I think that by the time I come back for him, you will have agreed to do what I want.'

Chapter Thirty-Seven

Night had fallen and Isarel had taken over the wheel again when they finally turned on to the carpark of the Black Duke, which was where Lauren, planning ahead with typical efficiency, had booked rooms.

'Below the castle but near enough to be convenient,' said Ciaran, stretching his cramped limbs and looking about him.

'In its shadow,' said Isarel, who had been silent for the last few miles. Moira glanced at him uneasily.

Moira was not very used to hotels, but she thought the Black Duke struck an eminently satisfying note. It was a low, rambling building, with the rooms pleasingly scented by old timbers and centuries of woodsmoke, and with uneven floors and small windows with criss-crossed leaded lights.

Ciaran said, 'It's eight o'clock. I don't think there's much we can do tonight, do you?'

'The concert starts the day after tomorrow,' said Isarel, nodding towards a familiar poster on the green baize board in reception, and Moira felt a chill.

'So I see.'

'Which means,' said Isarel thoughtfully, 'that we've probably got just under twenty-four hours to get Ahasuerus and find Kate before Eisenach is teeming with the faithful answering the call.'

'The f— Oh. Serse's People, yes, of course. Listen then,' said Ciaran, 'let's unpack, meet up for dinner and discuss what we'll do next.'

In the end, they ate in the bar: 'Where,' said Isarel, 'we might pick up a bit of gossip about the concert. How's your German, Moira?'

'Non-existent, I'm afraid.' German had not been thought a necessary language by the nuns. 'I did French at school,' she said. 'But I don't suppose that'll be much help.'

'You never know. I've got some German,' said Isarel. 'But it's rusty. Ciaran, do you have the gift of tongues, at all?'

'Far from it. I might make out the odd phrase or two.'

'We'll have to do the best we can.'

Moira enjoyed eating in the bar, which was full of local people and which appeared to be the focal point of the entire village. They were served home-made vegetable soup and huge puffy omelettes, with buttery mushrooms and crisply pink ham spilling out.

'We'll keep the dining room for when we celebrate Kate's rescue,' said Ciaran.

'And Vogel's downfall and Ahasuerus's re-interment,' put in Isarel.

'You make it sound like a task of Herculean proportions. Do you have to be so sepulchral?'

'Somebody's got to keep the party sober,' said Isarel, grinning.

'If you're keeping anything sober it'll be the first time in recorded history. Are we having coffee? Oh no, we can make it for ourselves upstairs. More private for the council of war.'

They held the council of war in Moira's bedroom which was the largest. Father would have had a fit at the thought

410

of his little girl entertaining two men in her bedroom. He would have had apoplexy at the sight of the bottle of whiskey which Isarel produced and poured into tooth mugs.

'Do you mind, Moira? It helps me to think.'

'Of course not.'

'If,' said Isarel, perching on the windowsill where Moira had left the curtains open so that she could see the sweeping forests outside, 'if the Serse Concert starts the day after tomorrow, we've got to get inside Eisenach beforehand.'

'You mean – go up to the castle openly?' Moira stared at him.

'Yes. I don't think we dare wait until the concert,' said Isarel. 'But if we go up tomorrow, there'll be preparations going on – people setting up chairs and lights, people delivering things. Maybe even rehearsals for the orchestra – yes, that's a thought, if there're rehearsals going on, we might even manage to play the music – the Piper music. I mean – virtually unnoticed.'

'Simply act as if we're part of it all,' said Moira thoughtfully.

'Yes, exactly. Vogel might be expecting an attempt to get Ahasuerus and Kate, but he'd probably think we'd wait for the concert to start. And even if we encounter him, he won't recognise us, he'll assume we're Serse's People. He can't possibly know every one of them.'

'He'll recognise you,' said Ciaran, looking at Isarel from under his lashes. 'Jude reincarnated. Or hadn't you thought about it?'

There was a rather abrupt silence. Isarel looked as if he was about to say something explosive, and Moira, hoping to head him off, said, 'Could we divide our strengths and two of us go openly into the castle as if we're part of the concert, while the other goes in separately and secretly? Because even if Vogel's expecting one attack, he probably won't be expecting two, and whoever stays out of sight might find out quite a lot about the rest of the castle.' The two men looked at her approvingly.

'That's a very good idea,' Isarel replied. 'A two-pronged assault. You and I had better be Serse's People, because of luring Ahasuerus—' He grinned at her suddenly. 'Red hair and Jude's shofar. My God, what a combination. Ahasuerus won't stand a chance. Ciaran, how do you feel about searching for Kate while we do the luring? You're maybe a touch – mature – to be an acolyte anyway—'

'I wondered when someone would say that,' said Ciaran. 'I might have guessed it would be you. Yes, all right. I'll do the dangerous, difficult part while you have the excitement and the limelight. But don't blame me if they think you're Jude's ghost walking.'

Isarel drained his whiskey abruptly. 'Do you have the feeling of a pattern being repeated here?' he asked. 'The concert and Vogel and Eisenach?'

'I do,' said Moira, at once. 'I feel as if we're falling into a time warp. It's Jude playing the *Devil's Piper* all over again, isn't it? The audience won't be as grand, but almost everything else will be the same.'

'And,' Isarel added, 'the intention behind it all seems to be sinisterly similar, have you noticed that as well?'

'I have,' said Ciaran. 'And that's the bit I like least of all. Conrad Vogel's using the music to gather young people about him.'

'Yes, but he only wants the best: the gifted, creative ones. That's why his concerts have been aimed so strongly at students.'

'He's being selective,' said Moira.

'Exactly. And over half a century ago a man called Karl

412

Vogel came to Eisenach Castle to set up a concert, and Karl was very close indeed to a madman who nurtured a warped plan of creating a Master Race,' said Isarel.

'Selective breeding,' Ciaran commented. 'Genetic engineering. Hitler's Golden Aryan People.'

Moira, listening intently, felt as she had felt before, the rapport between these two. They finish one another's thoughts. And then: yes, but it's Isarel who starts the thought. He pounces on your thoughts and understands them before you've even got them half framed in your own mind.

'I think Conrad Vogel is trying to do what Karl did all those years ago,' said Isarel. 'But on a – a more spiritual plane. I think that's what this Serse Cult is all about. The control of minds – young, gifted minds.'

'Dear God.'

'Don't blaspheme.'

'I'm not.'

Moira, leaning forward, asked, 'Who set that first concert up? Was Jude invited to Eisenach with an orchestra to – to perform, or what? I wouldn't know how these things work.'

'The story is that Baron von Drumm – the owner of Eisenach Castle – was so flattered at the request to use the Castle's name for the orchestra that he asked Jude to give the orchestra's first public official performance there. But in fact it was Karl Vogel who approached Jude while they were both in Vienna – my grandmother had letters from Jude describing the meeting, so it's documented. There was some kind of fairly formal lunch I think, thick with Schutzstaffel including Himmler himself.' He glanced defensively at the other two, and said, 'He kept questionable company, didn't he?'

'So do a good many people,' observed Ciaran. 'Including

monks and barristers and musicians.'

Moira, who was making coffee, said carefully, 'Would it help us to know about the lunch with the Schutzstaffel?'

'You mean, do I mind talking about it?'

'Well, yes, that's what I did mean.'

'Not if it will help us.' Isarel paused, arranging his thoughts, and then continued, 'Jude went to Eisenach like a shot. It was a very prestigious invitation, I should think, and the von Drumms were what would have been called part of the *ancien regime*. Angelika von Drumm was one of Jude's mistresses.'

He stopped, and Moira, drinking her coffee, glanced at him, hoping this was not difficult for him.

Isarel was aware of Moira's sympathetic glance, and he found it unexpectedly comforting. She was remarkably perceptive about Jude. She was perceptive about most things, in fact.

Isarel had found the letters at the same time as he had found Jude's scores, and he had read them seated on a broken chair in the attic of his father's house, with swathes of dust and cobwebs all round him and only a single candle for light. He could still feel the shadowed stuffiness of the attic, and he could feel the brittleness of the old paper in his hands. There had been a musty scent of age about the letters, but there had also been a lingering drift of the dried lavender that the dead Lucy Weissman had sprinkled between the pages before shutting them away in a small cedarwood box. Lavender had ever afterwards smelled of sadness and pain for Isarel.

Jude's letter had been faintly mocking about the lunch at which he had met Karl Vogel; he had made rather a good story of how Vogel had earnestly assured him, over pre-prandial sherry, that all the food being served was *kosher*. Jude, who had a broad-minded view of all religions and would eat anything put before him, had taken a malicious pleasure in disconcerting his hosts by expressing a liking for oysters served in the English manner – which of course meant wrapped in lightly-fried strips of bacon. He had related this in his letter to Lucy with mischievous relish, but even then he had clearly been more interested in the renovations being done at Mallow. He had insisted that the Bluthner was to be placed precisely as he had instructed – 'In the room on the left of the central hall, and angled so that the glow of the setting sun falls directly across the keys'. It was the shortest letter of the few that Isarel's grandmother had kept, but he knew why she had kept it. It was the one that had ended with the words, 'I believe I can't refuse the invitation to Eisenach Castle, since it comes from fairly exalted personages, and anyway it won't be for long. Light the lamps for my return, Lucy my love, because even if the world burns I will sleep in your arms at Mallow before the year ends.'

The world had almost burned, and Jude had assisted in the burning of thousands of its people, and he had never returned to Mallow. That letter had left Isarel with a poignant vision of his grandmother seated in Mallow's deep bow window, the lamps obediently burning, waiting for the return of the one who never came back . . .

Isarel frowned and shook off the lingering ghosts, reaching for the whiskey bottle again.

Ciaran said, 'Isarel, I'm the last person to preach about the evils of drink, but—'

'I'm drinking too much. Yes, I know. I'm drowning my glory in a shallow cup and selling my reputation for a song.' He set down the glass. 'You can lay the blame at Jude's door. He might as well add responsibility for my drinking to all his other sins.'

Moira said softly, 'It's like being haunted, isn't it? It's

like being shadowed,' and Isarel looked at her.

'Yes. Because wherever we look in this thing, we keep coming back to Jude.'

Jude had found the journey to Eisenach Castle unbelievably tedious, even travelling in one of the Party's railcars.

'Luxurious,' Erich von Drumm had promised him, puffing out his cheeks with importance. 'We look after our guests, Herr Weissman. You will enjoy the Castle, and Eisenach itself has many historic features. Links with Goethe and Schiller. And there is an ancient church where Bach played the organ.'

'Really, Baron? Which Bach?' Jude nearly said, 'And whose organ?' but von Drumm's sense of humour was virtually non-existent, and his musical knowledge was such that he would only be able to grapple with one Bach at a time anyway.

If the bone-rattling railcar was von Drumm's idea of luxury, a week's stay at Eisenach Castle was likely to be one of the minor tortures of the realm. Jude regretted agreeing to the concert already. It was remarkable what you would say yes to after a couple of bottles of good German hock. But the invitation had been persuasively and rather flatteringly couched. 'Baron von Drumm and his wife will place the entire castle at your disposal for the orchestra's inaugural performance,' Karl Vogel had said at the absurd, pretentious lunch in Vienna. 'A large house party: perhaps some hunting for the men, motor expeditions for the ladies. An *al fresco* luncheon. All the most influential people, my dear Weissman.' A small smile, the knowing nod as of one man-of-the-world to another. Jude waited. 'And,' Vogel said, after a moment, 'the culmination will be the performance of your own work.'

'The *Devil's Piper*? Yes,' said Jude thoughtfully, 'I

assumed that was what you meant.'

'But of course the *Devil's Piper*.' The smile that never quite reached Karl Vogel's eyes showed. 'What else?'

'What else indeed?'

'It will be the most glittering night Eisenach has seen for centuries,' Vogel said, and added in a voice of muted awe, 'even Herr Himmler may be able to come.'

'That, of course, would ensure a very memorable evening,' rejoined Jude politely.

'Certainly.' Vogel either did not hear or chose to ignore the edge of sarcasm.

'Also,' put in von Drumm eagerly, 'Angelika will be very pleased to offer you hospitality.'

Which meant that Angelika von Drumm was up to her old tricks again. She had offered hospitality to half of Western Europe if her performance in Jude's bed three years ago was anything to judge by.

'The hospitality would, of course, extend to your orchestra,' said von Drumm, and Jude refrained with difficulty from observing caustically that if Angelika was prepared to take on his entire orchestra, it did not sound as if she had changed much.

It was his own fault that he was being jolted into the middle of nowhere like this. You should never drink beyond your capacity with Germans and you should not allow your former loves to sway your judgement, either. His father would have said, with a sad smile, 'The heart dominating the brain.' His grandfather, vulgar old sinner, would have said, 'Cock ruling head.' His grandfather would have been nearer the truth.

As they neared Weimar the scenery started to get unexpectedly interesting and Jude put down the book he had brought to pass the journey – a new Leslie Charteris – and stared through the window. Darkling forests and glimpses of brooding castles here and there. Marvellous. Was it stirring something up in his mind? He frowned, forcing his mind to yield up the burgeoning images. Berlioz's *Damnation of Faust*? No, nothing so Mephistophelian. Something vaguely sinister by Paganini?

And then he had it. Of all things, it was Beethoven's Pastoral that was so imperatively demanding recognition. But it was a Pastoral that owed nothing to the conventional rusticity of buttercup-splashed meadows and babbling brooks; this was a darker, much older concept. Jude was sitting upright now, his eyes sparkling, his mind awash with images. It could be done. He could do it. Next spring in Vienna? He would sweep aside the shepherds and the haymaking and put in their place the dark old gods: creatures who owed their being to wild woodland paganism: cloven-footed Pan creatures who walked not on all fours like beasts, but upright like men. Stone circles that beckoned with long-fingered branches . . . He forgot about the journey and the scenery, and tore open his briefcase, grabbing several sheets of the blank score paper which went with him everywhere, scribbling with impatient haste, and then finally flinging down the papers and sinking back into his seat, half exhausted, half exalted.

The critics would hate it – Jude grinned with mischievous delight at the knowledge – they would berate him for reading into Beethoven's music things that Beethoven had not meant. But Beethoven, locked into his tragic silence, had known about the dark side of nature and he had known about the dark underside of music, as well, just as so many other great composers had known. What about Schumann swimming helplessly in and out of madness, writing some of his most remarkable music at the tide's turn? What about Mozart, so volatile as to be regarded by some as unbalanced? Maybe you had to be a little mad to compose

418

or to create. Was I mad when I composed the *Devil's Piper*? Or – disturbing thought – was I even possessed? If it had not been for that scrap of legend: the two or three pages of musical score handed down within his family, would he have conceived the *Piper* suite at all?

Coming out here to give a concert was more than a little mad, of course. Nobody who was anybody was going to trail out here for a concert, although a good many people who thought they were somebody might be there.

Jude did not much like Karl Vogel or von Drumm, but Vogel was entertaining company and the Baron was influential and might be useful. Jude's father would have said, 'Make use of them both, my boy.' His grandfather would have said, 'Bleed the *goyim* white.'

Goyim was not a word you dared use any longer, of course, although Jude's grandfather, fiery old rebel, would not have cared. But it was a word too tinged with Jewish contempt for these days. The Führer had a strong anti-Semitic streak, although Jude supposed that even Hitler could not expect the world to be purged clean of Jews just to suit his whim.

Chapter Thirty-Eight

After Conrad Vogel went out through the earth tunnel, Kate sank to the floor of the crematorium, shaking uncontrollably from the strain of pretending to be unafraid, wrapping her arms about her bent knees in an endeavour to force warmth back into her body.

She thought she could not have fought Vogel physically. He had had the gun and although he probably preferred to keep her alive, he would not have hesitated to use it. He had not used it, because he thought that shutting her away with Ahasuerus would make her give in and record his disgusting message for Richard. Like hell it will! thought Kate determinedly, standing up and pushing her hair back. I've survived this far and I'll think of a way to survive a bit farther.

She glanced through the steel doors to the gas chamber. There was still very little light, but she could see the vents: like yawning black maws in the shadows. All the better to eat you with, my dear . . . All the better to spew gas into your lungs, my dear . . . Yes, but it's not those things I have to fear, it's Ahasuerus. The Devil's Piper. Did Vogel mean that about him still finding females attractive? Yes, Kate, he meant it, it's no good deluding yourself.

It was very quiet. It was so quiet that Kate could hear small breathy sounds from beyond the crematorium. There was a faint echo down here, magnifying the sounds.

Kate scrambled to her feet and crossed to the outer doors, listening. The sighing sounds came again, louder, *nearer*, and with them, dragging footsteps. Vogel returning? You're deluding yourself again, Kate.

Because the sounds were the awkward footsteps and the ragged breathing of someone making a slow painful way through the dark tunnels. Someone who moved awkwardly because he was maimed, and someone who had to feel his blind, fumbling way because a mask impaired his sight.

Ahasuerus, coming to find her.

Kate moved by blind instinct. There was nowhere to hide, but she would have to find somewhere. She pushed the doors shut – they could not be locked from inside, but even shutting them might afford her a few precious minutes – and looked back at the room.

Three of the terrible ovens were open, dreadful yawning cavities, but two still had doors and Kate eyed them. They were roughly at waist height, and the bolts were steel and they had not rusted. But it must be five decades since anyone had tried to open those doors. She took a deep breath, and with her mind shuddering in disbelief, took hold of the nearest bolt.

It was harder than she had expected. She sobbed and threw her weight behind first one and then the second, forcing it back. Sweat trickled down her spine – partly with panic, partly with the frantic exertion – and her hands were scraping against the outer brick of the ovens, skin and nails tearing, but she was beyond feeling anything except mounting terror and a driving urgency to hide.

And then the bolt on the end furnace slid protestingly back and Kate gasped in relief, and dragged it all the way, prising the door open. There was a scream of sound and she winced again – would Ahasuerus have heard? A breath of stale, faintly warm air gusted out and something that had been piled softly against the door tumbled forward. There was a dry brittle sound, like twigs cracking. Bones. Brittle, charred bones. Kate stared at them and her stomach lifted with nausea. I can't do it! But I've got to. You can do it, Kate, and you must do it because there isn't anywhere else to hide. And after all it was only an empty furnace, long since cooled, and the poor incinerated bones could not hurt her. Poor dead creature, whoever it had once been. It had been huddled against the door, one skeletal hand raised. Trying to get out . . .? If I start thinking like that, I'll be lost. I'll keep remembering that gassing was appalling but it was effective.

But Kate still lost several seconds staring into the yawning blackness, knowing that hundreds – probably thousands – of people had burned in there. Yes, but they were dead when they were thrown in. I won't believe anything else. And the limping footsteps were already crossing the outer chamber and in another minute he would be fumbling at the doors. Kate took a shuddering breath and, placing her palms flat on the oven floor, pulled herself inside. Easy. Like levering yourself on to a low window ledge. So far so good.

She reached out to pull the circular door closed, and heard thankfully the dull clunk. The faint light shut off and Kate crawled deeper in, going hand over hand and foot over foot. Several times her hands closed on recognisable bones: long arm or leg bones, or thin brittle fingers. But I'm not noticing any of it. And even if I am noticing it, I'm not minding. Poor murdered creatures. Jews, almost certainly. Persecuted and exiled and deserving of all the pity in the world. At least there aren't any skulls. If I touched a skull, I shouldn't bear it. Yes, you would.

As she went farther in, there was a dreadful grittiness

under her hands: like feeling little piles of instant coffee granules. Cinders, that's all they were. Like charcoal in the bottom of an old-fashioned kitchen range. You drew out an ashpan at the bottom. Raking out, Kate's grandmother had called it, except that whoever had been in charge of this oven had not raked it out the last time it had been used.

The oven smelt exactly the way an ordinary kitchen cooker would smell if it had not been cleaned for a long time. Greasy. *Meaty.* If I reached out to the walls they would be smeary, thought Kate; they would be larded with the cooled fat of roasted humans. This is unbearable. This is like something out of Grimm. The witch in the forest who put children into cages and fattened them for her ovens. Yes, but this is real. And the alternative is to face Ahasuerus and Conrad Vogel, and even if I could defeat Ahasuerus, Vogel's armed and he'd shoot me.

There was only the thinnest spill of light in here, but Kate, going largely by feel, had the impression that the interior was larger than she had expected. But it would have to be large, of course. Hundreds of bodies would have been thrust in at a time. Concentrate on Ahasuerus. Is he in the furnace room?

But she had already heard him. She had heard the screech of the long-disused outer doors being opened, and the dragging gait coming across the floor. Would he guess she was here? Had Vogel told him? Would he sense her presence anyway? She crouched into the farthest corner, her knees drawn up to her chest, hugging her legs. It was like a childhood game. If I screw myself into a tiny ball in a dark corner and close my eyes tight no one can see me.

This would be a dreadful place to die. The smell was appalling; you could feel it and you could taste it.

The sounds from the furnace room were muffled by the thick door of the oven, but Kate's nerves were stripped raw, and it was very easy to conjure up the image of Ahasuerus prowling around the bare room, peering inside each of the ovens. Would he reach in? She remembered the dreadful hands that had scrabbled at the stone tomb in the crypt and a wash of sick fear engulfed her.

There was silence, and Kate strained to see through the darkness. Was the door being slowly opened from the other side? Was that a faint rim of light showing around the edges? No, she was imagining it.

And then into the waiting silence, came the sound she had been expecting and dreading.

The teeth-wincing sound of claws against steel. Ahasuerus was trying to open the doors.

Jude was beginning to wish he had not come. Eisenach was a fairytale castle, but it was from one of the grislier fairytales – Grimm, or Perrault. Bluebeard's lair, the retreat of Man-eating ogres. It reeked of ancient intrigues and blood-drenched legends and it was filled with whispery echoes and unexpected little twists of stairs. And draughts stirring behind the arras, thought Jude, amused. Have I fallen into a performance of Hamlet and not noticed?

There was an air of elegant decay as well, but this did not surprise him. Angelika von Drumm trailed with her an aura of casual extravagance, but Jude suspected that although the family might once have had old money, they were now *nouveau poor*. It had never stopped Angelika from being dressed by Schiaperelli, and wintering in Biarritz.

But for all that, Angelika – or someone – had got hold of a Bluthner which had been placed in the sitting room adjoining his bedchamber on the second floor, and which Jude observed with pleasure.

But it would have been so much better to have been in

Ireland. Mallow and Ireland and autumn – oh yes! Golden trees and crimson sunsets and the smoky scent of peat fires and the lashing wild Atlantic coast. Lucy seated in the bow window with the light falling across her brown hair . . . Instead he was holed up in this hideous castle with his orchestra scattered in various billets all over the village. The woodwind section had been allotted the local tavern, the Black Duke, which was unfortunate in view of the woodwinds' partiality for lifting the elbow.

And Jude himself was in a huge, brooding bedchamber with dark, red flock wallpaper and a massive tester bed and glowering mahogany furniture and a view over some kind of lumpen structure gouged out of the hillside on the castle's western boundary.

He studied this as he dressed for dinner the first night. There was no reason to find it vaguely sinister. Probably it was only an ancient barrow or a hill fort that had been excavated in the recent past. That would explain the freshly gouged look.

But hill forts surely had never had jutting brick chimneys or doors cut into the side of the hill itself? The sun was not quite setting, but it was beginning to sink and great crimson swathes splashed the skies, giving the countryside all around a brutish sulky appearance and pouring over the hill structure like a crimson river. Jude frowned and turned away, straightening his evening tie impatiently in the smoky depths of the mirror over the dressing table. Everything in the castle was either worn or faded or tinged with the macabre.

Angelika von Drumm was not faded or macabre of course, and only a purist would have described her as well worn, and even then it depended on your interpretation of the expression. As Jude entered the tapestried dining room, she was standing directly beneath one of the crystal wall

425

lights, her hair lit to a blazing aureole. He grinned inwardly. Still an eye for a good effect, Baroness. Knowing she had deliberately placed herself under the light did not stop him appreciating the effect it created.

She turned as he came in, holding out her hands, giving him the three-cornered smile that had once smiled up from his own pillow and drawing him into the small group standing about the fireplace.

'My husband Erich you already know.' A dismissive gesture as if von Drumm did not count, which as far as Angelika was concerned, he probably did not. 'And I think you have met Karl Vogel.'

'Baron. Vogel.' Jude nodded acknowledgements.

'You have had a good journey, Weissman?'

'Abominable. None of your trains run on time, Baron.'

'And,' said Angelika, her hand still on Jude's arm, 'Irma, may I present to you Jude Weissman. Jude, this is Madame Greise, who is staying with us for the concert.'

'Madame.' Where on earth had Angelika found this hungry-eyed lady with the over-painted lips and the greedy hands? Jude took Irma Greise's hand and dropped it as soon as politeness allowed. Harsh and dry. Like a claw. He disliked women who had fingernails like talons and enamelled them blood-red.

'And here,' said Angelika, 'is an associate of my husband's, Otto Burkhardt.'

'Herr Burkhardt.' Jude's first thought was that Burkhardt was Angelika's latest lover, but a closer look made him change his mind. Even in her wildest days, Angelika would not have gone for this cold-eyed, sparse-haired specimen. Burkhardt might have been asked to balance Irma Greise, or he might be exactly what Angelika had said: an associate of the Baron's.

The food at dinner was indifferent but the wine was

426

superb. Jude supposed von Drumm had inherited the wine but that the food had to be paid for. His orchestra would probably fare better than he would in that respect, then. The woodwinds would certainly fare better.

With the coffee and brandy, Karl Vogel steered the conversation to the concert and it afforded Jude a malicious pleasure to block his endeavours to discuss the *Devil's Piper*. Vogel said, 'I understand the inspiration was an old score that has been in your family for several generations.'

Jude smiled and said, 'Music is a tradition in my family. These things are often handed down. This is a very good cognac, Baron.'

'Will you have some cheese with it? Or perhaps a little fruit?'

'No, thank you.' The apples were puckered and the pears spotted with brown. The cheese looked as if it might crawl off the plate of its own accord.

'It is also said,' pursued Vogel, 'that an ancestor of yours was a close friend of Mozart.'

Jude regarded him thoughtfully. 'Mozart was prodigal with his friendship,' he said. 'But he died in poverty.'

'My dear,' said Angelika von Drumm, leaning across the table, 'we shall all of us die in poverty if the Party's present policies continue. It's all building autobahnen, and guns before butter and four-year plans these days. Too austere for words.'

'And if Herr Hitler forms this alliance with Mussolini—'

'Oh, Otto, *don't* drag Mussolini into it—'

'Well, at least he made the trains run on time—'

'The only way I can endure anything Italian is when it comes in the form of silk underwear,' said Angelika, and winked provocatively at Jude on the side the Baron could not see. Jude smiled rather perfunctorily and permitted the servant to refill his brandy snifter.

'Do you know Italy, Madame Greise?' he said politely.

'I do not. Nor the Italian people.'

'Oh. Irma has something of a yen for Hitler,' put in Angelika. 'Ever since she heard him speak in Berlin last summer. Personally I find him *sinister*, and just the tiniest bit *bourgeois*.'

'He has come from modest beginnings, of course,' put in von Drumm doubtfully, and Jude saw him glance uneasily at Burkhardt and Vogel. 'But he is an enthusiast and a visionary.'

'Master Races and stamping out people who aren't *pure* Germanic – my dear, if that isn't *bourgeois*, I don't know what is.'

'The mark of a parvenu,' murmured Jude, and Angelika said at once,

'*Precisely*. I told you at the time, Irma darling, it would be *déclassé* to sleep with somebody like that.'

Across the table von Drumm was looking even more uncomfortable, but Karl Vogel said smoothly, 'Herr Hitler is a considerable patron of the arts, Angelika.'

'Oh pooh.'

'Also,' said Vogel, watching Jude over the rim of his wine glass, 'he greatly admires your work, Herr Weissman.'

'Now that,' said Jude, looking up, 'I find surprising.'

'I believe he has even wondered about asking if you would consider a commission for a new national piece of music.'

'A German anthem?'

'Perhaps not quite that. But a— lodestar for our young people.'

'A rallying call,' said Burkhardt, and at his side, Irma Greise murmured, 'A call to the golden youth of Europe,' and looked very directly at Jude. It was probably fanciful to imagine she licked her lips.

428

'Darling, if Hitler or anybody else is really placing hopes for the future in *golden* youth, anything less like a golden youth than Jude would be hard to—'

'I regret,' said Jude to Karl Vogel, 'that I do not compose to order, Herr. If your master really does want a – what did you call it—?'

'A rallying call,' said Burkhardt again, and Vogel frowned.

'A lodestar,' he said severely.

'Ah yes, that was the expression. But rallying cries and lodestar calls are not my forte, Herr Vogel. You're talking to the wrong composer.' Jude sipped his brandy and added, poker-faced, 'Has Herr Hitler considered Schoenberg? Or even Hindemith?'

Vogel stared at him coldly. 'They would not be appropriate,' he said at last. 'Were you not aware that Herr Hitler has ordered the boycotting of Hindemith's works and that Schoenberg has been outlawed by the Party? Both gentlemen have left Germany.'

'Dear me,' said Jude, deadpan, and Vogel looked at him suspiciously.

But he only said, 'It is a pity you are not interested in the Führer's idea, Herr Weissman.'

'Isn't it? But I don't accept commissions.'

'Indeed? But even Mozart had to trim his sails to the prevailing wind, I think?'

Mozart again. Jude replied offhandedly, 'So it's said. And now I wonder if you will excuse me if I retire early? It was a long journey today and I shall need to begin work early tomorrow.'

'Ah yes, the rehearsals for your *Devil's Piper* performance.' This from von Drumm, his jowly face smiling.

Jude stood for a moment looking round the table. A smile curved his lips and he said softly, 'Dear me, were you expecting to hear that at the concert? Didn't I tell you I had changed my mind?'

'You have changed your—'

'Certainly,' said Jude. 'I've decided that we shan't be playing it.'

And made good his exit.

He went directly to his room, but he did not immediately go to bed. He hung up his dinner jacket and loosened the black evening tie, and perched on the windowsill, studying the hill structure, wreathed in shadow now, a crouching bulk against the skyline.

That last remark would certainly stir up those two rogues Vogel and von Drumm. There was no doubt but that they were after the music, of course: Vogel had given that away by persistently bringing Mozart into the conversation. Jude wondered how much Vogel knew and how much he believed.

'A lot of rubbish, of course,' Jude's grandfather had always said, drawing down his brows. 'I never believed a word of it.'

His father had said cautiously that it should not be forgotten that Mozart had been something of a prankster.

But Jude had always liked the legend of his own great-great grandfather in Vienna in the early nineteenth century, forming that tenuous friendship with Mozart's only surviving son, being given the two or three sheets of music score paper in return for some favour or other.

'Probably of no worth whatsoever,' his great-great grandfather was supposed to have said, handing the music on down through the family. 'Not even written by Mozart, of course; his son remembered him buying it from one of his disreputable associates while he was writing *The Magic Flute*. It might have come from anywhere.'

It was not difficult to visualise Mozart buying a piece of music from a starving gypsy or street ballad singer down on his luck, perhaps even cheerfully bestowing the last of his own dwindling resources in the process. But it was odd that he had apparently kept the single sheet of music so carefully.

It was at this point in Jude's thoughts that he became aware of a light burning within the hill structure.

As he leaned over, trying to see more, two dark-clad figures detached themselves from the shadows surrounding the castle and crossed the courtyard towards the lights.

Irma Greise and Otto Burkhardt.

Chapter Thirty-Nine

The Black Duke had the morning scents and the morning aura of every hotel Isarel had ever stayed in. Freshly ground coffee and a faint pleasant undertow of freshly baked rolls. People nodded polite 'good mornings' to one another on their way in or out of breakfast and collected daily newspapers which were neatly arranged on the reception desk.

As they ate breakfast, it occurred to Isarel that Moira was rather quiet and although at first he assumed this was because she was nervous about what was ahead, he revised this almost at once. Ciaran, carefully casual, had referred to a fiercely over-protective family background, and Isarel understood that Moira had hardly travelled beyond the small Irish village. She's being wary, he thought. She's unused to hotels and she's worried in case she does something wrong. The fact that Moira had naturally good manners and did not need to worry, did not come into it.

Isarel, buttering a warm roll, felt unexpectedly angry at the family – the father particularly, hadn't Ciaran said? – who had kept Moira in such a stifled, narrow environment. This was the twentieth century, for goodness' sake and Moira ought to be enjoying boyfriends and clothes and some kind of social life. Certainly she ought to be pursuing a job, if not a full-blown career: she was intelligent enough to make a university place a fairly safe bet, in fact.

Something ought to be done about it after this crazy adventure was over. Isarel was aware of an inward twinge of half-cynical, half-wry amusement. Pygmalion and Galatea at your age? Or even – God forbid! – King Cophetua and the beggarmaid? That would be very unwise indeed, that would be absolutely mad. And anything less like a beggarmaid— But Moira was so obviously intelligent and she was attractive and perceptive; Isarel thought it would afford anyone pleasure to bring her out of whatever narrow, unhealthy world she had been living in. Svengali and Trilby was probably nearer than King Cophetua, which brought them full circle to music again.

'Do we take the car?' he demanded, as they finished their coffee.

'I don't know. How far is the castle, have we any idea?'

'I noticed a turning off the main road a bit farther back,' said Moira. 'Just as we drove in.'

'Oh yes, I saw that as well – was that for the castle? Well then, it's only ten minutes' walk or so, but we'd better drive as near as we can, because we might need the car later. But we could park at the side of the road and walk up. All right, both of you?'

But it was to Moira Isarel looked as he said this, and Moira understood that it was his off-hand way of asking could she manage the walk.

She said at once, 'Great. Let's be as inconspicuous as possible.'

They came out of the Black Duke and into the watery morning sunlight, and as they drove down the road, they saw a small group of people going towards the castle.

'Serse's People,' said Isarel, pointing to them. 'They're beginning to arrive. So that's what they look like. They're not quite what I was imagining.'

'They're very purposeful,' said Ciaran.

433

'And if they're students, they're much less rowdy than any students I ever had anything to do with,' said Isarel rather wryly. 'They look smug, don't they? The chosen race, already. If people are going up there now, we should manage to gate-crash without too much difficulty. Here's where we turn off, by the look of it. Yes, "Eisenach Castle – private road".'

'And a poster about the concert underneath,' said Moira.

'With the symbol again. That group were all wearing it around their necks, did you see it? Like ikons on silver chains. Do we know what the symbol is? It's nearly the Aryan Cross, but it isn't quite. Ciaran, have you ever seen anything like it?'

'I have,' said Ciaran.

'Where?'

'Carved into the side of Ahasuerus's tomb.'

For a moment no one spoke, and then Isarel said, 'Is that meant to make us feel better?' He pulled in to the side of the road. There was no conventional pedestrian path, but there were areas of roughish scrubland at intervals, marked with tyre tracks and oil patches, as if cars quite often parked there.

'We're going in on a wing and a prayer, aren't we?' said Ciaran, as they got out.

'I'm afraid so. We'll have to be ready for anything. Try to look like a Serse, Ciaran, you don't know who might be watching.'

As they went up the track, Isarel felt the atavistic fear forcing its way to the surface again. Finally and at last, I'm approaching the nightmare mansion, he thought. I'm going back. For a moment he was unsure whether he was in his own time or Jude's and as they went up the rough track in the morning sunshine, the sense of dislocation increased, because the Eisenach he had known and walked through in dreams had no reality outside of lonely midnight shadows and creeping darknesses.

It ought to have been easy to dismiss the memories and concentrate on getting inside and rescuing Kate and capturing Ahasuerus. Isarel tried to do so, but his entire body was strung up to a pitch of such extreme anticipation that his heart was beating erratically and his stomach was churning. This is the place of dreams. The galleried hall where Jude gave that glittering concert; the tapestried dining room, the dark brooding bedchambers . . . In another minute we shall be round the curve in the track and it will be there.

He had thought he was prepared, but as they came round the curve in the road, the castle was suddenly in front of them: its huge, brutish outline rearing up against the night sky, the dark turrets silhouetted against the sky, the narrow windows like slitted eyes. The sight of it slammed so violently into Isarel's senses that the landscape blurred and for a moment a great weight seemed to press down on him. There was the impression of something dark blotting out the light.

It was Ciaran who said, 'Dear God, would you look at that,' and Isarel forced back the suffocating waves of the past. The present came jarringly into focus again.

Surrounding the castle was a high brick wall, black and forbidding and easily twenty feet in height. It was smooth and impenetrable, and it was topped with thick coils of barbed wire. Directly in front of them, set into the wall, were wrought-iron gates, lined with sheets of iron.

Moira said, 'They've shut the world out.'

'I think it's more than that,' said Isarel, staring. 'I think they've shut something in.'

'At least the gates are open.'

'Yes. Do we just walk in?' Moira was looking at the gates rather nervously.

'That Serse group's just walked in,' said Isarel, and nodded towards the group they had seen on the road who were going through the castle gates. 'If they can do it, so can we. We'll go in with huge panache and we'll get away with it. And if anyone stops us, we've come to find out about the concert.'

'And maybe join the faithful,' murmured Moira.

Ciaran, who was looking back down the track, said, 'I think this is where I melt into the background. Vogel will probably have his own people beyond those gates and we've agreed I'm to keep out of sight.'

'Where—'

'I think I'll walk all around the outside walls to see if there's a breach anywhere. If I find a back door, I'll go in. But from then on, it's anybody's guess.' He turned back and looked at them. 'God keep you both,' he said suddenly.

Isarel stared at him. I think that's the first properly conventional religious thing he's ever said to me. To his astonishment, he heard his own voice reply, '*Shema Y'Isroel, Adonai Elohaynu, Adonai Echod.*'

Moira said in a whisper, 'What is that?'

'I think,' said Ciaran, his eyes on Isarel, 'that it's the ancient Hebrew affirmation of the reality of God. But I could be wrong.'

'You're not wrong,' said Isarel shortly. 'Shall we get on with it?'

'All right.' Ciaran looked at them both, and Moira said, 'Please find Kate.'

'With God's help.' He smiled briefly and then turned away. Isarel looked at Moira.

'Ready?'

'Ready.'

436

Approaching the gates was the eeriest experience yet. Isarel was beginning to feel very cold, as if he was about to step into an icy landscape. As if sunshine and the birdsong would not penetrate beyond the iron gates and the wall. I'm going into the nightmare, but the nightmare itself is starting to distort, because it's bright daylight and there's the sound of birdsong overhead and scrunching autumn leaves underfoot. There's the faint drone of traffic from the highroad below, and Serse's People all around us.

Moira said very softly, 'We're going back, aren't we? It feels as if Time stopped here and never got wound up again.' Isarel glanced at her, and she continued in a more practical voice, 'And we'd better keep an eye out for Vogel, hadn't we?'

'Yes. You'll recognise him again?'

'I think so. Yes, of course I will. It'll feel odd seeing him in these surroundings, though, won't it? After everything we've found out and pieced together. And,' said Moira thoughtfully, 'I can't help wondering what that other Vogel was like. Karl. I know you said his name never got into any of the history books, but did you ever see any photographs at all?'

'No. And I don't know much about him. But,' said Isarel, staring up at the castle, 'he was the man my father blamed for Jude's death at Nuremberg.'

'Jude was executed at Nuremberg?'

'Yes.' Isarel glanced about them, but although a few more sets of Serse's People were coming up the hill behind them, they were well out of earshot. I'm getting paranoid, thought Isarel angrily, but when he spoke again, he kept his voice low.

'There was a series of minor trials after Goering and Hess and their ilk were sentenced; to deal with the smaller fry. They didn't get much publicity, but Jude's trial was made very public indeed. There was a huge backlash of feeling, and it was then that he was dubbed "Judas". My father once said that the whole world hated him.' He paused and then said, 'Jude was shot as a traitor in the yard of Nuremberg Prison in 1946 and his body was cremated. The world thought he was hanged from the same gibbet used for von Ribbentrop and intended for Goering and they were led to think it because it appeased their anger to rank Jude alongside Goering. But my grandmother had to be given the death certificate, and it stated quite clearly that Jude died from rifle-shot wounds.'

'You hate it, don't you?' said Moira. 'Jude's death? I would if he was my ancestor.'

'Yes.' Isarel registered her use of the word 'ancestor', rather than 'grandfather', and he guessed it was because she could not associate the dark romance of Jude with such an elderly expression. Was she so young that she saw Jude as romantic? But for all her youth, she was very far from naive. With some perverse idea of testing her, he said, 'Jude was an evil, traitorous bastard – that was proved beyond doubt. The weight of the evidence against him at Nuremberg was overwhelming. He helped to send thousands of Jews to the gas chambers, he actually took his orchestra into Auschwitz and gave recitals while they were gassing thousands of the prisoners and incinerating the bodies.'

'Why? To cover up the screams or what? I don't mean to sound flippant,' said Moira. 'Because I do know that what was done to the Jews was horrific and appalling. But I don't understand.'

'I'm not sure I understand either,' said Isarel. 'But according to my father, he played the *Devil's Piper* suite.'

'Oh!' said Moira. And then, 'To subdue the prisoners?'

'It's the likeliest explanation,' said Isarel dryly. 'He deserved to die and he deserved to be branded as "Judas".'

He stopped, and without hesitation, Moira said softly, 'But for all that he was a genius, a brilliant, charismatic musician and composer, and you can't bear to think of him being dragged out of some wretched cell at Nuremberg, and thrust up against a wall and shot.'

'No. How did you know?'

'I can't bear it either,' said Moira.

Ciaran had gone stealthily around the outside of the wall, keeping in its lee, but strongly aware of the towering bulk of the castle within. The size of the castle had surprised him: it was much larger than he had been expecting, and he had thought, although he had not said, that if Conrad Vogel was able to command the use of a place such as this for his concert, he was far more powerful and successful than they had been bargaining for.

The wall had surprised him, but he had been unsure of whether this was because of his ignorance of the world. Presumably people today liked privacy as much as they ever had, and anyone who owned a large estate would take precautions against burglars and vandals. But there was something harsh and cruel and forbidding about the wall and the barbed wire and Ciaran thought that if Kate was being held somewhere behind those walls, it was going to be very hard indeed to get her out. The thought of her helpless and frightened was almost more than he could bear. Had they been wrong not to involve the police? Ciaran was conscious all over again of his years inside the monastery, away from the world, and he thought with fierce bitterness that if Kate had been threatened by Satan or his emissaries, he could have fought them better than he could fight this impenetrable fortress. If Eisenach had a breach in any of its defences, they were not detectable.

And then he reached the outermost boundary on the

western rim, and saw the swell of the hillside and the jutting brick chimneys.

He stood for a moment, frowning, thinking he had surely seen something like this before – old newsreels? – and trying to see, as well, if this would provide a way of getting into the rear of the castle unseen.

There was a soft footfall behind him, and a voice said coolly, 'How very accommodating of you to walk up to the castle and save me the trouble of coming down to get you, Mr O'Connor. Or should I call you Brother Ciaran?'

Ciaran wheeled sharply round to confront a tall, cold-eyed man with close-cropped grey hair, standing behind him. In his hand was a gun.

It was clearly impossible either to fight or run. Ciaran considered it but knew at once it would be pointless. If this was Conrad Vogel, he would shoot unhesitatingly, and have an entirely plausible excuse for the incident afterwards. Or a means of disposing of the body so that suspicion would never touch him. Ciaran felt a shudder of fear, but he said quite calmly, 'Good morning to you. Mr Vogel, is it?'

'Of course.' Vogel glanced at the hill structure, and said, 'I see you are studying the place my grandfather caused to be built.'

'Your grandfather, was it?' Ciaran was trying to decide how much Vogel knew about them, but he did not let this show.

'It was,' said Vogel. 'And you still haven't told me how I should address you.'

'It doesn't matter in the least,' said Ciaran. 'If you are going to continue to point that gun at me, you can call me whatever you like, because I shan't bother to answer you. But I would like to know what that place is.'

'Were you thinking of trying to get inside?' said Vogel.

440

'How extraordinary. I was just thinking of taking you in there.' A thin smile. 'There are two doors and they can both be opened from the outside. But I am afraid that once inside, you will not be able to get out.'

'Why not?'

'Because the doors have bolts on the outside,' said Vogel. 'And I should have to bolt you in.' The thin smile curved his lips again. 'That is Eisenach's own private death house,' he said. '*Konzentrationlager Eisenach*. It has been disused for almost half a century.'

'But it will be interesting to find out if the ancient gas machines still function.'

Chapter Forty

Jude had not been precisely disturbed by the sight of Burkhardt and Irma Greise going towards the hill after everyone in the castle had gone to bed, but he had been curious. He was very curious indeed about the smeary lights burning from within the hill itself.

It would, of course, be the height of ill manners to follow them. Jude grinned and, turning away from the window, reached for a thick jacket. Life would be very dull indeed if everyone was perpetually well mannered.

The castle was silent as he stole through it, the rooms empty and still. The door was half open into the dining room, and he glanced inside. The room was empty, but Angelika's perfume lingered on the air, and he went swiftly down the elaborate marble and gilt stairway that led to the great hall, thinking that it was a florid monstrosity, but thinking as well that it might make a suitably dramatic background for his own entrance at the concert.

The hill was just outside the castle boundaries, but a small door had been left ajar in the brick wall surrounding the castle proper. He went through, keeping to the shadows, and padded stealthily towards the lights. As he neared them, he saw that they were, as he had thought, coming from inside the hill itself, and this puzzled him for a moment, until he saw that someone had built immense steel doors that apparently opened straight into the hill.

There was a faint drone of voices from inside, and Jude hesitated, looking about him. Nothing. He took a deep breath and went inside.

It was dark and dryly hot inside the hill, and Jude stood waiting for his eyes to adjust, aware that he was in a kind of tunnel. The lights were ahead of him, and the voices were louder now. To spy or not to spy? But I've come this far.

The tunnel was longer than he had first thought, and it wound down. Jude, keeping to the shadows, saw the inner chamber before he reached it: a long, coldly lit room with the doors ajar. If he stayed flat to the wall he could see in without being seen.

Otto Burkhardt and the hungry-eyed Irma Greise were seated at a table with Karl Vogel, and even at this distance Jude could feel the authority irradiating from Vogel. Facing the table were two young men and a girl, none of them more than nineteen or twenty, all thin and beaten-looking, but all glaring at Vogel with angry defiance.

Vogel was speaking and Jude received the impression that he had been speaking for some time.

'The regulations specify that any Jew can be killed in any manner considered most conducive to discipline and deterrence of further resistance,' said Vogel. 'That is why you are here. You are rebels and dissidents.'

'Disruptive influences within the ghettos,' nodded Burkhardt, with the eagerness of one keen to be identified with the sentiments of a superior.

The elder of the two young men stared contemptuously at them. 'You quote from the orders given to Heinrich Himmler's sadistic sycophants,' he said.

'Is that because you have not the originality of mind to frame your own words?' said the younger.

Anger flared in Vogel's cold eyes, but when he spoke again, he did so as if the interruption had not happened. 'You are all members of the ghetto resistance group,' he said.

'Yes. The *der schwarzer shtab*. Human beings against the animals of the Schutzstaffel.' The boy paused, and then said with angry pride, 'We are members of the Hashomer Hatzair,' and Jude thought in horror: Jews. The prisoners are Jews. But why don't they at least attempt to escape? They don't outnumber Vogel and Burkhardt and the Greise, but they match them.

Vogel rapped impatiently on the table. 'We shall not play at semantics. You are dissidents and you have been brought here to tell us the names of the other subhumans in the rebellion.'

'Subhumans?' asked the young man coldly.

'The term Jew is synonymous with the term subhuman,' said Vogel. 'There is no difference.' There was such icy dismissal in his voice that Jude's fingers curled involuntarily into fists.

The boy who had said, Subhumans? leaned forward, his hands flat on the table. 'If you insult us we shall return the insult,' he said with scornful hatred. 'But since we are Jews, we shall repay the debt with interest. That is what you would expect of us. And that being so—' He struck Vogel's face with the flat of his hand and a gasp of shock went through the chamber. 'That is for what you have said and that—' The sound of a second blow rang out, 'That,' the boy continued viciously, 'is for humiliating my sister.' The marks of his blows stood out starkly on Vogel's face, and Burkhardt half rose but Vogel waved him back.

'I am unhurt, Otto. And the creature will suffer a little more as a result. His sister will certainly suffer.' The light eyes looked at the girl and a smile curved his lips. Jude thought he had never seen such calculating cruelty in any face.

Vogel pushed his chair back from the table and walked round to stand in front of the girl. From his hiding place, Jude saw him thrust his hand down the front of her dress. 'I, also, can add interest to a debt,' said Vogel, his voice thickened with lust, but as he spoke the girl's eyes suddenly blazed with anger and she stepped back and brought her knee slamming up into his genitals. Vogel sprang back, doubling over and clutching himself.

Burkhardt and Irma Greise leapt forward at once, overturning their chairs, and there was a flurry of metallic clicks from the corners of the room. Jude inched forward and understood then why the prisoners had not tried to escape. At the chamber's far end stood six of the castle servants, all levelling guns. Guards, he thought. Not servants at all. And there are probably more of them inside the door, out of my line of vision.

Irma was tearing aside the girl's thin cheap dress, which Jude guessed to be some kind of prison garment, and her long painted nails raked the bare skin, drawing bubbles of blood. She moved behind the girl, hooking one arm about her throat from behind, jerking the girl's head back.

'For what you have just done, you should be forced to spend a night in *my* bed,' she said, her eyes burning and intense. 'And when I was surfeited, I would bite off your nipples and spit them on to the floor.' Her arm was still circling the girl's neck, but her free hand fingered the small high breasts, and then slid deliberately lower. The girl had been struggling, but as Irma's hand went between her thighs she froze, and a look of shuddering disgust showed on her face.

Irma pushed the girl to the floor, where she crouched for a moment, shivering and naked, her arms crossed over her

445

breasts in the age-old female gesture of protection. 'Weak,' said Irma. 'A cheap subhuman. Don't bother to save her for me, Karl.'

'Then,' said Vogel sarcastically, 'may we go on?' Without waiting for a response, he turned to the prisoners, his lips a thin line. 'Since we have seen extreme insolence from all three of these,' he said, 'and also violence, there is no alternative other than to extort the maximum penalty.'

'Death—' murmured Burkhardt.

'The maximum penalty,' said Vogel again, and looked at the guards. 'You understand the order?'

'Yes, Lieutenant General.'

Lieutenant General. Jude felt his blood chill at the words.

'Then,' said Vogel, a slurry note of anticipatory pleasure in his voice, 'proceed. Hang this insolent one and also the girl.' He looked back at the younger of the boys. 'But that one we will send back to his wretched ghetto so that he can describe to the other would-be rebels how we deal with their puny attempts to defy us.'

He pointed to the roof of the chamber, and for the first time Jude saw the row of huge iron hooks, the spikes glinting blackly in the cold light.

Jude thought that the people in the inner room were by now so intent on their grisly travesty of a trial that they would not have heard him if he had run down the tunnel in steel-tipped boots, but he was transfixed. He could see nothing he could do to help the prisoners but to leave was unthinkable.

The guards had lifted the first boy and were tearing off the thin prison trousers. They glanced to Vogel and Burkhardt as if awaiting an order, and when Vogel nodded,

446

two more winched down the hooks. Jude saw that there was a kind of pulley system affixed to the wall, with taut hawsers wound around wheels and secured to the floor. The hooks came down slowly and screechingly and with a dreadful inexorability. The spikes caught the light.

Two guards grasped the boy's ankles, and jerked them wide apart. A third dragged his hands behind his back and snapped thick manacles about his wrists.

'Spread his legs wide,' hissed Irma. 'Let the other two see. Let the girl know what's ahead for her.'

'Let him feel all of it,' echoed Burkhardt.

The boy was writhing and trying to escape the guards and the other two prisoners were struggling against their own captors, but Jude could see that the struggles were futile and that the prisoners must know it. His mind was tumbling, but he thought: if I went out there I should only be one more against them. And if I go back to the castle— But there was no one in the castle other than Angelika von Drumm and Erich and he was no longer inclined to trust anyone in Eisenach. Could he trust Angelika, even?

The boy's thighs were being dragged impossibly wide; the thin tendons in the groin must be stretching unbearably. As the boy started to moan, the guards lifted him, two of them still grasping his ankles, two more taking his thighs, and hoisting him, still firmly upright, over the point of the huge iron hook. Jude saw with sick horror that the hook's point was being forced upwards into the boy's exposed scrotum. His head was thrown back in fear and panic, the cords of his neck standing out, and although he was still struggling, the guards were holding him so tightly that he could barely move.

Karl Vogel leaned forward, resting his chin in one hand. 'To leave you like this for a time would be what the Chinese peoples term exquisite agony,' he said softly. 'But

447

we will be a little more merciful.' He nodded to the guards. 'Impale him.'

The two guards lifted the boy higher and a third held the hook steady. Jude had the impression of a warped surgical procedure about to be performed. And then they jammed the boy down hard.

The hook's point pierced his scrotum at once and burst through the lower part of his stomach. He toppled over at once, in an ungainly tumble, and hung upside-down with blood welling out of the deep, dark wound between his thighs.

The other two prisoners were crouching on the floor, shivering and helpless. The boy who would be sent back to the ghetto had managed to reach out a hand to the girl.

The impaled boy was still moving, his hands flailing feebly upwards to try to dislodge the biting agony of the hook. As the hook swayed and turned, he swayed and turned with it, and Jude, sickened and appalled, thought he was beginning to resemble nothing so much as a huge carcass of beef on a butcher's hook. Blood, streaked with seminal fluid and urine, poured down the boy's body, running into his eyes and soaking his hair, and then spattered wetly on to the floor. Jude felt his guts contract with the agony of it.

The boy had been panting and heaving in dreadful rhythm, but now he sagged and gave a choking gurgle. There was a whistling sound as air rushed out of his lungs and his eyes rolled up.

'Dead,' said Vogel dismissively. 'Now for the girl.'

It was at that point that Jude pushed open the door and walked into the lighted room.

The effect on the two men and Irma was electric. They rose from their seats at once, and then Burkhardt turned to Vogel as if awaiting orders.

Jude said coolly, 'Good evening. This is an interesting gathering.' He glanced to where the dead boy still swung gently from the hook. 'I shan't apologise for intruding, because if you really want to be uninterrupted you shouldn't leave lights burning or doors unguarded.' He paused, and then said very deliberately, 'I think we may be of some assistance to one another.'

Vogel and Irma exchanged wary looks. Vogel said, 'Indeed?'

'Indeed,' said Jude, 'because it seems—Do you mind if I sit down, by the way? And if that is cognac in that decanter— Yes, I thought it was. Thank you.' He sipped the brandy slowly, resisting the compulsion to drink it in one gulp. 'I suppose these are rebels?' he said surveying the prisoners. 'Well, it happens now and then. From one of the ghettos? Can I ask which one?'

Again there was the cautious exchange of looks, but Burkhardt answered readily enough. 'They are Lithuanian Jews. From Kaunas.'

'I see. And,' said Jude, 'you intend to return the one whose life you have spared to his people with the story of the punishment in store for rebels.' He leaned back in his chair, the fingers of one hand curled negligently about the glass of brandy. 'What about the girl?' he said in a drawl. 'You will execute her by the same method?'

'Yes.'

Jude looked at the girl, and his eyes travelled over her unclothed body slowly and rather insolently. He looked back at Vogel and the two others. The silence lengthened, but finally, Jude said, 'I will strike a bargain with you, Vogel. You want the music – the *Devil's Piper*. We can stop playing games: I know it and you know it. Well, I will offer you a *quid pro quo*.'

449

He stopped, and after a moment, Vogel said, 'Go on.'

'I could be persuaded into playing the music for you,' said Jude. 'But there would be two conditions.'

'Yes?'

'The first is that you give me the girl.' He caught an abrupt movement from the prisoners which he ignored.

'Why?' said Vogel instantly, and Jude made a brief gesture.

'She takes my eye. These things happen.'

Irma Greise regarded Jude hungrily and said, 'And also, the line between extreme pain and sexual arousal is a very fine one, is that not so, Herr Weissman?'

'As you say,' said Jude coldly, and looked at Vogel. 'Well?'

'It might be arranged.' Vogel glanced at Burkhardt and Irma, and then said, 'But before we go any farther, there is a condition I will impose in my turn, Herr Weissman.'

There was a silence in the room. Jude risked a covert glance at the two prisoners. The girl was trembling, but the boy was listening closely.

Vogel said slowly, 'You are right when you say we want the music. We do. We believe it can further Germany's plan for supremacy.' He paused, his eyes assessing Jude. 'But we also want to know how you came by it,' he said. 'And what you know about it.'

'You want the provenance,' said Jude thoughtfully, and helped himself to another measure of brandy. 'I suppose it's a reasonable request.' He sipped the brandy, frowning, and then said, 'The music came into my family during the early years of the nineteenth century. My great-great grandfather was given it in Eighteen-Fifteen or -Sixteen. I am not sure of the exact year.'

'By Wolfgang Mozart?' This was Burkhardt, his cold eyes avid.

'Mozart was dead by then,' said Jude. 'It was his son who owned the music – the only surviving son. There was some kind of business transaction with my great-great grandfather – a favour to be returned,' he said vaguely. 'The music was part of payment of a debt.' He saw Burkhardt and Vogel exchange sidelong glances.

'That,' said Vogel, 'accords with what we have heard.'

'Mozart is supposed to have acquired the music towards the end of his life,' said Jude. 'He bought it from a travelling musician whom he met while he was writing *The Magic Flute*.'

'Shortly before he died?'

'Yes.' Jude made an expressive gesture with his hands. 'It's as likely a tale as any other. On the one hand it could be argued that Mozart never needed to buy anyone else's music in his life, but on the other, he was generous to a fault. You can believe it or not, just as you like.'

'Do you believe it, Herr Weissman?' said Vogel.

'Not especially. Although I don't entirely disbelieve it.'

'But – you wrote the *Devil's Piper* around the music?'

'Oh yes. And it was plagiarism in its purest, most unabashed form. If you are going to steal, you make sure the booty is worthwhile. The legend tells how the music is far older than Mozart, of course, although that depends on which version of the legend you have heard,' said Jude off-handedly. 'There are any number, you know.'

Burkhardt said, almost stammering in his eagerness, 'But surely – the famous legend is how the music can summon the ancient High Priest who possessed the secret of immortal life—'

'Oh, you've heard that one, have you?' said Jude vaguely. 'Ahasuerus and the sorceress, Susannah. I expect that's as true as any.' He lifted the brandy glass again.

'Power over minds,' said Karl Vogel softly.

'Yes, that's believed to be another of the music's properties.'

'It is that that our masters covet,' said Vogel, and Jude regarded him thoughtfully.

'Yes,' he said at last. 'I imagine they would.'

'Also,' said Irma Greise, 'there is the power over bodies. Sexual potency.'

'Do they credit it with that?' said Jude, sounding bored.

Burkhardt leaned forward. 'You mentioned another condition?' he said, and Jude smiled and made the age-old gesture of rubbing his thumb and index finger together.

'Money,' he said. 'What else did you expect? If you proposition us, do we not bargain?'

He stopped, and Vogel said thoughtfully, 'Ah yes, you are also Jewish.'

'Are you thinking of throwing me into one of Himmler's work camps, Karl?' said Jude softly. 'But if you do that, you will never get the music.' He reached for the brandy decanter and refilled his glass as unhurriedly as if they were seated in Eisenach's dining room. 'My services are for sale to the highest bidder,' said Jude. 'But the bids have to be very high indeed.' He paused and then said, 'However, if you are prepared to meet my demands, I will put my music – the *Devil's Piper* music that has been handed down in my family – at the disposal of your masters.'

There was an abrupt silence, and then Vogel said, 'You know who our "masters" are, Weissman?'

Jude looked around the room, and glanced at the iron hooks and the armed guards and then back to Vogel himself. 'Oh yes,' he said softly. 'Yes, I know exactly who they are.

'And I am prepared to strike a bargain with them.'

Jude had never wholly trusted the thin legend that had come

down from his great-great grandfather, and he did not really trust Mozart's part in it either, because Mozart had possessed that Puckish sense of the ridiculous. Jude knew the legend of the *Black Chant* as well as anyone, and Mozart would have known it as well. The trouble was that Jude had never been able to entirely quench the sneaking suspicion that Mozart might have considered it a huge joke to bequeath to the world a worthless piece of music on the premise that it was truly the *Chant*, the ancient sinister sequence of notes that could call up the creature of the legends.

But it was astonishingly easy to visualise Mozart towards the end of his life, his money and his health failing, falling into the raucous motley world of his *Magic Flute* librettist and fellow Freemason, Emmanuel Schikaneder of the People's Theatre; enjoying the company of Schikaneder's disreputable, attractive actors and the ragamuffin gypsy dancers and acrobats and circus dwarves.

A travelling musician of Italian descent and dubious origin, Jude's great-great grandfather had said, and had told how the Italian boy had parted with the music very reluctantly indeed.

'Of great value,' the boy had said. 'In my family for hundreds of years.'

But he had been starving and Mozart, according to all the stories, had been generous to a fault. Jude had never been sure of the truth of it all, but he was inclined to tilt the scales just very slightly in favour of the story being true.

And if so, it looked as if the ancient music that so many musicians had believed to possess diabolic powers, that could call to men's minds and their bodies, and that was so immeasurably old its origins were believed to stretch back to before the days of Solomon and the Temple Magi, was about to be used again.

In the service of the Nazis.

Chapter Forty-One

Angelika von Drumm curled into a corner of the book room at Eisenach and said pettishly, 'My dear, I cannot imagine why you agreed to go to a work camp of all places!'

'I cannot imagine why either,' said Jude urbanely.

'Especially after your reception at the concert last night – *wasn't* it rapturous, I thought they would never stop cheering. And when those women started to bombard the platform with flowers – so extravagant and marvellous – of course, it was the *Piper* music that affected them, exactly as Erich and Karl said it would, and I know perfectly well that there is something *peculiar* about that music, although I can *not* decide what, but I must say—'

'A little champagne before you say it, Baroness?'

Angelika wriggled in delicious anticipation and held out her glass. 'Champagne in the afternoon – *sinfully* luxurious. I always associate it with you, not that one drinks champagne in the afternoon as an everyday thing of course, at least not if one is married to Erich— And of course, he will be your friend for life for bringing it, always supposing you *want* Erich as a friend for life— What was I saying? Oh, the concert. My dear, *wasn't* that Sonia Esterhazy creature *obvious* at supper afterwards? She did everything but take off her clothes and lie at your feet, too shaming, because she must be forty if she's a day, and I'd wager my last *cent* that she came to your bedroom later, not that you'd admit it—'

'It would be against my religion to admit any such thing.'

'Nonsense, you haven't got a religion, you're a pagan.'

Jude said, 'Some to Mecca turn to pray, and I towards thy bed, Yasmin.'

'Rubbish, you pray to music if you pray to anything,' said Angelika, at once. 'And I do think— Oh, this is *very* good champagne, Jude, trust you to have the best— Do you remember how we drank Bollinger that afternoon in your apartment in Vienna?'

'Clicquot,' said Jude.

'Was it *really*? And there was caviare and those *exquisite* Viennese *petit beurres*, and you played the piano so *violently* that I was positively *awash* with desire, in fact between Schumann and *lust* – or was it Schumann? I forget now – but what with Schumann and you, I couldn't *think* properly! If you hadn't picked me up and carried me into the bedroom, I should have *expired*. I promise you!'

'If memory serves, we didn't actually reach the bed that time—'

'Nor we did! Imagine your remembering! We had such fun, didn't we? I can still see that marvellous white silk rug—' She sipped the champagne, wrinkled her nose in pleasure and then said suddenly, 'Why are you really going to the work camp with Otto?'

'To give a series of Workers' Recitals.'

'Oh, Hitler's ridiculous idea of bringing culture to the masses,' said Angelika. 'Very *bourgeois* – I said he was a parvenu, didn't I? And I do think it *extraordinary* of you to have paid for that *odd* couple to travel back to their home. I know they are Jews, and that you all have this absurd fellowship, hugely admirable of course, but so *tedious* I should think! And I cannot imagine where you found them—'

'You would not believe me if I told you, Baroness,' said Jude.

'Which means there is some kind of secret going on,' said Angelika. 'Well, I do think you might tell me what it is, because everyone knows I am the *soul* of discretion.' She lay back on her cushioned sofa, regarding Jude from limpid, guileless eyes.

Jude smiled, and sipped his champagne with silent enjoyment, and presently Angelika said a bit crossly, 'Anyway, what shall you give the workers, poor dears?'

'Oh, something stirring,' said Jude vaguely. 'Whatever doesn't need orchestral back-up. Tchaikovsky might do. Possibly Liszt.'

'The *Piper* doesn't need orchestral back-up,' said Angelika slyly. 'And it's what they want, you know. Erich and Karl and that cold-eyed Otto Burkhardt – oh, isn't he boring that Otto? Did you ever meet *anyone* so charmless? How you are to endure him in that work camp I cannot imagine. Shall you do what they want?'

'Perhaps.'

'Which means,' said Angelika shrewdly, 'that you will do exactly what *you* want. I think you are really rather ruthless, Jude, darling. And as for Hitler's marvellous idea,' she said, holding out her glass for more champagne and digging out a hefty scoop of caviare to accompany it, 'if you were to ask *me*, I should say the entire thing sounds like force-feeding the poor souls.' She curled her feet under her, eating caviare with industrious pleasure. 'I was thinking,' said Angelika, her voice sliding down several octaves into an intimate purr, 'that I might invite you to stay for a while, Jude. After Erich has gone back to Berlin, you understand. Just ourselves, very *intime*.' Her eyes slanted with mischievous optimism.

456

Jude spread his hands. 'Forgive me, Baroness. You're very tempting, but I can't.'

Angelika regarded him, and for a moment something unexpectedly serious showed in her eyes. 'Is she very beautiful, your wife?' she said, and Jude looked up from refilling his own glass.

But he only said, 'Yes, very.' And waited.

There was a brief silence, and then with a return to her normal manner, Angelika shrugged and said, 'Oh, well if you must go to that dreary work camp, you must. The journey will be *appallingly* tedious you know. And when you do get there, there will be nothing to see.'

'Nothing at all,' said Jude expressionlessly.

'Well then, I cannot imagine why you should want to go to this – what is it called?'

'It's the largest camp of them all,' said Jude. 'It's in Poland near to a place called Oswiecim.'

'I've never heard of it,' said Angelika. 'Mark my words, it'll be precisely as I said, the end of the world, this— what did you say it was called?'

'Auschwitz,' said Jude. 'More champagne, Angelika?'

The journey to Auschwitz was exactly as Angelika had prophesied. It was long and tedious and uncomfortable, and the railway station, when they finally reached it, was cold and stark and grey. The colourlessness of despair, thought Jude, turning to oversee the unloading of his luggage from the guard's van. He had not brought very much, save a few changes of clothing and his music case; Burkhardt had promised that a piano would be available for the recital. 'Although I'm afraid a Bluthner may not be possible,' he had said, and Jude had stared at him coldly.

'I do not play anything *but* a Bluthner.'

Burkhardt was waiting for him on the platform, which

Jude supposed was inevitable, although he had not expected the presence of so many Schutzstaffel officers. Most of them wore the characteristic rounded helmets of Himmler's Gestapo and all of them were armed. They stood watchful and alert, stamping their booted feet on the ground, their breath turning to vapour in the sharp air as orders were rapped out.

'They are waiting for a new detachment of inmates for the camp,' said Burkhardt, escorting Jude out to a parked car with a chauffeur at the wheel.

'Jews?'

'Oh yes. They are to arrive on the next train.'

'Why are the guards so heavily armed?'

'Well, we do not anticipate any real rebellion,' said Burkhardt, after a moment. 'Because the Jews are happy to be leaving their ghettos, which are over-crowded and insanitary, you understand.'

'I'm sure they are ecstatic to be coming here,' rejoined Jude, and Burkhardt glanced at him suspiciously.

But he said, 'With so many numbers there may be isolated outbreaks of panic. Our aim is to ensure obedience and calm.'

'And with all those sub-machine guns you can scarcely fail,' said Jude politely. 'How many people are being transported?'

'About four thousand today. That is why the trucks are here. They could be made to walk to the camp, but trucks are quicker, and we can get a great many into each one.'

'Four thousand today,' said Jude thoughtfully.

'Five or six times that many are coming in total. All will be brought up during the two days.' Burkhardt glanced at Jude. 'You look as if you're doing sums in your head, Herr Weissman.'

'How perceptive of you, Herr Burkhardt,' said Jude.

Auschwitz Camp, when they reached it, was far larger than Jude had been visualising. He stared at it and felt a coldness enter his heart. This was surely the grimmest, most desolate place anyone could ever imagine. The end of the world, Angelika had said, but this was a world by itself, a stark, lonely world marooned amidst dank marshlands.

The gates opened for them and as their passes were inspected by the guard, Jude could see the serried rows of barrack buildings beyond. The entire compound was surrounded by what were plainly electrified wire fences, and set into the fence at intervals were guard towers with black-snouted machine guns. As they went inside, Jude experienced a sudden surge of terror: this is a fearsome place. This is like entering one of the cold, ancient hells of the poets. Dante's despairing stone-built Malebolge – 'Of iron hue, like to the wall that circles it about'. If I was writing music about this place, I should make it huge and dark with lots of bass – maybe a slow, sombre cello, maybe even an organ.

At his side, Burkhardt said, 'I think this is the first time you are to perform inside any of our camps, Herr Weissman? You do not object to doing so?'

Jude replied carelessly, 'If you prick us do we not bleed, and if you pay us highly enough do we not perform at your request?'

'You sound cynical.'

'Merely venal.'

Provision had been made for the recital to take place in a long, single-storey building on the edge of the main compound, which Jude assumed was some kind of mess-room for the officers and camp commandant. Armed SS guards lined the walls, and a platform had been erected at one end, with narrow, half-curtained windows behind. Jude glanced out. In the cold, raw air of this place, it was possible to make out long, narrow tracks in the ground, marked by rusting railway sleepers, leading to a group of brick-built buildings with jutting chimneys. There were eight or ten of them and they were perhaps half a kilometre away, a little apart from the main compound. Jude frowned and turned his attention back to the platform and the anxiously hovering Burkhardt.

'None of this is satisfactory,' he said coldly.

'I regret there was not very much time, Herr Weissman. And the facilities here are of the most basic— But you see there is a Bluthner.'

'Nevertheless it is what I am accustomed to.' Jude looked around the bleak wooden-floored room. 'It is certainly not what you led me to expect.'

Donning the arrogance and the *prima donna* mantle and seeing Burkhardt's worried glance towards the assembling commandant and camp officers drove the horror back slightly, but beneath it Jude was beginning to doubt if he could give a performance here at all. Music needed warmth and light and space; it was a soaring, marvellous thing, a thing of love and delight and peace. To play music in this terrible place, reeking of such despair, was so wrong as to be nearly obscene. He considered walking out, but as the guards brought in the prisoners, he knew at once he could not.

'The dissidents,' Burkhardt said, watching them, and lowering his voice, and glancing over his shoulders as if he had made a vaguely blasphemous observation. 'In every community there are always a few disruptive ones—'

'But in here you reward your rebels with piano recitals?' Jude waited to see how Burkhardt would answer that one,

460

but Burkhardt simply shrugged.

'We do not question orders,' he said. 'And Herr Himmler has many ideas which are regarded by some as—'

'Bordering on madness?'

'Progressive and modern,' said Burkhardt reprovingly. 'You should not let Herr Vogel hear you speak that way.'

'I don't care if the entire German High Command hears me.'

There looked to be about two hundred of the prisoners regarded as dissidents, but the hut was very large and they were huddled closely together so that it was difficult to be sure. Several of them clutched small bundles of belongings and all of them were thin and ragged. But an angry light burned in the gaunt faces, and when they looked at Jude they did so with unmistakable hatred.

The officers had seated themselves directly in front of the platform, courteously helping one another to chairs, Karl Vogel, his thin, austere face unreadable, among them. Jude stood at the front of the platform, his eyes going over the assembly, and then without any ceremony, he walked across the platform and sat down at the piano.

It was important to shut out the ragged, hollow-cheeked prisoners and the feeling of their hatred. It was important to shut out the appalling surroundings as well. The *Devil's Piper* suite was complex and powerful, and it took every ounce of Jude's concentration to control it. An orchestra would have helped, because the musicians would have shared the huge weight of the concentration, but Burkhardt and Vogel had been adamant. No orchestra. A piano recital only. And we are paying you very well indeed for it.

Jude half closed his eyes, forcing his mind to a single glittering point until he was aware only of the music and the creature waiting at the music's heart. The Piper, the eerie enigmatic being, waiting to prowl the world . . . Did

I truly create him or does he actually exist somewhere, as Mozart believed and as his Italian gypsy believed, and as my great-great grandfather believed?

There was no emotion quite like this, there was nothing in the world to compare with the moment when you deliberately drew together the glittering strands of your own creation and rolled them up into a prismatic globe, a huge, vibrant humming top, that you could whip into life and send spinning into the waiting silence in a cascade of pure sound. Jude took a deep breath and brought his hands down on the Bluthner's keys.

The eerily beautiful music – the music born from Mozart's ancient yellowing score; the legendary music that contained the medieval *diablo* chords, that was called by some the *Black Chant* and believed by others to have evolved from a harlot's dark passion for an immortal High Priest – poured into the room.

Jude fell fathoms deep into the music at once, going down and down into its allure, so that for a while he lost all sense of time and he certainly lost all sense of place. Nothing but the music. Nothing but the drawing out of the enigmatic creature from his lair. Nothing but the approach of the deep midnight when the Piper – bound by the music for ever – must walk, his footsteps echoing on the deserted cobbled streets, snatching victims from their beds: virgins for their blood, children for their souls . . .

The music went up and up: he began the toccata, the series of rising arpeggios, feeling them build, feeling the fearful anticipation spilling out . . . The Piper approaching . . .

Into the music, sinisterly in time with the rhythmic staccato chords that were the Piper's prowling footsteps, came a sound so alien but so intrusive that it scratched at

Jude's mind and broke into the chimerical world that he had been spinning. He frowned and went on playing, but the spell was splintering and the magic was lost.

A subtle change had come over the long, bare room and Jude, his hands weaving the music but his mind no longer inside its bewitchment, looked towards the inadequately curtained window facing him.

Filing through the grounds of the camp in terrible procession was a shivering, straggling line of humanity – several hundred prisoners at least – being driven forward by heavily armed, black-clad guards. Each prisoner wore the thinnest of rags, each head was bowed, all eyes were bereft of light and hope. Most of the prisoners wore the yellow Star of David, not defiantly or proudly, but in numb obedience to the Gestapo's ruling and although some were crying in a miserable beaten way, most of them moved in silence. As Jude lifted his hands from the keys, the sound of the shuffling shambling footsteps and the helpless sobbing swelled and ebbed on the air, like ritualistic keening. It mingled unexpectedly with low sullen murmurs from the angry-eyed men and young women, and Jude caught the words 'murderers' and 'butchery' before the guards advanced on the prisoners, raising their rifles threateningly. The prisoners cringed and fell silent, but although there was terror in their faces, there was still hard bitter hatred as well. At the front of the hall, Vogel and the officers had risen to their feet and as Jude took an uncertain step forward, Vogel bounded on to the platform, shouting to him to go on playing. His thin face was blazing with emotion, and his voice sliced through the charged atmosphere, escalating with exultant madness.

'Go on!' he cried. 'This is what we brought you here for! Play them to their deaths! Cow the subhuman things! Quench the rebels!' He looked down to the floor of the hut, where the prisoners were being herded through the door and a terrible gloating lust showed in his face.

The doors at the back had been dragged open, and Jude could see the tracks made by the black railway sleepers more clearly. The low brick buildings were perhaps half a kilometre distant, and the shambling shuffling line of prisoners was still going forward. Dreadful understanding assaulted his mind like a blow then, because he had heard the whispers and the rumours, although he had discounted them, because no one surely would commit such a huge act of savagery—

But the rumours were true. This was Hitler's solution to what he regarded as the scourge of Europe. Genocide. The murder of a people. The low buildings were gas chambers and adjoining them were crematoria. He was witnessing the annihilation of Jewry; it was happening while he stood here. And this was why Vogel had wanted the music. To drown the cries of the dying prisoners. Perhaps even to subdue the ones who are next. Yes, of course, to subdue the rebels.

Because the music has the charm to call up spirits, and to soothe pain with sound and agony with air . . . To lead lambs to the slaughter and Jews to the flames . . . My own people, he thought, the immense horror of it breaking against his emotions. My own people and I have helped them to die.

In here were the dissidents; the difficult ones he was supposed to soothe. Perhaps they were even the nucleus of some kind of underground resistance movement that Burkhardt and Vogel had uncovered.

At his side, Burkhardt, his voice thick with relish, said, 'Now you see how we deal with the problem of Jewry, Herr Weissman. Gassing and immediately afterwards incineration. Quick and easy and clean.'

'And now,' said Karl, his eyes as cold and as hard as agates, 'now, Herr Weissman, play on. Subdue them! This is what we are paying you for! Use the music!'

Jude, his mind spiralling from disgust to repulsion and then back again, looked across at the guards, weighing his chance of rushing the SS men and somehow leading the prisoners out. Would they respond? Would they follow him if he created a diversion? But he knew at once that it would be useless. There had been that spark of rebellion in their faces, but they were plainly half-starving and exhausted, and at the smallest sign of real mutiny the guards would gun them down without compunction and within seconds.

There was absolutely nothing to do but resume his seat and continue to play the music and try to drown the despairing sobbing and the piteous pleas of the doomed prisoners and the shuffling of their feet as they were crammed by the hundred into the gas chambers.

As the music spun to its final soaring notes, from beyond the hall, came the deep echoing sound of the gas chamber doors closing.

Chapter Forty-Two

Ahasuerus was no longer tapping against the door of the grisly oven, but Kate knew he had not gone away. She could feel him standing on the other side of the door: within a few feet of where she was crouched. He's working out how to open the oven, she thought in horror, and shrank back against the far wall, hugging her knees to her chest.

The bolts had halted Ahasuerus in his tracks. Kate had no idea if this was because he was unfamiliar with bolts or because he was physically unable to move them, and she shuddered, remembering the mutilated hands. The Devil's Piper might not be able to grasp the thick, awkward bolts in the way she had been able to grasp them, but he probably had sufficient strength to simply force them back and then pull the door wide. If he did that, was there any way she could hold the door shut from this side?

She crawled forward again, scarcely noticing the crunched-up spun-glass bones on the oven floor this time, and ran the palms of her hands over the flat, pitted surface of the door. At once Ahasuerus moved closer. Had he heard her? But he knew she was in here anyway. There was the sound of harsh ragged breathing – he's bending down, thought Kate, still pressing against the door, feeling for some kind of handle. He's peering at the unknown mechanism that's cheating him of his prey. He's *sniffing* at the edges of the door – I can *feel* that he is! If I had a weapon I could defend myself. Wild ideas of snatching up the poor, crumbling bones and using them as clubs if Ahasuerus opened the door coursed through her mind, only to be discarded. The bones in here were half a century old and they were as fragile as porcelain. But what about a shoe? Could she deal a good enough blow with the heel of her boot? She dragged one off, running her hand over it to convey its outline to her mind in the dark. Black suede, with high heels – she remembered putting them on to go to Conrad Vogel's office about a thousand years ago. They were not at all practical footwear to have on if you were trapped inside a Nazi incinerator with an undead corpse trying to get at you, but the heels were high and they were tipped with tiny steel caps. As makeshift weapons they were not at all bad. Who said vanity never paid?

It would make a terrific story if she got out. When she got out. There I was, she would say; trapped in an ancient crematorium oven with a corpse trying to get at me, and I escaped by hitting the creature over the head with the heel of a Gucci boot! It ruined the suede but it did the trick. For a brief, wild moment she could visualise herself at a dinner party – one of the kind she and Richard used to give and attend – burlesquing the tale, making everyone laugh. Trust Kate, they would say, grinning. Vanity of vanities to the end.

She took a firmer grip on the boot, and as she did so, the scream of tortured metal sliced shockingly into the thick stifling darkness. Kate shot back to her dark corner at once and crouched there, shivering and terrified, but still clutching the spike-heeled boot. One good blow to the temple— There was the really sickening noise of thick claws scraping against steel and every nerve in Kate's body flinched. She fixed her eyes on the thin smear of light that was the only indication of the door's whereabouts, and waited.

Inch by tortuous inch, the rim of light was widening; not normally and gradually as if the door was opening as it was intended to open, but jerkily and painfully. I was right! He's tearing the door away from its hinges! She could hear the snuffling, painful breathing much more loudly now, and waves of sick revulsion washed over her.

Light spilled in from the outer room: dim pale light, and there, framed against it, was the cowled head and shoulders of Ahasuerus. He stood for a moment, looking in at her, and Kate caught the glint of his eyes through the mask. She set her teeth and took a firmer grasp on the boot. One good blow to the temple, remember, Kate?

From the dark tunnels beyond the crematorium, came the sound of the outside door slamming, reverberating through the crematorium and the gas chamber dully. Ahasuerus froze, and half turned his head so that the hood fell back a little. Kate, her mind caught between fear and hope, saw that even with the thin clinging mask, his face in profile was extraordinarily clear. The thought that this had once been an extremely attractive creature brushed her mind and then vanished as she caught another sound. Footsteps. Someone was coming along the tunnel towards them.

Whoever it was, it was certainly not Vogel. The footsteps were too uncertain for that. And Vogel had said he would leave her in here with Ahasuerus all night. Time had ceased to be measurable or even noticeable in here and her watch had stopped, but Kate thought it had been early morning when Vogel came in, and that only a couple of hours had elapsed.

Whoever had entered the chamber was approaching. Kate could hear the footsteps more clearly now, but

Ahasuerus was still barring the path to the door, and she stayed where she was, straining every sense to hear, still ready to strike out if Ahasuerus reached for her. But Ahasuerus had moved away, and he was standing with his back to her, facing the door leading to the gas chamber beyond. Dare she creep forward and strike that blow now? But it would mean crawling awkwardly to the edge of the ovens, which she could certainly not do silently. And she had absolutely no idea who the footsteps might belong to.

And then a tall, dark-clad figure appeared in the half-open door, and Ciaran's voice said, 'Kate?' and the hooded, cloaked figure of the Devil's Piper flinched and half fell back. The sound of Ahasuerus's anguished breathing filled the chamber, and with it, a dreadful, imploring sobbing. Kate, her skin prickling with compassion and revulsion, her mind tumbling in disbelief, crawled cautiously to the edge and saw that Ahasuerus was backing away from Ciaran – what in God's name was Ciaran doing here? – and that he had thrown up his hands – oh dear heaven, the terrible claw-hands! – as if fearful of a blow.

Ciaran said in a curiously gentle voice, 'Ahasuerus – you must know I mean you no harm—' and stopped as Ahasuerus turned his head mutely from side to side, like a trapped animal. Ciaran advanced, and Ahasuerus moved instantly to the door, the awkward, deformed gait piteously obvious. There was a half-strangled cry, and then he was gone, his footsteps echoing limpingly in the outer room and then in the tunnel. Going away from them.

Kate fell through the opening into Ciaran's arms.

They were seated on the brick floor of the crematorium, their backs against the wall facing the ovens. Kate thought she had not really fainted – fainting was what dieaway Victorian heroines did for goodness' sake – but she felt a

469

bit odd, as if it might be better not to stand up yet. Ciaran's arm was around her and he felt warm and safe and masculine.

Kate said a bit fuzzily, 'You aren't a mirage?'

'Far from it, dear girl.'

'And – you do know where we are?'

'Certainly I know. In general, we're just outside Eisenach Castle, and more specifically we're in a disused death chamber.' There was the glint of a smile. 'And yes, you did faint, but you were only out for a few minutes. And no, I don't know where Vogel is, and I don't care at the moment. Ahasuerus is somewhere out there, but between us we'll think of a way to deal with Ahasuerus, Kate.'

Kate was still light-headed, but she stared up at him and thought: yes, that's how he talked, that's the soft, silver-tongued Irishness I've been remembering.

'What you are doing here?'

There was the smallest pause, and then Ciaran said, 'I followed Vogel.'

'Why?'

'To get you back.' His arms tightened about her. His thigh was six inches away from hers. Kate's heart began to race. 'Although,' said Ciaran, 'I'd have to say it was to get Ahasuerus as well.'

'I never really deceived you, did I?'

'Oh yes,' said Ciaran, his eyes on her. 'Oh yes, my girl, you deceived me all right. It wasn't until you'd gone that I put the pieces together.'

'He recognised you, didn't he? Ahasuerus, I mean. Just now?' It had been rather terrible to see Ahasuerus cowering like that. Kate hoped it was not going to be the one thing she would remember if they got out of all this alive. When they got out of all this alive.

Ciaran said, 'Yes, he recognised me. He recognised what I represented.' He looked down at her. 'Re-interment,' he said. 'He knows it's the vow we all take, and he knows because he's come up against it more than once.' He paused, and then said, half to himself, 'And the poor tormented thing will fight like a wild creature to avoid that.'

'How dreadful.' Kate could not tear her eyes away from him. Even in the uncertain light his eyes were cool and grey and clear. Eyes you could drown in. And that glossy beard, not quite red, but the colour of autumn leaves. It emphasises the lines of his face. Puckish. Satyr-like.

'You gave me a terrible fright when you passed out,' said Ciaran softly. 'Are you really all right, Kate?' His voice was like a caress. It was indecent the way the Irish could slide into that sexy purr.

'I think I'm all right. I think I'm fine,' said Kate, by no means sure that she was. 'I'm a bit cold,' she said suddenly, and he pulled her closer.

'Is that better?'

'Oh yes. Ought we to see if Ahasuerus has gone?'

'Yes, we ought. We ought to be thinking of a way to get out, as well.' He held her against him. 'I shouldn't be doing this.'

'No. I understand.' Neither of them had moved.

'I shouldn't be feeling like this, either. Kate, have you the least idea of the effect you're having on me?' His other arm came round her at the exact moment that Kate turned her face up to him and put her arm about his neck. The kiss when it came was tentative and exploratory, and then suddenly it was not tentative in the least. Explosive, thought Kate. Hungry. As if we've both been starving for each other. Like being drawn down into a whirlpool. I've never felt like this in my life. She forgot everything in the world except his lips and his arms and the feel of his body against hers. She forgot the creeping menace somewhere in the tunnel, she forgot about Vogel and Richard and Eisenach.

Ciaran said, as if the words were being torn from him, 'Oh Kate, I was afraid you were dead—'

'I nearly was.'

'You can't imagine the fantasies I've had about you—'

'All the things you're supposed to have renounced? I had a few fantasies on my own account, Ciaran.' Marvellous to say his name. 'Will you have to confess this?'

'I will.'

'Will you be punished?'

'Excommunicated, probably.' He kissed her again.

'I thought celibacy went with being a monk,' said Kate. 'Automatic impotence.'

'My darling girl, impotent is the last thing I am at the moment—'

Her skin was blazing with such passion that she thought if he touched her it would burn his hands . . . His hands . . . Sliding under the silk shirt, caressing her. He might have been inside a monastery for God-knew how many years, but he had the assurance and the gentle authority of someone very experienced with women indeed. Impossible to resist. I don't want to resist. But I should. I think I might faint again if he continues. But I think I'll die if he stops. But she summoned up the resolve to sit up straight again, and she put her hands flat on his chest and pushed him away. 'I'm stopping while we still can,' she said. 'You do understand?'

'I understand it all. And if I was to make love to you—' His eyes darkened and Kate's heart leapt. 'If I was to make love to you,' said Ciaran, 'I certainly wouldn't do it down here with the Devil's Piper prowling the tunnels, and with ghosts and agonies crowding us on all sides.'

So he had felt the ghosts as well.

'Of course I feel them,' he said at once. He looked at her

472

and Kate thought that the passion was like a tangible thing, hovering on the air between them. I don't know where he ends and I begin. I don't know where I end and he begins. I can feel his mind, flowing into mine and back again. It's the situation we're in, that's all. Propinquity created by danger. It's a well-known phenomenon to feel immensely close to people you share danger with, I believe. Comrades in the trenches. People risking their lives for fellow soldiers. *Iche hatte eine Kameraden.* You're kidding yourself, of course, Kate. This isn't *Iche hatte eine Kameraden.* This is something much deeper and something that's potentially very damaging indeed. Whatever it was, it bore no resemblance at all to the handful of light affairs she had had since Richard's accident: brief amusing interludes that had never hurt anyone and that had certainly never hurt Richard. Kate had always hoped that Richard, damaged in ways that did not show, might have understood about those occasional casual adventures. This feeling was not casual at all. It was something deep and strong and so fierce that it could hurt Richard very deeply indeed and it could hurt Ciaran and all of them. And I haven't the least idea what I'm going to do about any of it, thought Kate. I wonder if he has?

Ciaran had raised his head and he was staring towards the doors into the outer chamber.

'What—?'

'I'm not sure.' He got up and went lightly across the floor, and stood listening. After a moment, he put a finger to his lips, indicating, 'Be quiet.' Kate waited, and presently, Ciaran came back.

'I think something's happening,' he said. 'I think Vogel, may he rot in hell for eternity, is calling Ahasuerus out.'

'Well, can't we—' Kate stopped and shivered. 'Vogel has a gun,' she said.

473

'I know it,' said Ciaran worriedly. 'Do you think I wouldn't have jumped him if he hadn't?'

Kate said. 'He's come to get Ahasuerus because he needs him for his wretched concert.'

'No,' said Ciaran, rather grimly. 'Not yet. Vogel knows exactly what we've been doing – he's probably followed us and he's probably had his wretched Serse children spying on us. I think he's going to use Ahasuerus as bait for Isarel and Moira.'

He stopped and they stared at one another. Then Kate said in a whisper, 'The music— Ciaran, it's starting.'

From over their heads, they heard, quite unmistakably, the first faint notes of the shofar.

Chapter Forty-Three

Once through Eisenach's iron gates, Moira and Isarel felt unexpectedly better.

'Almost normal,' said Moira determinedly.

There were a number of Serse's People in the castle grounds, all of them engaged in various tasks which were plainly for the forthcoming concert. V-shaped display boards were being placed in the courtyard at the front of the castle's central portion, and two girls were fixing up small printed cards with arrows directing people to the different parts of the castle: the old stable block where drinks and food could be bought; the central hall where the actual concert would take place; the washrooms. The Serse ikon was everywhere.

No one took any notice of Isarel and Moira as they approached the castle's main entrance, but they were both uneasily aware of the towering walls and of the rows of windows. Any one of the rooms behind those windows might contain a watcher. At any moment, they could be challenged.

In front of them was a huge, oaken door with an iron ring handle, and Isarel eyed it and then looked down at Moira.

'This is it, isn't it?' said Moira, her eyes huge.

'This is it,' said Isarel. 'All right?'

'No,' said Moira. 'I'm not in the least all right. I'm

terrified to death. But whatever we have to do, I'll do it.'

'Good enough,' said Isarel, and reached down to the immense ring handle.

Entering the castle was like stepping fathoms deep into the past. The door opened straight on to an immense, galleried hall with a hammer-beamed ceiling and quatrefoil windows set high up. At the far end was a wide, curving stairway of marble and gilt.

Isarel stopped dead just inside the door. Mellow afternoon sunlight filtered in through the narrow windows and lay in soft, blurred pools everywhere, and there was a moment when he saw it as it would have looked to Jude: not dusty and untidy as it was now, but brilliant and shining; coruscating with the radiance of the women's jewels and the spun-sugar filaments of the crystal chandeliers, heady with anticipation and thrumming with excitement. And at the zenith of it all – insolently timing his entrance with exquisite precision so that every head would be turned to look at him – Jude.

Moira was right, thought Isarel; we really are going back. And Jude's very close. If I knew the right word of command or if I could somehow open an invisible door, he would be here. I'd see him exactly as he would have been that night, coming slowly down the marble stairway, amused and faintly arrogant, dazzling in black and white evening dress, as self-assured as a cat. Calling his orchestra to attention, affecting to hardly notice the audience, lifting the baton . . . And then the music, the huge, soul-scalding music swelling out and filling up the hall . . .

He blinked and looked about him. The chandeliers were still here, dulled by time and neglect, but suspended from the moulded ceilings beneath the galleries. And although the seething excitement of Jude's day had long since gone, the hall was filled with bustle and life. A dozen or so young men and girls, all wearing black T-shirts with the Serse ikon, were arranging rostra for the orchestra's platform at one end of the hall and there was a hum of workman-like sounds: hammering and the chink of tools; little bursts of conversation and shouted instructions; chairs being dragged across the floor; occasional spurts of laughter. Ladders stood at the opposite end to the platform, and several of the men were wiring up some kind of spotlighting. Lengths of green baize carpeting were being unrolled, and potted plants – ferns and palms – stood waiting to be banked against the front of the platform. Four or five more Serse followers were setting plastic-backed chairs into rows facing the platform.

Jude would have expected and got crystal chandeliers and hothouse flowers and an audience largely drawn from the aristocracy of the day. He would have played his disturbing, mesmeric music amidst a cascade of Worth and Dior gowns, and a flurry of expensive perfume: the Bright Young Things of *la belle epoque* had vanished by then, of course, but the Thirties had had their own svelte elegance. There would have been the creamy, expensive, froth of champagne at the interval, and later, at supper, the tables would have been set with the glistening shapes of whole salmon on beds of crushed ice, alongside silver dishes of Beluga caviare and Perigord truffles, with lobster and quail in aspic, and *foie gras* and out-of-season *fraises des bois*.

Moira said softly, 'Who will the musicians be? Would Vogel use different ones for each concert?'

'I think they'll all be Serse's People,' said Isarel, keeping his voice low. 'It would be the only way Vogel could trust them. Can you see Vogel anywhere, by the way? You'd better warn me if you do, because it's as well to know where the enemy's stationed, and I shouldn't know him from Lucifer. In fact of the two, I'd probably recognise Lucifer better.'

'I can't see either of them,' said Moira, deadpan, and Isarel smiled at her.

'I believe you're beginning to answer me back, my child,' he said.

'I believe I am,' Moira glanced about her. 'Where—'

'The stair,' said Isarel, without hesitation. 'Let's get it over with before anyone spots we're not of the faithful. And we're simply rehearsing for tomorrow, remember. With any luck, there're probably little groups all over the place doing the same thing.' He nodded coolly at the band of workers and walked confidently across the hall.

The stair was beyond the orchestra's platform, a little to its right, and it was a huge, wide sweep of marble and gilt with ornate balustrades and carved stone bas-relief and a high, soaring ceiling reaching up to the domed roof. I'll bet Jude came down that, thought Moira. I'll bet that fifty years ago he walked down those steps into an anticipation so strong you could slice through it. She was conscious of a sudden painful twist of longing: I wish I could have seen him! and then she remembered Isarel at her side, and for a moment past and present merged.

Isarel slid one hand casually into an inner pocket and Moira's heart lurched. The shofar! He's going to play the music! She glanced warily to the half-built stage, but no one was looking at them, and no one appeared to have seen anything to question in their presence. But Moira was strongly conscious of her heart beating fast, and with every minute she expected someone to come up and demand to know what they were doing.

Isarel had approached the stair almost without conscious thought and as he began to ascend the gilt and marble curve, Jude was with him again, walking at his side . . .

Haunting me as he did all those years ago . . . As he has never stopped doing. And fifty years ago Jude played his marvellous eerie music in this hall and now I'm about to do the same. Here I go.

He lifted the shofar to his lips and into the great echoing hall of Eisenach Castle floated the sweet, cool notes of the ancient music. Isarel's whole being was concentrating so absolutely on what he was doing, that he was scarcely aware of the half-turned heads below, and of Serse's People putting down hammers and straightening up from unrolling carpets or arranging plants. This is it, he thought. This is the ancient lure: the legendary *Black Chant* that stretches back and back over the centuries, linking Tartini and Berlioz and Paganini. Mozart and Handel and Liszt.

And Jude. Jude Weissman, writing his marvellous, compelling *Devil's Piper*, taking his orchestra into the Nazi death camps. Subduing the wretched, doomed Jews so that they would go unresisting to their deaths . . .

This is Ahasuerus's music, thought Isarel in awe, but in the same instant, doubt brushed his mind. It's not going to work. Nothing's going to happen. Panic swept in, and for the first time he became aware of the listeners in the hall.

The shofar's sound was light and thin in this vast place, but the music's beckoning and the sinister romance and the spider-web bewitchments were all there. Subtle. Soft. Wrapped inside the music, creeping into your mind, but doing it so gently and so insidiously that it fastened its claws into your brain before you realised it. The notes spun and shivered about the hall, and within them was a swirling expectancy, an immense anticipation that thickened the golden sunshine into the shapes of beckoning hands and crooking fingers.

He's approaching, thought Isarel, his mind swinging between panic and sheer blazing excitement. I was wrong

479

– it's working! The tension mounted up and up; painful, unbearable, stretching out and out until it was so thin and so taut that at any minute it would snap . . .

And then it did snap: with a single plangent note it snapped and something that had been shadow and blurred came sharply into focus at the head of the stair.

He was there. Ahasuerus, the renegade High Priest from two thousand years ago. He was coming across the galleried landing, but he was coming slowly and unwillingly, the hood that Isarel remembered pulled forward to hide his face. This is the legend, thought Isarel, the sheer awe of it gripping his mind. This is the rebel and the lover and the scholar who was cast out by the jealous Elders of the Temple, who was disgraced and exiled, and finally cursed with immortality by his own hand.

He quickened the music almost imperceptibly, and Ahasuerus lifted his head and saw Moira.

Moira was still frightened, but when Ahasuerus appeared she felt a bolt of exhilaration almost instantly followed by a rush of pity so overwhelming and so dizzying that she had to put out a hand to the smooth balustrade to stop herself from falling.

Ahasuerus was not tall and forbidding which was how Moira had been thinking of him; he was bent and hunched over, and most piteous of all, he was cowering. Isarel was nearly level with him now, and the music was going on and on – beautiful, heart-breaking music that you would follow into hell if only it would never stop – and Ahasuerus was cringing, flinging up his hands in the gesture that Moira remembered from the crypt. The immense compassion began to dissolve and flood her whole being, and she thought: whatever he is, whatever he's been, he's tormented and wracked with desolation . . .

Forced to walk the world to the music's command.

It was then that he saw her, and a stillness came over him. Moira saw the glint of his eyes within the hood and froze in panic.

She was dimly aware of shouts down in the hall and of doors banging and people running – Serse's People giving the alarm! – but she had eyes and mind for nothing but Ahasuerus. He was coming towards her, the dark cloak billowing. She thought Isarel was still playing, but she was no longer sure.

Ahasuerus reached out to her and there was such entreaty in the gesture that Moira felt as if she had been struck. Without having the least notion she was going to do it, she went forward into his arms and felt them fold about her.

He held her to him at once, bending his head, and there was the feeling of warm, strong masculinity and of gentle strength. Moira gasped and heard him speak in a struggling, blurred whisper:

'Susannah . . .'

Limpid eyes – cool grey, intelligent eyes – were looking at her through the eye-slits of the mask and for a moment, nothing existed in the world save the steady regard of those beautiful clear eyes.

Ahasuerus's arms tightened and he lifted her bodily, and then went with his terrible lurching gait back down the narrow, shadowy corridor.

The minute Ahasuerus scooped up Moira, Isarel had stopped playing, even though his mind had reared up angrily. You fool! This is precisely what you wanted! Ahasuerus lured by red hair once more! Get after him and get Moira before you're caught!

The people in the hall were already starting towards them – too late, we're discovered, thought Isarel angrily.

He looked down at them, and as he did so, the immense oak doors they had entered by were flung open and a thin-faced, cold-eyed man stood framed there.

Vogel! thought Isarel, and even at such a minute, even with frantic danger closing in, he was aware of black bitter fury against the descendant of the man who brought Jude to that sordid shameful death.

Vogel did not hesitate. He ran across the hall, ignoring the clustering Serse People, and started to mount the stair.

In his right hand he held a gun, and as Isarel turned to go deeper into the castle after Ahasuerus and Moira, he fired.

In the shadow-wreathed mind of the creature who had once arrogantly faced the Temple Elders in first century Jerusalem; who had bargained with Cosimo Amati for a night with his lady, and who had contemptuously dragged a Tudor King from Catherine Howard's bed, comprehension burned as strongly as ever it had done.

He had no idea of where or when this cold harsh age was, but among all the selfish-eyed, greedy-handed people, only one thing mattered.

Susannah.

Susannah, her red hair streaming, her eyes tilted at the outer corners, her clothes as strange as everything else here, but unmistakably and blessedly Susannah. Ahasuerus forgot the huge ugly castle, he forgot the shouting people, and stared at the slight figure in front of him, his heart and his mind splintering with pain and joy and sheer awe. Walking towards him, exactly as she had done all those weary centuries ago. In his arms again, as she had always promised him she would be.

The coldest of all the cold ones, the man who was called *Vogel* – the one who had a warped, blurred vision of Susannah's music – was coming towards them, and in his hand was the thick, squat instrument that Ahasuerus recognised as being a weapon. He did not stop to think: he pulled Susannah against him and so achingly sweet was it to hold her again, that for a few moments the harsh unknown world grew dim and he was once again in the Temple with Susannah coming through the little secret door.

He turned away from the shouting people and the cold evil-eyed *Vogel*, and went through the old castle, pausing at the far end of the corridor. Where to hide? Where to take Susannah to be safe?

And then he remembered the dark underground place where *Vogel* had locked him with the other prisoner, and he remembered that the heavy doors could be opened from without.

The instant that Moira had heard Ahasuerus say '*Susannah!*' she stopped being frightened, and the minute she looked into the clear grey eyes, a jolt of violent emotion shook her, and kaleidoscopic images tumbled across her inner vision, so brief that she could not be sure she had really seen them, but so vivid that they seared into her mind, like the blinding dazzle of the sun.

A tormented figure nailed to the cross, engulfed in flames and bleeding into the jagged red skies above, the pale smooth skin lacerated and torn to bloodied tatters . . . An agony so great it splintered your mind, and then the dreadful desolation of an underground cavern, lit to macabre life by dozens of flaring torches, peopled with black-clad monks, bending over a stone tomb, their faces avid and gloating in the flickering torchlight . . .

Because the walls of Time are as thin as paper, and if you can control the music you can control Time . . .

Control Time. Because Time's walls are as thin as

paper . . . She had never heard the words before, and no one had spoken them aloud. But if they're right, thought Moira, have I stepped through Time to him, or has he stepped through to me?

They were crossing the castle quadrangle; Ahasuerus was heading for an old, ivy-covered wall, and there was a minute when Moira thought he was about to walk into it. And then she saw that the thick mats of ivy concealed a low arch with an iron gate, and that the gate was open and beyond it was a narrow passage, like a covered walkway. Ahasuerus pulled the ivy aside impatiently and went unhesitatingly through the iron gate.

It was like plunging into a dim underground world. It was not absolutely black in here but it was dark and narrow and rather unpleasant, and there was a dank smell of wet earth and moss. But Moira, recovering her senses a bit by this time, thought they must be in-between an ancient inner defence wall and the new bastion she and Isarel had seen from outside. Whoever lived here wanted to keep Eisenach very safe indeed from the prying world, and whoever that someone was had constructed a second, parallel rampart to encircle the original one. Even in here, it was possible to tell that the new wall was very thick, very dense stone.

Whoever had built the second wall and created this half-secret passageway, had not joined the two walls at the top; Moira glanced up and felt a chill. Far above, meshing forbiddingly against the sky, were thick close coils of black spiked wire. If you were trapped in here, you might just about manage to climb up, making use of the crumbling patches of brick for footholes. It would take a very long time because both walls must be twenty feet high, but if you were agile and if you were driven by fear, you could do it. Yet it would avail you nothing, because you would be torn to bloody tatters trying to get through the barbed wire.

And I'm trapped in here with the Devil's Piper . . .

And then there was a stronger ingress of light, and the passage widened. On the right-hand side – the outer wall side? – Yes! – was another of the thick iron-sheeted gates. Beyond the gate was merely another of the walled tunnels, at right-angles to the one they had just come through. But at the far end were huge double doors, fitted with immense steel bolts. And the doors were open. Ahasuerus sent a quick look behind him, and then went through.

It was much darker beyond the doors and there was the abrupt, unpleasant sensation of burrowing into a subterranean underworld. Fear scudded across Moira's skin and her heart began to pound.

Ahasuerus set Moira down and stood back to watch her, his head tilted as if trying to hear her thoughts. In the thick shadows it was impossible to do more than make out the remarkable eyes deep within the hood.

From somewhere outside, Moira could hear the sounds of angry shouts and running feet, and the abrupt shocking explosion of gunshots, but it was like hearing it from a huge distance, or from under water. She could not take her eyes from Ahasuerus, and she felt as if she was falling down fathoms into a shadowy underworld, where there were strange eddies and currents, and where Time's walls could tear, and where there was no one and nothing in the world save the creature in here with her.

'*Susannah*—' It came again, filled with such love and such aching desolation that Moira forgot about this being the ancient creature of the legends: the fearsome undead High Priest, and reached up with both her hands to push back the hood. There was a moment when she felt the silky spill of black hair, and then he gave a low groan, as if he had been pushed beyond the last barrier of endurance, and cupped her face in his hands – pitiful burned hands!

485

thought Moira, helplessly – and drew her to him.

There was the confused jumble of sensations again: there was the sudden surge of longing and aching bitter-sweet regret – I was born too late or he too early! – and his arms went around her, and he was warm and masculine and there was the faint drift of something that reminded her of lavender or dried rose petals, or— Oh, how stupid of me, thought Moira, hazily; it's the scent of memories unfolding. Yes, but are they his memories, or mine . . .? Time's walls tearing . . . I believe I can almost hear it happening. Like old, old silk fraying, like cobwebs dissolving, like slicing through thin pure Spring water . . . But we missed each other in Time, my dear lost love . . .

Her heart was racing and her senses were spinning dizzily but her hands were perfectly steady as she reached for the concealing mask.

The first bullet missed Isarel by several feet and buried itself in the wall, but as he reached the top of the stair, Vogel fired again, this time only missing him by inches.

He went through the old castle by a blend of instinct and race-memory. Jude's castle . . . Ahasuerus had come in this direction, and although Isarel had no idea of whether he was on Ahasuerus's heels, he ran unerringly through the dark intersecting corridors and the galleried landings that Jude would certainly have known, several times dodging into the shelter of a shadowy stair or a deep alcove to miss Vogel and his followers as they pounded after him. I'm shaking them off, he thought with sudden hope. But I've no idea where I am really. Unless I've fallen through into Jude's time.

He half fell down a narrow winding side stair that debouched on to a small inner courtyard. Was this the western boundary of the castle? And some kind of half-hidden gate half buried in the wall where the ivy had been pulled aside? Is that the way they came? Isarel glanced about him, but there was no sign of Ahasuerus. Yet the ivy looked as if it had only just been torn back. Into the wall, then.

The green shadows closed about him at once, and he went forward cautiously, forcing his eyes to adjust to the dimness. The thought that he might be going into a trap was strongly in his mind, but it looked as if Ahasuerus might have come this way, and Ahasuerus had Moira. Isarel set his teeth and plunged forward. There was barely four feet of width between the two walls, and if Vogel followed and fired again, it would be impossible to dodge the bullets.

He reached the immense iron doors, and stopped short, eyeing them warily. Half-open doors. And unless he had completely lost his sense of direction they went straight into the hill on the castle's western side. Why would anyone cut doors into a hill, for heaven's sake? Isarel glanced helplessly behind him, and then took a deep breath and plunged forward. He was still fearful of a trap, but he would far rather pit his strength and whatever wits he had left against an undead High Priest from the past, than face a loaded revolver. Especially when the undead High Priest had got Moira.

Once through the doors, he caught a glimpse of light up ahead, and the sound of voices. As he moved towards them, there came from outside the pounding of feet in the walled passage and a scuffling. Isarel swung round – Vogel? – and heard with cold horror a huge hollow clanging reverberating through the tunnel, shaking the ground and dislodging little flurries of earth from the sides and the ceiling.

He stood very still, his eyes raking the darkness. That's

it then. Vogel and his minions have shut me in. Then it's onwards and upwards. No it isn't, it's onwards and downwards. I'll just hope that one of those voices is Moira and that the other is Ciaran. I don't want it to be Ciaran, because I'd rather think of him somewhere outside, still free. But he'd be an ally.

He went towards the voices, and the feeling that he had had earlier of walking farther and farther outside of Time returned. I'm leaving Time behind, he thought. I'm entering into something so drenched in agony and despair and desolate torment that it's scarcely bearable. If Eisenach has any ghosts, they don't walk in the castle: they're down here. God, this is a terrible place.

His eyes were still adjusting to the dimness, but he could see a door ahead, half open into a long brick-lined room. There was the glint of red hair, and Isarel felt the relief wash over him. Moira. Yes, but where's Ahasuerus? Isarel walked into the room, and stood for a moment, blinking.

He saw Ciaran with huge thankfulness mixed with bitterness – so Vogel got him, did he? – and he saw that with Ciaran was a young woman with straight black hair and smudges of exhaustion under her eyes. Kate Kendal, thought Isarel. Ciaran's lady, the one we've come half across Europe to find. She's not quite what I thought she'd be. But there's no sign of Ahasuerus. Then it's the four of us and the ghosts.

The ghosts . . .

Standing at the centre of the room, watching Isarel, was a thin-faced man with the translucent pallor of extreme age and smouldering dark eyes and long sensitive hands. As Isarel stared at him, the present began to dislocate again and to fuse with the past; the room started spinning so that he had to put out a hand to the wall to stop himself from falling. Outside of Time . . .

'Isarel,' said the old man, and his voice was like deep soft velvet. There was a pause, and then, 'Come inside and join our captivity,' said Jude.

Chapter Forty-Four

The room had stopped spinning at last, and Isarel was sitting on the floor along with the other three, his back against the brick wall. Jude was still standing at the centre. Position of authority, thought Isarel. I bet it's deliberate, as well. Good for him; I don't think I could stand up if my life depended on it.

There was still a strong feeling of distortion and he could not get a proper grasp on reality. He could pin down individual thoughts: important things like escaping and Moira and Ahasuerus – God yes, where is Ahasuerus? – but he could not make them link up in his mind.

He could only think that here in front of him was the legend. He didn't die, thought Isarel. All those years, all those stories . . . I can't take my eyes off him; I don't think any of us can. He glanced at Moira and saw that she was curled up in one corner, her chin resting on her bent knees, her hair tumbling about her shoulders. But she was not looking at Jude, she was looking at Isarel and this brought a faint, far-off comfort. In a minute his thoughts would start to mesh properly again.

For what seemed to be a very long time no one spoke, and when the silence was finally broken, Isarel heard with a shock that it was his own voice.

'You're alive,' he said. 'You didn't die at Nuremberg.'

And thought, Well, at least I can string a cogent sentence together.

'The Nuremberg Trial was a fake,' said Jude. 'I was never there.'

'You've been here all along? All these years—'

'Yes.'

'Vogel's prisoner,' said Isarel, and there was a long pause before Jude answered.

But he said, 'Yes. I have been Vogel's prisoner – the first Vogel, Karl, then later his son and now his grandson, Conrad. I have been their prisoner ever since the Nazis found out what I was doing.' He stopped, and Isarel thought: his voice is like no voice I ever heard. It's like deep blue midnight. Like vintage red wine or a cat's fur.

He asked, 'What you were doing . . .?' and Jude said,

'I wasn't working for the Nazis. I was working against them.'

It was as vivid as if it had been yesterday. All those years, all the decades inside Eisenach, a solitary castle prisoner, rather as Rudolf Hess had been a solitary prisoner inside Spandau. Karl Vogel and his family had allowed Jude to work and to compose, because they had never ceased to covet the *Chant*, and although the captivity had been absolute, it had been a silken one.

But it was still too easy to look back across the loop of time, to see the years melt and blur, until he might have been in Auschwitz with the sounds of mass murder echoing about the bare wooden concert hut.

When he had stopped being sick in the washbasin in the corner of his room in the officers' quarters, he lay on the narrow bed, drinking neat whiskey from the bottle. The fiery spirit burned his throat and scalded his stomach but it did not erase the nightmare images printed on his brain.

It was nearly midnight when Otto Burkhardt knocked on the door and by then Jude was so drunk that he could hardly stand up.

'What do you want?'

Burkhardt opened the door and stood just inside the door, looking down. Jude's hair was tumbling over his forehead, he had discarded his evening tie and his shirt was unbuttoned at the neck. He stayed where he was, supine on the bed, the whiskey bottle held loosely in one hand. It was the height of discourtesy, but he was too drunk to care about being courteous to this animal.

Burkhardt regarded him with the insinuating smile that Jude found so repulsive. 'I have come to convey to you the thanks of my masters, Herr Weissman,' he said. 'Your music made for a smoother operation than usual. A total of eight hundred—'

Eight hundred lambs to the slaughter. Suffocated and then shovelled into ovens and burned to charred anonymity.

'I have brought for you a gesture of our appreciation,' said Burkhardt and stepped back, so that Jude could see the young female Nazi officer who stood at his side. 'A token of gratitude from my masters for your performance.'

'Performance?' The word came out slurred but not as slurred as it might have been.

The smile deepened. 'The music,' said Burkhardt softly. 'We are immensely grateful to you, Herr Weissman.' He glanced at the girl. 'I find,' he said in a different tone, 'that executions often have an aphrodisiacal effect. And so—'

Jude looked at the girl and felt a sudden crude lust, born not of desire or simple sexual hunger, but of anger and hatred. He set down the half-empty whiskey bottle, and sat up, looking at the girl. A Nazi. It would be a small revenge, but—

He nodded dismissal to Burkhardt and pulled the girl inside, locking the door. She was thin and blonde, and she had cold, greedy eyes. She stood before him, her eyes raking his body, and then said softly, 'Anything you wish, Herr Weissman. I will do anything you wish.'

Jude, his lips set in a hard cold line, said, 'Will you indeed, my dear?'

A thin grey dawn was breaking outside when the girl finally stumbled from his bed. Jude, torn between fierce exultation and bitter self-disgust, waited until she had gone and then slid from under the sheets, and pulled on trousers and a thick dark sweater. He dashed cold water on to his face, and padded cautiously outside, scanning the camp for sentries.

A sprinkling of coarse ash covered the roof of the death houses, and a heavy, fat-laden scent clung to the air. Jude glanced at the narrow brick chimneys.

It was easier than he had expected to dodge the guards, and at this hour there were only a couple of token patrols. They marched exactly in step, and Jude, keeping in the shadows of the serried rows of barracks, timed the steps absently. If you were writing music to reflect this, it would be thin and metallic. Lots of tympani, maybe even one of those small hand drums called a timbrel. Very, very staccato. Concentrate, Jude. He crossed the deserted compound to the nearest of the prisoners' huts.

He had not dared to hope he would be able to get inside, but he saw at once that several of the huts had doors that rolled down from the roof and secured into the ground with bolts, rather like a huge roll-top desk. He crossed swiftly to the nearest, and bent to lift the bolts, cautiously pushing the steel shutter up until a band of blackness showed at the bottom. Enough to squeeze through but not enough to be noticed.

He crawled underneath, making as little sound as possible, and once on the other side, stood up, trying to get his bearings. The first thing to assail his senses was the smell: human sweat and unwashed human flesh and hair, and above it all, so strong that it was like a solid wall, the warm, fetid stench of human excrement. He stayed absolutely still, aware that there were dozens of people in here, but unable to see them and waiting for his eyes to adjust to the light.

And then out of the blackness in front of him, a voice said, 'There's somebody in here with us.'

It was unexpectedly eerie to hear that whispery voice coming out of the dark, but Jude stayed where he was, waiting and listening, trying to assess what was in here. After a moment, a second voice said, 'You're right. Somebody's crept in. Somebody's crept in from outside and is hiding in here listening to us.'

'A spy,' said another voice. 'A spy standing inside the door listening to us.'

Jude, trying to make out the direction of the voices, still trying to penetrate the dimness, said clearly, 'I'm not a spy. I want to talk to you. If you have any way of making a light, please will you do so.' There was a pause, and then the scrape of a tinder box. Three or four tiny candle flames burned up. Half a dozen or so faces swam through the darkness, lit from below to hollow disembodied life.

'It's the composer,' hissed the voice who had spoken first of all. 'The one who played earlier today.'

'The one who helped to send a batch of prisoners to the chambers.'

'He's one of Burkhardt's jackals.'

'Or one of Vogel's.'

'I'm not a spy,' said Jude again. 'Won't you believe that?'

'You're with the Gestapo.'

'We know all about you.'

Their voices were harsh with anger and bitterness and Jude took a grip on his senses. Speaking clearly and firmly, he said, 'Listen to me, please. I'm a Jew, like all of you.'

'If you're a Jew, you're a traitor,' said the one who had called for the candle to be lit. 'You're a renegade.'

'Here to spy out our secrets and go running to the Gestapo.'

'We know about spies and traitors in here.'

Jude said very clearly, '*Shema Y'Isroel, Adonai Elohaynu, Adonai Echod*—'

There was an abrupt silence, and then, the one who seemed to be the leader said, 'Traitors have quoted the Holy Word before. It means nothing.'

'I'm not a traitor,' said Jude. 'And I'm not here to spy on you. I'm here to help you escape.'

The flickering candlelight burned up more brightly then, showing the inside of the long hut, and Jude felt his senses reel because this was the worst thing yet.

Directly in front of him, perhaps two feet away from the roll-down corrugated doors, was a wall of steel and mesh extending out of the concrete floor and stretching up into the iron roof above. Thick bars were interleaved with spiked wire, and at the centre a tiny door had been cut, barely three feet in height, barely two feet across. It was impossible to avoid the impression of a cage with a hinged flap for a door.

But it's a cage for humans, thought Jude, appalled. The flap is for them to crawl in and out.

The prisoners were clustered at the bars, watching him, and at first sight there seemed to be dozens: thin, ravaged-eyed creatures, scantily clad in tattered shirts and trousers. There were no seats although a few bundles of rags had been arranged near the wall.

At the far end was a circular, wooden-sided barrel, about three feet high. A lid had been drawn across it, but even at this distance the stench of urine and faeces was overwhelming, and even in the wavering light of the thin dripping candles, it was possible to see where runnels of fluid trickled out between the seams.

At the other side of the hut, as far from the dreadful wooden barrel as possible, was a squat iron stove: a metal cup stood on it as if some liquid was being warmed, and several of the prisoners were huddled round it, their skeletal hands held out to it. Jude, trying to take everything in, had the fleeting impression of some kind of organised grouping, as if turns were taken to stand at the stove for a few minutes of warmth or a sip of the fluid.

A slow, deep anger began to burn, and he went as near to the terrible cage as he could, and said, 'I'm going to free you.'

'All of us?' said the leader jeeringly.

'No. But as many of you as I can.'

They stared at him, and without warning, the painful light of hope began to dawn in their eyes.

The spark of anger that had been lit in the makeshift concert hall at Auschwitz – the anger that was to stay with him through the years ahead – burned up into a steady strong flame.

He thought, afterwards, that at times it was only that pure clear flame of anger that kept him going. Certainly it spurred him on.

He had traded on the reputation he had already earned with the *Piper* suite, and it had stood him in good stead in those early days in Poland and Eastern Germany.

He maintained a cold arrogance towards Vogel and Burkhardt, and at intervals he made imperious demands. My orchestra has lost two violinists, a cellist; if you want me to go on playing for you, you must let me replace them with people of my choosing. I know of a very good violinist incarcerated inside Dachau . . . or Buchenwald . . . Once brought out, the musicians could be provided with papers and sent to safety in Switzerland or England and Canada. It was not a ploy that could be used many times, but it worked for a while.

Each time he went into the camps he had found a way to take or deliver notes between huts, even once to smuggle in small radio parts for the secret listening posts in the camps. There were knives for digging crude tunnels beneath the camp latrines, there were the locations of small partisan groups outside who could provide fake papers and false identities or simply shelter for a few nights. Every scrap of information was absorbed into the network, and Jude seldom knew how effective his contributions were. The network itself was pitifully ragged; the cobweb strands of plots often tangled with other cobweb strands, rendering weeks or months of dangerous intrigue worthless. How it did not unravel altogether Jude never knew, but incredibly it did not. Incredibly, between prayer and determination and courage of an extraordinary degree, it struggled on, even though its people had to move in extreme secrecy; even though to be caught meant death and, before death, brutal questioning. Reveal the names of your collaborators or we will tighten the thumbscrews, we will winch the pinions of the rack, we will operate the device that will mangle your hands and feet . . .

All of these or any single part of them were enough to stamp out the frail shoots of rebellion, but they did not.

Insofar as the Jewish rebels could risk a rallying cry, they risked one: *'Dahm Y'Israel Nokeam'* – 'The blood of Israel will take vengeance.' Later the slogan was abbreviated, using the first letter of each word, the Hebrew letters: *daled, yod, nun*, which spelled out another Hebrew word: DIN, meaning judgement.

The careful underground planning went on, and Jude, peddling his music, entering the camps wearing the falsest of all false guises went on with it. To most people by now he was a Nazi collaborator, one of Himmler's jackals, to be hated and feared. It was not unknown for his recitals to be greeted with sullen silence, or with jeers and cries of 'Traitor'.

He never quite despaired; he thought he never would despair because the music would always save him – Angelika von Drumm had not been so very wide of the mark when she had said if he had a god, that god was music – but at times despair came agonisingly close and at times he almost gave up. So easy to leave them to it; so easy to argue that it was not his fight and it was not his war, and the few prisoners he was smuggling out and the thin scraps of information he was carrying to and fro were so infinitesimal that they could scarcely count. So seductively easy to go back to Mallow where the pouring dusk was smudged with violet and indigo, and where the air was scented with woodsmoke. And where Lucy would be waiting, seated in the jutting bow window perhaps with the child, perhaps just reading or sewing, her hair turned to the colour of new-run honey by the glow from the lamps burning in the windows . . .

But he never did go back, and eventually, after the years of struggle and danger and intrigue, it was too late.

Chapter Forty-Five

'The little I did was never enough,' said Jude, looking at Isarel. 'It was nothing compared to the millions who died.'

Isarel was aware that his mind was starting to work properly again. He still could not concentrate on the menace in the dark tunnels beyond this room, but he knew the difference between the past and the present once more. He sat up a bit straighter, but it was Kate who spoke next.

'You used the music,' she said, and Jude looked across at her.

'I used the music,' he said. 'But not in the way the Nazis expected. Vogel and his people wanted the *Black Chant* very much, they believed it would give them tremendous power and I believed it as well. They wanted the Jews subdued – mesmerised – so that they could slaughter them wholesale and as well as that they wanted it for Hitler's mad fantasies.' He paused, and then said, 'By then Hitler was already enamoured with his insane dream of creating a new Aryan Race, and to place such power in such hands was unthinkable.' He spread his hands, and Isarel was abruptly reminded of his ancestry. 'And so I removed the heart from the *Piper* suite after the Eisenach concert, and then stitched the music up so that it wouldn't show.'

'You – could do that?'

'Of course I could do it,' said Jude, and for the first time, the arrogance was there.

'You went into the death camps and gave recitals,' said Kate, staring at him.

'Yes. It was the only way I could get inside.'

'That's – absolutely remarkable.'

'Not so very remarkable as all that,' said Jude. 'Mahler's niece, Alma Rosé, led an entire orchestra while she was a prisoner inside Auschwitz. And Furtwangler used his position as leader of the Berlin Philharmonic to smuggle Jewish musicians out of Germany. It was not generally known at the time, but he did it. I continued playing what Vogel believed to be the *Black Chant* in the death camps but it was no longer the *Chant* at all, of course.'

Ciaran said thoughtfully, 'You risked a very great deal.'

'I expect I did,' agreed Jude, sounding amused. 'There was no heroism, you understand, no bravery. It was little better than romantical idealism. Perhaps it was also vanity and arrogance. I believed I could save the world.'

Ciaran said, 'There's nothing wrong with idealism when it brings help and hope. There's nothing wrong with romanticism either. You must have an extraordinary story to tell.'

'So,' said Jude politely, 'must you. But we shall none of us have any kind of story to tell if we don't think about getting out of here.'

'And,' Isarel pointed out, 'the most immediate thing to think about is Ahasuerus.' He heard with relief that his voice was sounding very nearly normal. 'Moira, what happened to Ahasuerus when he brought you in here?' He indicated the half-open door leading to the tunnels. 'Where did he go?'

Moira took a minute to reply. Ridiculous to feel this strong sense of protectiveness, but in those agonisingly brief minutes in the tunnel something had been forged that she would not forget. Even the terrible burned face beneath

500

the mask had not had the power to make her flinch.

Because you remember me as I once was, Susannah . . .

His burned maimed mouth had twisted in the painful travesty of a smile, and Moira had managed to smile back, even though tears were spilling from her eyes and there was a hard sick lump of misery in her throat.

Because he was born too early and I was born too late and there is no way of crossing the huge gulf now . . .

There had been a sudden hard embrace and another of those brief flashes of memory – a young man with pale translucent skin and features purer and clearer than you could believe possible, and sensitive fastidious lips that could lift in mischievous passion – and then he had gone. But the glimpse had printed itself on her mind, and she thought it would always be there. Something to keep folded away for ever and never to share.

She looked at the others and said, 'Ahasuerus simply brought me here, and I don't know where he went. I couldn't see. He might have gone back to the castle—'

'Or he might be prowling out there in the tunnels,' said Isarel, glancing at Moira, and then away. Kate shivered and pulled Ciaran's coat more closely about her.

Moira said carefully, 'I don't actually think that Ahasuerus means any of us any harm.'

'I wouldn't bet the ranch on it,' said Isarel caustically. 'I wouldn't place any reliance on what Vogel might do, either.'

'Nor,' said Jude dryly, 'would I. You four must get out at once.'

'How?' Kate leaned forward and Jude regarded her and smiled. Isarel saw Kate blink and then return the smile, and thought: well, I was right about one thing at any rate: he's a killer with women. I can't begin to work out how old he'll

501

be – although he can't be less than eighty – and Kate's probably thirty-two or -three. But she's looking at him as if she'll be his slave for life. I expect I'm doing the same. I can't take my eyes off him – I don't want to take my eyes off him. I think he's a sorcerer or a hypnotist or something. And I still don't know if we can trust him, because for all we know he's working with Vogel.

Ciaran said, 'There isn't any way out except for the doors, surely?'

'There can't be,' said Kate. 'I explored the whole place when Vogel locked me in. I'm sure I didn't miss anything. And we heard the doors closing—'

'Vogel closed them, of course,' said Moira, and she, too, regarded Jude intently. Like acolytes hanging on to the every utterance of the Messiah, thought Isarel. If I'm not careful, I'll be falling for it as well.

Jude said, 'Yes, Vogel lured us all in here very nicely.'

'Including you?' Isarel heard the note of suspicion in his voice, but he couldn't help it. I don't trust him. I don't dare trust him. 'Why did Vogel put you in here?' he said sharply, and Jude turned his head.

'So that I should be out of the way for the concert. I've had a silken prison, Isarel, and I've had almost every comfort and luxury I could wish for, but it's been a prison for all that.'

Isarel said, 'You never tried to escape?' and there was a sudden silence.

'You don't trust me, do you?' said Jude, at length.

'Not entirely. I certainly don't believe that someone with your guts submitted to being a captive for so long without trying to get out,' said Isarel.

'How do you know I didn't? How do you know I didn't try a number of times and failed?'

502

'You didn't though, did you?' said Isarel, meeting the dark eyes.

'No.'

'Why not?'

Jude hesitated and then said, 'We're wasting time we haven't got. If you don't get out soon you may find you're Vogel's prisoners to a far more helpless extent than this.'

'Then,' said Kate, 'where is your way out? And how do we know we can believe you?' Isarel caught the note of aggression and understood that Kate also was distrustful of Jude, and that she was angry at herself for having succumbed to his charm earlier. The only one of us who does trust him is Moira, he thought. And that's very odd indeed.

'My dears,' said Jude mockingly, 'fifty years ago I was aware of almost every escape route out of almost every Nazi death camp. I may have been ignorant of one or two, but I certainly wouldn't have been ignorant of the one on the doorstep of my own prison.' He indicated the half-open door leading to the crematorium.

'The escape is in the one place that the Nazis never thought to look,' said Jude.

'Inside the ovens.'

'The prisoners built it over a long and tortuous period,' he said. 'They hid inside the ovens between mass burnings, and while the ovens stayed cool enough, they broke through the brickwork. They dug outwards using their bare hands and any scraps of instruments that could be smuggled in. The hole is very small but it joins up with the chimney flue and once in there, it's possible to climb up and come out on to the hillside beyond the castle boundary.' He looked at them. 'I'm simplifying what was a very complex operation, of course – they had to insulate the inner wall from the

503

tremendous heat when the furnaces were fired and they had to shore up the space beyond the oven wall and a dozen other things. But that was the principle.'

'That's— incredible,' said Ciaran, staring at him, and Jude again gave the shrug that Isarel suspected was partly assumed.

'There were far more incredible escape stories than that. The prisoners here worked at night, with only a single lookout to keep watch,' he said. 'Eisenach wasn't an especially large camp, and although it was sentried, it wasn't as heavily sentried as Auschwitz or Belsen or Dachau.' As he spoke, Ciaran was crossing to push open the door to the crematorium, and Isarel saw for the first time the gaping ovens. Horror prickled his skin and almost automatically he reached for Moira, pulling her against him. She felt light and fragile and unexpectedly familiar.

'The opening is at the very back of the largest oven,' said Jude. 'Near the floor. It will be difficult and I'm afraid it will be unpleasant, but if you can get through, you should be able to get to safety.'

Isarel started to say, 'What about—' and then stopped as they heard a sound from beyond the underground rooms.

Ciaran said, 'Ahasuerus—?' and then stopped, because it was certainly not Ahasuerus.

Kate said, 'It sounds like – car engines being revved. Several of them, very close to us.'

'It is car engines,' said Jude, his eyes on the half-open door. 'And can you hear the other sound above it?'

'A thin hissing,' said Isarel after a moment. He looked at Jude. 'It's coming from the outer room,' he said and a terrible comprehension began to unfold.

Jude said, 'That is a sound I have not heard for fifty years, and it's a sound I hoped never to hear again.' He looked at them. 'The gas machines have long since fallen into disuse, but unless I'm mistaken, Vogel has connected car exhaust pipes to the vents. He's pumping in pure carbon monoxide.'

Isarel said, 'But that means—'

'That means that however crude and however makeshift, Vogel is resurrecting the gas chambers, and that you probably have no more than thirty minutes to live.'

Isarel and Ciaran moved as one, slamming shut the chamber doors.

'Will it seal us from the gas?' said Moira, her eyes on the door.

'I've no idea,' said Jude.

He glanced at Isarel, who answered, 'It's not very likely, is it? Whatever seals there were will have disintegrated years ago. Vogel's probably used rubber tubing to run from the exhausts to the vents themselves, and it's not foolproof, but it's pretty damn close. We haven't got any time to waste.' He moved to the largest of the yawning ovens, repressing a shudder. Difficult and unpleasant, Jude had said. 'It ought to be ladies first, but in case we meet anything unexpected, Ciaran or I had better lead the way.'

'You lead,' said Ciaran, at once. 'You're thinner, and it's fifty years since this thing was used. You might have to force a way through—' He glanced at Jude, who said,

'The hatch is very small. The prisoners were severely under-nourished and emaciated. But I think you will manage it. If Isarel goes first, Moira and Kate can follow, and Ciaran can bring up the rear.'

Isarel looked at him. 'And you?'

Again the characteristic spreading of hands. 'I must stay.'

'Why?'

Jude glanced uneasily to the outer chamber. The hissing of the fumes was faint, but it was discernible. Thirty minutes . . . And several of those minutes had already gone. 'There's no time to explain,' he said.

'Explain,' said Isarel angrily, and Jude made an abrupt gesture uncannily like Isarel's own. Speaking rapidly, he said, 'It took the Nazis a long time to realise what I was doing, and when eventually they did discover it, they were in an awkward position. They couldn't kill me because they still wanted the *Chant*, but they couldn't let me remain free either. And towards the end of Nineteen Forty Four, Karl Vogel and his creatures took me to Auschwitz.'

The savagery in his voice and in his eyes as he said *creatures* was so brutal that Isarel stared at him and felt something painful close about his heart. *This* is what I was waiting for. This is the real Jude; the angry, idealistic young man who fought Hitler's Third Reich and stormed Nazi strongholds and carried prisoners out under their noses. This is what I wanted to feel. I wanted a hero; it looks as if I've got one.

'In Auschwitz, they tortured me,' said Jude. 'They wanted the original music of course, but more than that they wanted the details about the escape network – about what was called *DIN*. I managed – somehow – to keep silent. But inside Auschwitz there is a device called the boot,' he said. 'Not a new device, the Tudors knew about it, and the Nazis never disdained to steal ideas. It's a mechanism that crushes bones and tendons and muscles beyond repair.' He stopped, and for the first time emotion showed in his dark eyes.

Isarel said in a whisper, 'They crippled you. They crushed your feet. Dear God, that's why you could never escape.'

'Yes.' Jude glanced at Moira, and unexpectedly he

506

smiled. 'I think you had already guessed,' he said.

'Not entirely. Perhaps a bit.'

Kate, who had been staring in horror, said, 'They left you the ability to create music, though.'

'Oh yes. You find that surprising?'

'Cold and calculating,' said Kate, and Isarel saw her shiver. 'Vogel and his people still wanted you to work for them, didn't they?'

'Yes. They left my hands and my mind whole,' said Jude. 'And for that I have never ceased to thank God, because without music – without the ability to compose – I should not have survived their imprisonment.' A sudden reminiscent grin lifted his lips, and he said, 'A very remarkable lady once said that music was my only real god – forgive me, Ciaran – and I was to prove her right.'

Isarel, mindful of the seeping, choking danger, but still unable to stop looking at Jude, said, 'You continued to compose? Inside Eisenach?'

'Certainly. I demanded – and got – a Bluthner. I demanded gramophones and recording machines. The compositions are all in my turret rooms. Symphonies, concertos, two operas, even some jazz, although that is perhaps not— Were you thinking of your inheritance?' he asked politely.

'God, no—' Isarel broke off and said angrily, 'We'll manage a way to take you out with us.'

'You will not. I should be the most appalling handicap and you would never get out. You must go without me.'

'I can't leave you here— I *can't*—'

Jude said impatiently, 'Isarel, for the last fifty years, I have not been able to do more than drag myself across the room. You have to leave me behind.' The sudden mocking smile showed. 'In all of the best escape stories, the weakest gets ditched,' said Jude. 'Ditch me.'

'But all those years—' Isarel was terribly aware of the minutes running out, and of a thickening staleness already gathering, but he said, 'All those nights when I was aware of your presence—'

'Yes. I was there. I don't understand it any more than you do, but it doesn't matter. We both know and we both understand, and nothing more needs to be said between us.' He looked at Isarel, and finally and at last, Isarel moved to him. There was the brief feel of Jude's arms about him, hard, strong, and then Isarel stepped back, and grasping the edges of the terrible oven with both hands, hauled himself inside.

Chapter Forty-Six

The interior of the oven was an appalling place: dark, meaty-smelling and stifling. The floor was level with the opening, and although this was apparently the largest of the four, it was still barely more than five feet high so that none of them could quite straighten up. As Isarel went deeper in, the rancid blackness closed over him and he was aware, as Kate had been, of the lingering agonies pressing in on all sides.

The other three had scrambled after him, and their presence was enormously comforting. But Isarel's mind was still filled with Jude, and he was agonisingly aware that they had left him alone in the brick chamber. I've left him alone with the Devil's Piper and with the ghosts of thousands of butchered men and women, he thought. And with death trickling in and filling up the room . . . Yes, but if we're quick, we can get to the outer doors and unbolt them. Thirty minutes, he said. It's probably twenty now.

From behind him, Ciaran said, 'Mother of God, it's as black as the devil's forehead in here. Isarel, take my torch and switch it on, till we see where we're going.' His voice was deliberately down-to-earth, but tiny echoes bounced whisperingly off the sides.

'And,' said Moira, 'the better we can see, the quicker we can be.'

'It's all very well to shout instructions from the back,

but it's damned difficult to do anything in here,' said Isarel, and was thankful to hear that his voice held the old sarcastic edge. He flicked the torch switch and at once wished he had not done so, because the thin beam of light showed up the black cinders crusting the underside and the scattered piles of charred bones, some still lying in the faint but discernible outlines of human shapes. They disturbed flurries of evil-smelling ash as they went forward and felt it shower into their hair. Kate and Moira flinched and shuddered and once Moira put up her hand to wipe her eyes.

'Keep your heads down,' said Isarel, glancing back over his shoulder. 'The roof's lower than it looked and we can't cope with anyone getting knocked out. Jesus God – saving your presence, Brother Ciaran – but this is like walking into a tunnel of hell.'

Moira said, 'But not everyone who came in here died in here. This is how a lot of them escaped – Jude helped them to do it. Let's think of it as a way out.'

'A way to freedom,' said Kate. 'Some of those poor wretched prisoners got out – maybe quite a lot of them. We'll get out as well. And then we'll go back for Jude.'

'I'll go back on my own,' said Isarel, at once. 'There's no need for anyone else to get into any more danger.'

'Stubborn to the last,' remarked Ciaran. 'If we don't hurry none of us will get anywhere. Is that the hatch over to your left? Down by the floor. Shine the torch till we see.'

Isarel directed the torch as well as he could in the cramped confines, and there near the floor of the furnace, was a small opening hacked out of the brick, a rough and ready aperture that looked as if it had been made by the roughest tools imaginable. It was no more than three feet wide and at the sight of it Isarel felt his resolve waver. I've got to squeeze through there – we've all got to squeeze through there – and God alone knows what's on the other side. Whatever escape route there was might long since have caved in. The torch picked out an oblong sheet of metal lying on its side near to the gaping hole, its surface pitted and scorched.

'They must have used that to cover the hatch in between escapes,' said Ciaran, scrambling forward. 'And to insulate the escape route.'

'It looks a bit makeshift.'

'It was probably more effective than it looks. Ready, Isarel? I don't think there can be much time left.'

'Of course I'm not ready.' But Isarel was already lying flat on the oven floor, preparatory to squeezing through. 'But here I go anyway. Moira, can you or Kate take the torch and bend down to shine it through the opening as much as possible— Thanks.'

He began to inch through the narrow opening, using his hands to pull himself forward. His face was almost flat to the uneven smeary floor and the stench was in his mouth and in his throat, and beneath him was the crunch of macabre piles of ancient brittleness: the cinders of human bones and nails and flesh. His hands closed on the unmistakable outline of a skull, his fingers sliding inside the eye socket before he realised it, and he drew his hand back at once, sickness welling up in his throat. Unbearable. But don't think about it. He forced his way through the small opening, and felt, as he did so, the ghosts of the long-ago prisoners pressing in on all sides. The urgency and the frenzy that must have driven their own escapes bore him forward, and so vivid was it that for a second he almost felt thin, emaciated hands pulling him through. There was a faint breath of cool, fresh air on the other side, and Isarel stood up cautiously.

He was in the crematorium shaft. He was standing

inside a dark narrow chimney, a nightmare place, echoing with the fear and urgency of the escapees, and blackened and charred with a thousand burnings. Isarel pushed the crowding horrors back, and forced himself to look upwards. A cascade of black cinders gusted into his face, rasping at his throat and half blinding him, and he gasped and choked, rubbing his eyes clear with the backs of his hands. We're almost there, we're going to get out, he thought determinedly. But the minutes were slipping away and he was dreadfully aware of how little time there must be left to save Jude, and there was still Ahasuerus. Isarel could not begin to think what they would do about *him*.

The shaft was narrower than he had been expecting – no more than four feet across – and the uncertain torchlight showed up the black pitted iron of the walls. A little trickle of cold air was still coming from above.

He felt warily all around the sides of the shaft for rungs or footholes, and found them quicker than he had hoped, scraping his hand against a jutting iron stave and snatching it back with a curse. He bent down again and called back through the hatch for Kate to tilt the torch upwards, and at once saw the iron staves jutting from the sides of the chimney. A rough and ready ladder driven into the lining of the shaft. But serviceable. Praise God and the Zionist Resistance Movement. How had they managed to drive staves into iron under these conditions? In secrecy and danger and with the constant threat of an appalling death hanging over them? Don't wonder, just be grateful. He tugged on the lower rungs, dragging down with his entire weight and thought they were safely embedded still. So far so good. Don't die, Jude. I'm almost there.

He called through to the others again. 'I'm in the crematorium chimney, it's appallingly narrow and it's pretty nasty, but there's iron rungs driven into the sides and I think we can climb out. But the shaft is only about four feet wide and we'll have to go up in single file.' His voice echoed in the enclosed space, and came back at him hollowly.

There was a hasty consultation on the other side of the hatch, and then Kate called back, 'We understand what you mean, and we'll come through the hatch one at a time. We'll pass the torch back as we come, so that whoever's next can direct it up the stack to show the way. All right?'

'Good idea. Try to time it so that there are only two of us in the shaft at a time. The rungs feel firm, but they're fifty years old. I bet you never thought you'd escape up the flue, did you?'

'That,' said Kate, 'sounds like a very suggestive music hall joke.'

'Well, tell Ciaran to send up a prayer that we'll all get out to laugh at it.'

Kate said, 'Get on with it and don't waste any time.'

'I am getting on with it,' said Isarel, who was already starting up the lower rungs.

The chimney stack was about twenty feet in length, although it was difficult to be precise in the near dark. Whoever had positioned the rungs had not just set them in a straight vertical line, but had splayed them out so that you could hold on to the two above you and work your way up with your feet. The shaft was narrow enough for it to be possible to lean back against the other side as you climbed. But the pull on the muscles of arms and thighs was grindingly hard, and Isarel knew that Jude had been right to say he would never manage it. Had he managed to get out of the gas-filled chamber to near the outer door where the air might be better? We should have helped him into the tunnels, he thought with a sudden pang. But it was so rushed, so frantic. And there was so much I wanted to say.

They crushed his feet because he wouldn't betray his people. They rigged the trial at Nuremberg – how? a dupe? a double in the dock? – and so for half a century, the world thought he was a traitor. I can't begin to grapple with it. It's too enormous.

He stopped again and looked down at Moira, who was beginning the climb. The wavering light of the torch from below picked out her upturned face, and Isarel said with sudden irrelevancy, 'You look like a chimney sweep's urchin.'

'I don't care what I look like at the moment.'

'Neither do I,' said Isarel softly, and although the echo missed it, he saw that Moira had heard. Her eyes flew up to meet his, and Isarel at once said in a practical voice, 'If you keep climbing it's easier than it looks. But I'll come back down to help you if— I mean – is it awkward for you?' He hoped this was sufficiently tactful, but Moira said,

'It's probably a bit harder for me than it is for the rest of you, but I can do it. Jude would never have managed it, would he?'

'No.'

'Will we reach him?'

Isarel heard the uncertainty in her voice and the fear behind it. He was angrily conscious of wanting to get her out to safety, and he was very conscious indeed of his earlier thoughts about her. But this is neither the time nor the place, Svengali. Get on with the escape from Colditz, and with rescuing Jude, and finding Ahasuerus, and then have a look at the idea again.

He said now, 'We'll try to reach him, Moira. Onwards and upwards. Upwards in particular.'

From below, he heard Kate say, 'I don't suppose we'll ever know the name of the poor souls who built this, but whoever they were I hope they all got out and lived in

514

luxury and idleness until they were a hundred and ninety-two,' and he smiled despite himself.

His shoulders and wrists were aching abominably, but he thought he would willingly endure the torments of the damned if it meant reaching the top. He could see daylight now; a faint, grey spillage of light, and he thought it was the most beautiful sight he had ever seen.

And then, marvellously and unbelievably, he was there, he had reached the top, and the grey afternoon was all about him, and there were ordinary things everywhere: trees and birds singing, and the muted sound of the traffic from the highway below the castle.

He bent to help Moira out, and said breathlessly, 'All of you stay up here. We're outside the castle boundary by the look of it – yes, there's the wall over there.'

They had come out on the far side of the gentle hill-rise that concealed the grisly underground chambers, and the entrance was on the other side. Behind them was a small copse and in front of them the castle's bulk reared up grimly. Even from here, Isarel could see the four vehicles – two large vans and two old German Army-type trucks with canvas sheets across the backs and flaking camouflage paint still visible. They were parked near to a steel door opening into the hillside. Isarel eyed it, trying to gauge the distance. It was a much smaller entrance than the double doors he had found in the walled walkway, and it had probably been how the SS officers had come and gone when Eisenach had been a death camp in its own right. Whatever it was, it was much nearer than the concealed entrance in the castle wall. Could he get to it without being seen?

He looked back at the trucks. They were backed up to where a series of black-mouth spouts protruded from the hill, and long black tubes snaked from the exhaust pipes and clamped around the spouts. Gas vents, thought Isarel, feeling cold horror close about him. And the engines are still running. I think we're going to be too late.

He said urgently to Moira, 'Get into the shelter of the copse, make Kate and Ciaran go with you – Kate anyway – and for the love of God stay there!' He looked at her, at the smudges of soot and the tumbled, tangled hair, and reached out a finger to rub the smuts from the tip of her nose. The light, half-affectionate, half-teasing gesture which was all he had intended, suddenly turned into something far deeper and far more important, and almost before he realised it, he had pulled her against him and kissed her hard. There was a second or two of surprise and then he felt her response. He held her for another precious second, and then put her from him. 'That's in case I don't get the chance again.'

'Oh, I hope you do—' said Moira, delighted colour staining her face, and Isarel thought: God, she'll be an absolute knock-out with the right clothes and hair— No, I'm wrong, she's a knock-out anyway, even grimy and sooty and dishevelled.

And then he was running across the hill slope, every muscle feeling as if it had taken a beating, but beyond caring and almost beyond feeling. Only one thing mattered now and that was reaching Jude.

The first person he saw as he approached the narrow entrance was Vogel. He was climbing out of the nearest truck, a couple of young men wearing the Serse emblem with him, and he seemed to be calling directions as he came. Isarel could see that each of the vehicles had three more Serse followers inside, and although he was frantically aware that the underground rooms must be choked with carbon monoxide by now, he forced himself to halt. If

Vogel still had the gun – and of course he has, you fool! – there was no point in going straight up and getting shot. He stayed where he was, crouching low, scanning the grassy hillside.

Vogel's people were disconnecting the pipes from the exhausts leaving them coiled like black serpents under each of the spouts, and turning back to the trucks. Isarel risked a glance at his watch. Almost thirty minutes since it had started. Did Vogel think he had pumped in enough fumes to kill them all, then?

Four of the young men were bringing six or eight objects out of the vehicles, and Isarel, trying to edge nearer, trying to see what they were doing, felt impatience and frenzy beating a frantic pulse in his head. Go *away*, damn you! Whatever it is you're doing, stop it and go away! He wanted to go hurling across the stretch of ground and drag open the tantalisingly near doors and reach Jude, but he forced himself to stay where he was.

And then he saw what had been carried out of the backs of the trucks, and understanding slammed into his mind.

The objects were five-gallon jerrycans: probably relics of the war, and while two of the young men reached for the disconnected hoses, two more were undoing the caps. A pungent unmistakable smell reached Isarel, and his mind rocked in horror. Petrol. And from the awkward careful way the men were carrying them, each of the cans was brimful. At a rough calculation Vogel and his minions were pouring between thirty and forty gallons of petrol down the vents and straight into the underground rooms.

It was makeshift and it was a weak echo of what had been done here fifty years ago, but the aim was chillingly obvious. Vogel was resurrecting the crematorium, the Nazi ovens – exactly as a short while earlier he had resurrected the gas chamber. He was going to set fire to the

517

petrol and flames would rage through the underground rooms. If Jude was not gassed by now, he would certainly burn.

Even as Isarel's mind struggled to accept the reality and to grope for some kind of plan, Vogel and his people retreated, leaving the youngest of the men behind. Suicide mission, thought Isarel, staring in disbelief as the boy wrapped a rag around a long stick and bent to soak it in the petrol dregs. God yes, I believe that's almost precisely what it is! He remembered Kate's story of the suicides, and of the fanaticism displayed by Serse's People and also by Vogel himself. Was this boy really going to risk immolation, actually burning alive, purely to further Conrad Vogel's distorted nightmare vision of a new Golden Race? He might manage to get clear once he had thrown the burning taper in, but it was going to be a very close thing.

The boy was looking back to where Vogel and the rest had taken cover, and held the stick aloft, plainly indicating: Almost ready! With his free hand, he brought from his jacket pocket a cigarette lighter.

There was no time to think, no time to consider danger from guns, or from leaking carbon monoxide, or even from petrol explosions. Isarel flung himself forward across the grassy slope, shouting for all he was worth.

'Stop! For Christ's sake, man, stop! We've escaped – we're all out, and the only thing left down there is your wretched Devil's Piper! If you light that thing, you'll blow Ahasuerus to hell!'

He was halfway across the hill when he saw he was too late. The boy had already flicked the lighter, and the petrol-soaked rag had caught, burning up with raw scarlet and yellow flames in the cold autumn afternoon. The fumes from the vents must already be rising, and at any minute the entire hillside would erupt in flames.

Vogel had heard him. He turned, and Isarel saw, even at this distance, the cold fury in his face.

'Stop!' yelled Isarel, again. 'You crazy, murdering madman, don't you understand! Ahasuerus is down there – everything you've been working for is about to blow up in your face!' He kept running, but he kept his eyes fixed on Vogel, formless frantic prayers scudding through his mind. Please God, let him believe me – please God, don't let him shoot me – and above everything, please let me reach the doors and get Jude before the petrol ignites, and let Jude be all right— He was dimly aware of Ciaran running down the slope towards him, and of Moira and Kate watching, their arms about one another.

Vogel had understood. He was running down the hillside, shouting to the boy as he came, and the hill was suddenly alive with Serse's People, some going in the direction of the gas chamber, but others running away. The boy who had fired the petrol-stick had flung it to the ground and he was stamping frantically at the flames, but even through the panic, Isarel could see that it was still burning, and at any minute – oh dear God, at any second – the gas chamber would blow.

He reached the steel doors at the same instant as Vogel himself, and by now uncaring of who and what Vogel was, dragged at the bolts. As the doors yielded, thick choking carbon monoxide and petrol fumes belched out and Isarel staggered back as if he had been hit, gasping.

But Vogel did not hesitate. He went forward, as if he was mad or possessed, his hands raised above his head in blind consuming fury. Isarel, still gasping and half-blinded, received a brief dreadful glimpse of another man who had stormed like this, and who had held dark sinister sway over a nation, and who had pursued a cruel warped dream of creating a perfect race . . .

There was just time to think: Vogel's going inside, he's going into the gas chamber to get Ahasuerus, and Isarel heard Ciaran coming towards them, shouting to them to get clear.

The words were lost. There was an explosion of sound, and a huge, ear-splitting crackle. A livid wall of scarlet and yellow flame shot upwards, searing their vision. Half of the hillside burst open, and showers of earth and boulders and huge burning clods rained down upon them.

A terrible scream from within the gas chamber rent the air, and in the seconds before Isarel blacked out completely, a figure that had been huddled on the other side of the doors, fell forward and lay on the ground.

Chapter Forty-Seven

A pall of black smoke hung over Eisenach Castle, and the acrid stench of burning was still thick on the air as Ciaran and Kate walked slowly out of the Black Duke and up the narrow cart-track. The castle itself was untouched: grim and forbidding against the morning sky, and the gaping hole where the underground rooms had been was not visible from this side.

'Over,' said Ciaran, stopping halfway up the track. 'Isn't it?'

Kate stared up at the rearing outline, and shivered, pulling her coat about her. 'I think so. I hope so. Yes, of course it is; it has to be. Vogel's certainly dead. We saw his body.'

'And several of his people.'

'Yes.' She was still watching the dark silhouette. 'Some people might think Vogel got his come-uppance very neatly.'

'The cleansing flames?' said Ciaran, a note of amusement in his voice. 'And you a cynic and a sceptic, Kate.'

'I know one thing,' said Kate. 'Moira was right when she said Ahasuerus never intended to harm any of us. He'd tried to get Jude to the outer door, hadn't he? Where the air would stay fresher.'

'Yes,' said Ciaran softly. 'We can't know exactly, but I think he had.'

'Even when Ahasuerus was trying to reach me while I hid in the ovens,' said Kate, repressing another shiver, 'even then, he was trying to help – I see that now. If he could have called out, he would have done. But he had no knowledge of our modern speech—'

'And perhaps speech was difficult for him anyway,' said Ciaran carefully. 'He had been dreadfully mutilated already.'

'Yes.' Kate felt a coldness, remembering the thin, pale mask with the eye-slits. How had Ahasuerus really looked? She said, 'I'd like to have seen him as he really was. I mean at the very beginning.'

'In first century Jerusalem.'

'Yes, Moira saw him, didn't she? That's why she wouldn't say much about him.'

'I think so,' said Ciaran softly.

'The priest and the lover and the rebel.' Kate glanced at Ciaran. 'Maybe I'm not quite such a cynic as I like to think. I should like to have seen Jude as a young man, as well. He must have been pretty astonishing.'

'He was pretty astonishing in the underground room,' said Ciaran.

'Yes. Moira was absolutely spellbound, wasn't she?'

'Moira,' said Ciaran, 'is spellbound by Jude's grandson, only I'm not sure if she's wholly realised it yet.'

'I noticed that as well. It's mutual, isn't it?'

'It is. And if anything comes of it, they'll have battles royal, because Isarel doesn't know yet what kind of cat he's got by the tail.'

'They'll love every minute of it,' said Kate, smiling.

She looked up at him, and Ciaran said softly, 'And now what about us, Kate?'

'Is there an us?' Kate had known they must have this conversation since approximately three o'clock in the morning when, exhausted by the police interrogations, and still filthy from the smoke of the explosion, she had climbed wearily into bed at the Black Duke. She turned to face him, searching his expression. 'You're going back, aren't you?' she said. 'You're going back to Curran Glen.'

There was a long silence, and then Ciaran said. 'Yes. I'm going back.' He looked at her. 'And so, I think, are you.'

'Yes.'

'To Richard?'

'To Richard,' said Kate. 'There was never really any other option, Ciaran. I wish there could have been.'

'I liked him very much,' said Ciaran, his eyes on her.

'Yes. I like him very much as well.'

Ciaran paused, and then said gently, 'My darling girl, I don't believe anything else was ever really possible. I wish it could have been. If we had been different kinds of people—'

He stopped, and Kate said, 'The trouble is neither of us could compromise. And certainly neither of us believe that a promise can be qualified. That's what this is about, isn't it? Whether you make the promise to God or to a husband, you don't say, Yes, I'm going to make this promise and I'm going to keep it, but only so long as such-and-such doesn't happen.' She made an impatient gesture. 'Since Richard's accident there've been one or two—'

'Adventures?'

'That's as good a word as any. Yes, adventures. But they didn't mean anything. They wouldn't have happened – at least I don't think they would have happened – before the accident. And they didn't touch what I felt for Richard. I kept the vow according to my own lights.'

'"To thine own self be true."'

'Yes, exactly that.' Kate thought she should have known

that Ciaran, with his quick intuitive mind would understand.

'But you – you'd be dangerous,' she said. 'You'd walk into my mind and you'd take it over. You'd smash everything up, the fragile relationship I'm managing to sustain with Richard— Forcing him to stay hopeful, at times simply forcing him to stay alive—' She stopped and then said, 'I can't leave Richard – I can't ever leave him. I think I can allow myself the occasional fling – I don't think that's breaking the rules – but you wouldn't be just a fling. You'd be so overwhelming that I wouldn't have any mind left for anything else. I'd be breaking my own rules.'

'Dishonouring the vow.'

'Trust a religious to put it in a high-minded way. But yes. Even if you— dishonoured your own vow, I couldn't do it, Ciaran. And,' said Kate, 'I don't think you will. I don't think you could square your conscience with— what ought I to call it? Revoking? Renouncing?' She looked at him, and waited, as if saying: all right, that's my side: now it's your turn.

Ciaran said, 'Since entering Curran Glen there've been one or two ladies who've tempted me. And I have to be honest and say that several times I've come dangerously close to abandoning celibacy. But those ladies didn't— impinge on my mind. They certainly didn't seriously endanger my vow to God. But you did. The barriers went down when we were both trapped in the underground room, but I don't dare let them down any further, Kate.'

He stopped, as if considering whether he should say any more, and Kate said, 'That's the strength of the vow, isn't it? Sometimes you have to fight to stay inside Curran Glen, but it's a fight you want to win.'

'Yes.'

'Will you remember me?'

'Every day. And,' said Ciaran, and then the sudden,

slant-eyed glint showed, 'also every night, may God forgive me. I'll pray for you, of course.'

'Well— thank you.' Kate found this disconcerting, but she managed not to show it. He's retreating, she thought. He's deliberately drawing the folds of his monastic life around him. Get you gone, lady, you get no more of me . . . I can't think of a single thing to say. All the rivers of sorrowing verse written, all the torrents of anguished sonnets penned down the ages, all the scholars and the poets and the philosophers who wrote their scalding words about parting, and I can't find a single thing to say to him.

But he made it easy for her. He took her hands and looked down at her very intently, and said, 'You will be in my thoughts and in my prayers for a part of each day, Kate. May God bless you always, my darling girl.' His eyes were serious and intent, and Kate stared at him. This is how I shall remember him. In the months and the years ahead when I have to force Richard to live and hope, and endure more operations and re-enter the world, this is how I shall remember Ciaran. Not as the charismatic Irish monk, silver-voiced and far more worldly than is strictly safe for him, but as the man of God. The committed devout religious. Praying for me, praying that God – his God – will bless me.

As they walked slowly down the road, Kate said, 'Do you know, I feel extraordinarily light-headed. It's a bit like being drunk.'

'Ah, you're suffering from a rush of morality to the soul,' said Ciaran promptly. 'It's a wonderful feeling: it comes from the awareness of self-virtue and the gift of chastity, although as somebody once said, that's a thing I wouldn't have as a gift—' He smiled at her, and Kate thought: it's going to be all right. I think I'm going to cope. And then, with sudden angry determination: of course I'm going to cope.

They walked back towards the Black Duke. Richard was flying out to join them; if his plane had been on time, he might be there already. He might be waiting for me, thought Kate, with a sudden uplifting of her emotions.

There was an unexpected balm in the knowledge that Richard would be waiting for her.

Finale

The windflowers and the wood anemones had thrust their way out of the ground, and the jagged tear in Eisenach Castle's western side had already been softened by a sprinkling of bellflowers and primroses.

Memories skinning over, thought Isarel, standing in Eisenach's massive marble and gilt hall. Wounds healing and ghosts banished.

The ghosts were still here, of course; they might fade in time, but they would never quite go. Isarel could feel them crowding into the already-packed hall, jostling for place with the living, as if they were saying: but we have as much right to be here as all of you! We made the past and we created the present, and this is our night as much as anyone's!

It was a night for ghosts and it was a night for memories to be unrolled and spread out like faded cobwebby tapestries.

It was a night when, if you could reach out and scoop up a handful of the atmosphere, you would find that cupped in your hands were old agonies and new loves and ancient curses and lingering bitternesses.

And threading it all together, the haunting, legend-drenched music.

And if you could really have taken that pot-pourri handful of tonight's ambience, you might also have received a full-volt electrical shock, for Eisenach Castle was so heady with anticipation and excitement, it was thrumming with such expectancy, that every brick seemed to be sizzlingly alive.

In the great domed roof the newly cleaned chandeliers sparkled and coruscated, illuminating the trailing microphones and TV leads and camera flexes. The cameras and the microphones and the spotlight-hung gantries were jarringly out of place here, of course, and they were violently at war with the ghosts, but they had been unavoidable. Every TV station and radio station from three continents had bid for a place here tonight; every branch of the media had been determined to capture tonight's concert for all time. Reputations might be made or ruined out of tonight's events.

'The cameras will capture the living,' said Moira softly, at Isarel's side. 'But I'm glad that the ghosts will elude them.'

It was comforting that Moira could feel the ghosts as well; Isarel thought he ought to have realised she would be aware of them, but he was grateful to her for acknowledging them, nevertheless.

Champagne was standing ready in ice-buckets in the ballroom beyond the hall, and it was Clicquot and Bollinger because anything else would have been unthinkable. The long table had been carefully and lavishly set by the deferential caterers, and there were glistening salmon and trout on beds of crushed ice; lobsters and quail in aspic, silver dishes of Beluga caviare and Perigord truffles; *foie gras* and out-of-season *fraises des bois*.

Hothouse flowers were banked against the orchestra's platform, and the heady scents mingled with the expensive perfumes of the female guests. Isarel did not know whether the gowns were Worth or Dior as once they would have been, but he thought that most of the exclusive designer

528

houses of today's *haute couture* would be represented.

He was scarcely aware of taking his seat below the orchestra's platform, along with Kate and Ciaran and Richard and Lauren, and when Moira put her hand on his arm, and said softly, 'The orchestra's tuning up,' he felt the present blur and fuse with the past again. I'm going back once more, he thought. Only this time it's different.

As the Deputy Leader gave the A from the gleaming ivory and black Bluthner, the babble of talk and laughter and the hum of speculation stopped as abruptly and as completely as if a door had been slammed shut.

There was a spatter of polite applause for the Leader who came quickly into the hall, acknowledging the audience with what was very nearly apology, as if, despite his knighthood and his long distinguished career, he knew himself necessary but unimportant tonight.

Every eye was turned to the stair now, and the anticipation had returned, a hundredfold. The suspense was building up and up, becoming a tangible thing, stretching out and out . . . Unbearable, thought Isarel.

And then, between one heartbeat and the next, he was there. Standing at the head of the sweeping marble and gilt stairway, exactly as he had stood fifty years earlier. Judas returning . . . Jude Weissman, avenged and revenged . . . This is it, thought Isarel, staring at the thin, upright figure. This is it, the justification, the vindication, the single, marvellous moment when all of those years are going to be swept aside, and when an evil reputation is going to be smashed once and for all, and a new one forged out of a dark romantic exile. Take this moment and hold on to it, because never in the whole of your life has there ever been anything like it, and never, not if you live to be a hundred, will there ever be anything like it again.

Jude was moving forward: assured and elegant in the

sharp formal evening clothes, walking sufficiently slowly to recall the torture of Auschwitz, but exuding that remarkable charisma, radiating the astonishing confidence. Arrogant! thought Isarel, feeling a thick choking knot of emotion start to form in his throat. He's milking it of course. Playing to the gallery. I don't blame him one bit. He's stunned the audience into silence but at any second, they'll erupt. It'll be like uncorking a huge bottle of the creamiest, fizziest, most vintage champagne in the world. Yes, I was right, here it comes . . .

Jude was halfway down the stair when the silence broke, almost hesitantly at first, as if no one dared shatter the spell, and then gathering momentum, erupting into a great deafening wave of sound, a mammoth shooting fountain of emotion that went up and up, louder and louder, finally bursting in a great firework explosion of delight that cascaded across the ceiling and showered over the entire hall. People shouted and cheered, and overhead spotlights flared and cameras swung and TV and radio announcers gabbled delightedly.

Jude reached the foot of the stair calmly and stood facing the cheering throng, as composed as a cat, his eyes raking the assembly, a smile curving his lips.

Isarel was between Moira and Kate, both their hands clinging to his, and he could feel the tears pouring down his face and he knew that Moira and Kate were crying as well, openly and unashamedly, and he knew that probably every person here tonight was close to tears by now.

As the house rose to its feet, Jude bowed with perfect courtesy and unruffled poise, and smiled again, almost as if he might be saying: ah yes, this is how I remember it, and then walked with slow careful tread to the waiting Bluthner.

The cheering and the applause stopped at once, and the silence came down again. Isarel saw Jude's eyes narrow in concentration, and knew that for him the years of exile might almost never have been, and that there was nothing in the world for him save the music. The music saved me, he had said. The music kept me sane.

The leader looked to Jude, and lifted the baton. And then the downbeat was given and Jude's hands came down on the Bluthner's keys. The music, the marvellous, soul-scalding music that had pulled a dazzling, rebellious High Priest from beyond the grave, that had cuckolded a Cremona lute-maker and charmed a Tudor King, that had fooled Nazis and helped lead Jews to safety, flooded the ancient castle, as, fifty years after he had first entered Eisenach, Jude Weissman again played the *Devil's Piper*.

Epilogue

The BBC newsreader came out of the meeting preceding the evening's news bulletin, and sat down at his computer terminal, assembling his notes and his thoughts.

There was the usual depressing procession of items. The Economy failing, the Government making contradictory statements, the latest round of peace talks in places with unpronounceable names . . .

A short piece on the Memorial Service at Westminster Abbey for Jude Weissman who had died last month – 'Peacefully in Ireland after a brief illness'.

The newsreader enjoyed good music and he felt a pang of loss. He had attended two concerts, one in London and one in Galway, where Jude Weissman's music had been played, and he had thought the music disturbing and beautiful.

He scanned the notes handed in by the research team, making sure that nothing had been missed.

Nothing had. Some of the stuff had been culled from the ready-prepared obituary, of course, which had been used when Weissman's death was announced last month, and which had been on file for just over ten years, ever since that extraordinary business in Eisenach Castle. The story of how the Nuremberg trial and execution had been faked, and how Weissman had been a prisoner for half a century had been on every news bulletin in the world and there had been an explosion of emotion.

The obituary had been pretty comprehensive. The announcer keyed in the appropriate commands and brought it on to his screen to refresh his memory. Yes, it was all there. The dazzling successes of the Twenties and Thirties; the war years with that remarkable plot that had cheated the Nazis. And then Weissman's gradual return to the world after his rescue: TV interviews, one or two carefully planned public performances. Every concert hall had clamoured for him, but he had been sparing with appearances. St Martins-in-the-Fields and the Vienna State Opera House. The Barbican and Festival Hall. One or two more in Ireland. Two of the major publishing houses had brought out books on his experiences: one with Jude's collaboration and permission, one without. The unauthorised version had outsold the authorised, of course: the announcer had only been a young brash reporter just beginning to make his way in television journalism, but he could remember the furore. And then three years ago, BBC2 had prepared and screened a documentary about Weissman and his work, which had been highly praised. He turned back to his notes.

There would be some footage of the Memorial Service, which apparently included a good clear shot of Isarel and Moira West arriving at the Abbey, with their daughter, Susannah. Nice that the old man had lived to see the birth. The luminaries of the music world had all been there as well, of course, and were mostly captured on the short film; the announcer checked names.

At the bottom of the researcher's report, was a hasty scrawled note from the director of the OB camera crew.

'I managed to get just about everybody who was anybody,' she had written. 'With the exception of one gentleman who sat apart from the rest at the very back of the Abbey and spoke to no one. I have no idea who he was, other than that he was crippled and leaning on a stick, and obviously elderly.

'I didn't pursue him, because I had the feeling that he might be some kind of religious recluse, or even a hermit.

'He wore a long cloak with a monastic-looking hood completely shadowing his face.'

Dan Simmons

THE HOLLOW MAN

AN UNFORGETTABLE JOURNEY INTO THE DARK HEART
OF MORTALITY FROM AWARD-WINNING AUTHOR

All his life, Jeremy Bremen has been cursed with
the unwanted ability to read minds. He can hear
the thoughts behind the placid expressions of
strangers, colleagues and friends: their dreams,
their fears, their most secret desires.

For years his wife Gail has served as a shield
between Jeremy and the world's neurobabble;
her presence has protected him from the intrusive
thoughts of those around him and allowed him
to continue his work as one of the world's
leading mathematicians. But now Gail is dying
and Jeremy comes face to face with the horror of
his own omniscience.

Jeremy is on the run – from his mind, from his past,
and from himself – and his treacherous odyssey
takes him from a fantasy theme park to the mean
streets of an uncaring city, from the lair of a killer
to the gaudy casinos of Las Vegas, and at last to a
sterile hospital room in search of the voice that is
calling him to the secret of existence itself.

FICTION / GENERAL 0 7472 3814 6

A selection of bestsellers from Headline